Praise for

Return of the Sword

~ ~ ~

"...***Return of the Sword*** **is a wonderful collection of sword and sorcery short fiction**...some of the finest examples of the genre that I've read in a long time. Sword and sorcery has come a long way since the days of the "noble savage" wrecking havoc, but that hasn't stopped it from being a lot of fun and overflowing with action. If you're looking for a wonderful break from your daily grind, **I can think of nothing better than this collection of mayhem to take your mind off things**."

~ Richard Marcus, *Blogcritics Magazine*

"**If you like sword and sorcery fantasy, you will like this anthology**....Overall, I enjoyed the anthology and read through it quite quickly, proving to me that I was having fun. And that is what this first offering from [Rogue Blades Entertainment] is meant to do. ***Return of the Sword*** **is meant to entertain, and it succeeds...**"

~ John Ottinger III, *Grasping for the Wind*

"**I highly recommend...*****Return of the Sword*** to anyone who appreciates a straight-forward adventurous tale, and I applaud the effort to present some quality sword & sorcery tales in a market where the sub-genre seems all but forgotten. **I hope more publishers will follow suit and give us more new S & S books.**"

~ Greg Hersom, *Fantasy Literature.net*

"...[A] fine collection..."

~ Janice Clark, *The Fix*

"All around great reading wonderfully written in bold and strong voices....[Rogue Blades Entertainment] has been trying to present and create a place for Sword and Sorcery. They have met that goal and gone beyond it as these stories are indeed fine heroic tales and are of a quality that extends beyond a genre offering. **The book has language to thrill...**"

~ Dan Nelson

"***Return of the Sword*...deserves accolades** for...such a large number of quality stories [in] a single publication. This rivals (and even surpasses) some entries in [the] *Swords Against Darkness* series, of which I'm also fond....every story in this anthology...brought something to the sword-master's table. **Do yourself a favor and procure a copy for your bookshelf, today.** Otherwise, I'll tell Solomon Kane that you're a werewolf."

~ Wesley Lambert, *The Star Road*

"If you have a craving for sword-and-sorcery, straight-up no chaser, then you'll find it in...*Return of the Sword*, the new anthology from [Rogue Blades Entertainment]...[that] has gathered together nineteen short stories...of heroic fantasy. The key word here is "heroic"; with a few interesting exceptions, the offerings on display make no delay hurling their courageous warriors onto the front lines to let them carry out their bloody business to our old-fashioned delight. There are fiends to slay, damsels to rescue, and titanic battles to win, and **none of [the stories] wastes the readers' time getting to the juicy red meat."**

~ Ryan Harvey, *Black Gate* Magazine

Praise for Stories from

Return of the Sword

~ ~ ~

Jeff Draper's "The Battle of Raven Kill"
"…a masterful job of giving a very realistic description of close and horrible infighting..." ~ Richard Marcus

"The Lair of the Cherufe" by Angeline Hawkes
"…quite tasty; if you want the heroic goods delivered, this is the place to start." ~ Ryan Harvey

Bill Ward's "The Wyrd of War"
"…the surprise, for me, was the kick in the stomach I felt at the end, even though I half-expected it. Very well done." ~ Janice Clark

"To Be A Man" by Robert Rhodes
"…an easy 5 stars and then some." ~ Greg Hersom

Jeff Stewart's "Mountain Scarab"
"Greed, swordplay, treachery, humor…has it all." ~ Wesley Lambert

Michael Ehart's "To Destroy All Flesh"
"…an excellent introduction to Ehart's characters…His writing is fluid and his characters heroic with a twist." ~ John Ottinger III

"An Uneasy Truce in Ulam-Bator" by Allen B. Lloyd & William Clunie
"Lots of fun adventure, here. I hope to see more from this duo – the characters, *and* the authors." ~ Wesley Lambert

Phil Emery's "The Last Scream of Carnage"
"I thought I had it figured out, but there's a nice little twist at the end. I do love surprises." ~ Janice Clark

"Valley of Bones" by Bruce Durham
"…Mr. Durham…has a talent for telling stories at a dizzying pace. This one is no exception." ~ Wesley Lambert

Christopher Heath's "Claimed by Birthright"
"…straight ahead wizard vs. warrior and it is exciting." ~ Dan Nelson

Steve Goble's "The Mask Oath"
"...one of the most intense and violent selections...it...up-ends readers' expectations about its avenger's true motives." ~ Ryan Harvey

"Fatefist at Torkas Nahl" by David Pitchford
"...wisdom and stupidity, barbarian boastings and civilized chivalry, courage and skill, and a vicious demon sword..." ~ Janice Clark

Stacey Berg's "Altar of the Moon"
"...about the price a warrior pays for being a hero...not your typical adventure story..." ~ Richard Marcus

Ty Johnston's "Deep in the Land of the Ice and Snow"
"...perfectly captures the popular sword-and-sorcery concept of the hero who won't let anything, not even the gods, restrain him." ~ Ryan Harvey

"The Red Worm's Way" by James Enge
"...a clever tale with an unusual twist...Morlock...is truly a unique character in literature, let alone heroic fantasy." ~ Dan Nelson

Thomas MacKay's "Guardian of Rage"
"...there be swords and darkness and cramped spaces, and a beastie straight out of Lovecraft's nightmares." ~ Wesley Lambert

"What Heroes Leave Behind" by Nicholas Ian Hawkins
"...the strongest characterization in the anthology. [Hawkins] delves into a realistic portrayal of an aging hero..." ~ Ryan Harvey

"The Dawn Tree" by S.C. Bryce
"... [a]story about betrayal, but this time about a hero being tricked into betraying himself. This was an excellent story..." ~ John Ottinger III

"The Hand that Holds the Crown" by Nathan Meyer
"Great battle descriptions. In fact, practically the entire story is one big brawl." ~ Wesley Lambert

"Storytelling" by E.E. Knight
"For anybody with any aspirations to storytelling, no matter what the genre, it's an invaluable piece of writing." ~ Richard Marcus

"...a great straight-forward style guide..." ~ Dan Nelson

"...an excellent article on the basics....if you're an aspiring writer at any level, you'll find this well worth reading." ~ Janice Clark

Rogue Blades Presents

RETURN OF THE SWORD

AN ANTHOLOGY OF HEROIC ADVENTURE

Edited by Jason M Waltz

Milwaukee, WI

Published by
Rogue Blades Entertainment
5234 S. 22nd Street, Suite 401
Milwaukee, Wisconsin 53221
USA
www.roguebladesentertainment.com

Cover Artist: Johnney Perkins
Interior Artist: Mike Jackson
Interior Graphics: John Whitman

Rogue Blades Presents
Return of the Sword: An Anthology of Heroic Adventure

ISBN-13: 978-0-9820536-0-7 (paper)
ISBN-13: 978-0-9820536-1-4 (electronic)
Library of Congress Control Number: 2008937015

First Edition: March 2008
Second Edition: November 2008
Printed and Bound in The United States of America
0 9 8 7 6 5 4 3 2

Rogue Blades Entertainment
Putting the Sword back into Swordplay; the Hero back into Heroics!

Return of the Sword

Rogue Blades
ENTERTAINMENT

Acknowledgments

It has been my great privilege to gather this collection of tales for you. Yet without the guidance of certain individuals it would not have happened. Far more than I can ever list here were either influential in or directly supportive of my obtaining this opportunity. However, there are a specific few the trail leads directly through whom I would like to expressly voice my gratitude to.

George R.R. Martin instigated this culmination of events in November 2005 while autographing books for a young author who had just admitted he was trying to write a novel as pleasurable to read as Martin's own *A Game of Thrones*. Mr. Martin kindly looked this author in the eyes and told him to write some short stories. Told him to write and submit and learn from each of the rejections encountered in pursuit of publication. Told him to make a name for himself in the world of small press and magazines. Whether such advice holds as much weight now as it once did is moot. What matters is that this author went straightaway home and discovered an online fellowship of like minds he never knew existed.

That night I found (the now defunct) Pitch-Black Books, their "Icons" themed anthology, www.swordandsorcery.org and the *Flashing Swords* ezine, and www.SFReader.com. I never went to sleep; instead, I read everything on those websites and at work the next day I wrote my 9,000-word "Icons" story. That Daniel Blackston rightfully promptly rejected – with a terrifically helpful personal note. And so began my short story writing.

Through interactions via the SFReader.com Forum I met and furthered my relationships with Daniel, Armand Rosamilia (of Carnifex Press), James Boone Dryden (now of Sheer Speculation Press), Kelly Christiansen (of Cyberwizard Productions), and numerous other fine editors, authors, and reviewers. These connections led in turn to progressive opportunities: fantasy book reviewer in the Carnifex Press magazine *Clash of Steel*; book reviewer for SFReader.com; fantasy acquisitions editor for the Sheer Speculation Press magazine *Staffs & Starships*; assistant managing editor for the very same *Flashing Swords* ezine I discovered that pivotal night and newly resurrected under Cyberwizard Productions; promotion to anthology editor then managing editor of the new imprint Flashing Swords Press; and now editor and publisher at Rogue Blades Entertainment, my very own publishing house.

I would also like to extend my gratitude to the members of this anthology, for without them it would definitely be a book most boring. They created the art you now hold; all I did was find the pieces and help each one complete the whole. Each author and artist within these covers has been a pleasure to work with. Many of them have surpassed my expectations with their offers of assistance and continual encouragement. I've a sneaking feeling, though, that I'll discover the lot of them has spoiled me when it's time for the next anthology. *Hmm.* I suppose I could avoid that by keeping the team intact and inviting them all back.

There are, of course, those persons in the background to whom I owe even more. These are the ones who endured my many requests to "view this" and "hear that;" were forced many a late night (and even early morn) to pry my drooling face from my keyboard and rouse my sleeping figure sprawled across my desk; were obliged to tolerate the grumpy bear I then became during daylight hours; were asked to cover for my absences at family events.

These are also the ones who were witness to my bursting excitement when I rushed to share the latest story I'd selected; who saw my exuberance when the completed cover art arrived. As I sit here now and type these words, I realize I will probably never know just how much work my editing of this anthology caused my family. I can only pray that all the rest to follow do not pose as large a burden. So I pen this first of hopefully many dedications foremost to my three ladies:

TRW
BRW
SRW

Jason M. Waltz

February 2008
(edited October 2008)
Milwaukee,
Wisconsin

Artists

Cover Artist

Johnney Perkins

Johnney has been a loyal fan of fantasy and sci-fi ever since the age of five, when he saw his first Frank Frazetta works. His paintings of fantasy locales and pinups are spectacular, but it was his works with characters from J.R.R. Tolkein's *The Lord of the Rings* and his warrior themes that led me to him. When I was too late on purchasing his "Into Battle" for the cover of this anthology, I asked him about creating a similar piece of art for me. The rest, as they say, is history. Johnney was a pleasure to work with, especially as neither one of us had done a cover like this one before and there were times changes had to be made. Despite it all, he delivered a terrific piece of art – just as he promised. I look forward to working with Johnney on several more covers in the years ahead. Find more of Johnney's works at http://www.myspace.com/jperkins24 and at http://www.fantasyartists.org/Gal30_Johnney_Perkins – the online artists' gallery I first discovered him in.

Interior Illustration

M.D. Jackson

M.D. Jackson draws his visions with a passion, without a choice. Which in truth he does not have, for he knows his head will simply explode if he does not rid it of each new vision in preparation for the next. When he reads a story, a single, powerful image usually grips his imagination and compels him to work on it until it is right. I enjoyed working with M.D. and am grateful for his many efforts – especially the creation of our Flashing Swords Press logo (on the title page). To see more of his fevered imaginings, read previous issues of *Flashing Swords* or visit his gallery at http://community.imaginefx.com/fxpose/mdjacksons_portfolio/.

Transitional Icons

John Whitman

When I showed my friend John this page crediting him for my line break icons, he asked me not to list him. He claimed (with a sheepish grin) that if he had known I was going to attribute them to him, he would have done a better job. Once I recovered from my shock, I said, "Too bad, John! I'm publishing my appreciation of your help whether you like it or not – but next time you owe me your best work!" In all seriousness, John is a terrific artist who has created several works for me in the past – and may just be doing so again.

Here's to you guys!

Forward:
Swords Drawn

A Tale of Heroic Promise

by Jason M. Waltz

I am excited about this book you hold. It is my belief no finer compilation of heroic tales of action and adventure exists.

Herein lie sensational records of legends old and new, myths forgotten and freshly spun. Here be tellings of the spectacular and the supernatural – and the grotesque and the grim. For alongside the glories and triumphs of heroics come acts desperate and mundane. It is not all fanfare and beauty.

Return of the Sword contains adventure at its most basic. Heroic tales of adventure. Heroic persons do not plan heroics. They simply react and do those things that need being done, sometimes despite their own goals, most often in conjunction with those basest of all desires – the pursuit of women, wine and wealth enough to procure more of both.

True heroes are usually found in the grit. In the muck and grime of the battlefield; in the commonplace of the tedious. They are the everyday people pounding out survival who inadvertently protect the welfare of others in spite of disgruntled disclaimers they but protect their own interests. They are dirty. They suffer domestic in-tranquility and shortened life spans. They do not seek praise, though it often comes as a by-product of their deeds – it is less desirable than coin. What heroes do is simple to describe and hard to live: Heroes continue to do the ordinary in extraordinary times and do the extraordinary in ordinary times.

Being heroic does not make one fearless. On the contrary, it is fear that makes one act heroically. Fear demands a choice be made, an intent declared. Fear is to heroics what light is to darkness: there is no such thing as the latter – just less of the former. Heroes are those courageous enough to act despite their fear.

Whether that means standing up to a horde of marauding Vikings ... to an army of jackbooted thugs ... or to a gang of schoolyard bullies. Whether it means denouncing slave markets and gladiator combats . . . or racism, censorship, and public malfeasance. Heroes are those who choose to face their fears, to struggle through them, fight through them, and finally triumph over them. Sometimes triumph.

Winning isn't a requirement for being a hero. Many a hero has fallen mid-combat, often without anyone knowing until the battle is over. The result is not necessarily important, though the more successful the victory the more beautiful the heroics, the louder the praise. But not every hero wins public accolades or even bears a famous name.

Who witnesses the personal struggles through soul-searching gut-checks that require immediate action? Who is there to see the silent triumphs . . . followed by the shattering failures? For that's the other part of this heroic equation. Heroes aren't always 'heroic.' It's not a default title. At any given moment they face the same choices those less heroic – those more fearful – do. Both must decide to be brave, to move forward, to do an action regardless of the potential cost . . . or not.

Heroes are those who continue to do the ordinary in extraordinary times, and to do the extraordinary in ordinary times.

Return of the Sword is the flagship of the new "Rogue Blades Presents" series of anthologies and collections published by Rogue Blades Entertainment. Our mission is to meet the continuous need for quality adventure entertainment. Yes, the need.

Society has a deeply rooted want for tales of the heroic. Heroic adventure enables readers to vicariously triumph over not just 'the bad guy,' but over the guy who's holding us back, keeping us down. Over the guy who is *us* – but 'worse' than we are. Heroic literature is clearly not about life's elites, nor is it about the very well-defined war between good and evil, white and black. It is about battles in the gray and the people in the middle. About the common people performing the uncommon: surviving.

Humans need to be reminded such possibilities endure. The storytellers who once orally passed along generations of these tales no longer exist. Yet there are still storytellers in the world – twenty-four of them right here inside this book.

Our storytellers have shared the tales and art that burned within their souls and coursed within their veins, demanding to be heard.

These stories aren't just strings of words accumulated for the sheer production of it. This art isn't just pixels and hues randomly combined. All are exclamations of discourse designed to reveal passionate meaning and force each reader, every viewer, to lay claim to a heritage of heroism.

Looking for heroic adventure? Turn the page for twenty opportunities to relive your life without once leaving your easy chair, without once risking it all like each of the following protagonists. If you're not drenched in the sweat of fear and battle lust, panting for breath in the aftermath of survival, exhausted from the never-ending slinging of steel, and flushed with the adrenaline of victory upon finally closing the back cover – well, then, you haven't learned how to really live!

I dare you to bare steel and stride forward. I promise you will not be disappointed.

What happens to the weapons and the heroes who wield them after the battles are over? They aren't always paraded down the streets nor hung above the mantel. This story explores one possibility as it speaks of a heroine weary of carrying the sword that carried a nation to survival. Hers is a tale about the aftermath of heroics, about responsibilities unsought and lonely vigils stood – about the enforced separations that exist between 'normal' folk and heroes. It is also a tale of promise, for the ultimate understanding it impresses upon us is that both weapons and heroes return in time of need.

Stacey Berg writes from Houston, Texas, where she lives with her partner and three cats. A scientist, gardener, and aspiring surfer, Stacey is hard at work on her third (as yet unpublished) novel. She writes because she needs to read the stories living inside of her.

Altar of the Moon

by Stacey Berg

Keren rode into the darkest part of the forest just before midnight on the day before the full moon. *Only desperation,* she thought with a flicker of briefest amusement, *could induce anyone to follow a trail seen only in a dream.* But she was nearly beyond desperation, let alone hope; and she could not bear to think what she would do if the trail proved false. So she urged her tired horse forward, letting him pick his own way through the undergrowth, always heading west. She wondered when the last human had ridden this way. The trees were ancient, huge and gnarled, and more than once she had to work back a little distance to get around some fallen giant that blocked her way. The branches tore at the moonlight, leaving her only the shreds to travel by, but it would be enough for a few more hours' ride.

The sword's voice was barely audible this night as it sang softly to itself. Sometimes it was so loud that she could hear nothing else. The war was over, her people safe, but the sword gave her no peace.

Her horse's ears flicked forward just as forest unexpectedly gave way to a meadow. Keren blinked, dazzled by the sudden brightness of the unfiltered moon. For a brief moment she thought the meadow was empty, and then her eyes adjusted. A woman stood just at the margin of the forest, so still that she might have been carved from one of the ancient trees. She wore plain leather and no weapons, and faced the way Keren was coming with her feet apart and one hand clasped over the other like a palace guard, yet she did not seem to notice Keren at all. She bore a sense of patient, timeless waiting, and in the last second Keren had to think, she wondered if the woman had been standing there forever.

Then the woman's gaze came suddenly alive, fixing squarely on Keren's face.

The sword leapt unbidden into Keren's hand.

"My name is Veray," the woman said as she rubbed down Keren's sweaty horse with a cloth she had produced from somewhere unseen. She did not seem to need a reply. She had asked nothing, only given Keren some bread, freshly baked, though Keren could not imagine where it came from, and water that was clear and sweet. Keren sat by a fallen log to one side of the meadow, eating absently, still trying to shake free of the last tendrils of the sword's madness. The woman only lived because she had not so much as flickered an eyelid when Keren rode at her. Faced with that stillness, Keren had managed to turn the blade at the last moment. For once. Her head ached. The sword was back in its scabbard, leaning up against the log an arm's length away. That was as far as it would let her set it aside, these days. She rubbed her eyes. Still dazzled by the moon-light, they would not clear.

The woman, Veray, hummed softly as she worked. Keren did not recognize the melody, but somehow she found it comforting. Closing her eyes, she let the song drift into her mind, where it mingled with the sword's voice, fitting itself around that harsh rhythm like water flowing around broken rock, filling crevices, smoothing jagged edges, until the two together formed a kind of harmony that was nearly silent. She let her head fall back against the tree, content simply to rest here while she could, in the closest thing to quiet she had known in longer than she could remember. Eyes half closed, she drifted like the moon she watched crossing the cloudless sky.

Veray finished with the horse, setting him loose to graze on the tall grass that carpeted the meadow. Keren frowned, coming back to herself a little. The open space, small as it was, still seemed unnatural in the midst of such a dense wood. The grass looked as if it had never been touched by an animal before. Veray seemed to have no horse. In fact, Keren realized, there was no sign of habitation here at all. Unwilling to break the quiet mood, she nonetheless found herself curious to know what this strange place was that she had stumbled into, and who this strange woman was who gave back a precious moment's peace in exchange for an upraised blade. She was trying to frame a question when Veray said casually, "Tell me about your sword."

Keren froze. "What about it?" She glanced warily at the sword, willing it not to awaken. It – she – had almost killed the woman once tonight already, although Veray seemed strangely unmoved. For the moment, the sword remained quiet, still lulled by Veray's song.

Veray cocked her head. "A blade like that is certain to be surrounded by stories. I may even have heard some of them."

Keren felt herself relax a little. The usual preposterous amalgamation of fairy tale and legend had nothing to do with her. The war had been simpler than that, and far worse. "People make up stories," she said. Bitterness crept into her voice. "You should know better than to believe them."

Veray looked down at her. The moonlight seemed to shine from her eyes. "Tell me yours."

A stillness fell over the clearing. Even the moon seemed to wait, as if the movement of the night skies hung in some delicate balance. Keren looked up at the strange woman, wondering. "Tell me," Veray said again, softly, irresistibly.

And Keren did.

It was a simple enough tale, for all the blood and pain. Keren spoke calmly of the unknown girl who had followed a song only she could hear, and found an enchanted sword on the night of the new moon, with her country poised for a last stand against an invading horde. The sword sang all around her, making her invincible in battle, and together they had cut down enemies beyond counting. In that first dark night they saved the castle, and in that year the kingdom. And finally one morning the enemy was gone, and the girl, sick of the slaughter, had thought only to return to her peaceful life. But the people made her a hero, and the sword's voice would not be quieted. It sang of blood and death, and gave her no rest. She searched the kingdom for anyone, anything that could rid her of her burden, and found nothing but despair, until at last she fled for her sanity.

Keren wondered if she had lost or found it here.

"You still hear the sword's voice," she heard Veray say distantly. It was not a question.

"Even in my dreams. But not right now," Keren suddenly realized. Her heart quickened, in fear or hope, she could not tell. "What was that you were singing?"

Veray ignored her question. "What does the sword tell you?"

"I don't know. It isn't words, it's just . . . What it feels, somehow. Wants. I can't explain."

"Did it tell you to come to my clearing?"

Keren sat up straight, frowning. "I don't know," she said, wondering why she had not thought to ask herself that. "I had a dream one night. I was desperate. I—a dream, a vision, I don't know. A delusion, probably. It showed me a trail." *And it showed me a death,* she did not say aloud, *though I could not see whose. My own,* she felt certain, *and I will welcome it.* She ignored a sudden chill and continued. "The trail led to an altar. I laid the sword down by it, and the sword stopped singing. It was the most wonderful silence in the world." She shook her head disparagingly. "When I woke up, I decided to follow the trail. I didn't think it could be any worse than aimless running."

"What does the sword say now?" Veray asked softly.

"Nothing," Keren answered, puzzled. "I told you—there aren't words."

"But what does the sword say?" Veray asked a third time. Her voice echoed oddly in the moonlight.

Keren started to protest, and then could not. Instead she heard her own voice take on the lilt of prophecy, and she intoned: "The sword may be wielded for good, but it is not good. It may save the kingdom, but it will be its downfall. No harm may befall its bearer, but it will destroy her." She looked up at Veray, heart pounding. "It sang those words to me the day I found it. It has never said another word that I could understand, but only that."

"Oh, but there is one more line," Veray said intently. "I know."

Keren stared at her. "I swear," she said, suddenly very frightened. "That is all I ever heard."

Veray looked up at the bright disk hanging oppressively over the meadow. For a moment the harsh light turned her face into an unreadable mask. Then she looked down at Keren, and all that showed in her face was a gentle sadness that frightened Keren all the more. "Unless she sheath it in the altar of the moon."

"What?"

"That is the final line. 'Unless she sheath it in the altar of the moon.' "

Keren felt a strange, wild hope rise in her heart. "What does it mean? How do you know?"

"I know," Veray said again.

Keren's heart squeezed painfully. "Can you take me to this altar?"

Veray looked away as if the question hurt her. She shook her head. "You will find it for yourself, soon enough."

Keren dropped her head in her hands in despair. "I am so tired of all this." She wiped her eyes angrily. "If you won't show me, I don't care. Just tell me where to go. I'll leave now."

"Tomorrow," Veray said.

Keren shook her head wearily. It was too much effort to stay angry. She asked incuriously, "What will be different tomorrow?"

Veray did not answer her for a long moment, only stared down at her soberly. When she spoke, it was reluctantly, as if whatever she had to say went much against her will. "For one thing, the moon will be full."

"What difference will that make?"

"For another, there will be an altar." Keren's head snapped up. She felt a sudden foreboding of something terrible. The bleak expression on Veray's face confirmed her fear even as Veray said, "One last thing will be different tomorrow, too."

Keren's gut tightened. "And that is?"

"You will have to fight me."

For a moment it was as if Keren's every muscle had frozen as she sat. The last hope she had died within in her with a terrible sharp pang. She came to her feet in a rush. "Why?" she cried.

Veray's eyes were distant and full of pain. "You think that only you can hear. But the sword sings to me as well."

Keren drew the sword in a rush of despair. Bad enough it had forced her to kill in the war, enemies too many to count. At least that had been in the service of her people, without regard for her own life. But to be challenged by a fool who thought the stories romantic, who coveted the burden Keren would do anything to escape, was an outrage she could not bear. Keren raised the blade to Veray's throat. Fury made it shake. "I would give it to you if it let me," she snarled, "But it won't. If you want it, you'll have to take it. Just get it over with."

Veray shook her head. "Not tonight."

Keren gestured with the tip to distract herself from the overwhelming urge to run it through Veray's heart. The rage she felt was all her own, and none of the sword's. "Why wait?"

Veray smiled again. Her sorrow and compassion washed over Keren's fury. "Many reasons. The moon is not yet full. You are very tired. And I—" A tuft of cloud passed over the moon. For a moment Veray's eyes dimmed. "I am in no hurry."

Keren felt the blade fall away with her anger. She was suddenly so tired she could barely keep her feet, and the moonlight burned her eyes. She thought she heard Veray say something from somewhere far away, and then she was falling into the dark.

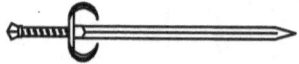

She awoke in twilight. Her head was pillowed on meadow grass, and a soft cover kept her warm in the evening breeze. She heard a reassuring whicker from her horse grazing placidly nearby. She stretched languidly, enjoying the peaceful moonrise.

Then she remembered.

In a panic she reached for the sword, sure Veray would have taken it from her, but it was there by her side. She arose more calmly, well aware that Veray could easily have killed her as she slept. Keren scanned the meadow in a slow circle, searching in the shadows for any sign of the other woman.

She almost failed to see her. Only when the moon, just sliding above the canopy of trees surrounding the meadow, cast an oblique ray into the fringe of the wood did Keren see the slim figure standing still as she had seen it when she first burst out of the forest. As if the kiss of the moonlight brought her to life, Veray stirred and walked forward into the meadow. The light turned her pale leather to silver, marred only by the dark slash of the sword she now wore. When she stopped, they were separated only by the long length of Keren's shadow stretched on the ground between their feet.

"Did you dream?" Veray asked quietly.

Keren thought about it as if it were the most important question in the world. "I don't think so," she said, surprised. "No. The sword was quiet."

"That is good," Veray said with a satisfied nod.

"What did you dream?" Keren asked, but she already knew.

Veray's eyes grew huge, reflecting the whole of the rising moon. "Death," she whispered, and drew her sword.

The first clash of weapons startled the horse, which let out a bellow and shied away across the meadow. Veray attacked fiercely. Keren had no time to think or choose. She fought by instinct, every move dictated by necessity and the sword. The war had been like this, men mowed down beneath her blade before she even saw the threat, movement so fast she barely saw the enemy's terrified face, the sword's voice so loud in her ears she barely heard the bright clang of metal or the screams.

But this fight was different. The screaming was all in her own mind, outraged protest against a battle she could not refuse to fight. And Veray's face she could see, though it held no terror, only a fierce bright satisfaction, as if an eternity of waiting had finally come to an end.

They were surprisingly evenly matched. Even in Keren's greatest battle there had never been a single opponent who could face the sword so long. She and Veray were partners in a furious dance, thrust and step and parry, both part of a single pattern. Keren listened in amazement as the sword's cry turned from rage to wonder and finally to a hopeful eagerness she had never felt from it before. Woven throughout was Veray's song, answering note for note as swiftly as their weapons crossed. So entranced by it all, Keren had no power to stop what happened next.

There was a thrust, an answer, another stab and hiss of blades. Keren came between Veray and the moon, her shadow falling dark across the other woman's face. Veray began to pirouette away, then stopped mid spin and stood up very still. She never even tried to block as Keren's sword buried itself deep in Veray's chest.

They stood locked together for an infinite moment of total silence. Veray smiled. Then her knees buckled. Unable to withdraw the blade, Keren went to her knees with Veray in her arms. "Why didn't you move?" she cried accusingly. "You wanted this to happen. You wanted to die."

"No. But . . . necessary." Veray drew a choked breath, squinted painfully up at Keren. "Sorry . . . you had to do it."

Keren moved a little, shielding Veray's eyes from the merciless light. "But why?"

Veray smiled again, gaze unfocussed. She murmured, "When the sword is needed, it sings to the one who can wield it. But when the need is past, it longs for the one who can sing to it . . ." She coughed, bringing blood.

"Quiet," Keren said. "Be quiet."

Veray nodded slightly. "It will," she whispered. Her hands locked around the blade, clutching it to her like a child. "I will sing it to sleep. Sheathed . . ." Her breath went out on a sigh.

Keren shivered, understanding at last. "In the altar of the moon," she said wonderingly. "You." Veray did not answer. Her sightless eyes reflected the full moon back at Keren.

Keren knelt there for a long time with the silence echoing in her head. Finally she stirred, closing Veray's eyes against the brightness. Then she went to look for her horse, and the long trail home.

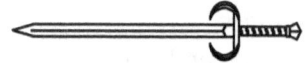

Of what value is self-benefiting sacrifice; at what price is sacrifice too costly? This tale returns the sword with a vengeance. It drives its point home with stunning force and leaves an aftertaste so haunting you go back to read it again despite the bitterness burning in your gut – despite the sullen fear you feel that you would do no different.

Bill Ward pens a helluva striking story. I've had the pleasure of reading several of his works, each one slamming me in the gut and demanding my attention. A self-described omnivorous bibliophile, Bill admits to being fascinated by the people who create the books and stories that he loves. He wants to be just like them when he grows up. Bill has penned numerous short, battle-heavy stories for gaming publications, but this was his first on spec piece ever sent to market. Of course, it was summarily rejected, but like the warrior in this tale, Bill kept on pressing forward. You'll find several of his tales in issues of Flashing Swords *magazine, and his website at http://billwardwriter.com.*

The Wyrd of War

by Bill Ward

It was the autumn of the world. On the hard earth of Toth, where the bones of twice ten thousand lay broken and scattered upon the plain, great hosts marched to war. From the north came proud armies beneath banners of rust red and red-gold and the stark white of wasteland snow. Assembled from fenland and mountain dale, city, town, and freehold, the able few of all tribes and nations stood within its ranks. They were the last of their kind upon the lands, the last to stand against the Animus – the living shadow at world's end.

It had waxed strong, this unseen power, sweeping armies from the field and devouring whole kingdoms in its wars. It had spread across the lands, a blight, enslaving those it did not destroy. Now on this, the last day, the Animus brought forth its force of beasts and bestial men upon the parched earth of the ancient battle-plain, and there made war for the fate of all.

At the northern army's leftmost point stood Vendic and his fate-bound brothers, eying the vile host that surged across the plain – a patchwork mass uncountable and chaotic, as inconsistent in its component parts as the hoardings of a madman. It held no common step, no order of march, no signal banner. Among its many files and divisions jungle savages cavorted before the stately remnants of baronial armies, somber steppe horsemen canted side-by-side with stave-ribbed wolves, and baboons in leathern armor ambled soberly amongst mobs of blood-mad berserkers. Still stranger things moved within this vast and many-headed shadow, half-men and unmen, unnatural fusions of man, beast, and *other*, creatures warped and debased by the energies of the Animus.

The sky above the horde was filled with raucous birds, a million bits of dirty rag caught swirling in a maelstrom.

Perhaps it was the dark sorceries that now dominated Vendic and his comrades that allowed him to view the approaching host without fear. Or perhaps it was a still larger fate than that demanded by the necromantic charms he wore beneath his skin, a world-fate of supreme indifference, that provided the anchor for his own fatalism. No matter.

As if seized by a single impulse Vendic and his battle-brothers, the forty-nine men of the Wyrdkin, strode forward, leaving behind the defending line of spearmen and archers of the left flank. They would be the first to meet the enemy, the first to die. The first to test fate – to find their *wyrd*.

Unaccompanied by the bray of horn or the pounding of drums the onrushing horde charged.

The wild, loping things that ran to meet the Wyrdkin were Oolugoi, beings twisted by long service to the Animus. Each hunched form bounded forward with a clumsy, sideways gait, leading with their shielded flanks – distorted growths of bone blooming like fungi from their fused and torso-locked right arms.

Vendic felt the compulsion take hold of his body as the skirmish line of Oolugoi neared – the necromantic charms he had allowed to be nailed into his flesh, the dread *geas* of battle they contained, overwhelmed and transformed him. As one body the Wyrdkin sprinted into the oncoming line, striking the unmen with a force not seen in the turning of an age.

The leading line of Oolugoi fought with lengths of bladed chain, wove and whipped into an intricate, ever-moving blur. No man would charge such a thing – a weapon-snaring, strangling flash of steel. Into this Vendic ran, directly and at speed. He struck the nearest fiend's darting chain squarely with his heavy blade, cutting it, sending a half-length skirling into the distance. Its wielder Vendic smote, slamming the misshapen thing broken and bleeding upon the ground.

Behind the line of whirling chains more Oolugoi irregulars moved to meet the Wyrdkin, giddy with bloodlust. With steel hatchets and cumbrous glaives they set upon the outnumbered men, surrounding them entire.

Vendic slapped aside a glaive and clove the closest foe, shearing bone-shield and flesh clean through. The compulsion of the *geas* steadied him, while the blade he bore struck and struck again. Such artifacts made ordinary men into gods on the field of war, but exacted a heavy price.

Willingly the Wyrdkin had accepted this burden, that of the dread charms and fell blades, counting it toward the balance of hate owed their foe. With it came certain death and a destiny rewritten in accordance with the *wyrd* of war. But it was the damnation of forgetting, of losing one's self to the charms that ate at the mind, that to Vendic seemed the ultimate reward, the ultimate pardon from the cruelties of life. It, as much as the desire for revenge, had been why he had chosen to assume the mantle of Wyrdkin, to trade his life and soul for sweet oblivion.

Arms numb with the shock of impact, Vendic parried the glaives and axes of the Oolugoi with tireless, borrowed skill, each threat countered by a sword wise in war and older than the oldest man. Closing his eyes, fighting blind, he raged – screamed – a lone voice merging with the din of battle to weave a fatal song.

He longed to live only here, in this moment of forgetting, but the *geas*-laden iron charms that had been hammered beneath his flesh had not yet robbed him of everything – for even as they stole his mind they left within him a core of will pared down to its essentials. As he struck blindly about him, wielded by his weapon, he knew little of his past pleasures or pain. Only the single haunting image of twin gray-eyed girls dancing the length of a winding mountain trail rose to meet him from the depths of memory.

He opened his own gray eyes.

The Oolugoi had dispersed; their misshapen bodies littered the ground, the remainder driven off by allied light cavalry as the defenders rushed forward to reinforce the Wyrdkin's startling success. Vendic's brothers had lost fully a third of their number, for even eldritch swords cannot protect a man surrounded. The blades and charms, priceless relics from an elder age, would be reclaimed should victory be achieved. The men, those bleeding on the plain and those that still stood, had been lost at the trumpets' first muster

– for that is what it meant to be bound by fate's *geas*, to kill and to die to the last man.

Regrouping, the flank secure for the moment, Vendic and his comrades watched the battle intensify in the distance. Through the dust haze he saw phalanx upon phalanx of northern pikemen press the center, pushing a churning mass of lightly armed infantry slowly back. Such a mob could not match the discipline and steel of the pikes, for they were not soldiers but slaves, as bound to their fate as Vendic and his companions. But unlike the foul Oolugoi, who revered the disembodied force of the Animus as a tribal god, those men and women slowly ground down by the allied pikemen had been taken from village and town and turned, by whatever dark power the Animus wielded, into the fodder of war.

Vendic shuddered, remembering the tandem flight of twin gulls, white wings streaking behind them in a stream of silver; the pale hair, pale eyes of his beautiful daughters, running.

Discordant shrieks – sounds Vendic mistook for memories until they loomed close – wrenched him from his thoughts. The Oolugoi had regrouped, and now moved upon the flank alongside larger forms, hulking silhouettes in the swirling dust. Northern spearmen marched forward to block the advance, their captain exhorting them to stand firm. The Wyrdkin remained in reserve – far enough away to ensure they would not feel the irresistible pull of the *geas* until the spears had had their chance to blunt the Oolugoi's momentum.

As the foe drew near the agonized shrieking grew stronger – the collective wailing of a thousand damned souls. With dawning dread the flank's defenders learned what new horror they faced.

The giants lurched forward with an ape-like stride, forelimbs twice as long as rear giving them an erect posture but little grace. Each was a mountain of raw flesh, a densely woven mass of skinless muscle and bone that glistened wetly, trailing plumes of steam in the chill air. But each of the six was but an imperfect machine, a crude construct. The Oolugoi called them Skollogim and held them sacred, legend named them juggernaut and warned that they could crush a man or drive him mad. Each massive form was a patchwork conjoining of dozens of men and women, all alive in agony. All screaming.

Vendic watched as the monsters waded into the thin line of spearmen, scattering those they did not flatten outright. The compulsion seized him, the *wyrd* of battle again called Vendic and his comrades to war, heedless of their chances for victory.

This, then, would be his end. So be it.

The juggernauts trampled forward, shaking the earth with their blunt, pounding limbs. Vendic shoved a fleeing spearman aside, a ghost face white with terror, and bulled through the frightened pack that blocked his advance. Some few of the panicked soldiers thoughtlessly brought their spears too close to a Wyrdkin and were struck down by magic blades that saw them as a threat – though most had dropped their weapons as they fled, and nearly all feared the fate-bound and their cursed steel as much as the fleshy creatures of the Oolugoi and scrambled out of the way.

A red cliff of seeping flesh reared above Vendic. He charged, penetrating the aura of terror surrounding the juggernaut, his body shuddering from the tortured dirge of the construct's chorus. He hacked at the nearest limb as one felling timber, chopping a wedge in the unprotected meat. Close now to the beast Vendic saw the individual contours of people entwined in its sickening mass – skinless tissues melding, entire bodies stretched into tendons driving dense clumps of muscle – layer upon layer of manlike shapes slithering above and beneath one another in a nightmarish parody of human anatomy. Through the clot of blood and lymph that clung to the great composite beast, scores of faces wept and screamed.

These too had been taken as the Animus had infected the lands of the south and east, made slaves by a force that could not be seen or felt and given to the Oolugoi as raw material for their infernal rites. All here now on Toth, all who still lived, whether free or slave, were here. All were damned.

Two pale shapes dancing, receding in the distance. Vendic shook as the charms burned his mind for fuel against his human frailty, but he no longer wished to forget – would not forget the crime done to him, the theft of his family, the theft of himself.

He brought his blade up hard against the stomping forelimb of the juggernaut, splitting a cluster of jointed bone. The creature jerked its half-severed arm upward, clumsily, sending Vendic sprawling to the earth. He lay dazed, the charms demanding action of his unresponsive flesh. Around him the Oolugoi rushed to slay those warriors that had not fled or been trampled. He saw one of the Wyrdkin decapitated only to fight on, a headless marionette

flung about by his own sword, killing the foe beneath a geyser of blood until his *wyrd* released him and he crashed to the earth.
A juggernaut rose above Vendic where he lay, its bludgeoning arms poised to fall.

He closed his eyes as the world grew bright.

A blast of heat buffeted him and the roar of flame filled the air, replacing the sounds of battle as surely as day replaces night. Vendic shielded his face, rolled, and crawled blindly away from its source, feeling his clothing catch fire, his skin blister and burn. He dragged himself back toward his lines; forcing his limbs mechanically forward, uncaring if it was his *geas* that preserved him or his own reawakened will to live. Rolling painfully on the hard, corpse-littered earth, he extinguished the wreath of flame that had clung to him like a curse.

His skin was tight, charred into black scales that split with the slightest movement. He opened his good eye, the other a dark and smoking hollow in his skull, and saw an orb of fire trail across the overcast to impact amongst the spreading conflagration he had escaped. Burning men and Oolugoi fled the flames, trailing smoke and fire. No juggernaut could be seen emerging from the blaze – the long-delayed northern artillery train had arrived in time to stall the Animus's flanking advance.

Vendic stood, tasting ashes, and watched. A swirling melee had engulfed the center of the battlefield, the discipline of the pikemen had broken and they now fought wildly with stabbing swords against heavy infantry of equal skill. The newly arrived ballistae shifted focus, hurling fire into the enemy rear until an explosion rocked the battery, engulfing the machines in crimson flame. The black birds that filled the air above the clashing armies had descended as a body upon the battery, upsetting the braziers used to ignite the missiles and igniting the artillerists' supply of naphtha. Beyond the flames and dust, Vendic glimpsed a mob of mounted easterners steal behind the north's entrenched right flank to pour flights of black-fledged arrows into the defenders' unprotected rear.

A few survivors filtered past him, their horrified shock as they sighted Vendic told him all he needed to know of his own condition. He was alive only through the will of the *geas* – like the headless Wyrdkin he watched swinging to the last, Vendic had remained standing despite his wounds. He saw no other member of his cursed band, and no free soldier chose to stay by his side amongst the smoke and corpse-stink of the smoldering left flank.

He stood alone, quietly; his flesh a smoking cinder, his ancient blade fused with the meat of his hand. He had been given a gift of sorts, for he would be the last of his band to strike the enemy, carrying their cause on his shoulders, until he finally sunk beneath a storm of blows, defiant to the last.

Vendic thought now of his daughters, dear twins, fey and changeable as the mountain breeze of his home. He could almost see it, could almost bid farewell to the place and the people he was so close to forgetting forever. But they were gone, only his girls remained to him, stolen though they were, likely slaves of the Animus if they lived at all.

A stirring caught his attention, somewhere out beyond the smoke and smolder. Up and down the line the forces of the Animus prepared their final assault. Vendic saw massive shapes looming in the middle distance, nearing the battle's center. Columns of slaves edged forward, dragging three colossal sledges with a groaning of iron and wood that filled the plain with the roll of thunder. Upon each platform sinuous, tentacled things stretched heavenward, tall as towers. The northern line dissolved at the sight.

The sound again, and in the smoking ruin of the Oolugoi advance a new force crept forward, charred bone snapping beneath their feet. Vendic gripped his blade and stood waiting, hoping for the compulsion that would speed him forward to meet these, the last of his foes.

He would hold his girls to the last, he knew now; neither *geas* nor war could take them from him again, the children that so briefly shared his life. Perhaps, even now, it was their strange charms that remained with him, charms that went beyond mere beauty or the mystified love of a father for so delicate a pair of creatures to capture something of the essence of the world, another kind of underlying *wyrd*. Their potent magic lingered, embraced him.

Vendic whispered an inaudible challenge, his cracked lips bleeding. The foe drew closer, slowly, a crowd of vague shapes in the smoke beneath a darkening sky. He stumbled forward, begging the *geas* to take hold one last time, to propel him toward his destiny before his body failed him. To get him close enough for the hungry blade to do its work.

It happened as a lightning strike, one moment he was weak, dying, in the next the *geas* was jerking him forward, lending quickness to his ruined limbs. Sending Vendic, alone, toward the approaching foe. He raised high his scarred blade.

Hundreds of them, small, slim from hunger, trailing the rags they had been wearing when last at their parents' side. Hundreds of children faced Vendic, an idiot slackness in their features, their eyes lamps of hate.

As he ran closer, appalled and powerless at his fate, the sea of small faces parted to allow the emergence of two pale sylphs, children themselves, dread power embodied in their dead gray eyes.

Vendic howled as he killed. And killed.

Can raw strength coupled with fanatical belief carry a warrior through every fight? What happens when one of these traits fails? Survival comes from having a bit more substance, a little bit more something, *down deep within one's core. The preceding tales established that heroes are created by circumstances outside their control. Chosen by events, they are selected by default for simply being the only ones in the wrong place at the wrong time with the capabilities to effect change. Believing the opposite is what makes them heroes. Believing they but do their jobs, they shoulder the responsibility to see things through and carry along those around them. Such heroism requires uncommon character. Character built or broken upon the ability of the anvil of one's faith to absorb life's blows. This next tale, in my opinion, is the most powerful tale in the anthology. For the Carnage-Lord, though supremely confident and a truly impressive and terrible warrior – the most fascinating character for me in these pages – is not heroic. Not in this tale. By his very being, he negatively proves my assertions. By his every action he counterdemonstrates my logic. Yet still the potential to prove heroic is his.*

Phil Emery's fascination with the possibilities found in Sword & Sorcery is so strong he finds it easier to write than to not – a distinctly advantageous position to be in when simultaneously teaching writing and working on a novel in pursuit of a PhD. Among the characteristics of Sword & Sorcery which fascinate Phil most is the lyrical language of legend so closely entwined with such tales, and the ability to influence the reading experience through novel ideas in presentation. I found Phil's choice to italicize dialogue rather than bind it within quotation marks, and his desire to vividly draw the reader down into the depths of Darkmaw through textual interaction to be visually stunning contributions to the impact of his tale. Phil's previously published novel Necromantra *(Immanion Press, 2005), is available through Amazon.com.*

Editor's Choice: The Last Scream of Carnage

A Tale of the Carnage-Lords of the Valac

by Phil Emery
& illustrated by M.D. Jackson

For generations after they would talk of it. They would talk of it as a last resort to frighten children into obedience, use it – in day – as an oath, and they would talk of it on nights when other, lesser screams echoed from the cavern.

They had never seen a man like the Carnage-Lord of the Valac before that evening. He rode into their village as the sun sunk into the hills, splashing the sky with pale blood.

Food and a rest-place!

They obeyed without protest. Even here word of the unconquerable Valac had reached. Word of warriors riding horses huge and hard and wild as themselves, plunging from warships and surging out of the seafoam, ravening across the land. Word of army after shattered army sent reeling by those who rode with carnage in their eyes and in their scabbards.

And the Carnage-Lord was their eyes.

The Carnage-Lord was the one who scouted ahead of the main force of the Valac, looking not for danger but prey. And if he should be slain the Valac would simply shrug and choose new eyes for their war. For the Valac only paused in their bloodquest to spit upon death. They held their souls greater than the souls of others, for they swelled them with slaughter.

That night screaming echoed out of the hills. In the fallen quiet in the hearth-hall where everyone had gathered, where hearth had been lit and food readied, where only the youngest children's wide, wondering eyes met his, where even the snarl of a dog toward him was wary, the Carnage-Lord broke the hush like a neck – without care.

He asked of the screams.

Only the screams themselves, riddling the night, gave him reply.

These people, he mused with pity and contempt, must honor weak gods. If the gods are strong the people are strong – if the gods are weak. . .

Finally, the scraggy mouth of a stooped and puckered village elder reluctantly began to work.

For time beyond memory there have been nights when screams rise from Darkmaw. On the mornings after such nights, from a village, from a farm, someone is gone. Someone never found, never seen again. Something comes from Darkmaw. Something which takes man . . . takes woman . . . takes child . . .

The words were a challenge to the Carnage-Lord. He would not fail the god of the Valac by refusing it. His faith gave him no choice, nor did he wish any. He laughed.

Take me to Darkmaw!

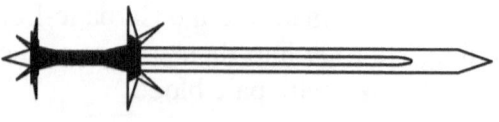

The villagers had shuddered, aye, but the scabbarded threat on the Valac's great thigh was nearer than the screams – the screams that still riddled the night as the Carnage-Lord, torch in one fist, reins in the other, a village youth crouched behind him, thundered his mount into the hills.

The night's half-moon
the severed pate of a skull
glowed whitely
was lost as dark clots of cloud harried the sky
glowed whitely
until the Carnage-Lord yanked his mount to a raking halt before the gape of Darkmaw. It was as though the cavern had swallowed part of the night.

Another scream, deafening, tore free.

The Carnage-Lord dismounted, took hold of the youth by the scruff, plucked him down, rammed a kiss on his mouth.

You seem the bravest of your kind. Come with me.

The Carnage-Lord allowed him to twist free, watched him rush like terror wetting itself, back to the pricklings of light dotting the lower lands. The Valac wristed the taste of the lad from his lips, let them curl between grimace and sneer, turned his back, unsheathed his sword.

Torchflame stabbed at the dark and it yielded. The cavern was huge. It reminded the Carnage-Lord of magnificent worship halls in cities the Valac had sacked – instead of fancy jeweled or bronzen lamps,

Darkmaw's clammy roof
suspended
stalactites.

Weaving his way between their sibling stalagmites he moved deeper, until cavern crouched into dank tunnel,
twisting,
darting,
shifting direction like a narrow frightened animal,
always
descending, always going deeper.

A scream
now and then
rushed past on its way to the sky
deafening

flailing at the hearing of the Valac
Carnage-Lord.
Each time he would bend,
let torch and sword fall, jam fists against ears.
The space between the echoes of torment increased
as the Carnage-Lord went deeper.
But
then
came another sound.
Faint to begin, growing louder as the
Carnage-Lord went still
deeper,
an almost-sound.
Almost like the myriad cicada-chitter
on the summer hillsod of the Valac homeland.
Almost like
the swarm-sound of locusts over the
southern plains.
Almost.
Creeping louder until it was a huge,
high-pitched whispering clamor.
Time
and time the Carnage-Lord would
plunge
around a twist in the rock, girding to confront
the makers of the almost-sounds.
Time and time
there was only the tunnel,
void,
deepening.
Time and time the torch revealed less. It
was beginning to falter. But still the
Carnage-Lord went on, until finally,
with death's
inevitability,
as he knew it would, the flame
failed.

Darkness.

The chittering stopped.

The Carnage-Lord dashed the spent torch away. It struck something not rock – chipped away a fragment of pain – not a voice – almost a voice. Other almost voices joined it, swelling, and the Carnage-Lord realized that the chitterers had been waiting for an ally, an ancient ally, the dark. But the Carnage-Lord's god Val could see, was watching him as he watched all Valac, judging their courage. He laid his other hand on his sword-hilt and roared into the crescendo of almost-voices.

For the glory of Val and Valac!

A sea of things surged over him. Hands? He felt bony pieces which were surely fingers, with hard-edged bits like nails that tore at him. He swung his sword. It journeyed only inches before digging into something. He knew the feel – knew it well. Strength drove the blade through meat and bone as if through straw.

He rejoiced.

Chittering bodies clogged the limestone narrow like thick, unbreathable air all around him, all over him, crushing, gouging, mauling.

Still
he
swung
his sword,
hauling it through clammy strata of
meat, blood, bone,
meat,
blood,
bone.

He joyed at the even higher pitched chittering which was, he knew, not almost, but truly pain.

Slaughterfever pounded his temples. The familiar passion of the hard carnage. The pulse of the Valac.

Always new hands tore at his body, his face, and from this he ripped grim satisfaction, knowing the new would have needed to squirm through the corpses of their shuddering fallen.

After a time-drowned-in-blood-ecstasy, as he knew it must, there came the first quiver of weakness in his arms. Still he arced his blade through meat,
blood,
bone, and

meat,
blood,
bone, but
slower now.

Anon, skin soaked in sweat and blood, he felt his legs buckle and he slid through the almost-live, almost-dead smother to his knees.

Heaved upward
every seething splinter of will urged into numb sinews. His legs straightened. Surged up again, gasping his god once more into the still fierce chittering. His sword arced again,

but slowly,

slowly.

A bony forearm jammed across his windpipe. Fingers yanked, nails clawed. The blackness deadening his sight seeped further inward.

The Carnage-Lord was surprised to awaken.

Air bristled up over his wound-crusted body – not rank, not savage in force – malevolent in some distant way, like the cruel core of the world dreaming threats.

There was no ground below him.

The weight of his body clustered around his wrists and ankles, clustered and burned. He was held by them against rough sheer rock. Held by them by feverously green glowing worm-things coming out of rock and coiling around wrists and ankles and sinking back into rock.

Burning. That was what burned.

Their glow was sickly, quickly failing.

Above, dark. Below dark.

Darkmaw.

And all around, his captors, clustering on the rockface, clinging without effort. Eyes glimmering like points of midnight moonlit tarns. Restless. Eager. Anticipating? Small. Man-like and yet not men.

Almost-men.

Hundreds – male, female, even smaller things the Carnage-Lord imagined were spawn. He tried to reckon the number he had slain before being whelmed.

But for the dark you'd not have taken me so easily!

The words echoed strangely, plucked by the air from his battered mouth and carried curling upward like defiant smoke. The Carnage-Lord imagined them making their way through the passages of Darkmaw for a while, then dying.

Dying.

The creatures began softly chittering in their stabbing almost-language. It had a new quality – like vocal drooling. And he saw they had teeth – like little sharpened stalagmites and stalactites.

So

he nodded

man-eaters.

He guessed why they had not slain him before. They preferred their meat warm.

Suddenly came a shrug of movement. To the right the Carnage-Lord saw, in a gap in the almost-men's numbers, their last victim, worm-shackled some ways along the rock.

A man?

The screams that had issued from Darkmaw earlier that night had not sounded like a man.

You live?

The groan was weak, hardly audible, somehow in some way hollow. More hollow than Darkmaw. The Carnage-Lord scrutinized him as best he could in the palsied wormglow.

They

have feasted

on me . . .

The Carnage-Lord's heart curled in contempt. There was no wound, no mark whatever on the weakling's flesh. He had been sent mad with fear.

The Carnage-Lord turned back to his captors. The crust of blood over his body cracked and flaked.

You'll have no screams from me. When a Valac dies their soul is taken by Val to Gemmorn, the afterworld, to eternally feast and drink and battle and ravish other worthy souls in the soft carnage.

He jerked suddenly – pulling the worms taut. His wrists and ankles still burned, though there was no flesh left on the bones. He laughed. The almost-men startled back.

May my meat turn your stomachs!

From far away came the other captive's last words, void of hope, void of something more.

Your soul will never reach any afterworld, Valac . . . It is not your flesh they intend to eat . . .

The almost-men's needle-mouthed chittering grew louder as they came close again, closer than ever, breath-close. Then, as those mouths opened wide, they stopped.

The hunger in the tarn-glimmer eyes faded and heads twisted, puzzled. They edged around him on the rockface like bewildered spiders – peering, listening, smelling, touching

silent.

Then they slipped away dejectedly, one by one, into the sheer dark, appetites thwarted, unable to find their true prey.

And that was when it rushed out of Darkmaw, out of the hills and into the night, torn-throated with outrage and despair – voided of hope, pride,

belief.

The last scream of carnage.

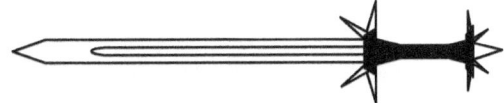

What fills the mind of one who waits upon death? Who waits, not upon a nameless foe or an unknown fear, but upon a specific and overwhelming opponent devoted to one's elimination? Perhaps nothing, for it is not logical to willingly choose to stand alone against such a juggernaut of doom. It takes something unique uniting mind and heart to enable one to do so. It takes adherence to something more meaningful than simply self. What follows is an exploration of duty and the value we ourselves attribute to it.

Jeff Draper writes – not for noble or even monetary reasons – but because he is a man who believes everything could be done better, especially if he were controlling things. Even storytelling. He believes this so strongly, he spends hours twisting his children's bedtime tales until all but the youngest can grasp the intricacies of why the Dark Faerie Queen wages eternal war on Little Baby Zebra. For more about perfect bedtime storytelling or about this story (including Deleted Scenes!) and some rather interesting commentary on writing, visit Jeff's blog at http://scriptoriusrex.blogspot.com.

The Battle of Raven Kill

by Jeff Draper

Rocks fought the incessant crash of the swollen river, rising above the water like knuckles of the Earth. Oth stood at the foot of the bridge, stout leather boots caked with mud and blood, and watched the tattered remains of his clan disappear into the night. They sought the safety of the moors beyond the river while Oth turned and sought signs of the invaders driving them from their homelands.

Moments before he had stood amongst his clan, adjusting a bloody bandage wrapped around his arm, as they filed past him across the bridge. A girl of ten summers lingered by his side. He knew he should push her away and force her to flee with the rest of his people but when she did he'd be left with nothing but noise and cold night. For these last few moments he drew warmth from her very presence. When the last clansman shuffled past, Oth looked down at her and said, "You have been a good daughter." He sought to reassure the child with his rumbling basso voice and its simple strength. It seemed to work.

"You chose well," she said with a smile. Before he could tell her to leave she held up a small necklace. "I made this for you while we ran."

Oth took the charm in his hand and smiled back. It would never fit around his neck. Twined from her own hair, it held bits of bark and flowers found across the hills. He reached up and tied it to his torc of iron braid.

She glanced over her shoulder at the disappearing clan and seemed to set her resolve. “The other children have always whispered you cannot die. Is that why you are staying to fight the Pechts?”

“There is no time for this, child. Run with the clan. Stay close to them.”

“But—”

“Do as I say!”

She backed up a step, startled. Without another word she turned and ran.

Oth watched his adopted daughter vanish into the dark. The charm dangled over his heart and he brushed at it with a hand that would soon be drenched in blood. He bent to gather his weapons and prepare himself for the coming fight.

A slow, cold breeze blew down from the mountains while he waited. Pale light from a partially hidden moon drifted across the landscape. A tower shield lay ready at his feet. In his right hand was a stout hard oak rod that ended in a fist-sized ball of studded metal. The foreign trader had called it a mace and so that was what Oth called it. Mace. In his left hand was Stick, a similar sized club that ended in a squat metal point.

The bridge over Raven Kill was not much wider than an oxcart and it had no rails. Ice runoff from the mountains and the recent rainstorms had created a torrent of frigid water roaring between the large, smooth rocks. Raven Kill could not be crossed without the bridge, and to fall into it would be certain death, either by drowning or by being dashed against the stone. The raiders would have to cross the bridge and to do that they would have to kill him. “I will not die here tonight,” he whispered.

To get a feel for the battleground he stepped onto the bridge. It consisted of simple, flat stonework, built with no art and no love; a utilitarian reminder of a utilitarian people. It created a path to link moor with mountain. Barely visible among the grasses and reeds sat the foundation stones of a trading post that had been abandoned by the utilitarian people when his grandfather was a boy. They had left, but the bridge remained.

Oth knelt and laid his clubs beside him. It would not do to pray with weapons in his hands. “Great God of sky and stone,” he muttered. Although the thundering waters erased the sounds of his words, he knew they were audible where they mattered. "Our enemies strike like snakes, quickly and without mercy. We have fought and we have run and now we are here. Give speed to the clan. Take speed from our enemies. Give strength to my arms. Harden my weapons."

He recited some other prayers, searching for the words that would bring him victory. Finally, at a loss for anything else to say, Oth realized what had been welling up in his heart all night. "I do not understand your ways but I ask you to not abandon me here. You've given me this duty and I meet it willingly. This . . . " He choked on his words and tried to steady his voice. "This may be the moment I was created for. Stand with me and do not let me falter. Do not let me give up. Do not let me make the choice that will doom us all."

With that he looked up and saw movement on the rise. Oth grasped his clubs and stood, slipping his hands through their leather straps. The shield he rested against his knee. *And so it begins.*

Shadows appeared and disappeared along the shelf of higher land that bordered the broad riverbed filled with brush and small stands of trees. They moved cautiously and paused often, like fat blackbumbles flitting from flower to flower.

Scouts.

They should have seen him by now, clearly exposed beneath the shifting moonlight and against the gray stone of the bridge. He hoped they suspected an ambush. *Let them keep suspecting that.*

A low, bright star had moved from one side of a tree to the other by the time the scouts filtered down to the valley floor. Four distinct shapes moved through the brush and stopped below the same point Oth had first seen them. He knew they had pondered the distance to the bridge and came to the same conclusion he had long ago: It was much too open for them to cross unseen, and much too long to risk throwing a spear that would likely miss and be lost in the river. They would be muttering all this to each other right now. Oth smiled as more time passed.

Then Oth saw them break from the brush and run at him. When they had covered half the distance, he saw they carried no spears but were armed only with hunting knives. These scouts sought glory. They wouldn't slow for one man guarding a bridge between them and their prey slipping away on the other side. They would strike him down and clear the path for their brethren.

Exactly what Oth desired.

One of the Pechti stumbled on the loose river rocks. Oth let the shield drop to the stones behind him and stepped forward. Three continued their rush to close with him and Oth watched them calmly. In the moonlight they did not look like men at all. Whorls of ink and ritual scars darkened their appearance and broke up their patterns.

He raised his clubs. The scout to his right lunged.

Oth stepped left and let the man slip past him. He thrust both clubs into the face of the next one, causing him to slip and stagger. Swinging backward with his right arm, Oth slammed Mace into the back of the Pecht's skull. The solidness of the blow and crunch of bone told him the man was dead.

Oth drove Stick into the thigh of the stumbling man, sending him to the stone, and swung an overhand smash with Mace at the next. The scout raised his free hand in an involuntary effort to block. The club broke his arm and continued down into his forehead. Bone shattered like a wasp's nest and the man crumpled into a heap at Oth's feet.

The scout on the ground tried to swing his knife but Oth knocked his hand aside with the follow through from Mace and drove Stick into the man's chest. The last scout regained his charge, but came to an abrupt halt after seeing the first three killed so quickly. He stopped too close. Oth did not hesitate. Another step forward and another swing with Mace dropped the man dead.

Oth looked back to confirm that the first scout lie face down in the water and then relaxed and lowered his clubs. Four less Pechti raiders for his clan to face. An idea came to him as he glanced over the bodies and the far edge of the riverbed. He needed every advantage he could create.

First he gathered the knives of the dead raiders and threw them into the river. Then he dragged their bodies several paces before the bridge and laid them with their heads touching and their feet pointing into each of the four directions. Oth smiled. *Let the superstitious Pechti destroyers ponder that.*

Resuming his place on the bridge, Oth thanked the Great God for each moment given; for each furlong his clan put between them and him. "I will live tonight," he said to himself. *I will live this night.*

The low, bright star slipped closer to the horizon before movement and shadows again appeared on the rise. Countless and continuous both came, spreading to either side along the ridge. Soon one long, dark mass stood assembled atop the rise. It appeared to Oth as if a giant spider slowly crept over the rock and now tensed to spring upon its prey.

He stood at the bridge and waited.

The shadow paused. Most likely their war leader wondered why his scouts had failed to report this defended bridge. *Do they see their bodies yet?* An order must have been given because the shadow slipped down the ridge to the edge of the brush. Oth watched them assemble. Numbers of raiders were left behind, as smaller shadows separated and spread out along the route. *Defending against the non-existent ambush.* Oth reached up and with a rough tug ripped the bandage off his newly scarred but whole arm. *Take your time.*

The mass of men left the shelter of the brush and flowed forward, halting halfway to the bridge. The flanks spread even with the center, forming a long line facing the river. Oth stopped counting at fifty. At this distance he could make out single figures and saw them pointing toward him and gesturing to each other. They'd seen the bodies. The roar of the river swallowed their words, and Oth could only guess at their fear and anger.

Two forms plunged forward; shoved from behind. Oth watched their resistance change to acceptance as both raised high their spears. He crouched when they quickened their pace, snatched up his shield when they simultaneously launched their spears. The shafts disappeared into the night sky and Oth held the shield before him, angled to his left in anticipation of their fall. Both spears struck the heat-tempered hard oak and glanced off, slicing through nothing but river water.

Oth remained crouched and backed a few steps further onto the bridge. He peered around the shield and saw more gesturing and animated conversation. It seemed two of their best spear throwers had just lost two steel-tipped spears. *How many more will they chance wasting so?*

His answer came almost immediately as he heard a great shout and the mass of Pechti charged. Oth studied their advance, their tattoos blending with the night and giving motion to the blackness. He pushed his shield higher on his left arm, holding both Stick and shield strap, and backed up a few more steps. "Great God strengthen me."

The Pechti screamed, their savage wail cutting through the cold air. Designed to make enemies empty their bowels in fear, it only made Oth grip his weapons tighter. He settled into a loose crouch and watched the raiders in the center of the mass. They would be the ones to come out onto the bridge. Oth bared his teeth in a ruthless smile. They could only come at him two at a time.

The throng slowed near the strange placement of their dead, then parted and moved around it. The two center Pechti reunited and ran straight at Oth while the rest slowed to a halt, their screaming battle lust denied release. All eyes watched the advancing raiders reach the bridge. Just before they set their front feet to leap into battle, Oth jumped forward and to the right, forcing their spears to his left with his shield and bringing his right hand around in a wide swing. The club smashed into a tattooed shoulder, shattering bone and crumpling the man's arm. The momentum of the blow drove the Pecht into his fellow warrior and both of them tumbled into the upstream side of the river, taking their spears with them.

Two more raiders replaced them. Mace knocked a spear aside and smashed into a man's face, breaking his nose and snapping his head back. Oth swung at the next raider while the first staggered backward and impaled himself on the spear of the man behind. Bodies tripped and tumbled. Confusion spread, stopping the attack as swiftly as a pen stopped a herd of rushing sheep.

Three overhand smashes created three more corpses at Oth's feet. A raider jumped over the bodies and Oth ducked low, swinging his club into the side of the man's knee. The joint bent the wrong direction just as the Pechti landed on that leg with all his weight. His battle cry became a scream of pain and the man tumbled head first into the fast moving water.

Oth could see the Pechti lining the riverbank, shouting at him and raising their spears in anger. Two-by-two they continued to come. He retreated a step with every kill he made, hoping to string the fight out on the bridge before some of those on the shore decided to risk losing their spears. In front of him a snarling mass of enraged warriors, unable to charge him, instead thrust their spears forward three and four at a time. Oth blocked with his shield and swatted with his club and continued to back along the bridge.

A spear came in low and sliced into Oth's calf. He grunted in pain and dropped to one knee, bringing the shield down hard. It snapped the head off that spear, but another came over the top of the shield. Oth barely twisted his head out of the way. The shield moved oddly on his arm and he realized a spearless raider had grabbed it. Already low to the ground, Oth used his solid leverage to wrench the shield to his right, across his body. He dragged the Pecht through the other lancing spears, knocking at least one into the river before throwing the raider after it.

But he was now on his knees. Oth sensed a shift in the battle lust of the Pechti. They thought they had him. The lunges began anew as three raiders crowded together on the bridge and pushed their spears forward. Oth turned the shield sideways and thrust it up to meet them. He pushed hard with both of his legs and rose quickly. Spears and arms collided with his shield and he forced them away. A low swing with Mace caught legs, breaking some and bending many others in pain.

Another spear came in low and stabbed him through the top of his foot. Oth brought Mace over and down, connecting with the top of the Pecht's head and collapsing the man's neck into his chest cavity. The lifeless body dropped and rolled from the bridge.

Oth limped back another step. A spear jabbed forward and stuck in the shield. Oth whipped his club up, breaking the shaft and leaving the head embedded, then struck at another Pecht with the backhand. The warrior frantically dodged the club and slipped on the edge of the bridge. He scrambled for a handhold but tumbled over anyway.

The momentum of the attack stalled again and Oth lashed out, breaking a forearm. The closest raiders started falling back, only to meet resistance from their brethren still pushing forward. Oth lurched to his left and shoved a warrior off the bridge with his shield. A looping underhanded swing with Mace caught another Pecht squarely in the jaw and flung him back into his friends. Oth had now struck four or five unanswered blows and the entire mass of raiders surged away from him.

He limped after them with a few more swings, until he saw they'd pulled back onto the muddy riverbank. Sudden movement at his feet made Oth look down. Tattooed arms, glistening in the moonlight, clung to the bridge, muscles flexing as they grasped for further handholds. The Pecht looked up with a snarl. His snarl became a howl when Oth stamped on his wrist and bones snapped; a strangled scream when Oth kicked him in the face. The man fell into the water and the forceful current yanked him under the bridge. Without a second thought, Oth turned to face the raiders again flanking the far edge of the river.

A large figure wearing a metal headpiece and holding an elaborately curved dagger stepped onto the bridge. He shouted in an odd accent, rough and sneering. "Dirt man! Why do you stand?"

Oth remained silent. He glanced at the wounds on his legs and saw only smears of dark blood. Without the threat of more enemies to distract him, Oth felt his strength slowly leak away, along with his rage. He heard the panting of his breaths and realized how exhausted he'd become. Surprised at how heavy his clubs were, Oth lowered his arms. His clarity of mind seeped away and he wondered if this was what it was to die.

The raider chieftain called out again. "My stones will crush you! Do not stand! You will die a worm's death!" He followed this with a few more words in the Pechti's guttural language.

Oth wrenched his senses away from concentrating on his own body and focused on the enemy. He could only guess at some of the chieftain's meaning, but he knew the savage mountain people thought little of anyone who lived below their heights.

"I will stand," he shouted back. "And only I can choose when I die!"

The chief looked side to side. Oth realized what they were about to do and started to back up. The raider shouted and raised a fist. The long line of Pechts drew their arms back.

Oth watched their arms surge forward. Spears flew from the shadows. He hesitated, then raised his shield and looked away from the falling spears. Backing as quickly as he could over the countless dead, Oth felt many of the spears fly past him and many others glance off his shield. Trying to count them was useless.

He felt the slice of a spear across his elbow. Twisting away from that side, he felt another sting his lower back. Oth kept retreating. More spears collided in front of him and clattered off the shield. The howling cries of the Pechti followed him above the roar of the river.

Then a spear came down through the darkness and pierced his thigh, right below the frame of the shield. Oth could not stop a yelp of pain as he staggered back and fell. The spear passed through his leg and its point lodged among the stones of the bridge. Searing pain shot through his body and he started to curl up in agony. Oth let go of the shield strap and it slid over his club to fall into the water. He clutched at the shaft of the spear, sending new waves of pain through his body.

Howls of victory crossed the noisy water. The throng of Pechts poured onto the bridge and ran at him with knives drawn.

"No," Oth grunted. "Not yet."

Oth released his other club and let both hang from their leather wrist straps. He gripped the bloody spear on either side of his leg. "God, do not leave me!" He gave the spear a violent twist and screamed as he forced the tip deeper into the rocks. New runnels of blood cascaded over his hands. The Pechts sprinted at him.

"God, I beg of you," he shouted. "Help your servant!" Oth twisted the spear again and felt the spear head snap off. With a violent tug he ripped the shaft back out of his leg.

Get up, get up, get up he thought. New strength flooded into him, as powerful and unstoppable as the river he laid so close to. Oth used the spear as a lever to raise himself onto his knees. The first two Pechts closed fast and lunged forward with knives outstretched. Oth swung the broken spear at their shins. One jumped it and tried to get past him. The other took the spear against his legs and staggered to the side.

Oth rocked to his left and shouldered the passing raider into the river. A knife swiped out and stuck Oth high in the arm. He thrust the spear shaft into the nearest face, and lurched to his feet. Clubs dangling from his wrists, Oth swung the spear into someone's head. Two rapid thrusts of the broken spear made the attack stumble and break once more. The Pechts gathered on the bridge were again unable to get past him and remained bottled up by their own front men.

Rage filled the night sky and Oth could see the Pecht war leader a few ranks back urging his men forward. Oth whipped the spear around and let it go, aiming for a head. He bent below a lunge and grabbed for his clubs. A raider rolled over his shoulder and Oth stood, sending the man tumbling awkwardly into the river.

Oth could no longer see the far side of the river, but it looked like every last Pecht was on the bridge and pushing forward. A few even tumbled into the river as the mass of them surged forward. He limped backward, swinging his clubs in tandem but landing few blows. The press of bodies kept forcing him to lose ground and Oth didn't know how much bridge he had left.

Too many. There are just too many.

Oth saw it in their faces. They knew they could beat him. The end of the bridge must be close. They would simply push him back and get around him. Then they would be on him like a pig in a snare.

The clubs weighed heavy in Oth's hands. His legs ached and sharp pains radiated from his many wounds. Oth saw his blood flowing from those wounds and his eyes followed the trail of death in his wake, straight into the horde of Pecht raiders. He spied the Pecht leader still only a few ranks back and saw clearly the only chance he had. He charged.

Two huge steps and Oth watched fear blossom in their eyes. Two of the raiders in front of the leader still held spears and raised them in desperate defense. Oth swung downward and shattered one spear, then shouldered the man off the bridge. His other arm struck straight toward the next Pecht and Stick pierced him high in the shoulder. A sweep of the legs with Mace brought the man down, screaming from a doubled-back knee. Oth bulled into the next two men. Spearless, they stabbed at him with knives but he got inside their reach and pushed them both outward and into the rushing river.

The next two men suddenly found themselves face-to-face with Oth's savagery and lashed out in panic. A blade nicked Oth's forearm. He ignored it and lurched on. The press of bodies pinned his clubs close now, restricting his options to pushing and kicking. Still Oth strove to reach the chieftain.

Knives lanced at his face and he ducked. Distracted, his rush stopped and once again Oth felt himself step back onto blood-slicked stone. A whimpering moan told him he had left a man alive on the bridge behind him. He caught sight of the writhing form in the corner of his eye and struck downward, crushing the back of the man's skull.

Another Pecht lunged forward, swinging a knife. Oth could not bring his clubs up fast enough. The knife caught him along the ribs and scored a long, bloody mark. He gasped and pushed out with both clubs, barely injuring the man but forcing him back. Then a spear thrown from behind the front rank sliced deep into the bones of his left shoulder.

Oth staggered back and knocked the spear away with Mace. When he did, Stick slipped from his grasp and dangled by its strap. He couldn't close his fingers on the handle. He looked down and watched Stick slide off his wrist and drop to the bridge.

He could almost hear the gasp of the warriors and then everything else seemed to quiet. Oth looked up and saw the Pecht chieftain step between the two lead raiders, a smile of victory creasing his face.

"You fight," shouted the chieftain. "But you no fight no more."

Oth could hardly keep his legs locked and steady. He felt as if any moment his knees would buckle and he swayed to the right and left, trying to find a balance that would keep him standing. Pain raced through Oth's whole body and he knew more would soon come. Without the strength to stop them, they would spit him with their remaining spears and toss him off the bridge. The rocks would break his bones and his lungs would fill with water while he tumbled all the way to the sea.

Mace slid off his other wrist and fell to the stones.

It would be so easy to give up now and avoid it all. Defeat was moments away. Just give up and let the pain go away. Oth glanced above the ranks of tattooed men. The star he'd been watching had set behind the ridge.

The war leader watched Oth's still form. When Oth did not respond to his further taunts, the Pecht stepped forward and drove his knife straight out.

Oth felt the blade pierce his skin, break through his chest bones, and split his heart in two.

The pain was incredible and he gasped, unable to scream. He felt his lungs flood with his own blood. Oth looked down and watched the severed charm fall to the mud at his feet. The chieftain let go of the knife and Oth dropped to his knees. He heard a violent cheer from the Pechts as he fell backward. His head struck the muddy riverbank with a splashing thud loud in his ears. Stars wheeled in the broad, black sky above.

As his eyes fluttered closed he saw the raider chief step over him and turn to face his followers. The man pumped his fist in the air and another victory cheer greeted his triumphant display. Oth's hearing faded and the roar of the cheer became the roaring drone of the river.

Oth thought of his village and the helpless cries of the dying. He remembered the flight across the foothills to get to Raven Kill where he knew he could make his stand. He pictured the eyes of his adopted daughter as she asked about the secret he had guarded all his life. Oth blinked the sweat out of his eyes and with sudden shock realized he did not picture his daughter's eyes in mere vision.

She lie huddled behind a large rock not five yards from him.

"No," he mouthed. She was a shivering bundle of leather scraps and dirt, sitting on the cold ground with her arms around her knees. Wide-eyed terror gripped her face and she looked close to screaming.

His duty was not complete. Not tonight. Maybe not ever. He could not give up. *Great God damn me for a fool for ever thinking I could.*

His right hand twitched, then planted against the stone and pushed. Oth rolled to his side. The cheering stopped.

Oth rose to his knees, pulled the knife out of his heart, and swung the curved blade up at the raider chief turning to face him. It slid deep into the man's belly and Oth forced the point upward. The chieftain reached down with both hands and clawed at the dagger's hilt. An expression of stunned surprise froze on his face and dark blood spurted around his fingers. Then he fell backward onto the mud on the moor side of the bridge.

Oth stood up and spat blood into the river. In a wheezing rasp he said, "I told you only I could choose when I die." He coughed roughly to clear further blood welling from his lungs and watched the war leader's eyes drift into death.

A great shuffling of feet sounded behind him. Oth turned and looked at the mass of disbelieving Pechts. He balled his fists and limped forward.

They turned and fled as one.

Oth paused then and let the weariness creep over him. He staggered to the rock and knelt by his daughter. Coughing, he spit more salty blood onto the ground. "You should not have seen this."

He sat heavily against the rock, his entire body caked with blood and mud, and watched the tattered remains of the Pechti tribe disappear into the darkness. His daughter touched his shoulder and he felt a rush of warmth from her presence. Around him, all that remained was a death filled bridge and rocks rising out of the river like knuckles of the Earth.

Rogue Blades
ENTERTAINMENT

What is the legacy of a hero? A dented shield and worn blade? A song briefly upon the lips of the masses? How about a mindset, an approach to life that does not change despite circumstances. But what if the hero changes? Can one still be heroic without the proper tools? The hero certainly believes so. Heroism inspires – sometimes the very person being heroic. And sometimes the most heroic moments of a life don't arrive while being 'heroic.'

Nik Hawkins writes and edits at a large university in the Midwest, where he lives with Loki the cat, an enchanting fiancée, and a gnawing hunger for the tales of myth and heroic adventure. As most such tales focus on protagonists in the prime of their youth, Nik decided to find out what tale an aged hero might have left in him. To see what other thoughts might come his way, visit Nik's blog at http://nihawkins.wordpress.com.

What Heroes Leave Behind

by Nicholas Ian Hawkins

On a cold seaside morning, when the gray cliffs wept for the passing of summer, a hero awoke to a reflection he did not know.

A feeble light seeped though the window as Tolasun rose from his bed. He shuffled stiffly to a stone basin and washed the dreams from his eyes. As the dark water calmed, he waited to see the familiar gaze of a warrior. Instead, a tired, wavering stranger stared back.

His bright hazel eyes had gone dull and yellow. Where they once shone through russet locks, they now hid behind wispy strands of gray. Ragged scars decorated his face like the red paint of war, and flesh sagged beneath his once proud chin. Within the merciful illusions of sleep, he had forgotten how swiftly the years passed. Had it truly been so long?

He could remember at least sixty Iron Seasons, though he had no doubt weathered the bitter cold of a few more. In those long years, he had forgotten his home, and why he had left it. For the moment, though, home was the Salty Brine Inn, a stout, dockside building of rough-hewn stone soaked in mist from the sea. He had visited the place often in his younger days for ale and women and rest from the road. He knew not why he had strayed here this time. Long ago, he had learned to follow the pull of his spirit. He moved as his soul moved, for it brought him where he was needed most. Now it seemed he moved but to fill empty spaces.

A knock on the door echoed in the lonely room, but Tolasun did not hear it. He gazed past his aged reflection into the dim light of his past, to the roar of battle, the ring of steel. He drifted back to the years he had spent with the Wintermen of Sard, to their raids on the rich Parnan missions filled with fat, self-righteous priests. He recalled months of errantry with the liveried knights of Paltra, when he had driven back a tide of vicious Celembri bent on conquering the world.

He saw himself as he once was, striding boldly across endless leagues, facing down countless trials with ferocity and will, with nimble feet and a dancing sword. In those days, the skalds and minstrels had sung his praises. Swift as his deadly strike, his name had become one with savior and justice and hero.

But that was another age. Now his enemies had dwindled and hid in dark places. Years had passed since he had donned his armor or drawn his sword. His deeds had faded into forgotten legend, and his name rarely graced the songs of the bards. Few knew he yet lived.

Another knock on the door chased away visions of the past. He straightened himself with a groan and hastened to pull a tunic over his growing girth as he made his way to the door.

A dark-haired woman he had known well in his younger days waited outside the door, awash in the gray light of the morning. For a thrilling moment, he thought she had come to him, as she had on many hot nights in the past, and he felt the youthful lust rise within. But he soon remembered she had married the village blacksmith decades ago, and they had had many children to fill their lives with smiles.

"Liel," Tolasun said. "It is good to see you." He held the door to let her pass into the small room.

"I scarcely believed it when they said you had returned, Tol," Liel said. "But I am glad to know it is true."

Tolasun smiled. Liel's beauty still shone through the wear of time. Though gray streaked her hair and creases lined her face, youth yet graced her movements, and the wisdom behind her eyes lent her fresh allure. Tolasun stood admiring her when a stern, well-dressed youth entered the room.

"My eldest son would speak with you, Tol, about a threat to our village," Liel said. "Will you hear him?"

"Of course, of course. Please, speak."

Tolasun examined the young man. He wore a black cloak over gray tunic and breeks and was armed with a long hunting knife. He stood eye-level with Tolasun – a full six feet – and well-groomed brown hair hung to his shoulders, framing the strong outlines of his face. The lad had seen probably twenty Iron Seasons, maybe twenty-five, but his determined hazel eyes revealed maturity and ambition. This was the reflection Tolasun had expected in the washbasin only moments ago. As he pondered this, the young man spoke.

"Greetings, Tolasun," he said with a slight bow. "I am Ebren. While I do not know you, there are still some in this village who remember your great deeds, and I have learned of them. They are truly the stuff of legend. This is why I and the other village leaders seek your aid in a matter of grave urgency."

Tolasun had almost forgotten how this felt. He basked in the nostalgia, barely concealing the excitement that brewed inside him. "Tell me of this matter."

"We have ill tidings from the Sovan monks in the Mountains of Morning. Several days ago, a group of brothers went to gather building stones from the ruins of Ustrien. They have not yet returned to the monastery. Some monks have explored the outskirts, but do not dare go nearer. They tell me it is surrounded by an eerie silence. Not a bird sings, not an insect hums. The deer no longer drink from the stream that runs through the ruins. Not even the crag cats stray too near. We fear that whatever evil has taken root in the old fortress will soon come for us."

Tolasun considered the request for half a moment. "Ebren, tell the others I leave for the old fortress tomorrow. I will find what troubles Ustrien." As he spoke, he felt the hole inside him begin to fill.

Liel smiled in relief, and Ebren failed to hide his surprise at the warrior's quick decision. "Thank you, Tolasun," he said. "The village will rest assured that such a great warrior goes to defend us. I will tell the village leaders the good news. Should you need anything to aid you, you have but to ask. I wish you luck, Tolasun."

Ebren strode from the room, leaving Liel and Tolasun in silence. After a long moment, Liel spoke. "The village leaders – they thought you would take to him because of our . . . past."

"I'm still taken with you," Tolasun said, mischief in his voice. She gave him a dubious look, and Tolasun cleared his throat.

"Well, he seems a good man, your son. Strong. Looks familiar, too."

"He is not yours," Liel said quickly; she had always known his mind. "You may think so because his features are so like yours, but that is the look of his father, as well. And he has his father's sense of responsibility . . . and commitment. He is not yours."

Tolasun nodded; Liel went on. "But he is willful, restless. He will go to Ustrien, despite the urging of others that he stay. Please, you must keep him from doing so."

"Why?" Tolasun asked. "He seems quite capable, and the monks could use the help." Wode knows I could, as well, he thought. "Perhaps you worry too much."

"But my worry has merit, Tol. Not long ago, one of the fish-wives heard Manira calling my name from the sea, so she took me to the shore. She carved runes into pieces of driftwood and whale-bone, tied them together with kelp, and threw the bundle to the tide as an offering. I saw a yellow serpent rise to swallow it and take it below. The next morning, I came upon a giant oyster washed ashore, and inside I found this." She reached into her cloak and pulled out a smooth red orb the size of an acorn. "It showed me an awful vision."

She held it out to Tolasun, but he hesitated. "I know these pearls. Corlunes, they are called. They are said to hold the future."

"Yes. Take it, and behold the vision I saw."

Tolasun grasped the pearl, and the world turned black. But soon a distant light appeared, like the far-off mouth of a cave seen from deep within the darkness. He began rushing toward the light, floating like a spirit, and it grew larger and brighter. Soon, the glow surrounded him.

He found himself in the midst of a battle, viewing the carnage through the eyes of a stranger. The stranger's hand came into Tolasun's view. It grasped a long hunting knife, much like Ebren's, and the wrist bore three long streaks of blood. Beyond the hand, a blanket of smoke covered all else.

Out of the dense grayness, a snarling warrior rushed at the stranger, whirling a wicked sword. Tolasun's vision turned to the pale sky, as if the stranger were falling backwards. Above, he saw the bloody hand lose its grip on the hunting knife. Then, as suddenly as he had arrived, Tolasun floated back through the darkness, the light dwindling before him until he was again standing with

Liel in the small room in the Salty Brine Inn. Tolasun wore a haunted expression.

"So you saw it," Liel said. She took the pearl from Tolasun. "I know it was Ebren's fate. The knife is his, without a doubt. And I know his hands like I know no others. I held them when he cried; I watched them grow."

"This vision could mean many things, Liel – they are not always as they seem." The furrows on her brow remained deep with concern. Tolasun sighed with quiet pity. "If I see Ebren on the path to Ustrien, I will do my best to send him home."

"Please, do what you can. He will not listen to me, nor will he heed his father. Could a hero sway him?"

Tolasun smiled inwardly at the word "hero." Perhaps all the land had not forgotten him yet. "Maybe. I know that youth often ignore wisdom from the mouths of mothers and fathers, regardless of the sense it makes. Perhaps it is well, then, that he is not mine." Tolasun placed his hand gently on Liel's shoulder. "But perhaps . . . perhaps he should have been."

Liel turned to face him, lovely and soft in the brightening dawn, and smiled. "No. You were meant to leave a different kind of legacy in this world. Your heart is pure, but it will not let you be still. And now you must go again."

She traced the long, bright scar that stretched from ear to mouth on his left cheek, a gift from the fire hydra, Lursus. Long ago, he had defeated the beast and saved the village. When he returned from its lair, he had made love to Liel for the first time.

Liel took her hand from the scar and gazed out the window. "It's a lonely sea," she said. She kissed Tolasun lightly on the cheek and left him with the ghosts of regret.

He leaned on the windowsill and looked out at the water, toward the hazy gray infinity where the sky drinks the sea and the sea drowns the sky. "Yes. Lonely." He lingered for a sad moment. Before long, though, pride and confidence surged within his soul. Once again, he was needed. Once again, he had reason to move.

Tolasun dragged a bundle of animal skins from beneath his bed and unfolded it, revealing his battle-worn armor of thick iron scales on a backing of supple leather. Fitful care had left it slightly dull and splotched, but at the shoulders unyielding mother-of-pearl spaulders – plundered long ago from the den of a sea witch – still glimmered with many colors.

Next to the armor rested his steel falchion, forever keen and wanting for blood – yet for years, settling for little more than dust. He caressed the worn leather of the pommel, darkened and molded to his grip with the grime of battle. A sword master of Paltra had forged the falchion for Tolasun after he had fought off the Celembri. The steel blade, folded innumerable times in its forging, was light as wind, strong as the bones of the earth, and unequalled in quality. He had never named it, for no name seemed worthy.

Beneath his armor and sword he found his round, oaken shield, covered with the gashes of old battles, but still stout and solid. As the day wore on, he meticulously cleaned, polished, and sharpened his tools of war until they shone like his eyes at the cusp of battle. When he finished, he held his sword to the light of the dying fire to examine the fine edge. His gaze turned to his hands.

Much like his sword, his hands appeared strong and untouched – the one part of him that still felt young. But his eyes moved to his arm, to the creeping sag of his muscles, and he thought better of climbing the mountains to face whatever evil lurked within the ruins of Ustrien.

Tolasun had little experience with self-doubt, and he found the feeling unsettling. He opened the cedar chest, intending to pack away his weapons and armor, but he paused when the hollow sound of panpipes drifted through the window. They breathed a familiar, high tempo tune, one he had heard on many nights in his younger days. He went to the window in time to catch two young boys, one the piper and the other the singer, as they danced by in full song:

When Tolasun and Lursus met
In cold and rain and murky wet,
Lursus lost four heads of five
And ran into the marsh to hide.
Then Tolasun returned to Vore
To love a lass and drink some more!

He has no weakness, knows no fear.
He loves the wine, the mead, the beer.
His sword will slay our enemies,
Great Tolasun will make us free!

Vore, Tolasun thought. The name of the village. Such trivial things escaped him. But whatever the village's name, he cared for its people – folk who had not forgotten him yet, as so many others had. He had saved Vore once, and he would do so again. For a man without weakness – without fear – there was no other choice.

The next day, the sun burned away the clouds and brightened the world. Tolasun pulled his armor over his scarred body – a snug fit, but acceptable – and covered the iron scales with a long cloak of wolf hide. Hefting sword, shield, and a sack of provisions, he began his trek on foot, for a horse would only burden him in the mountains.

At the edge of town, the villagers had lined up to wish the warrior well. Their encouraging words carried respect and admiration, but a dolorous feeling struck Tolasun as he passed: he knew their faces, and even some of their names, but he did not know their hearts.

Tolasun's roving spirit would not allow him friends or a wife or wealth – that which would hold him in one place. He had accepted gifts of treasure in his time, but no more than he could carry. He had walked proudly under the gaze of admirers, bled with comrades-in-arms, delighted in many lovers. But he had never known true companions. There had been no time.

To push away his regret, Tolasun scooped up a small village girl in his strong but tender hands and kissed her on the forehead, then placed her back in her mother's arms to the cheers of the crowd. The innkeeper handed Tolasun a flagon of ale and he drained it with a speed befitting his legend. With a final salute to the gathering, he prompted another round of cheers, and walked on.

The young piper from the previous night danced alongside Tolasun for half a league, blowing the same upbeat tune on his battered pipes. Tolasun sent the boy back to the village with a playful swipe and continued toward the green foothills beneath the Mountains of Morning.

The cool sea breeze at his back urged him on, and the sun, cresting the mountains ahead, called him hither. With the thrill of new adventure, the vigor of his youth returned. Under the soft warmth of the early Fading Season, he sprang through the grass as light-footed as the Fay, scattering the dew like shivered gems. The grinding in his joints vanished, replaced by the familiar creak of leather, the rattle of iron scales. Life burned fiercely in his breast.

Soon, the path grew steep, and the foothills loomed dauntingly ahead. Tolasun's springy step turned to a trudge as he made his way over the rolling slopes into arduous terrain. His shadow grew long as the sun descended at his back. When the warrior reached the first gray face of the mountains, his energy was already sapped, so he chose to rest until morning at the base of the spires. In his youth, he would have traveled through the night, but his brief respite from old age had ended, and he felt again the full weight of his years.

The next day, Tolasun was greeted by a creeping ache in his joints and limbs. He ignored the pain and ate a meager breakfast in the shadow of the mountains. Daunted by his fatigue, though, he decided he could not manage the eastern route to Ustrien. Although the most direct, it was far too steep and dangerous. Instead, he began a lateral climb south to the Sovan monastery. From there, he would have an easier trek to the ruins.

Tolasun followed narrow crevices that wound between sheer cliffs. He skirted along treacherous ridges. The agonizing climb taxed him to his limits, for he carried more weight and less muscle than his younger self. When he felt his body would surely give out, the white stone obelisk of a Sovan fane caught his eye, and he stumbled on, desperate for the solace he would find within the monastery walls.

After a final struggle up a steep chute of loose boulders, the terrain flattened, and Tolasun staggered into the monastery grounds, gasping for air in the fading light. A gray-robed brother drawing water from a stream noticed the haggard warrior and came to his aid.

"Let me help you," he said, and lent Tolasun his shoulder.

Breathless, Tolasun could only give thanks with a nod. The young monk half-dragged Tolasun to the main hall of the monastery and eased him down beside the glowing hearth in the center of the room. He covered the warrior in a wool blanket and brought him a bowl of hot porridge.

Tolasun accepted the gifts gratefully, but with stinging pride. "Your name, brother?"

"Wenlos. And yours?"

"Tol . . . Tolasun," he said as he drifted to sleep.

The monk's eyes showed no recognition. "You are safe here, Tolasun. For now."

Tolasun's only response was the steady breathing of a deep, exhausted sleep.

Tolasun awoke to a fiendish cold. It filled the room with a dankness that chilled his bones like the northern seas. A shiver rippled through his body and amplified the familiar pressure on his bladder. He couldn't remember having slept through an entire night in the last decade without waking to piss. Agitated, he shuffled into the frigid night to relieve himself. Frost blanketed the ground outside and coated the scrubby mountain trees in gleaming crystal. As Tolasun struggled to make water, he noticed a shadow before the low moon – a vague shape like a man crouching.

"Show yourself!" Tolasun called.

The shape stirred and sprinted along the cliff's edge with the spryness of youth. Tolasun saw the outline of a sword, the silhouette of a shield, and the contours of taught muscle. He pursued, but the shape disappeared suddenly. Surprised, Tolasun skidded to a stop at the edge of the chute of loose boulders he had climbed the day before. He caught his balance on the trunk of a thick stone oak growing through a crack in the rock shelf.

Tolasun heard scrabbling below and shouted down the chute, "'Tis wise to run from me, prowler!" Feeling old and out of breath, he knew he could not catch one so young. He decided to return to the hall, a warmer and more defensible place. On his way, stimulated by the excitement of the chase, he emptied his bladder in a flood of relief.

When Tolasun returned to the hall, the hearth fire had reduced itself to embers and only the light of the half-moon lit the room through its narrow windows. The air felt even colder than the night outside, and the hairs on the back of his neck stood on end. Wary, Tolasun scanned the hall. A ghostly puff of breath floated through a beam of light in the southeast corner. He was not alone.

A scuffle like leather soles sliding on stone echoed throughout the hall, followed by a soft but menacing cackle. A voice creaked from a throat dry with death. "You fool warriors are all the same. You think you can outrun me? Hide from me? Will me away from your soul?"

A man-shaped shadow moved through the dark. Another cackle drifted out of the gloom, but it was drowned out by the sound of a thousand fluttering, membranous wings. Swift as the wind, the shadow enveloped Tolasun, its claw-like hands grasping at his throat. It rasped again, "Sooner or later, you all must face me!"

A pale face emerged from the shadow's hood, revealing a malign, toothless grin – an abomination of every old man Tolasun had ever seen, but surely not a man at all. It hissed with breath from the grave. Tolasun fell to his back and the aged thing pinned him to the floor. He turned his face away from the hideous stench and saw his falchion leaning on the hearth, just out of reach.

The shadowy thing possessed an obscene strength in its gnarled hands. It dragged them downward, carving red streaks into Tolasun's neck, and stopped at the warrior's heart. Tolasun felt a tremendous weight press down on his chest, like a wagon rolling over him, and his ribs began to yield to the pressure. He gasped in vain as sparks burst before his eyes. This, he thought, would be his last adventure. But his warrior's spirit cast thoughts of defeat aside. He reached deep within himself, past the lost strength of his youth, down to the vim he had kept hidden from time and age.

With a surge of maddened power, Tolasun grasped the shadow's wrists and pushed upward, bending the thing backward at its waist. The bones of its arms snapped like twigs and its crooked spine creaked in protest. A grisly crack echoed through the hall, and the thing screamed. Tolasun grabbed a log from the hearth and shoved it into the shadow's wrinkled face. Its black cloak lit up like a torch. It ran from the hall into the frigid night, fanning the flames and shrieking in pain and rage and surprise.

Out of the darkness, the crag cats roared in reply.

Just before dawn, Brother Wenlos found Tolasun curled and shivering in a corner of the hall and gently nudged him awake. The warrior veered from deep sleep to lethal alertness in half a moment. Startled, Wenlos stumbled backwards. It took Tolasun only another instant to take in his surroundings and realize where he was.

"Apologies, Brother Wenlos," Tolasun said. He lifted his aching body from the straw-covered floor. "An old warrior's habit, that – startling those who wake me."

"No apologies necessary, Tolasun," the monk said. He made his way to the hearth. "But why are you sleeping there in the corner? It is much warmer near the fire."

Tolasun recalled the abomination he had fought during the night. "I doubt you would believe me if I told you, brother."

Wenlos gave him a puzzled look and began to prepare breakfast. Tolasun moved closer to the fire and sat on the edge of the hearth. He looked himself over to see if he had sustained any grievous wounds and was shocked to see the scratches on his neck had disappeared. But he still felt the awful, crushing weight on his chest, the shortness of breath. He rubbed above his heart and hacked painfully until his mouth filled with phlegm.

"Your cough troubles me," Wenlos said. "It was a cold night. Perhaps you caught a chill."

"Perhaps, though—" Tolasun's words were lost in another fit of coughing.

"I know what will help." Wenlos left the hall and returned with a handful of dried yellow flowers and crackling green leaves. He tossed them in a bowl of boiling water on the hearth. "Foalsfoot. It will ease your cough."

Wenlos let the mixture bubble for several moments then urged Tolasun to drink. He did, and warm relief spread through his insides like mulled wine. He took long, deep breaths into his clearing lungs, and the crisp morning air lent him strength.

Tolasun and Wenlos were mid-way through their porridge when shouts drifted in from the monastery grounds. They could not make out the words, but understood the urgency in the tone. Then a robed brother burst into the hall.

"To arms!" the monk called to no one in particular. "Raiders have come to sack the monastery!" He ran off to spread the alarm elsewhere.

Raiders? Tolasun thought. The man he chased during the night must have been a scout. *But what of the ancient shadow?* He rubbed his chest and coughed again.

Wenlos gave Tolasun a grave look. "We have little with which to defend ourselves, Tolasun. A few of us were once warriors, but we cannot hope to fight them off. Will you help us?"

Tolasun lurched to his feet. He did not seem himself, weak as he was from his journey. But the porridge and herbs had strengthened him, and a battle waited. He nodded at Wenlos, took up his falchion and shield, and ran through the door of the hall.

Outside, the thatch roof of a small outbuilding blazed, covering the monastery grounds in dense smoke. Torches carried by invisible raiders hovered and shifted in the soot and added their glow to the early dawn. The scant light revealed scattered bodies of dead and dying monks, their warm blood melting the blanket of frost on the ground. Enraged, Tolasun strode toward the nearest torch, intent on slaying its bearer, but a familiar face emerged from the smoke.

"Ebren!" Tolasun yelled. "What in Wode's name are you doing here?"

Ebren stopped several yards away, a confused look on his face. "I arrived an hour before dawn to tell the monks you went to Ustrien, to give them hope. Why are you here, and not there?"

Before Tolasun could explain, a hulking shag of a man rushed out of the smoke toward Ebren, bellowing like a berserker and swinging a bearded axe. Two other ragged men armed with clubs swarmed upon Tolasun.

Ebren ducked beneath the axe swipe, drew his long hunting knife, and turned to face his assailant. But the hairy raider was swift and grappled Ebren in a ferocious bear hug. Ebren stabbed the raider again and again – in the back, the shoulder, the kidney – but he only squeezed harder. After piercing flesh half a dozen useless times, the blade lodged itself between the raider's ribs. Ebren lost his grip on the knife. Defenseless, his bones began to give in to the vicious embrace. Breath surged from his body.

Then Tolasun was there. He stormed through the drifting smoke, two raiders bleeding out their lives on the ground behind him. With his bloodied falchion, he hacked the shaggy raider behind the knees and drove him to the ground. Tolasun shifted to an overhead swing and brought the blade down upon the raider's neck. It bit deep. The man shuddered and fell forward upon Ebren.

Tolasun dropped his falchion and shield to lift the heavy corpse off of Ebren, but the shaggy raider felt like a slab of lead. As Tolasun struggled with the weight, Ebren's eyes widened in fear, and Tolasun knew danger approached from behind. He tore the hunting knife from the corpse, turned, and sprang to his feet just in time to see another savage-looking raider emerge from the smoke, swinging his sword low.

Reflex spurred Tolasun into an evasive roll. As he crouched and fell backward, the world slowed. He had the disquieting sense that he had witnessed this all before. And he had. Just as in the vision of the corlune, he saw the sky brightening through the smoke. He saw the hunting knife in his grasp and three red streaks trickling from the hilt, down across his wrist. When he hit the ground, the impact jarred the knife from his hands – young hands, like Ebren's. So the vision was right, and wrong.

Tolasun rolled to his feet, unscathed. The raider's sword had passed harmlessly above him. But now half a dozen more raiders closed in, cautious but brimming with menace. Without sword and shield, Tolasun felt like naked flesh in a winter storm. He glanced at Ebren; the lad appeared to be unconscious. Hoping the raiders would think the young man dead, Tolasun ran. The raiders followed, shouting war cries and swinging blades.

Tolasun dashed as quickly as his aging legs could carry him toward the chute of boulders at the outskirts of the monastery grounds. As his wind left him, the lip of the chute appeared through the smoke, recognizable only to one who knew it was there. The raiders were gaining ground. Tolasun gasped, stumbled. His momentum carried him forward with long, staggering steps. The nearest raider lifted his sword. Tolasun jumped.

His leap carried him over the lip of the chute toward a broad, overhanging branch of the stoneoak. But the distance seemed too great. Tolasun stretched, groaning with the strain. He hovered for a terrible moment over the emptiness beneath him and sent a silent prayer to Wode. Then his forearms struck the branch. He grabbed hold and lifted his armpit over the sturdy limb of the tree.

Behind him, blinded by smoke and unaware of the drop off, the raiders plunged headlong down the chute. Tolasun could not see the carnage as he fought to hang on, but he heard their horrible shrieks, followed by the sickening crunch of bone and the pulpy pop of broken skulls. He smiled in grim satisfaction.

When Tolasun returned to the monastery grounds, the monks had subdued the few remaining invaders. Ebren had regained his wind and freed himself from the death grip of the shaggy raider. He gave Tolasun a thankful nod.

Wenlos had just finished binding the hands and feet of a surviving raider when Tolasun approached. "We believe this one leads the rabble," Wenlos said.

Tolasun peered down at the captive, a middle-aged man with blond hair and dark eyes. He wore slightly better rags than the rest and seemed decidedly calm despite his predicament. He stared evenly back at Tolasun and smiled.

"Tolasun?" the captive said. His smile widened to reveal teeth like mud. "Could it be you?"

"I am called Tolasun," he said. "Who are you?"

"I knew you when I was just a lad. By Wode, you were old then, and now you look worse for the wear. Certainly not worthy of the songs the skalds left in your wake. If they could see you now, they'd rethink their praises."

"Andred," Tolasun said. "I knew you in Sard. It seems you have fallen far since then. Sacking Parnan churches is one thing, but attacking helpless monks devoted to the gods of your people? This is not the action of a true Winterman."

"Ah, Tolasun. Always judging, as if you were the very voice of justice. Why don't you leave justice to the gods you speak of? You are just a man, Tolasun, as I am – no better, no worse. And these are hard times for my people, times that will drive a man to do what he must. So cease your preaching."

Tolasun shook his head sadly then addressed the gathered monks. "When he recovers from his wounds, have him build pyres for the dead and repair what he has destroyed. Then do with him what you will. But keep a leash on him: he is treacherous."

Andred's cockiness turned to anger. He struggled with his bonds. "The crag cats take you, you self-righteous bastard!"

With the thrill of battle gone, Tolasun's blood had cooled, and the pain in his chest returned. He walked away, so the others would not hear his croup, and sat upon a small boulder. The smoke had cleared, and the sun had risen fully over the mountains. Tolasun gazed up the slopes toward Ustrien. There, a tendril of smoke rose like a crooked white pillar. Wenlos and Ebren approached and followed Tolasun's gaze.

"The smoke began a few days ago," Wenlos said. "It is not dark like burning wood, but cloudy, like a hot spring. We do not know what it portends."

"Well, I go to find out," Tolasun said.

"Tolasun," Ebren said, concern in his voice. "You are about finished. How will you have strength left to fight, if you must? Wait a while. Rest. The monks will understand. So will the people of Vore."

"It's not the going I fear will do me in." Tolasun grimaced and rubbed his chest. "It's the waiting too long."

"Then I go with you," Ebren said.

Tolasun coughed again. "No. I promised your mother. Stay here or we'll both have Liel's wrath to face. I fear her more than some unnamed menace in the old fortress up there."

Ebren protested, but Tolasun silenced him with an unyielding stare. The old warrior clasped Ebren on the shoulder, recovered his shield and falchion, and prepared for the final ascent to Ustrien.

The climb from the monastery to the ruins was less arduous than the trek from Vore. But pain nagged Tolasun through every step. Before leaving the monastery he had taken another draught of the foalsfoot elixir, which eased the pressure in his chest. Still, the ache would not subside, and spread slowly to his left arm. Tolasun had known old men to die this way, a death unbefitting a hero. He would rather fall while swinging a sword.

Adrift in his misery, Tolasun lost track of time, and soon he found himself standing before the crumbling walls of Ustrien. Built as a bastion against the legions of Sule during the height of that empire, the old stronghold was now barely distinguishable from the mountains upon which it stood. Wind and water had worn it down to a great stone heap. The stillness of the place was like a deep winter night, the silence unnatural. The courtyard gateway still stood, and Tolasun walked through.

A white mist like the steam in a Mesrani bath had settled upon the grounds. Through the haze, Tolasun could see a mountain stream that had long ago carved a path through the middle of the fortress. It fell from the cliffs in a glittering cascade, cut through the roof of the main keep, and flowed out the gate into the courtyard. The pillar of white smoke – which Tolasun could now see was steam – rose from the top of the keep.

Tolasun drew his falchion, waded through the stream, and halted at the keep's gate. He clutched his left arm and fell to a knee, coughing and wheezing. After several tortured moments, the spasm passed, and he continued on his path.

Inside the keep, Tolasun heard the soft splash of water. Light flooded through the broken roof, pierced the murk, and shimmered upon the falling water, revealing the source of the mist. Tolasun could scarcely believe it.

Beneath the waterfall lay the fire hydra Lursus. Pale vapors billowed from its mammoth-sized body as water swept across its deep gray scales. Once again the beast bore five heads: the four Tolasun had taken in their first encounter had grown back, as hydra heads will. Each was attached to a long, serpentine neck covered with tufts of wiry black hair. The necks lay upon the keep floor, bridging the stream like fallen towers. One of them – the one Tolasun had failed to take – stretched out well beyond the others. The beast's body rose and fell with steady breaths; it appeared to be sleeping.

Tolasun knew a bit of hydra lore – at least enough to deduce what was happening. Like heroes, fire hydras also succumbed to old age. After several hundred years, the organs in their throats that mix the elements of flame begin to fail. They burn from within until the creature overheats, or the elements smolder through. Lursus rested under the waterfall to cool its feverous body.

"So you crawled your way here from the stink of the marshes to plan your revenge, only to be taken by old age," said Tolasun. The hydra's ten eyes flashed open and ten nostrils flared like snorting bulls. But it did not move, it only watched.

"How did it come to you, Lursus? In a waking dream? A wrinkled old serpent like a sheath of dead snakeskin? The withered bastard tried to end me, too, but I sent him away screaming. Just like the last time you and I met." Tolasun pointed to the long scar on his cheek. "You gave me this, but I left you cowering in the swamps with but one head remaining. It seems you've licked your wounds and come back here to breathe fire upon us once again, eh? No matter. New necks will yield to my blade as easily as the old."

Recognition and hatred flared in the hydra's many eyes. Lursus gave a low growl and a shudder as if gathering itself for one last bite – or one last burst of flame. Age had not sucked the fight from it yet. Tolasun crouched and circled, ready to defend or strike. His blood boiled. He asked only that his heart carry him through this battle, whatever its end.

The hydra pounced like a crag cat. Tolasun warded off one set of jaws with his shield and dodged two others. He spun away, crouching again, and noticed that two of Lursus's heads sagged uselessly, each with gaping black holes where its fire organs had burned through. At the same time, Tolasun's exertions brought the pressure back into his chest, the rack into his left arm. He dropped his shield and fell to his knees. The hydra lumbered toward him, three slavering maws open wide for the kill.

Tolasun dipped a shoulder to roll away. He wasn't quick enough. Something gripped his thigh and hip like a vise. Searing pain coursed through his body. Then he dangled upside down, trapped in the jaws of one of Lursus's minor heads.

With a barbaric growl, he thrust his falchion upward into Lursus's nearest eye until the sword bit into brain. The beast yowled and released Tolasun. The warrior landed painfully on his back, the blade still in his hand. He dragged himself away from the hydra; a wide smear of blood glistened behind him. Swearing through the pain, he stood to face the next rush.

Lursus came slower this time, three of its heads now merely dead weight. Tolasun felt his confidence rise. "Down to only two, Lursus! Is this feeling familiar?"

The hydra's largest head shot forward. Tolasun sidestepped the snapping jaws and brought his falchion down upon the neck like an axe. The blade cleaved deeply and a shower of viscous black blood sprayed like a geyser. The hydra roared; Tolasun silenced the beast with two quick slashes that fully severed its head.

Tolasun stepped back, his guard relaxed for but a moment when the mouth of the hydra's remaining head clamped upon his shoulder. The mother-of-pearl spaulder burst into glittering shards. Lursus lifted Tolasun, shook viciously, and flung him away. The stream broke the warrior's fall, but blood flowed from his wounds, forming a pink cloud in the water around him.

Already pale, Tolasun waded to the stream's edge and leaned upon the steep bank. Lursus came again, belching smoke as its body – too long out of the water – began to overheat. Tolasun could no longer lift his sword. He braced himself for a brutal bite, and then the end. It would be a satisfying death.

The hydra was almost upon him when Tolasun heard a low rumble from above. He watched in disbelief as a boulder the size of a warhorse plunged from the roof, careened into the hydra's back, and snapped its spine like a wooden rafter. The boulder came to a rest upon the blackly bloodied remains as Lursus gurgled its final hot breath.

Tolasun thrust his falchion point down in the sand next to him and lay back on the stream bank. Above, Ebren leaned over the edge of the great gap in the roof, waving and shouting words that did not reach Tolasun's ears. Tolasun returned the greeting weakly and closed his eyes. The pain had left him, and his heart still beat. When he opened his eyes again, Ebren was gone, and a shaft of sunlight shot into the ruined building, casting a rainbow in the mist.

"Tell me I have led a good life, Wode," Tolasun whispered. "Make me believe I did not squander my days; that I did not pass on what I should have seized. Tell me I will be remembered."

Tolasun thought of Liel and Ebren, of the people of Vore and the Sovan monks. He thought of the joy they would know at being free of the black weight of menace. Remembered or not, at least he had spent this day well.

The mist had almost cleared from the room when Ebren stepped into the dancing rays of sun and crouched beside Tolasun. The warrior looked into Ebren's eyes, the very eyes he had expected to see reflected in the water on that morning two long days ago. He grasped Ebren's hands in his own, and for a moment, their entwined fingers looked like the hands of twins gathering something precious. Then Tolasun placed Ebren's palms on the falchion's hilt.

"The sword passes to you, Ebren."

Tolasun let his hands drop, smiled, and closed his eyes. As he relished his last breaths, he thought he heard voices drift in from outside, singing in time to the fading beat of his heart . . .

. . . Great Tolasun will make us free.

Can a single moment define a person – or is that one instant merely part of the definition, simply a bookmark in a lifetime of events? Certainly a prettier bookmark, perhaps even a valuable one, and definitely an important one. But when the book is full of them, what gives that particular placeholder any more consequence than another? Who does this defining, or the placing for that matter? And finally, when a bookmark is placed, is anyone at that moment even aware of its importance? I wonder if many of the participants in this battle on the plains of Torkas Nahl fully grasp the import of that which they do . . .

David Pitchford is a man of much variety. Prolific novelist, epic poet, on-call editor; overall stand up fellow. One half of the team that got me into this business (the 'Pitch' of Pitch-Black fame). David claims his writing is not a product of his imagination – he is the product of his writing. Writing is as much what he is as what he does. You'll find the proof of these assertions at his blogs: poetry at http://fringemonkey.wordpress.com *and all the rest at* http://bitterhermit.wordpress.com.

Fatefist at Torkas Nahl

A Tale of Arnoux Trav

by David Pitchford

Galwa spat from his high perch atop the wall of Torkas Nahl. His eyes narrowed. He gazed into the distance, into the dying sunlight of day's end. Two armies besieged the ancient city. Primus Keinwhid of the Lands of Sunset had brought his son for his first blooding. Rajan Vace, second emperor of Maltopia, marched his armies opposite the Keinwhid forces, his renowned Maneguard clustered strategically on his front lines.

"Bring the Fist," Galwa ordered a young monk in a cinnamon smock.

"Why the boy?" asked Badru Ibn Abbas, Prince of Torkas Nahl. "I am the general of my armies. I shall ride my chariot out and reclaim the splendor and glory of my ancestors."

"You are welcome to your foolishness," Galwa replied. "That is your choice."

"What auguries?" Badru asked the aged priest, turning the conversation to avoid his own annoyance. He wondered again how a withered, ancient man could hold such personal presence. Even Badru's father, Abbas Ibn Sayyid, had not been as imposing.

"The falcon flew south. The dove huddles in her cage. Ra promised blood in the dawning," Galwa said calmly. "Dawn's kid bleated on the altar; its gall bladder was filled with stones and the artery of its heart was curved backward. Its brain was enlarged but perfect."

A tall, hooded figure in a simple gray robe approached in respectful silence. He bowed to each.

"Prince Badru Ibn Abbas," Galwa motioned to the cloaked figure. "This is Arnoux Trav."

"My dear Trav," Badru bowed. "It is my great pleasure to meet you. Great and many have been the words of praise I have heard from my friend, Galwa. May it please the gods you are equal to this task brought to test you."

Trav bowed politely. Badru recoiled at the other's silence, expecting verbal acknowledgement. He looked to Galwa, Teacher of the Mikari.

"He has taken an oath of silence . . ." Galwa began.

"A mute? Camel dung! I have had enough of foolishness!" He turned and gave orders for his army to assemble behind the gates.

Galwa turned back to watch the troop progressions in the fields around the city.

"Take this lesson to heart, Trav. Gaze out now and note the troops, their arrangements, the way they spread to cover their weakness and show strength. How will you exploit their softness – turn their power against them and win from them their victory?"

Trav pulled the hood back to improve his field of vision. His shaven pate brought a sense of timeless youth to his hard-angled face. Blue-gray eyes gazed placidly out of a serene, untouchable countenance.

Down at the gate, Badru rallied his troops and arranged them for a sally against the Keinwhid forces. He commanded his lancers to attack Keinwhid's cavalry, the Koenigsguard, his mounted archers to ready themselves to rain hell into the flank closest to the Maltopian Maneguard. Twelve-thousand lightly armored militia footmen were commanded to hold the main gate, leaving only volunteer militia to defend the city should the gate be breached – that and the 600 Mikari monks Galwa had committed to the defense.

"Should the city fall," Galwa said mildly to Arnoux Trav, "we are here to assure it falls to Keinwhid and not these savage Katchka." He used the race name for the brutal peoples that comprised most of the Maltopian Empire.

Trav motioned to the other, weaving his hands swiftly in a language used only by the Mikari.

"Your vow is fulfilled," Galwa said. "Speak."

"Yes," Trav said, his voice a husky whisper unused for seven years. "I thank my teacher. These lines are wise, yet unwily. Keinwhid is too cautious, Rajan of the Katchka overconfident."

"Then you have a strategy?"

"Many," Trav nodded, watching and plotting as he conversed with his mentor.

"Questions cloud your aura," Galwa commented.

"I am young," he kept his eyes on the activity below. "Unblooded as that prince of Keinwhid . . ."

"And yet wiser than either general," Galwa nodded. "You have studied seven years the histories, the philosophers, the scriptures of civilizations long fallen to the dust of memory. You are well prepared – and though unblooded, not untested."

"Say your will," Trav bowed. "I am but a tool in the broad hand of providence."

"Tools are only as useful as those who wield them," Galwa chanted the axiom like a mantra.

"I am the will and the guide of providence," Trav set his jaw, inhaling deeply to calm his mind. "What outcome do you desire, Teacher?"

"Let the Orbs roll their dice," Galwa sang again in axiom. "Vace has no love of learning; he fears rebellion should his hordes learn their own ignorance. Should he win Torkas Nahl, the library and temples of art shall be destroyed by fire and ignorant superstition.

"I forbid that should happen. We care not otherwise who is victor – nor whom vanquished."

Trav signaled for an acolyte, ordering the Mikari to the walls. He had them station themselves as closely as possible to each other to provide cover fire with their slings. Though the slings were ideal for the mountain campaigns the Mikari normally participated in, Trav was less than certain the height of the wall would help to make them as formidable as the bows below. His orders were simple: *prevent any outsider from entering*.

He watched as the gate opened to emit a host of horsemen as Badru charged out to form lines. Torkas Nahl's army fanned out as if to face both armies, stretching from the unscaleable Cliff of the

Sun on the north to the Butte of Gods, an extinct volcano, to the south. These natural fortifications had proven horribly effective for time immemorial, just as the western rear of the city was protected by the desert of Jyne Din's nagas, serpents that swam the desert like eels feeding on everything that came to the sand.

Trav noted with wry satisfaction that both besieging armies continued to form ranks such that they were best defended from each other's treachery. Trav's predictions were forming before his eyes just as they had in his imagination. He looked on in stony silence, internally adjusting the details of his strategy to fit reality.

The plains of Torkas Nahl fell silent. Comfortably outside bowshot, a champion from each camp strode forward and cast a javelin in the ancient tradition. Parties from each army rode out to meet within the triangle bordered by the javelins.

"Terms!" Badru barked.

"Keinwhid offers life and liberty to all who concede," said Primus Keinwhid.

"How kind," Badru said dryly, his lips curling in contempt.

"Rajan Vace offers swifter death in his inestimable mercy," offered the dark emperor. His eyes broiled with hatred, malice, and ambition enough to send a shiver through the whole group.

"Another magnanimous offer," Badru said, this time in soft scorn.

"What terms offers the glorious and terrible Badru Ibn Abbas Ibn Sayyid Ibn Din?" Keinwhid bowed, his voice toned for calculated diplomacy.

"To Keinwhid," Badru smiled and bowed in the manner of his people. "I offer one fresh horse from my own stable and leave to retire to his own kingdom – having remunerated the lands and people of Din Aashra.

"To Vace," his eyes flashed menace. "Withdrawal in full and I shall require only a trifle to repay abuses to my peoples – the life of Rajan Vace, Usurper of the Katchka!"

"We are agreed then," Rajan drew his sword and saluted. The others returned his salute, and each moved to join his respective army and await what promised to be the monumental battle of the age.

"Tell me of the blade Angra Mainyu," Trav said respectfully to Galwa.

"What is to tell? It is a sliver of metal beaten by a smith, honed to severing sharpness, and soaked in the blood of heroes and villains."

"It lives," Trav stated dully. His eyes remained on the unfolding events in the field. Ranks of soldiers, horses, and others moiled into final preparations. Their commanders poised stoically, ready to lead them into battle.

"Angra Mainyu is a demon," Galwa said neutrally. "It is said that the demon possessed a smithy in the time celestials roamed the earth. Through the masterful skill of the smithy, *Mainyu* forged the sword to perfection. Taking it up, he struck down the nine sons of Bishma-Tizaree and Hymnia-Sylth, princes and godlings all. In his revenge, Bishma sought to destroy the blade, but Hymnia sang the sacred Lyric of Bondage and bound *Mainyu's* spirit into the sword itself."

Trav pondered the story while the armies below came to a standstill. Thunder rumbled from the south where clouds had gathered as though to witness spectacle. Dust settled across the plain under a harsh sun grown hot in the later throes of spring. Trav felt the calm creep along his nerves like the breath held in anticipation of meeting The Maker.

"Today shall matter little in this conflict," he pronounced, defying his own instinct toward awe.

From the hour following until the sun set like a fiery egg nested in the city's western heights, the armies swirled and bucked and strew death and injury over the plain before the gates of Torkas Nahl. Though the separate leaders strove with great might toward each other, the armies rallied time and again to throw back their foes. As the city's shadow began to pool like blood seeping from its walls onto the field, Badru Ibn Din called the remnant of his army back into the gates.

"Three thousand? In one day's battles? How can this be?" Badru's scratched but freshly cleaned face shone pale in the lamplight of his council chamber.

"It is so," Galwa reported calmly. "Keinwhid lost fewer, Vace many times more."

"Yes," Badru protested, "but that evil blade, Angra Mainyu, took no fewer than five-hundred of my best horsemen! How can such be defeated!"

"Do you ask my council? Or rave 'gainst the gods?" Galwa remained nonchalant.

"Yes!" Badru spat. "Yes! Damn you. Impart to me some wisdom with which to defeat my enemy."

"You must first rule yourself," Galwa said, his eyes catching the lamplight in an odd flash.

"I shall have you flayed," Badru clenched his jaw, biting the words out one at a time.

"Flay me if you wish," Galwa shrugged. "An unwise course of action. But now I choose to take offense and recognize that you and I have lost respect of each other. Seek counsel elsewhere."

Galwa walked from the room unswerving and unassailed. Though Badru motioned the guards to detain the ancient Master, they found themselves compulsively unwilling to carry out his will.

"Fetch his mute!" Badru raved.

"I am here," Arnoux Trav made his entrance.

Badru's eyes widened in surprise, though only rage shone in his countenance. Trav had changed from his pilgrim robes to a suit of armor Galwa had requisitioned from a local craftsman. A brushed steel breastplate topped his fine chain tabard, his hips and legs were plated appropriately for cavalry, and he carried a sheathed sword buckled neatly at his left hip. The sword's hilt was plainly polished bone or ivory, as was the hilt of the matching dagger sheathed on Trav's right thigh.

"You," Badru arched his eyebrows. "You have broken with the priests?"

"I am no longer a monk," Trav bowed. "Your highness, Badru Ibn Din, I am Arnoux Trav, Fatefist of the Mikari."

"Well met!" Badru smiled gleefully. He had been raised on stories of the ancient order of Mikari Fatefists. Reputed as the greatest warriors in the world, each was marked for it from the time they were left on the steps of any Mikari academy. Over a hundred years had passed since anyone was chosen – most surmised this to be a result of the Mikari fading into history.

"Do you place your army in my hands?" Trav asked, looking the monarch in the eye unflinching.

"By no means," Badru smiled. "Nevertheless, my heart praises the Lord of my ancestors for blessing the sons of Din with such a tool."

"What do you wish of me?"

"You," Badru paused momentarily, his brow furrowing. "You shall be my Flank and keep my life."

"So be it," Trav bowed, intoning the ritual acquiescence. "So is it. So shall it be."

"What action suggest you for the morrow?" Badru's eyes shone.

"None," Trav said decisively.

"None!" Badru looked to the guard. "Do you hear? The Fatefist would have us idle away our time while Keinwhid and Vace decide which portions of my city to possess."

"Torkas Nahl shall fall to no foe," Trav stated flatly.

"How can I defeat my foes from the craven's post?!"

"They shall grow restless and turn upon each other in the manner of scavengers." Trav pointed to the map rolled out between them on a large cedar table.

"Keinwhid has his army at hand. Rajan Vace is not so bold; despite superior numbers, he has left substantial reinforcement back at the fords of the Godsblood. That force is nearly equal in number to Keinwhid's as it stands."

Badru staggered under this revelation.

"You tell me Vace has another third of his army – another thirty-thousand in the Waterhorse plains?"

"It is so," Trav nodded. "I took their measure when passing."

"Gods of the desert! Gods of the plains!" Badru spat as he screamed his frustration. He cursed vociferously several minutes before taking a deep breath.

"You pronounce my defeat."

"I report your challenge," Trav shrugged.

"How old are you, boy?" Badru glared at him hotly.

"I was brought to Mikari-Jedra nineteen years ago," Trav answered flatly.

"By your age," Badru moved in close enough for Trav to smell the peppers and clove on his breath. "By your age, I had killed four-hundred bandits, led two campaigns against the infidel armies, and sired three sons."

"I have not accomplished as much, my lord," Trav looked him steadily in the eye. Though he was much taller than the prince, he was nearly as trim. Each bore himself with the confidence of royalty: one from the confidence of his birth, the other from the confidence of self discipline.

Badru's eyes flashed dangerously. He forced out a loud, raucous guffaw.

"You have a spirit of iron, boy," Badru slapped his shoulder. "Be wise enough to never again challenge me in my own city. I rule here. Keep it in mind."

"Thank you, emir, for the sage advice," Trav bowed ceremoniously. "Have you further desire of my counsel this night?"

"Yes," Badru snapped. "Advise me as to how I may wreak havoc on my enemy – without hiding behind the monuments of my esteemed and most worshipful ancestors."

"Let the Mikari stand as they did today, holding at bay with their slings all too eager to await your invitation," Trav began. "In your endless generosity, grant them the morning to grow curious. Once the sun has risen beyond its blinding rise, let the desert's heat assault their courage and sap their strength while your armies bathe and oil themselves in the city's luxury."

"This seems . . ." Badru opened his hands and spread his arms wide.

"Once the sun drops to first bleed shadow from the city's wall," Trav continued, "bring your horsemen against the border of the two armies like a wedge. Drive in with vengeful fury and howling to wake the sands. Then, just as quickly, turn and flee like a fox with his tail afire. The armies will close on you and each other, and there each of your warriors acts as three by drawing the foes..."

"Aha!" Badru clapped his hands. "Masterful!"

Understanding that he was dismissed, Trav bowed and made his way out.

"He is unwise," Trav told his mentor. "Impatient."

"Why?" Galwa asked.

"He makes himself small by the greatness of his ancestors." Trav said, thoughtful. "That is, he perceives himself small and strives to greater glory. Saving Torkas Nahl is secondary to personal glory. He would play the hero, but fears his fate is otherwise."

"Yet, he has some measure of wisdom, does he not?" Galwa sat in a meditative trance.

"He does," Trav conceded after a moment.

"What wisdom has he shown?"

"He did not linger in the field as a more rash man might have," Trav said, searching his own thoughts. "Perhaps he is more wily than wise; and yet, is this a sort of wisdom? He has insight into the soul of men such that he may lead or control . . ."

"And?"

Trav mulled the thought. Galwa's candles burned down nearly a finger's breadth before he spoke again.

"He has put his trust in you, my Teacher."

"No, Arnoux Trav," Galwa said sagely. "The emir has put his trust in you – the Mikari Fatefist. Shows he proper respect?"

"Badru respects little," Trav gazed into the flicker of his mentor's candles. "Badru loves only Badru and all he envisions himself to accomplish."

"How does this serve our purpose, Fatefist?"

"Badru's unreasoned quest for glory is a flame in the fire of our torch," Trav intoned, visions of battles and strategies forming like mist beneath the placid glaze of his eyes. "He shows wisdom also in this, that he commanded that I should be his shield and flank."

"You assented to this?" Galwa inflected the statement so slightly that only Trav would recognize its implications. Still, he seemed motionless, suspended by invisible strings in his meditative pose.

"He wishes to test my mettle." A flicker like a sudden smile flashed across Trav's face, hinting at youth in his hard-edged, handsome features. His smoky blue eyes narrowed at the corners subtly.

"Seeing the Dance of a Thousand Strokes in tomorrow's battles, he will grow ambitious and change directives."

"Perhaps," Galwa dismissed him.

Trav's gelding stamped impatiently beside the emir's stallion. Though the afternoon grew hot in the still air, Trav remained unperturbed. He cooed to his horse by name, Tabanyor, and prepared his mind. Something like an excited thrill ran deep through his heart, though no thought or emotion shown on his marble features.

"It is time," Badru growled.

"No," Trav replied in a low, toneless voice. "At the whistle of Mikari slings . . ."

"I command here!" Badru bit out the words.

"As you choose, emir," Trav nodded acquiescence.

One thousand horsemen waited behind them – one hundred with long spears, behind them two hundred with drawn scimitars, behind them five hundred with the famed Aashran bow, followed by the remaining lines alternating lancers and swordsmen.

"Command the gate!" Badru told the stony youth.

Trav did as ordered.

"Command the march."

It began.

Trav launched himself into the path of four Maneguard as they bore down on the emir. His mind noted but dismissed the intense messages from his nerves – exhaustion was overcome by the discipline of Mikari training. For the thousandth time today, he raised his heavy blade and arced it with deadly intent upon the enemy.

Despite his respect for their reputation, Trav was surprised and impressed with the Maneguard. They were well armored, but more than that they knew how to use their armor – knew how to shift minutely, and with an economy of motion to conserve strength while absorbing blows. No other group of warriors on the field had fared so well against him. No other now dared to move within reach of the Fatefist.

Trav let the weakest of the four past him, allowing others to assist in the emir's defense. He shifted to bring a broad swing down toward the strongest of the Mane, but curved the stroke an inch from the knight's upraised shield and diverted the momentum to a sweeping backhand slash at the Mane closing on his right. Steel blade bit through iron plates to shatter that knight's collarbone and slice deep into his throat as he left himself exposed by overreaching to attempt a deathblow to Trav's neck.

Hooves came down on Trav's shield as a knight risked his horse in a rearing attempt to unsaddle the Mikari Fatefist. Trav let his left shoulder relax to absorb the blow while tensing his right and bending forward at the waist to leverage the horse aside. The horse stumbled. Its rider disengaged fluidly, unharmed, as only a Maneguard could.

"Badru falls! Defend! Defend!"

Trav dropped from his horse as gracefully, perhaps even more fluidly, than the Maneguard. He spun and leapt in a series of attacks that took him to Badru's side.

"I bade you defend me!" the wild-eyed emir screamed.

"You remain unscathed," Trav's voice was hoarse. He realized for the first time that he had been shouting and screaming throughout the hours of combat. His detached self noted the clear sky darkening with the shadows of late afternoon. He killed four men with a fury of blows, and then stood alone to scan the field.

Emir Badru's personal bodyguards had dwindled in number from two dozen to nine. Each was exhausted, barely able to stand when not engaged. Though the lines were well-formed for the time they'd spent in combat, Trav could see that most of the forces were exhausted from heavy engagement. Blood flowed across the plain; a mist of it seemed to rise with the dust from horizon to horizon. The dead and wounded lay in a chaos of heaps and clusters interspersed with the mayhem of ongoing battle.

"Sound the horn: withdrawal!"

"I have not begun to tire!" Badru raved savagely. "I shall drive every Daeva, druj, and yatu from this land and into the abyss of Asha's vengeance!"

Trav dropped the final Maneguard within reach of them and turned to the emir's bodyguard, Dupda Ibn Ghadja.

"Blow your horn."

Dupda nodded his head slightly and reached within his dun robes. He pulled the horn free as another enemy squad approached, this time Keinwhid forces.

"I forbid you!" Badru eyes flashed madness, the pulse at his temple throbbing like a threat of divine rage.

"Nevertheless," Trav snatched the horn from Dupda's hand and blew three series of short bursts: *withdrawal.*

"Impudent . . ." Badru attacked him.

Trav took a quick step to his right and pulled the scimitar from Badru's grasp. Part of his mind worked on the problem of the advancing enemy.

"Impossible!" Badru gaped, wide-eyed and disbelieving, at his own weapon in Trav's hand. "That is a blessed weapon; divine will holds it to my hand – none may disarm—"

"Yet it is so," Trav said calmly. He tossed the blade back to its owner and turned to face the oncoming knights.

He held up his hand, "I challenge you to the Rite of Masters."

Keinwhid's knights stopped. The lesser soldiers made way. One disengaged from the rest.

"Your terms?" The knight raised his mesh visor. Trav noted the silver coronet artfully worked into the knight's helm. His shield was emblazoned with the Keinwhid dragon.

"The day is tired," Trav said. "And gorged on the blood of heroes. Let us decide today's balance. Each shall retire to his respective place and disengage from battle with the other."

"So let it be," Keinwhid the Younger nodded, smiling.

"I am the son of Keinwhid; who may I say was fool enough to challenge me?"

"You do not share your sire's caution," Trav observed. "I am Arnoux Trav, Fatefist of the Mikari and lately guarantor of Badru Ibn Abbas and the sovereignty of Torkas Nahl."

The two champions saluted with their swords and stepped into an intricate dance of martial triumph. They seemed almost choreographed as they stepped, lunged, and whirled around – toward, then away from each other. Their swords flashed. Steel sang with their innumerable attacks and ripostes.

"You know the Dance of a Thousand Strokes," Trav smiled.

"Yes," said Keinwhid the Younger. "I have studied many lores of the sword."

Crowds grew around them as exhausted soldiers and knights broke off to watch the spectacle of the prince and priest. Their fluid dance, seemingly unencumbered by the plates and coats of armor each wore, mesmerized the watching warriors. Silence spread from the circle as the number of onlookers grew and word spread throughout the ranks.

"Cease this travesty," a low, thunderous voice cut through the ringing song of the swords and the low mutter of the crowd's appraisal. Rajan Vace stepped out of the crowd, the crowd having fallen away from the threat of his dark, blood-covered blade.

Trav brushed off a powerful slash and disengaged. His placid battle smile turned to a disgruntled frown, then to a placid mask of marble invulnerability. He stepped back from Keinwhid the Younger, opened his left hand and pointed his sword at the ground in a gesture of disengagement.

Keinwhid the Younger sheathed his sword in a blurred motion and lifted his visor. Trav noted now that the prince was no older than himself. Keinwhid the Younger was flushed from the exertion of their battle; sweat streamed down his face, his breath came in ragged gasps.

"You have no right to the Contest of Champions on a field of three armies," Rajan glared at them contemptuously. "Or form you an alliance against me?"

"Perhaps . . ." Trav said quietly, willing his own breathing to calm. "Perhaps we are even now deciding that."

"I suppose," interjected a voice from the Keinwhid side of the circle. "I suppose that this could be decided presently."

Keinwhid the Elder stepped into the circle and made polite gestures to respective commanders.

"To my ears, *Katchka* king," he growled in a low baritone, "that rings of challenge. Is it your wish that the fate of this siege be here and now decided?"

Rajan Vace smiled. Knights and warriors trembled and pushed against each other to give the king – and themselves – more space. Vace stepped into the circle. He threw his helm to the ground. Taking Angra Mainyu in both hands, he whirled his infamous blade above his head with a sound like locusts swarming.

"I shall eat your heart, Keinwhid," he bared his teeth in an expression that could never be called a smile. "And you, False-fate of the pumpkin robes, I shall eat your eyes."

"And what would you have from Torkas Nahl?" Badru stepped in, eyes smoldering, scimitar point weaving figure-eights.

"There is no part of Badru *ibn ibn ibn* Din worthy of eating," Rajan Vace spat.

"We have our terms, then?" Keinwhid the Younger had caught his breath again. He stepped forward brazenly.

"These terms," Trav stepped in. "We shall strive against each other. The last standing shall have his terms. Name them now."

"My terms are the surrender of all to me," Rajan Vace seemed somehow to shadow the sun itself in his assertion. "Khalil, my heir, shall flank me – his terms are my terms."

"My terms are the head of Rajan Vace and the surrender of Torkas Nahl," Keinwhid the Elder said.

"Immediate withdrawal of all troops," Keinwhid the Younger asserted. "I require the head of Rajan Vace and the shards of his broken sword; of the noble armies of the Mikari and Torkas Nahl, I offer the mercy of full service to Keinwhid or immediate, branded exile without return."

"I require the heads of all marshals of the field not allied to Torkas Nahl," Badru said darkly. "Enslavement for the footmen, and knights may buy their freedom at one-hundred golden Dinri."

"Torkas Nahl and the withdrawal of all persons less their greater arms," Trav said, nodding as though it were already decided.

"By what right!" Badru fumed. "What right have you as my flank to name your terms?"

"None – as your *Flank*," Trav replied. "I fight for Torkas Nahl. I do not serve Badru."

Badru stood shaking for a moment as though given to fits of apoplexy. Rage overcame him. He charged the Fatefist. Trav brushed the attack away lightly and turned to face the greater threat of Angra Mainyu in the hands of Rajan Vace.

Badru gained control of himself, realizing his situation, and used his momentum to engage Keinwhid the Elder. He feinted a direct jab at the king and then spun into a great arcing roundhouse slash powerful enough to decapitate a horse. But Keinwhid was not there when the blow whooshed through empty air. Badru fell to the sand as Keinwhid landed a deft blow with his sword hilt on the back of Badru's head. He hit the blood-soaked sands unconscious.

Keinwhid the Younger began his dance again, this time fighting Khalil. He was only to the fourth thrust of the Dance of a Thousand Strokes when he broke through the young prince's defense and jammed his sword through the scaled armor and into Khalil's left side. When Khalil swung in desperation to avenge the attack, Keinwhid the Younger used a double-fisted cleave with his blade angled; he broke the man's arm instead of severing it.

Trav was on the defensive. He had begun a variation of the Dance, but Angra Mainyu was ready for it – obviously familiar enough with it to exhaust him. He switched to an ancient dervish style, then through a succession of all the styles he had been taught and practiced for endless hours. Rajan Vace scoffed, cajoling him with every passing flurry of blows. The sword itself seemed to mutter gibberish within his mind, a language he could almost recognize.

Trav began to evolve a style of his own. He drew first blood from Rajan as Angra Mainyu cut through the shoulder of his breast plate and skimmed aside on hitting the chain beneath.

The Keinwhids joined in against Rajan and his cursed blade. In some part of his mind, Trav noted the honorable means by which each had made his way to the current melee. He knew that trained men were even now kneeling to tend the wounds of Badru and Khalil. He formed no thoughts, but observed it in the high redoubt of his mind.

Rajan lunged suddenly away from Trav, sweeping two blades away before slashing in a lightning-fast attack that shattered Keinwhid the Elder's sword and sank into the older king's helmet and head. Blood jetted from the wound. It ran down the man's face, into eyes now glazed with sudden death.

Attack the man, not the sword. The gibberish in Trav's mind suddenly shifted into crystal clarity. Angra Mainyu spoke to him.

Your hand would so much better grip my hilt. Seductive as only power can be.

Trav batted away a sweeping stroke of Rajan's sword and lunged to ram his shoulder into the tyrant's ribs. He spun to meet the returning arc of the enchanted blade, keeping his guard constant and vigilant. Despite Trav's mastery combined with Keinwhid's, Rajan was drawing ten times more blood. And the wounds he inflicted were far worse. Trav's armor was tattered, his robes shredded; Keinwhid had dropped away at some point to discard his breastplate, it being so dented as to encumber him.

Drive in and kill him, Angra Mainyu sang like a siege against Trav's Mikari discipline. *He is unworthy. Slay him and set your hand to me. We shall take his empire and spread it tenfold . . .*

"Silence!" Trav redoubled his efforts. For the first time in several years, he felt the weight of his own limbs. His training was so severe that he had grown used to the physical labor of hefting a sword in full armor for the whole of any given day. But this was not training. Angra Mainyu hit with fiercer blows than anything he had known.

Keinwhid the Younger went down under the next onslaught. Trav could not tell how badly the prince was injured, but for the first time on the field he felt – he *felt*.

His crystalline redoubt crumbled. Passion gushed like adrenaline throughout his being. He kicked out to stop the killing stroke, striking Rajan's left elbow with bone-shattering impact.

"No!" he screamed. "Honor is the only power I crave!"

He pressed his advantage against Rajan, inventing new series of attacks and defenses as he spent himself. The gibberish began again within his mind, but he pulled the fire of his passion up to clear the clutter from his soul. He cleansed his mind with the passion's ferocity and poured it like fuel into his will.

Rajan spun suddenly into a double-fisted roundhouse and knocked Trav to the ground. His head spun with impossibilities of unconsciousness. He stared aghast, realizing that Angra Mainyu had changed tactics. The cursed sword had repaired Rajan's shattered elbow. It hungered to consume Trav's blood and soul.

He rolled to evade blow after blow rained down with rending strength and murderous intent.

Near the end of strength, Trav gazed up at the orange glow of Rajan's sword as it descended unimpeded toward his head.

You are mine . . .

A blade suddenly intervened. It knocked Angra Mainyu aside enough that it bit deep into Trav's left shoulder instead of through his helmet and skull. Trav rolled with the impact and got to his feet, too caught up in sudden hope to acknowledge the timeliness of Keinwhid's intervention.

Three blades flashed in the daylight's dying embers. Sudden bursts of passion ignited in the two sorely wounded young warriors as they faced the older despot and his demon-possessed blade. The blade itself seemed to shimmer toward a climax of hatred and fury. Rajan Vace's eyes were vacant, grown vacuous with the full possession of the demon.

Trav spun to knock aside a vicious sweep and came around full into a roundhouse kick to Rajan's head. Rajan fell for the first time. The crowd of warriors watching in rapt concentration cheered. Keinwhid feinted a blow at the fallen king's head, then whipped a slash down on both his wrists. Rajan's left hand came free – but his right stayed somehow attached and clutched to the sword.

Comprehension dawned on Trav as he watched Rajan bring his stump together with the severed hand in a bright orange flash. His hands were whole again.

Trav lunged, twirled, and suddenly held two swords. Keinwhid sprawled toward the crowd's edge. The crowd gasped in mixed awe and trepidation.

Rajan, maniacal grimace now painting his features with madness and demonic glee, charged at Trav. He spun a net of steel around him. Trav worked both blades with equal alacrity, though the strength of his blows suffered. He wove a net to counter Angra Mainyu's – spin, duck, dodge . . . tumbling like some manic acrobat.

Finally, Trav found his opening. His mind wrapped around the sequence of the demon's attack; he understood its strategy. He dodged a brilliant arc and sweep attack, caught the unholy blade on the flat of his left-hand sword, and slammed the Mikari sword down with all his might on the blade of Vace's enchanted weapon. The three blades shattered with a bone jarring shriek and a tinkling like coins dropped on cobblestones.

The final rays of sun passed beyond the horizon. Silence fell like a veil with night's sudden darkness. Trav knelt in the sand, his hands blistered to the elbow as though basted in coals. Rajan lay still. Keinwhid had risen and now held the emir's scimitar, stooped in a battle stance as though it were impossible that nothing threatened.

"What will?" Trav croaked through cracked lips.

"What?" Keinwhid the younger looked around wildly.

"What will?" he repeated.

"This is not my victory," Keinwhid said, shock plain on his features.

"It is," Trav stated flatly.

"No," Keinwhid replied. "I surrender myself."

"You cannot."

"I do," Keinwhid asserted. He walked over and pulled his erstwhile foe to his feet.

"You have slain our common enemy. The old kings have passed; let us build the kingdoms now in our own image."

"I seek no kingdom," Trav shrugged.

"Then you shall share mine," Keinwhid signaled for someone to tend their wounds.

"But then . . ." Keinwhid winced as an apothecary touched a burning salve into his deepest wound, then smiled at Trav. "But then, I guess a Mikari Fatefist has no use for kingdoms."

"You guess correctly," Galwa came forward from the crowd of watchers.

"A Mikari Fatefist has no use of a kingdom. However, Arnoux Trav has sufficed. I release him to his own."

Galwa strode to Trav and took the young man's hands tenderly, carefully in his own. He bent his head forward and muttered several prayers. Their hands glowed swirls of iridescent blues and greens as Trav closed his eyes and breathed his way into familiar trance.

Have I shamed you, Master? Trav sent his voice timidly into their internal melding of light.

Shame is not for the enlightened.

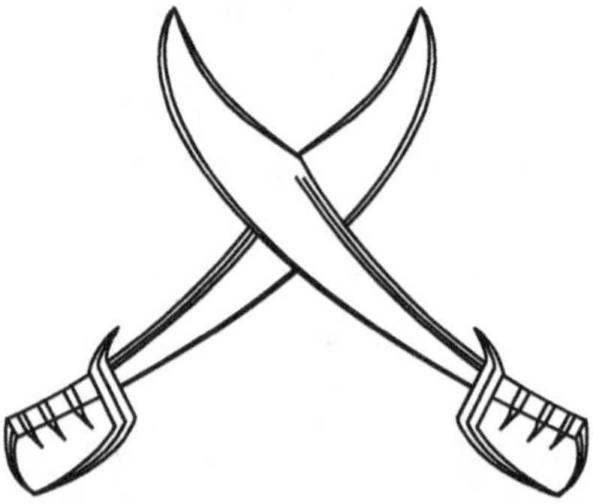

How much deference should be paid tradition? Traditions often dictate decisions and behavior simply through the copouts of ease, comfort, and status quo. Today's traditions are many times simply engrained rites meaningless in their automatic use. How strict an allegiance should we demand of ourselves – our leaders?

Ty Johnston knows that writing is all that keeps him sane. He could no more not write than he could not breathe – and he cannot understand anyone who doesn't have the same urge. Ty recently finished writing a trilogy, and Belgad, one of its major characters and the protagonist of this tale, demanded more attention. He asked Ty to explore his past and find out what had shaped him into the character he is in the trilogy. This is but one of those explorations – you can find more at Ty's blog at http://tyjohnston.blogspot.com.

Deep in the Land of the Ice and Snow

A Tale of Belgad of Dartague

by Ty Johnston

The wolves were too many. Belgad knew that as soon as he spotted the beasts. There were nearly a score of them, and the creatures were huge, nearly the size of a riding pony. What was worse, the wolves were quiet and had managed to surround him without his spying them sooner.

This was no ordinary pack. They had appeared from nowhere, and they had no qualms about scaling the side of a mountain for their human prey.

Belgad forced himself to climb higher, the bitter cold winds whipping at his long yellow hair. His fingers, the tips protruding from rags he had used to swaddle them, gripped the edge of another boulder and lifted him with the help of solid placement from his fur-lined boots.

On top of the rock, Belgad found a flat spot and sat, letting the cold air fill his tired lungs. His body needed rest after days of hiking dense forests and climbing steep hills, but he would not close his eyes; the wolves were drawing nearer, below and above. It would only be a matter of time before they would attack.

After what felt like hours to the big man wrapped in furs, one of the wolves, the largest, began to creep its way along a narrow path toward him.

Belgad watched the animal with anticipation, knowing soon he would be in battle.

Eventually the wolf was below the Dartague barbarian, just out of reach of the man's legs hanging off the side of his stone seat.

"Will you eat me today, wolf?" the large man said to the animal.

The wolf's only reply was uplifted ears and a tilted head.

"I think not," Belgad said, drawing in his legs and pushing off them so he stood on the boulder.

The wolf blinked, and for the first time Belgad saw it had eyes the shade of morning blue ice.

"I think not," Belgad repeated. With hands numb from stinging frost, he reached behind his head and pulled forth two swords. Gripped in his right hand was the long, heavy blade that had been handed down to him from his father; resting in Belgad's left hand was the shorter, wider sword taken from a Truscan mercenary during Belgad's first raid as a boy.

A low growl from behind made him turn his head to the side. "Tricky beasts," he said as he spotted another wolf above him choosing its steps cautiously in the rocky terrain.

Suddenly the wolf below sprang up, its claws digging into the side of the boulder and pulling itself to a firmer standing.

The movement was so swift Belgad had no time for a full swing with a sword. Instead he punched out with his shorter weapon's hilt, smashing the blue-eyed wolf across the snout and sending it sprawling back the way it came with a gash of blood across its muzzle.

The wolf above took that moment to launch itself, landing on the barbarian's back and sinking in its claws.

Belgad screamed out and raised his swords high above his head. The wolf on his back clawed at the man's fur coat, trying to get a firmer grip.

The barbarian slashed over his head in a downward stab at his back and the wolf there. The short sword caught the monster in its jaws and sliced its mouth to give the thing a wider grin. The wolf howled in pain as Belgad shook and twisted to one side, sending the injured animal plummeting to its wounded companion below.

Not taking time to notice the pain of his wounds, Belgad glanced around to see the rest of the wolves moving in through the trees below. He dared a glance over his shoulder and found no more of the beasts above, only a ridge a good distance away.

Without another look at his closing foes, and without sheathing his swords, Belgad darted up the steep incline to the ridge. This part of the world was foreign to him, and he knew not what lay on the other side of the mountain, but he could not make a stand in the open. He needed a cave or a steep valley, some place where his foes would have to come at him one at a time.

The wolves followed.

His lungs running out of air and his legs cramping, halfway to the ridge Belgad lost his footing, his boots sliding out from beneath him on gravel covered with frost. He would have fallen and tumbled back down the mountainside if he had not dropped one of the swords, the shorter blade, and grabbed hold of a gnarly branch sticking up from frozen ground.

Hanging there on the side of the mountain, his feet out over a lip of stone in open air, he heard the wolves howl. They were near, much nearer than Belgad would have thought.

His only hope was the mountain ridge. It was the only path open to him not layered with the monsters.

Belgad yanked on the frozen root and pulled himself near to standing again. Another howl, closer than before, had him glance down the mountain.

The wolves were coming. The bitter north winds shook the gray hair on their backs like a summer storm blowing across fields of grain. The nearest was only a dozen yards below.

Belgad sheathed his heavy sword in its scabbard on his back and pushed himself forward, more climbing than running now. His numb fingers dug into frozen dirt and lifted him another few feet. He kept clawing away and kicking with his feet, not daring to look back.

On his hands and knees, Belgad pulled himself the last little distance to the top of the mountain. Once there, he paused to catch his breath, staring down at his frozen hands and the gray stone beneath them. He almost wished the wolves would hurry and catch him. He had had enough, but first he would look over the edge.

Belgad raised his shaggy head and peered out from between the layers of golden hair that cascaded around his face. The view did nothing to improve his mood. Immediately in front of him was a drop he guessed to be three hundred feet, then a narrow beach of gray stones and chunks of ice. Beyond, stretched out before him as far as he could see to the horizon, was a flat, dead, cold ocean. No waves roiled, nor sea birds floated. There was nothing.

Glancing back over his shoulder, Belgad saw the wolves were wary in their climb. He had hurt two of them, and the others appeared in no hurry to feel the bite of his weapon. Slowly, with stiff joints, Belgad rolled over and withdrew his remaining sword. He sat there staring at the wolves working their way toward him. He was tired, true, but the lust of battle was beginning to boil in his blood again. He was sure he would die that day, but he had not traveled so far from home to die without putting up a fight. Let the wolves come, he told himself.

The wolves did come, but it took them nearly an hour, a few of them working near to their prey, then backing away once they drew his dark gaze. Eventually the blue-eyed wolf, the leader of the pack, and two others had the barbarian surrounded, the leader in front of the man. They stood their ground a dozen feet from Belgad, their gray paws digging into what little soil remained on top of the mountain.

"Come on, then," Belgad whispered to the pack's chief.

The ears of the wolf with blue eyes pricked up as if catching the soft words.

"Finish this!" Belgad roared.

The two wolves on the man's sides backed away with their tails between their legs, but the leader growled in the back of its throat.

"Bah!" Belgad said, pushing himself off the ground to stand straddle-legged atop the ridge. He waved his sword at the wolves. "If all you are going to do is stand there, I might as—"

The lead wolf cut him off. The creature charged, lunging the last dozen feet in one bound to reach the yelling man. Belgad brought up his sword, slicing into the animal's side but doing no real damage. The wolf slammed into the man, sending them both reeling backward.

Belgad barely managed to stay on his feet, the animal clawing away madly at his chest as it tried to pull him down. The barbarian brought back his sword for a mighty stab, but another wolf smashed into him, causing all three to plummet backward.

The cold air rushed past Belgad's face as he fell, bringing tears to his eyes. The last thing he remembered was the pain of a wolf tearing through his fur coat and into the flesh of his chest. Then darkness.

The barbarian woke to a dull orange glow shifting before his eyes. He lay unmoving, not knowing where he was and not wanting to alert anyone he was awake. Keeping his breathing shallow, he stared ahead at the light dancing before him. After long seconds, he noticed the sound of crackling flames at his back and realized the glow was that of a fire behind him reflecting off the stone wall inches from his face.

"No need for deception, son of Thunder," an ancient, cracked voice said. "I know you wake."

Belgad rolled over to face the speaker and discovered he lay upon the floor of a small cave. Sitting on a rock on the other side of the fire was an old man, stringy gray hairs hanging from his balding head and rough robes of wool hanging from his frail frame, the eagle, hammer and bear patches sown into its sleeves faded yet still discernible.

Belgad blinked, but did not move.

"You are wondering where you are and who I am," the old man said. "To answer the first question, you are in my home, and you have rested here for four days. To answer the second question, I am the one you have been seeking."

The young warrior's eyes grew wide as he shifted his body to sit on the dry hay with his legs crossed in front of him. "You are the skein weaver?"

The old man nodded. "You have been sent by your father," he said, pointing toward the pile of Belgad's clothes to one side of the room, the barbarian's heavy sword resting on top. "I recognize the weapon from days long past. You are of Clan Thunder."

"My father is ill," Belgad said. "He had not long to live when I set out."

"I am no healer," the skein weaver said, "though I did manage to tend your wounds."

"That is not why my father sent me," Belgad explained. "He told me you could unravel the skein of my life, telling me what awaits me in days to come. He said it was my final obstacle to becoming chieftain."

"That is true," the old man said. "I have told the unseen for many a man, including your father. It is tradition among the Dartague chiefs. They come to me as boys, and I prepare them for manhood."

Belgad crawled to his furs and rummaged through them, finally lifting a small leather pouch. "I have your offering." He withdrew a small, white chunk of bone.

"The knuckle of a warrior you have slain in combat," the old man said.

"Yes." Belgad held out the item.

"I need no such thing."

The younger man looked bewildered. "But my father—"

"That was a different time, and there was a different cost," the weaver said. "Your price shall be much higher, Belgad of Clan Thunder, for your future is far greater."

Belgad let the knucklebone fall from his fingers. "I do not understand."

"Of course you do not," the old man said with bitterness. "There are few today who understand the old ways. The world has moved on, the southern fools worshipping their new god, this Ashal."

"My people have remained true."

"As true as you can," the old man said. "In days past you would not have had to ride across wood and snow to me. I would have been ensconced in one of the great chiefs' mead halls, servants at my calling."

"My folk are no worshippers of Ashal."

"Your folk stood by as the Eastern church gained in power," the old man said, "as the last of the weavers and the skalds were driven into the wilds."

Belgad crossed his arms and raised an eyebrow. "You've told me of the past," he said, "but I'm here to find out the future. Either tell me, or let me be on my way. I have been gone long, and my father may have passed to the halls of our ancestors. My people will need their new leader."

The old man cackled. "You are a feisty one," he said, digging in the pockets of his gray robes. "I have already seen the future of the one called Belgad. I know why you seek my council."

The old man withdrew a clawed hand from a pocket and held up a small, gray ball of clay.

"What is that?" Belgad asked.

"It is a weapon," the old man said with a squinting eye. "I brought it from far Hipon a hundred years ago, when I was still young and traveling the world."

"It looks like a stone."

"It is much more than that," the old man said. "It is my deliverance, and it will be your tool."

"Tool? Tool for what?"

"To kill a witch," the old man said. "That is what I seek for your offering. You must kill a witch for me, then I will tell you your future."

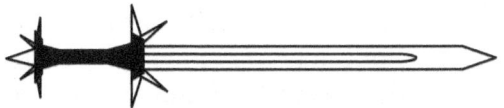

Other than the mountains to the north and a line of dead trees to the south, there was nothing to see but snow and the occasional glimpse of cold stone ground. Belgad grimaced as he lifted one foot ahead of the other and continued to trudge across vast tundra.

The skein weaver had told him the Ice Witch's hut of tree limbs, woven together by magic, rested on this tundra.

Tromping along, the barbarian wondered at the small clay ball he had stuffed into a purse on his belt. The weaver had said it was a magic weapon of flame that could destroy the witch. The old man had gone on to explain that Belgad would have only one chance to use the weapon, and then he must toss it directly at his foe.

A bump on the horizon caught Belgad's eye. He glanced up to see a small hill far away in the chilled flats.

After walking for what felt another hour, the barbarian was close enough to see the hill was the hut of branches, a door of ragged cloth hanging over the entrance. The yellow of fire glowed around the edges of the curtain, and a line of black smoke swirled its way through a hole in the roof.

"At least the witch is home," the Dartague muttered as he fished out the clay ball and drew his sword

He took another step and stopped.

On either side of the hut appeared two of the giant wolves, the four animals slinking their way out from behind the witch's home.

Belgad stood his ground and watched the creatures make their way to the hut's entrance where they sat on their haunches, their flat gray eyes glaring at the big man.

"Come out, witch," the barbarian hollered, "or hide behind your pets. It is the same to me. Today you die."

Nothing happened. The animals sat and watched him while a chilled breeze played with his hair.

"Have it your way, witch!" Belgad began to march forward.

Growls brought him to a quick halt. The beasts had not moved, but the hair on their backs was raised like pikes in formation.

The curtain over the door was thrust aside, and there stood a woman nearly as tall as Belgad, with skin a pale azure like a summer sky. Her slender arms and legs stretched from beneath her gown of black and gold as if she felt not the frigid air; entwined with the black of her long hair was a coronet of gold thread mingled with holly. Her ears were long and sharp. The beauty of her face was only marred by a dull scarlet gash across her forehead. Her eyes were the blue of a storm, edged with coal and familiar to the northern man.

"I know you," Belgad said.

The woman nodded. "Yes, Belgad Thunderclan, we have met. It was you gave me this scar."

"You were the wolf."

The woman nodded again.

"You should have died when you went over the cliff with me," the barbarian said.

"My lieutenant suffered a quick death," the witch said. "I became a hawk, drifting away on the wind."

Belgad rolled the clay ball in his hand and his courage grew.

"Did the wizard tell you why he wanted me dead?" the witch asked. "It's because I stole his magic. I sucked it out of him like a night hag stealing the breath of a baby. He didn't even know until he woke."

"You lie."

"No, Dartague warrior, I speak truth," the woman said. "You came to the skein weaver to have your future handed to you like a suckling pig served on a gold platter. How would I know? How would I have known your name?"

"You have your own magic," Belgad said. "The old man knew who I was. He knew to expect me."

"Only because he had foreseen your coming years ago," the witch said. "He knew of you before I took his magic. He knew of you before you were born."

Belgad didn't know if she was telling the truth, but he decided it did not matter. He had been told to kill her, and he would. If the skein weaver could not do as he had promised, Belgad would seek a refund in his own fashion.

The barbarian slung out a hand, flinging the clay ball.

The witch shrieked as the orb sailed through air.

The wolves dove forward, charging.

The first of the animals slammed into the northern man as the ball smacked into the witch, cracking on impact and spewing flame. The fire exploded around the woman as if she were made of tinder, eating away at her silky gown and melting the flesh of her arms and legs.

Belgad had no time to notice. That first wolf had knocked him back, but he managed to remain on his feet. He stabbed out with his sword, plunging the weapon to the hilt in the animal's side. The wolf fell away howling and spewing blood.

The other wolves were more cautious, forming a tight circle around their prey, looking for an opportune moment to spring to the attack.

Belgad allowed his eyes to wander to the burning witch. The fire had already eaten her down to bone, leaving a blackened skeleton standing in her place. The curtain too was burning, and the flames were working their way through the twigs that made up the hut.

A second wolf pounced. Belgad was ready. He dropped to one knee and slashed over his head with the sword, nearly cutting the giant beast in half. The animal landed in the snow next to its dead brother. With another slash of his heavy blade, Belgad put the animal out of its misery.

Seeing their mistress dead and two of their pack in pieces, the last two wolves turned from the battle and trotted away, glancing over their shoulders to see if the northern man would follow.

Belgad did not follow. He stood his ground, feet apart and balanced with his sword held before him in both hands, his look daring the animals to attack.

The wolves moved on.

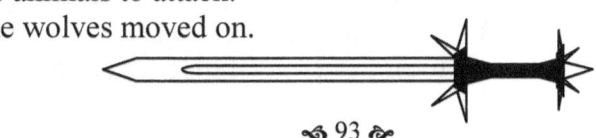

A land of ice and snow stretched behind Belgad as he climbed the last stone steps to the entrance of the skein weaver's cave in the side of a mountain. He knocked aside the curtain of deerskin that blocked the cold breeze, and tramped his way inside the tunnel, knocking white powder from his boots with each heavy step.

Belgad found the old man still sitting on a rock, huddled next to his small fire.

The barbarian tossed the black, burnt skull of the Ice Witch at the old man's feet.

"I knew the moment she died," the skein weaver said, staring at the death head.

"Your magic returned."

The weaver gave the younger man a dark look. "What would you know of it?"

"She told me before I burned her," Belgad said. "She told me she had stolen your powers."

The old man grumbled.

"Why would you have had cause to learn of me before now?" Belgad asked.

The old man's eyes darted about the small cave as if seeking an answer.

"What are you not telling me?"

"I unraveled the skein of your father's life long ago," the weaver said. "That is when I learned of you."

"Why did you not tell me you had lost your powers to the witch?"

The weaver averted his eyes.

"There's something about my future you are not telling me," Belgad said.

"I haven't told you anything," the weaver spat. "I have yet to unravel your life's skein. If you want me to do so, then remain quiet while I draw upon visions of your future."

Belgad shook his head. "No."

"No?"

"My future is my own," the barbarian said.

"You are speaking against tradition!"

"Whose tradition?" Belgad said. "Mine? I will make my own tradition. As for my father and my people, you were right that we no longer follow the old ways. We don't even know the names of the old gods. If the gods want to be worshipped, then they need a better speaker than you, an old man who lives in the hinterlands because no one will put up with his foolishness."

"You mock the gods."

"I don't worship them," Belgad said. "Let them worship me."

"Your shamans will not tolerate this."

"The shamans will believe what I tell them," Belgad said. "Besides, what good have your talents brought my people. We still trudge away at life. We still fight off our enemies. We still die. Knowing one's future will not help us. I can rule without your aid."

The old man stared into the crackling flames before him without saying another word.

With one last look at the weaver, Belgad turned and strutted out of the cave, leaving the curtain hanging open behind him.

After some little while, the weaver moved to the entrance of his cave. He reached to pull the curtain closed, but before he could he spied Belgad far off in the distance, traveling one heavy step at a time through the barren snowy land.

Staring at the back of the barbarian, the old man grinned. "And that is why, Belgad of Clan Thunder, you shall be the most powerful of Dartague chieftains."

Is there ever honor among thieves? There can be, though it's not common. By whose definition of honor and under what conditions shall we judge? Honor is built upon respect, predicated by integrity, and a companion to friendship. With such origins, it is a characteristic able to carry over into any aspect of life, thievery and crime included. It's at the core of what each of us is made out of, after all. The implication that one's profession or status in life somehow dictates whether one is honorable or not is staggering. The consistency of one's actions, either in specific moments or over a lifetime, should determine whether one is considered honorable or not.

Jeff Stewart is not a writer. He is a teller of tales. He is a man simultaneously apart from and at one with the great outdoors, a hunter whose prey is more often pried from experience and observation than from forest floors and mountain passes. He is a lore-giver, and his is an ancient profession.

Mountain Scarab

A Tale of Sigurd Grimbrow

by Jeff Stewart

The first guard died with an arrow through his throat. Before the startled members of the caravan could react, a screaming mob of Peshmerga tribesmen descended the steep rocky hills on either side of the pass. There was time for only one flight of arrows and javelins, and then the raiders were upon the merchant train.

The wiry mountain tribesmen swarmed over the defending guards, dragging them off their mounts and plunging daggers deep into the struggling lowlanders. Near the rear of the caravan, a lone Valkyrion from the North waded through the battle, his steel helm and war axe distinguishing him from the other raiders. Dark of hair and grim of visage, he stalked the bloody ground in silence, a stark contrast to the howling warriors around him.

The fighting ended very quickly. The surprise had been complete and the tired guards had been no match for the ferocious mountain tribesmen. The noise had not abated with the end of the battle. The mules brayed, frightened by the smell of blood, and the few women in the train screamed as they were gathered by the victors. The Peshmerga moved among the wreckage of the mule train, collecting arms and valuables from the dead.

Sigurd Grimbrow, the Valkyrion, scavenged for booty with the rest of the raiders. He moved among the mules, looking for anything of extraordinary value. He pocketed a handful of jeweled rings, plucked from the hands of a fat merchant who would no longer need them. His gray eyes surveyed the wreckage without pity. He moved further up the line, looking for baggage that had not been previously ransacked.

He spied a mule lying on its side off the beaten trail. Two black arrows sticking from its body told why it no longer huddled with its braying mates. Its cargo lay untouched. Moving off the trail, Sigurd approached the dead mule. A flash of movement alerted him to danger hidden behind the fallen animal. He hefted his axe and advanced cautiously. Spying the source of the motion, he gave a sudden oath.

The girl, realizing she had been discovered, quietly returned his gaze. He grunted in approval of her appearance: young and pretty, with brown curls, brown eyes, and full curves. Her clothing, while of good quality, was not expensive. Nor did she have any visible jewelry other than a simple necklace of blue beads. Although she had been hiding, she did not flinch when the tall man with the bloody axe approached. She sat up from behind the dead animal and returned his frank inspection.

Evidently making up her mind, she spoke in the common trader tongue. “You are not Peshmerga.” The Northman was just under six feet, below medium height for a Valkyrion, but a full hand taller than the wiry mountain tribesmen. His black hair jutted from under his steel cap while his cool eyes studied the girl in front of him.

“And neither are you,” answered Sigurd in the same tongue.

“Will you kill me now?” asked the girl. Although pale and obviously frightened, she faced him with courage. He found himself admiring her pluck, her daring to question a mountain raider while surrounded by the chaos of a deadly ambush.

“I did not plan on it. Should I?” The girl found herself at a loss for words at this question. “Do you have any weapons?” asked the warrior.

“I have a knife,” she answered.

“Give it to me.” He tucked the weapon into his girdle and gestured her to the side, while he moved to begin searching the dead mule’s pack. Finding several bolts of rich cloth, he stripped out the most expensive looking ones and set them to the side. A harsh laugh from the roadway caused him to reach for his axe.

"What have we here? Saving this one all for yourself, northern dog?" The newcomer was a wiry Peshmerga, dressed in filthy furs and a spiked cap. His fighting knife was crimson with fresh blood.

"She is mine, Hiwan. If you want her you shall have to wait until the spoils are shared out. Go find another to rut with, you ape-faced runt!"

A loud call from a ram's horn trumpet cut off the mountain raider's retort.

"Just wait, Valkyrion. I will wear your head on my belt before the new moon." The northern warrior simply stared impassively at the Peshmerga. Seeing that he would not be rewarded with a response and unnerved by the quiet stare of those impassive gray eyes, the filthy man grabbed the bolts of cloth and ran toward the assembling raiders.

"Damn!" Sigurd turned to the crouching girl. "Come on, if we don't hurry all the horses will be gone." He grabbed her slim hand and hauled her along at a pace that forced the girl to sprint. His iron grip pulled her remorselessly and kept her from falling when she stumbled. Coming to a horse, he cut its reins from the dead fingers of its former owner and vaulted into the saddle. Reaching down, he swung the girl up behind him.

"Hold on," he instructed. "We will cover some wild road, but if you fall you are on your own."

The next two hours were terrifying to the young girl. Rather than follow the caravan route through the pass, the raiders headed straight up the side of the mountain. They moved along narrow trails invisible from below, twisting this way and that, always climbing, clinging to the rocky face of the mountain. She ferociously hugged Sigurd's waist. At times one foot scraped the granite wall while the other hung over a sheer drop. Finally they arrived before a spring and a shallow cave in a small saddle among the peaks.

The Peshmerga visibly relaxed as they entered their hideout. The raiders unloaded their spoils and began caring for the captured mounts. The girl hovered close to Sigurd as he worked, stripping the saddle and grooming the lathered horse.

"My name is Simone. I am Aragonese." She took the Valkyrion's silence as permission to continue. "My father is a merchant. He has arranged my marriage to a minor noble of the Confederation. I am traveling north to meet my father. He is returning from a trading trip with the Rus. He was gathering the gold, furs and turquoise that will be my dowry. I am afraid my husband-to-be is not very rich. He is just a minor noble. Still, our children will be of the nobility."

"Best look around you girl," grunted the Northman. "Your immediate future is unlikely to include Confederation nobles."

The young girl blanched at this cold statement of fact. Frantically her mind worked to devise an escape. She knew she must have an ally. "What about you? Will you help me?"

His cold laughter crushed her budding hopes. "Me? And why would I do such a thing? Did you not see me crushing skulls with the others? I am with the Peshmerga, girl."

"You are not Peshmerga. You have the look of the north about you. A Valkyrion, are you not?"

"Aye, and if you know that, then you know I am even worse than these mountain raiders. A Valkyrion does nothing for free."

"But there will be a reward. I must get to Konnigsberg. If you help me, my father will reward you. Have I not told you he is gathering my dowry? He will give you a handful of gold for my release."

"Aye, and Yaseem will give me a handful of steel in my guts if I try to run off with you."

"Will they not allow you to escort me to Konnigsberg? Not even for ransom?" asked the girl.

"Not a chance, lass." His perpetual scowl deepened at her persistence. "They do not trust each other, let alone me. Two weeks ago I was a caravan guard also. They spared my life when they butchered the caravan, but only because I accepted their offer to join them. I am still an outsider. They will not trust me."

"But you could explain who I am. My betrothed would surely add to the reward. It should be enough to satisfy even these mountain dogs!"

The quiet warrior stopped combing the standing horse and turned his gaze upon the girl. She shivered at a sudden chill, as if the temperature had dropped unexpectedly. "Perhaps you did not understand me," he said coldly. "I am a Valkyrion. A Northman. I do not belong here and they know that. They let me live because of my fighting ability. But I have no other currency here, and no interest in your offers."

Simone felt her hope begin to die. "Then take me," she pleaded. "I will give myself to you. Just keep me as your own."

"You will be given as Yaseem deems fit, along with the rest of the spoils," he snapped. "I will not be killed trying to defend your honor, girl! You will live, unless you do something foolish. You will even learn to cope with the Pesh. Do not worry about your honor. Only a few rats like Hiwan would force themselves on you, and then only if he thinks he will not be caught. You will be a servant, or if you strike some warrior's fancy, a wife. It may seem horrible now, but it is better than dying."

Simone collapsed, sobbing into her arms. All of the terror and violence she had witnessed finally overwhelmed her and she cried uncontrollably. Sigurd calmly brushed the horse, studiously ignoring the girl. After several minutes the sobs stopped and her breathing quieted. Eventually she wiped her eyes and sat up, once again calm and in control.

"Very well. I shall do as you suggest. You should know one thing, however. I have a chest of jewels that belonged to my mother. Good jewels, not large, but of fine quality. If anyone gets me to Konnigsberg, I will give him those jewels."

"And those jewels?" he asked, pointing to her breasts.

"No! You lost any chance for those. I will bite any man who touches me, and if I can get a knife I will kill him!"

"Whoa! Where did this little wildcat come from?" The Valkyrion surveyed her with renewed interest. "A moment ago you were crying your eyes out, and now you want to kill a man. I think you are yelling into the wind, little girl."

"I care not what you think. I am simply telling the truth."

"Well, you better not tell anyone else your version of the truth," he said glancing around. "Most Peshmerga are not as patient as I am."

Finishing his chores, the grim Valkyrion took some bread and dried meat from a bag and walked toward the nearby fire. Simone hesitated, and then followed him. Sigurd picked a spot near the rear of the shallow cave, and reclined on the saddle blanket he carried. Simone settled into the small space behind him, watching the Peshmerga camp.

The raiders were finishing their care of the captured animals and were beginning to congregate around the small fires that had sprung up in the sheltered clearing. Food was prepared and wine skins were brought out. Simone recognized three of the caravan's former guards, bound and guarded. Several other women had been taken captive, also. Some of them sat, shaking and crying, oblivious to the world around them. Others sidled up to the various raiders, trying to gain protection with their charms. Fear of the unknown was alive in their eyes, bright and palpable.

A tall, wiry Peshmerga moved among the raiders. He would stop at each fire and talk to the men. Patting some, checking their wounds, he would laugh with others at some unheard jest. Simone guessed him to be the leader of the group. He moved with an easy, confident grace that gave her the impression of a cat. He was dark skinned and handsome, with a dazzling smile. Yet the smile never touched his black eyes, which were cold and calculating. Sinister was the word they brought to mind. This was truly a dangerous man, she thought.

Simone felt an itch between her shoulder blades. Suddenly uncomfortable, she shifted her position, looking around for the source of her irritation. Sweeping her gaze around the circle of firelight, she was caught off guard by a gaze of animal fury from across the flames. Hiwan, the ugly Peshmerga, leered at her with undisguised lust. His face looked even more grotesque in the flickering firelight. Broken teeth and bristling hair gave the impression of some wild animal, snarling at the fringes of civilization. Simone shivered and averted her gaze. She moved closer to the recumbent form of Sigurd, seeking refuge from the naked aggression in the tribesman's gaze.

A murmur announced the arrival of the handsome Peshmerga as he moved into the circle of their firelight. "Is that the chief?" she whispered in Sigurd's ear. He nodded as he sat up.

"Yaseem. He is the leader."

All eyes turned to the new arrival. He smiled easily and looked about the circle. He turned and spoke to the Peshmerga standing behind him. The stocky man began clapping his hands and calling aloud. The scattered warriors moved to the sound, gathering at their master's call.

Yaseem sat on a nearby rock, raising him above the others seated on the ground. Space cleared as the warriors formed a circle facing the leader on his granite throne. Hiwan moved in the background until he stood beside the Peshmerga chieftain. His blazing eyes never left the Aragonese girl.

"Now they will divide the spoils. You may be given as a servant to another warrior, but you will not be badly abused or killed unless you force them to it. Whatever happens, girl, face your fate bravely. The Peshmerga respect strength and courage. They will turn savage at the first sign of weakness." Sigurd spoke quietly and never turned his head toward her. She knew he was trying to avoid calling attention to her. She resolved to face whatever happened with valor. These mountain barbarians would not break her!

Yaseem spoke an order and the three guards from the caravan were brought forward. Yaseem spoke, for the first time using the trader tongue.

"You have trespassed upon our mountains and we have broken your back. Yet you three fought bravely. You now have a choice. I shall ask each of you. You may accept our mercy and join our small band, or you can join your brother lowlanders in a quick death. But if you choose to join, you are Peshmerga. You will be allowed to live and fight with us, but at the first sign of treachery, we will skin you slowly over a low fire. If you are strong, you might take up to three days to die. Think about that before you agree."

Turning his back on the prisoners, Yaseem tore a piece of dried meat with his teeth. He chewed strongly, then gulped from a wineskin. Wiping his hands upon his vest, he belched loudly and advanced on the waiting guards.

Stopping in front of the first man, Yaseem placed his hands on his hips. "Well," he demanded. "What say you?"

The Aragonese guard said nothing for a long moment. Then, he leaned forward and spat in the Peshmerga's face. There was a flash of movement and crimson blossomed. The caravan guard sagged and fell. Yaseem stood over the body and wiped the spittle from his face. He gave a harsh laugh and turned to the next in line.

"And you? Do you have your friend's courage?"

"I . . . I wish to . . . to join," stammered the guard.

"Very well. But remember my warning." Yaseem spoke a few words in Pesh to the waiting warriors who quickly cut the bonds of their new comrade. The third guard also elected to join and the group's attention turned to other matters. Yaseem spoke to his lieutenant. A shout went up and all of the spoils of the recent raid were gathered in the center of the circle. Yaseem looked at each offering, taking some for himself and giving the rest back to the warrior who brought it forward. At times there would be discussions and witnesses would be called forth.

"What are they doing?" she whispered.

"Yaseem is weighing the behavior of each man. If he has been brave, he gets a larger share. If he has acted cowardly or shirked the fight, he loses his share. At times the witnesses are needed to prove a point."

When it was his turn, Hiwan brought forth the bolts of cloth he had taken from Sigurd. The Valkyrion quickly rose and addressed the chieftain. "Those spoils do not belong to this coward. He stole them after I had killed the guard. He did not earn that cloth, but instead hid like a jackal until it was safe, then snuck out to steal from the lions."

Hiwan argued angrily at these accusations. Words flew back and forth over the fire, but all in Pesh so quickly that Sigurd could not understand the details. The idea, however, was crystal clear. Eventually the stocky Peshmerga that shadowed Yaseem leaned forward and whispered in his ear. Yaseem nodded and turned toward the crowd.

"Dara confirms the Northman's story. Hiwan, you did not earn these spoils. But Sigurd, you would not have lost this treasure if you had not been chasing that little skirt." Laughter arose from the assembled warriors at this revelation. "I will take this cloth to teach you both a lesson. That is my word."

Hiwan cursed and moved to the rear of the crowd. Sigurd merely nodded impassively and returned to his spot. When it was his turn, the Valkyrion presented his rings and was allowed to keep all but two, which struck Yaseem's fancy. The rest of the division was uneventful, but across the fire Hiwan's eyes watched the Valkyrion with violent intensity.

At the end, Yaseem rose and addressed the crowd. "Today was a good day. We killed many and few died. We have new property and servants to enjoy. Let every man who brought a woman keep or sell her as he sees fit. Slaughter two of the mules and break out the wine. We shall have a feast to celebrate our victory!" A cheer arose in the night sky at this announcement and the crowd dispersed to the various camp fires.

"What now?" asked Simone.

"It looks like you are in luck, girl. Yaseem has seen fit to leave the women with those who caught them. You are mine until Yaseem changes his mind. Since I am not a rapist, you have little to fear. If you work hard, I may not even sell you. You are safe, at least for a day or two."

Simone merely nodded. She knew this was merely a reprieve, and not a release. But now she had time. She would have to take advantage of this opportunity.

The pair ate, surrounded by the Peshmerga. Simone sat quietly, not understanding the Pesh tongue. Sigurd said not a word, merely eating in silence and watching the drunken Peshmerga. Simone was suddenly struck by the image of a wolf, fresh from the forest, alone amongst a pack of wild dogs. She knew then that he would never be part of this wild tribe. He would forever be apart, alone and solitary. There was an opportunity there. She just needed to find a way to take advantage of it.

She suddenly noticed a stillness in the Valkyrion. Following his gaze, she saw Hiwan whispering intently in the ear of Yaseem. The chieftain stared over the fire at her. His eyes seemed to bore right through her. She did not need to hear what was being said to know it meant trouble. She felt a sudden chill and averted her gaze.

Yaseem leapt to his feet and strode around the fire. Conversation died as the tribesmen realized something was happening. Yaseem stopped in front of Sigurd, staring down at the recumbent Northman. Sigurd did not even look up, but chewed nonchalantly on his meat.

"Northern dog," shouted Hiwan from across the fire, "the chieftain has decided to take your woman. Since you are not even man enough to have a wife, give her to a Pesh who knows how to treat women."

"I know how to treat you, little man," responded Sigurd. Laughter arose at this taunt, and even Yaseem smiled.

"The little man is right, however," spoke Yaseem. "You do not have wives or a family. You have no need of a servant girl. Women are scarce in the mountains, and soft lowland women do not last long. I cannot afford to let one go to waste. Since you cannot provide for her, I will do the honors," he said reaching for Simone.

Simone gasped and lurched backward, evading the Peshmerga's hand. Cursing, Yaseem raised his hand to slap the woman. His hand was halted in midair by the hardened grip of the Valkyrion.

Realizing too late what he had instinctively done, Sigurd dropped his hand and backed away from the angry chieftain. But it was too late. Screaming with rage, Yaseem grabbed Simone by the hair while gesturing for his guards to seize the Northman. The surrounding warriors grappled with Sigurd before he could reach his axe and hauled him after their leader.

Yaseem moved into the circle of firelight, dragging the struggling girl by her hair. The surrounding fires thinned as word spread and the warriors all gathered to witness the gory spectacle about to occur. Yaseem threw the girl to the ground where she lay, sobbing in fury. The chieftain drew his razor sharp knife and advanced on the Valkyrion, held tight in the grasp of several Peshmerga. Grasping the struggling Sigurd by the hair, he stared deep into the smoldering gray eyes and raised his knife to the bared throat.

"Barmengara!" shouted the desperate Sigurd. "Barmengara!"

"Well, well," chuckled Yaseem. "It seems our northern friend has learned something of our language after all. So be it. A challenge it is. You and I, to the death. But you know that no foreigner can ever lead a Peshmerga tribe. So if you win, I decree that you shall simply go free, released from your oath to us."

"With the girl!" gasped Sigurd, struggling against the hairy forearm across his throat.

"Ha! Very well. The girl shall go with you. Dara, you are my witness."

"It shall be as you say, Yaseem," agreed the stocky lieutenant.

"Let us prepare," ordered the savage chieftain.

The tribesmen gathered in a rough oval between two fires. Dancing flames sporadically lit the quickly cleared space as the two antagonists stripped to pants and boots. The jostling crowd called out wagers as they scrutinized the duelists. The whiteness of Sigurd's skin contrasted sharply with the butternut color of the Peshmerga. The Valkyrion, broad shouldered and barrel-chested and possessing the thick arms of a seaman, stood a full hand taller than the Pesh. Yaseem was wiry and supple, his movements like a dancer's. Scars crisscrossed both men's torsos, telling the crowd that this would be no easy match.

Dara stopped Sigurd when he reached for his deadly axe. "No axe. This fight is Peshmerga fight. You will use the Peshmerga knife." So saying, he handed a foot-long single-edged knife to the Northman. The famous Peshmerga knife, forged of mountain steel and honed to a razor's edge, was given each tribal son at his manhood ceremony. The knives were carried until death, and most were buried with their masters. An often-heard Peshmerga adage claimed *You can steal a man's woman or even his horse, but never his knife*.

Sigurd felt a cold dread when Dara placed the hilt of the knife in his hand. With his axe he would have given himself even odds, but not with this weapon. The Peshmerga were raised as knife fighters from childhood, and Yaseem was one of the best. Sigurd knew he had the greater reach and possibly more strength, but Yaseem was as fast as a striking serpent. Sigurd would need all his years of battle savvy to survive this fight.

The two combatants were brought to the center of the ring formed by the spectators. Simone wormed her way to the front of the crowd. Onlookers threw catcalls and challenges as bets were placed. Sigurd and Yaseem ignored the cacophony as each silently prepared for the ordeal ahead. Sigurd knelt and crushed the sandy soil in his fingers. He wanted no slippery grip during the coming contest. The wiry Peshmerga leaped and stretched while the stocky Valkyrion merely paced in front of the fire. At length, Dara beckoned them to the center of the open area and signaled the start of the duel.

The two fighters circled each other warily. A feint here, a stuttered step there, as each tried to gauge the man he faced. Finally satisfied, Yaseem launched a series of attacks with blinding speed. Sigurd survived the attacks only by giving ground as fast as he could. Hoots and jeers came from the crowd and more bets were hurriedly placed.

Once more Yaseem advanced. His knife flew in a flurry of strikes, but each was neatly parried a hair's width from Sigurd's body. The Northman stood his ground during the assault and when the momentum of Yaseem's charge carried the men chest to chest, Sigurd broke the attack with a crushing head butt to the nose of the startled tribesman. Yaseem sprang back, blood pouring from his nose. The chieftain wiped the blood from his face, spat, and grinned. He yelled something to the crowd that produced peals of laughter.

Yaseem stalked toward his opponent, this time slowly and deliberately. The two circled and feinted. Attacks were launched, met, and disengaged. The two men moved with grace and economy, each knowing that a sudden burst of speed might be needed at any moment. Minor cuts appeared on both men, but neither could find a fatal opening in his opponents guard.

Yaseem, seeing an opening at last, leapt forward with a savage thrust. Sigurd barely managed to parry the blade, but in so doing his foot stumbled upon a rock, and the Valkyrion fell heavily to the earth. Instantly the cat-like Peshmerga leaped and struck at the Northman's exposed chest. Sigurd managed to twist himself at the last minute and Yaseem's blade buried itself in the heavy muscle of his left shoulder. With a grunt, the Valkyrion threw the Peshmerga off his body and rolled to his feet.

The two fighters began to circle once more. Yaseem grinned broadly at the blood flowing freely down Sigurd's arm. The Northman flexed his fingers and assessed the damage. The blade appeared to have missed the bone and arteries, piercing only the thick muscle of the shoulder. But the arm had little strength left, and blood was flowing freely. This fight would have to end soon if it were to end in Sigurd's favor.

Yaseem danced in the firelight, enlivened by the sight of his enemy's blood. He circled and struck, forcing Sigurd to keep moving, never giving the Northman a chance to stem the flow of blood. Sigurd realized the end drew near, as his wounded arm barely allowed him to hold his own. He held no hope of launching an attack against the wild tribesman.

Yaseem once more advanced in a flashing series of slashes and thrusts. Back and back he drove Sigurd, inflicting more minor wounds to arm and torso. Finally Sigurd was driven to bay with his back to the roaring fire. Seeing his opponent trapped and off balance, Yaseem prepared to deliver the final thrust. In desperation, Sigurd threw himself onto the chieftain. The two collapsed into a whirling ball as they rolled away from the flames.

The burly Sigurd, muscled from years of pulling an oar in the northern seas, would normally have had an advantage over the wiry mountain chieftain. Handicapped by his wounded arm and weakened from loss of blood, it was all he could do to hold his own. He lost his knife in the initial scuffle, and was forced to use his one good arm to hold Yaseem's knife at bay. Over and over they rolled, kicking, cursing and bleeding.

Finally, the chaotic mass came to a halt. The two combatants lay locked in a deadly embrace. Yaseem strained with all his strength to finish the fight, his razor sharp knife thirsting for the

Northman's blood. Sigurd held the deadly blade away with his good arm, his wounded limb limp at his side. His legs were locked around the chieftain's torso, pinning Yaseem's free arm against his side. The spectators held their breath at the straining impasse. Yaseem was unable to drive the deathblow home, yet Sigurd could do nothing except hold his enemy in place.

The two men strained against each other until their breath came in ragged gasps. Muscles quivered with exertion and cold sweat covered their furrowed brows. Sigurd felt himself weakening. He knew he must do something to break the deadlock. He broke the bond of Yaseem's glare and glanced around for anything that might assist in the struggle. His eyes locked on a black speck in the firelight. Recognizing the shape, he lifted his injured arm and reached for the object. Scooping the sand, Sigurd whispered something to the straining chieftain and placed the black speck on his face.

The Peshmerga screamed in terror. His face frozen in a mask of horror, he dropped the knife and began clawing at the black spot which had begun crawling on his cheek. Sigurd swept up the fallen blade and plunged it deep into the chieftain's chest. Three times Sigurd struck, until at last Yaseem collapsed with a rattle, still clawing desperately at his face. Dark blood stained the mountain soil as the Peshmerga chieftain's life leaked from the grisly wounds.

Sigurd staggered to his feet, exhausted by the deadly struggle. The crowd of Peshmerga waited silently, shocked by the sudden climax. Dara stepped forward into the firelight. "The Valkyrion has won his challenge. He is free to go." The murmurs began as the crowd dispersed and the gleeful winners extracted payment on their wagers.

"No! He cheated! He murdered Yaseem!" The shrill voice of Hiwan cut above the din.

Dara wheeled to face the accuser. "It was a fair challenge and Yaseem met his doom like a man! You are to blame for this, you sniveling dog!" Hiwan shrank from the wrath of the Peshmerga lieutenant. "Do you think I do not know why you goaded Yaseem into this fight? It was your greed and lust that led to this. You will be gone by dawn, and if I ever see you again, you will die!" Dara spun on his heel and walked away from the pitiful creature. Hiwan shuffled towards the horses as those near him shrank away, not wanting to be contaminated by his shame.

Sigurd staggered back to his saddlebags and dug out an old shirt. He tried to tear the cloth into bandages with his teeth and his one good hand.

"Let me do that," a quiet voice said. He turned to find himself staring into Simone's brown eyes. She took the shirt from his hands and grabbed a knife from his gear. She sat near him and cut several squares of cloth, then folded them into a pad. She pressed it against his wound. "Hold this," she ordered. While he held the pad in place she cut several long strips and began binding the bandage in place.

"What was it that you did to him?" she asked softly.

"I took advantage of his friendship," answered the warrior.

"What do you mean?"

"Last week we were sitting around after a raid. Everyone was very drunk, and we started a game. Each man had to confess his greatest fear. Yaseem confessed that his greatest fear was the mountain scarab."

"You mean the beetle?"

"Yes, the common black beetle. It seems that in Peshmerga lore, the mountain scarab eats the eyes of the wicked after they are dead. This leaves the wicked souls blind in the afterlife, doomed to wander eternity without sight or kin. I knew that I could never beat Yaseem in my condition, unless I out-thought him. When I saw the beetle on the ground, I knew it was my only chance. I asked him if he was ready to wander the earth in darkness, then I simply placed the scarab on his face. The man's own fears killed him. I merely provided the opportunity."

"I see that I misjudged you. I thought you a simple reaver, but you are cunning as well. My father would reward you for my return, and mayhap there would be a position waiting for such a man as well."

"Enough, woman! Do not badger while I still bleed."

The girl's rejoinder died upon her lips at a movement to his rear. Turning his head, Sigurd saw Dara outlined by the firelight.

"Your time here is done, Valkyrion."

"It was a fair fight," answered the Northman.

"It was, and cunningly done I might add. But Yassem has many relatives here and some may feel they owe you a blood debt.

I think it is best if you go tonight." Sigurd sighed wearily. "You may take a horse and what gear you have. Here are the other rings Yaseem took from you. Consider it a farewell gift. Be gone before dawn." Dara turned to walk away.

"What about the girl?"

Dara halted. The pause stretched into a long moment. Simone realized she was holding her breath.

"Take her." The Peshmerga walked away without a backward glance. Simone let out a sigh of relief.

"It looks like you will get to marry your noble after all," Sigurd rumbled.

"And it looks like you will get your jewels after all," she responded.

"And my other reward?" he teased.

"I told you that you had lost your chance for that," she said while smiling sweetly and wrenching the knot on his bandage so that tears sprang into Sigurd's eyes. She finished the bandage and they began gathering the loose gear. Sigurd chose a long-legged gray gelding for himself and a sure-footed mountain pony for the girl. He saddled the horses with Simone's help.

"I was not jesting about the position," she said while they worked. "My father will give you many honors if you join our consortium."

"All I want is to get out of these damned mountains and get my ship under my feet once more," answered the Valkyrion. "Then I will go back to the north seas where I belong, with the spray in my face and the wind in my hair, where a man can die an honest death and not worry about bugs eating his eyes."

Finished preparing the mounts, he swung into the saddle and headed out onto the trail. Simone scrambled onto the pony and kneed its belly to catch up. The moon shone brightly, easily lighting their way as they descended from the high meadow. They rode in silence with only the creak of leather for an accompaniment as they followed the trail to the main caravan route.

"You never did tell me what your greatest fear was," prodded Simone.

"You are right," answered the Valkyrion. "I never did."

How do you ask a friend to lay his life on the line for you and yours? Yet when your friend is a renowned hero, how do you not? The root of my query is this: To what ends should you expect friendship to go? I don't think it's too presumptuous to question expectation. It's certainly not a given fact that everyone's friends would die for one another, though it is easy to assume such acts of love would occur – when we don't have to test them. What follows is a fun romp of a tale that at its core reveals much about friendship.

Angeline Hawkes cannot conceive of life without writing and she's been entertaining readers since 1981. Angeline combines her love of ancient history and archeology with her love of fantasy to create rollicking adventure tales. She believes these tales allow her readers to relate to her character while still escaping from the reality of their 9-to-5 lives. Angeline's publication credits are extensive, ranging from several novel-length works to hundreds of short stories. Visit her websites at http://angelinehawkes.com and http://fulbrightandhawkes.com for further adventures.

Lair of the Cherufe

A Tale of the Barbarian Kabar of El Hazzar

by Angeline Hawkes

The boastful tales of the cutthroats, thieves, and neighborhood roughs populating the old pub flowed as fast and as weak as its ale did. In a dim corner, Kabar, his brother, Aeneas and fellow mercenary and friend, Traken, sat sullenly watching the drunken locals boast and brawl. Men of few words, they preferred observation to idle conversation.

A gust of wind at the sudden opening of the tavern door drew their attention. A man clad in velvet robes staggered in with the icy blast. "I look for a man, a Kabar of El Hazzar? Is he here?" the man shouted above the din of the tavern.

Aeneas perked up. "Who asks?"

"Are you him?" the velvet-clad man asked.

"No. I am just asking who wants him."

"King Dorhling is of need of his services."

Aeneas looked at Traken and then at Kabar, who drank deeply from his ale, indifferent to the conversation concerning him. "And what services might those be?"

"King Dorhling's daughter, Laraine, has been abducted by Caspian of Sard—"

Kabar stood before the man could finish. “I am Kabar of El Hazzar.”

The messenger bowed in acknowledgement, looking to Kabar in relief. “King Dorhling says you and he once fought side by side and that you would come.”

“Dorhling speaks the truth. Take us to the king.” Kabar plunked two coins on the rough-hewn table and followed the messenger from the tavern, Aeneas and Traken beside him.

The king was overjoyed to see Kabar. Kabar strode down the marble hall toward the throne of the King of Korbesh with a smile on his face. Aeneas and Traken stood beside the huge door, allowing Kabar to meet with Dorhling alone.

“Hello, old friend!” the king shouted and got up from his throne, stepped down the dais steps and made his way to Kabar.

“It has been many years,” Kabar said, nodding his greeting.

“Too many, my friend. Time escapes quickly!” the king said and gestured that Kabar should follow him to a lounging area where silk couches littered the floor. Kabar sat, sinking deeply into one, and grimaced, unused to such finery. He much preferred the solidity of a wood bench to the soft enveloping couch.

“Your messenger tells us that Laraine has been abducted?”

“Us?” Dorhling asked, looking around the great hall until spotting the two men as large and as powerfully built as Kabar.

“My brother Aeneas, whom you may remember, and Traken, our friend and fellow mercenary in your army.”

“Have them come over with us, please.”

Kabar beckoned the men to the couches. As soon as they were settled, Dorhling turned his attention back to the matter at hand. “Caspian of Sardiel, the vile dog, has abducted Laraine and intends to sacrifice her to the monstrous beast, Cherufe.”

“Why Laraine?” Kabar asked.

“He needed a virgin of royal blood to appease the beast. He came under the guise of proposing an alliance between Korbesh and Sardiel to be sealed with his marriage to Laraine. Then he and his dogs stole her away. I received this the next morning.” Dorhling drew a scroll from his robes and tossed it onto the low table in front of Kabar.

Kabar's eyebrows rose as he reached for the scroll. Unfurling it, he read the few scrawled lines but learned nothing new.

"I wish you to bring my daughter back to me."

"Why me?"

"I learned of your employment in my army a few days ago. I can trust you to bring back my daughter with her virtue intact and I know if anyone can bring down that beast Cherufe it is you."

Kabar grunted. "Will you hire the three of us?"

Dorhling looked over the other two. "Aeneas I know, cut from the same cloth as you are. What of you, Traken? Can you protect my child, return her, unmolested, to me?"

Traken laughed. "I prefer the arms of women, not girls."

"Laraine is of marriageable age and beautiful. I have killed many a man who had foolish notions of his place with my daughter."

Traken grew serious. "You have my word upon my honor that I will return your daughter in whatever state we find her in."

Dorhling nodded. "Then three of you it is. There is only one way that the Cherufe can be defeated, and that is by the Singing Sword of Varquest."

"Is it still in Varquest?" Kabar asked.

"Aye, it is. The sword lies within a tomb in a ruined temple consecrated to the demon god Vorsh, deep in Varquest Forest."

"The Forest of Varquest? Some say it is haunted!" Traken hissed.

Kabar scowled. "I have never met anything that cold steel could not quiet. Haunted? Haunted by thieves and murderers, maybe. Know you the way to this temple?"

King Dorhling removed a smaller, plainer scroll from his robe and handed it to Kabar. "A map. Not a very good one, I am afraid, but I should think that the landscape has not changed much."

Kabar loosened the leather cord and unrolled the scroll atop the table. He studied it closely. "What do you know about the temple?"

Dorhling relaxed deep into his couch and accepted a goblet of wine from a servant. "Legend tells of a guardian."

"I expected as much."

"Though details on what the guardian *is* have been lost over time. Lots of speculations as you can imagine."

"I can imagine," Kabar said.

"I will provide horses and supplies to last you into the Eastern provinces. Anymore than that would slow you down and if I remember correctly, you do not like to be delayed."

Kabar nodded, a slight smile on his face. "I have heard there is a secret to wielding the Singing Sword of Varquest. Do you know this secret?"

Dorhling smiled. "I do. But, I am bound to repeat it to only one man."

Aeneas looked at Traken and stood. "We will wait for you by the fountain, Kabar."

King Dorhling nodded. "Thank you."

The king dismissed his servants and he and Kabar waited as Aeneas and Traken exited through the vast door. When the hall was empty, the king turned to Kabar. "Come close and I will tell you the secret."

Kabar leaned his ear to the king.

The overgrown forest was thick and unyielding. The three found it necessary to dismount and hack their way through the vegetation, pulling their horses along. It was obvious the path had not been used for a very long time.

"I tell you, this place is haunted. I feel something watching us," Traken said, stopping to search the emerald green of the forest with uneasy eyes. "Something watches from the trees."

"Probably birds or bats," Kabar said, and swung his arm down upon a thick bush that had spread across the path.

Aeneas chuckled and continued slicing through leafy branches. It was slow going and they moved only a foot or two at a time. The horses whinnied behind them.

"Even the horses sense it," Traken said as he scanned the woods again.

"The horses are impatient," Aeneas said laughing.

"As am I. Enough talking, more cutting!" Kabar demanded and brought his axe down on another tangled branch.

"Well, look at that!" Aeneas said in awe, pointing upward above the tree branches.

Before them, over the thick branches and bushes, rose the top of a mighty temple. Crumbling columns encircled the round building and from where the three stood they could see that statues and engraved runes surrounded the top frieze.

"The temple of Vorsh!" Traken whispered.

"It looks like Vorsh has lost his followers. That temple is near collapse." Kabar hacked another mass of leafy overgrowth. "At least we know it is right in front of us. If only we could get through this twisted path!"

Traken remained frozen in position, still staring upward at the temple standing between them and the sun and casting them into its dark shadow. Here and there, slivers of golden sunlight sliced through the forest canopy, bathing the visible ruins in a yellow glow and providing bursts of bright light that illuminated whatever was beneath it.

"We could use your arm, Traken," Aeneas said, breaking Traken from his trance.

"I am uneasy," Traken said. "I sense a presence not of man."

"It's probably Vorsh," Kabar said, whacking a viney extension that curled around a dead limb.

"You say that easily enough. Vorsh is a demon god. Doesn't this unnerve you just a little?"

Kabar shrugged. "Demons can be killed. It's just more difficult."

"Kabar the great demon killer!" Aeneas laughed and shoved his brother.

Kabar gave a heaving swing of his axe and brought down a cluster of ivy and leafs entwined on dead wood. The path gave way into a clearing leading toward the temple ruins.

"There it is," Aeneas said, lowering his axe.

Kabar sniffed the air and surveyed the clearing. Eyes trained for sudden movement studied the wall of forest that surrounded the clearing. The front of the temple still stood, its columns erect but teetering, threatening collapse. The back portion of the temple had already collapsed upon itself centuries ago and the forest had reclaimed the stone. He felt the *something* Traken feared – an animal presence watching them, lying in wait. The hair on Kabar's body stood on end. Dropping his axe, he slowly pulled his sword from the scabbard strapped upon his back.

"What is it?" Aeneas whispered, also pulling his sword free. He tossed his axe onto the ground beside a nearby tree.

Traken swung his axe into a fighting hold and stood ready. "You feel it now, don't you?"

Kabar nodded and continued to search the forest wall.

Without warning a blur of brown streaked past, above their heads. Instinctively they turned and followed the motion of color. An ear-splitting roar rent the air and the tawny streak lunged again – this time snatching Aeneas and dragging him into the clearing. There it stopped, Aeneas' throat and one shoulder in its huge jaws. One bite and it would snap Aeneas' neck like brittle wood.

Kabar stared. Before them, salivating over his brother's face, was a legendary Manticore. The massively muscled lion's body crowned with the face of a man held its scaled tail and its ball of poisonous quills arched high. One launch of those darts and the Manticore could kill them all. Three rows of razor sharp teeth teasingly clenched Aeneas, toying with him like a cat does a mouse. Traken and Kabar froze.

The Manticore growled. Aeneas lay as still as he could, terror blanketing his face. Kabar's mind raced. This was the temple guardian. Were there more? His eyes quickly moved around the edge of the clearing, finding nothing. He studied the Manticore in front of them, saw its patchy fur, yellowed teeth – age betrayed it.

Kabar turned his head slightly so he could see Traken's face. With his eyes he indicated Traken should move toward the left side of the clearing. Traken nodded and, carefully lifting one foot from the tangled path, began moving toward the goal.

The Manticore watched Traken moving, and another growl rolled from its throat. Kabar remained frozen in place. The Manticore's eyes shifted from Kabar to the slow moving Traken, and the beast gave Aeneas a slight shake. Aeneas whimpered and reached up with his hands to grab the beast's head. The human face looked down and seemed to smile at Aeneas.

Kabar eyed the Manticore's tail. He could tell the beast wasn't sure at which man to aim its poisonous barbs. The creature was sizing up the two men, determining the larger threat. Kabar tried to catch his brother's attention, but Aeneas was moving around too much and Kabar couldn't make eye contact with him.

The Manticore dropped Aeneas, snapped its tail backward and loosed its barbs toward Traken. Traken dove to the ground, narrowly escaping the volley. Aeneas took the opportunity to roll to his feet, but the Manticore roared in frustration, and sunk its teeth into Aeneas' upper arm. Aeneas shouted in pain.

Kabar reacted to his brother's cry and leapt through the air, prepared to plunge his sword into the growling beast shaking Aeneas back and forth. He landed backward astride the beast's body. Quickly twisting around, he clamped his powerful thighs tight to the Manticore's sides. Down he plunged his sword, again and again, impaling the beast on the steel. The Manticore let Aeneas fly with a toss of its head and wildly thrashed, trying to free itself of the warrior on its back. Roaring in anguish the beast ran toward the temple, crashing against the wall in an attempt to knock Kabar loose. Kabar plunged the sword into the tough hide of the beast and clenched the steel in his fist.

Boom! Boom! Boom! The Manticore roared with each jarring thud against the side of the ruined temple and stone and dust crumbled and crashed to the ground around them. Kabar held on.

The Manticore drew sideways to slam itself yet again into the side of the temple, when Kabar let out a primal war cry as terrifying as the creature's scream and thrust the cold steel of his blade into the heart of the vile beast. He jumped free as the Manticore's knees buckled and it collapsed to the earth. He glanced at Traken and saw his friend helping Aeneas onto a horse. Kabar turned his eyes back to where the Manticore lay amidst shattered stone and mewed and groaned in agony. He raised his sword high to strike off the beast's head, but life left the creature before its head did.

Kabar fell to a knee, bloodied and exhausted. He leaned over his sword, stuck tip first into the ground, and tried to catch his breath.

Traken led the horse to Kabar. "Your brother needs a healer."

"I will get the sword and go to Sardiel. You take Aeneas back and seek a healer." He panted. "We will meet again in Korbesh when my journey is done."

"You cannot do this alone!"

"I can, I have, and I will. I have made a promise to Dorhling and I will not fail him. Take Aeneas. Find a healer." Kabar stood and yanked his sword from the soil. "I am off for the sword."

Traken stared as Kabar entered the temple. He looked as if he watched a madman, but he knew better than to argue. He turned to Aeneas who slumped in the saddle of his horse.

"We wait till he comes out," Aeneas said hoarsely.

Traken nodded and turned to retrieve the brothers' axes from where they lay. He strapped them to the horses and waited.

The temple smelled of rotting vegetation and dampness. Scattered around the stone floor were the bones of small animals that had crawled inside the shelter of the temple and died over the centuries. Kabar walked to the dais in the center of the building and studied the Singing Sword of Varquest that lay atop a decaying velvet pillow. Looking around the temple, he discerned no traps nor sensed additional watchers or guardians.

Gingerly he reached a hand out and grasped the jeweled hilt of the sword. With a swift yank, he cleared the pillow and leapt from the stone dais.

Not waiting to see what would happen, Kabar ran from the temple. Outside, he turned and crouched, expecting resistance or some form of attack. Nothing happened. He stood, both swords in his hands, and watched. And waited. Traken spoke first.

"Looks like the Manticore was the only guardian."

"And he was old," Kabar said.

"Teeth still hurt like hell," Aeneas said with a weak chuckle.

Traken turned. "We will leave now. Shar guide you, my friend."

"Shar guide you both. Stay strong, my brother," Kabar said.

Aeneas nodded and closed his eyes as Traken mounted his own horse and pulled Aeneas' along by the reins.

Kabar watched them go. Then he left the forest, making his way back to the road that would take him to Sardiel.

He headed straight for the wharf as soon as he reached the busy port town. Kabar hadn't been to Sardiel in years, but the Black Lion pub should still be the best place to catch up on the local gossip. Drunken men tell many tales, after all. Listening to the crowded room, he was able to discern that Caspian of Sardiel had been rather boastful about his abduction of the King of Korbesh's daughter and that he was holding her in the palace as a royal hostage. Kabar ordered another ale as he mentally sifted through and discarded several plans of rescue. As he asked the tavern's serving wench to bring him some roasted meat, he spotted a familiar face near the fire.

"What? Ho! Moya!" he called toward the thin man.

The wiry man looked up from the fire he was huddled by. A big smile spread across his toothless mouth when he recognized Kabar. He got up from his bench and crossed the room to Kabar's table.

"Moya! My old friend!"

"Kabar of El Hazzar! What brings you to Sardiel?" Moya sat next to Kabar.

"Ah, I am here for a friend."

"What does your friend want from this stinking place? Because if it isn't fish, he will be out of luck." Moya laughed loudly and reached for Kabar's ale. Kabar snatched it from his grasp.

"Still a thief I see." Kabar laughed and guzzled his drink.

"Well, you know, it is a living." Moya shrugged.

Kabar's brain still raced with ideas on how to sneak into the palace and rescue the princess. He narrowed his eyes and glared at Moya.

"What? Why are you looking at me like a crazy man?" Moya asked with a nervous chuckle.

Kabar put four gold pieces on the table. Moya's eyes opened wide. "I have a job for you, Moya," Kabar said softly and leaned toward his friend. "That is *if* I can trust you?"

Moya laughed. "You know you can trust me, Kabar. I owe you for saving my life in Medina, remember?"

"I always remember, my friend. That is why I trust you with this job."

Moya nodded.

"I have a sword that I need taken to a certain location and hidden."

Moya frowned. "Just left?"

"Yes. It needs to be hidden where I can find it, near the top of the volcano of the Cherufe, do you know where that is?" Kabar asked.

"The Cherufe? Are you crazy, Kabar? That is the lava monster Caspian sacrifices to every year!"

"I do not need you to go near the mouth of the volcano, just close enough. I need the sword hidden beneath a pile of rocks and then you can leave. I will give you these four gold pieces now and you can meet me in Korbesh for riches that you could never imagine! Your days as a thief will be over and you can live in comfort as a nobleman. What say you to this bargain?"

Moya's mouth hung slack and his foul breath wrinkled Kabar's nose.

Moya cleared his throat. "Where is this sword?"

Kabar pulled it from the second scabbard on his back and handed it to Moya who eyed the jeweled hilt greedily. "Do it now."

Moya stood and bowed low, smiling. "I go now, and then I ride for Korbesh! You can trust in me, my friend."

Kabar watched him scurry from the wharf tavern like a rat running from a ship. "I better be able to trust you, Moya," Kabar said in a hiss as he took another drink.

The plan was simple. He knew he must get inside the palace. The best way to do so was to get captured. One way or the other he had to reach the volcano and the Cherufe. Kabar knew Caspian intended to sacrifice Laraine there, so he knew eventually the girl would be on the volcano. With the Singing Sword of Varquest hidden near the top, he could find it and free the girl. The in-between parts of the plan were still being worked out as he paid for a new mug of ale, but Kabar was determined on one point. He would go into the palace as a thief. Hopefully no one would recognize him before tossing him into a fetid cell somewhere.

Under the cover of darkness, Kabar crept through the city streets. The moon illuminating the narrow roads hung like a heavy pearl on a strand of starry diamonds. Closer he came to the palace walls, careful not to tread where people might be – but keeping to the back alleys where only the sleeping drunks and horses dwelled. Soon, he was close enough to hear faint music floating on the breeze above the walls. He looked for an ill-used gate or door to slip through and found one near the kitchens. A single guard was on duty, sleeping soundly, on a stone bench inside of the alcove where the door was tucked away. Kabar slit his throat before the man awoke.

Opening the door just enough to slip through, Kabar found himself in a dark corridor lit by torches. Water dripped down the stone walls and the floor was slimy with food refuse. This was obviously where the kitchen garbage was tossed. He stayed close to the wall and continued through the hall, snaking through the inner maze of the palace. He knew he was in a servants' tunnel when he began seeing secret doors that opened into crevices and other inconspicuous places for serving the nobility. He peered through a tiny peephole in one door to see where it went. A bedroom. Luxurious and comfortable; but not what he sought. Kabar crept onward until he heard the sounds of muffled screams and dull kicks coming from another door. Peeking through the peephole, he beheld a beautiful woman seated in a chair close to the fire, near enough for warmth yet safe from errant sparks. A gag covered her mouth and her hands and feet were bound to the chair. No one else was in the room.

Unless Caspian had other young women clothed in fine attire tied up in his palace, Kabar knew this must be Laraine. He contemplated his next move. There was a slight chance they might sneak out the same way he had come if they were quick enough. If they could get there before the dead guard's replacement came around.

He eased the door open and stepped inside. The woman in the chair stopped kicking and screaming and looked at him with wide, terror-filled eyes. Kabar held a finger to his mouth. "Ssh, princess! I am Kabar. Your father sent me."

The woman nodded fervently.

"I am going to take off your gag. Do not scream!"

She nodded again. Kabar cut the gag with his dagger and it fell onto the floor. She moved her jaw around and licked her lips with her tongue. "Where is my father?" she whispered hoarsely, voice scratchy from screaming.

"It is too dangerous for the king to come. We are old friends. We fought together in our youth. You will be safe with me." Kabar worked quickly as he spoke, cutting the ropes around her wrists and ankles. She stood, wobbly at first, and then reached for a nearby table to steady herself. She stood there for a moment.

"We need to hurry. I do not know how long the dead guard will go unnoticed."

"Dead guard?" she asked with a horrified expression on her face.

"Come," Kabar said. He didn't have time to discuss details with her. She looked afraid, but she followed him anyway.

Halfway through the servants' tunnel, Kabar heard the commotion. Either the guard had been found or the princess had been discovered missing. Either way, it was obvious the palace troops searched for someone. Kabar was pretty sure that someone was them. "Keep walking, princess," he whispered. He could tell she was fearful of what lie ahead within the tunnel and anxious about all of the noise from the halls and rooms without it. They reached the dank, putrid kitchen corridor and Kabar knew they would soon face a problem. There was little chance the dead guard had not been found, for by now all of the palace doors and gates would have been checked and locked. Even if they managed to creep undetected out of the kitchen corridor, there was little chance they could get outside the palace walls without being noticed.

This left as his only option the plan he had originally devised: allowing himself to be captured and then rescuing the princess from within the palace. It wasn't a very good plan, but it was the only way Kabar could remain close enough to Laraine.

Kabar grasped Laraine's hand and, sword held ready, emerged into the small, open passage between the kitchens and the outer palace walls. With quick steps he led their way to the gate where he had slain the guard earlier – and was surprised to see the dead man still slumped upon the stone bench. Kabar did not pause, and pulled Laraine through the gate.

Soldiers instantly surrounded them. It had been a trap. Kabar looked from face to face as more than twenty soldiers encircled him and the princess.

"Throw down your sword!" a burly soldier in the center commanded.

Kabar sized up his odds and though he believed he could take the men, with a shrug he slung the sword to the ground. Then they were on him. He heard Laraine scream as she was led away and he was yanked toward the palace dungeons. He didn't resist, just stumbled along wordlessly.

Down a dark, cold corridor they walked, deeper into the belly of the palace. The stench hit him before he could actually see the barred holes Caspian called cells. A heavy door was pulled open, groaning loudly on its ancient hinges. Kabar and his guards trudged onward.

He glanced into the fetid cells they passed, taking mental note of the prisoners behind the iron bars. Feces-laden straw covered the floors and wild eyes stared from the shadows. Some of the captives looked as if they had been imprisoned for years.

The soldiers halted in front of an empty cell and shoved him inside. Kabar lurched forward, catching at the wall to stop his fall into the filthy straw. He straightened and scowled at the soldiers as they locked the door and marched away.

A rickety wooden bench stood against one stone wall and Kabar crossed the small cell to sit upon it. He rested his head against the cold stone and listened to the dungeon sounds. Groans, wails, and faint crying could be heard above the rattle of chains and the clank of cell doors. Places of misery and woe were dungeons, and Kabar had seen his share of them – but none ever held him long.

With nothing better to do and not knowing what fate held in store for him, Kabar closed his eyes and fell asleep.

The clanging of keys on iron woke him. Kabar opened his eyes and glared at the men entering his cell.

"Who are you?" Kabar asked the lavishly dressed man smelling of cloves and spices.

"I am Prince Caspian," the man answered. "And it is I who should be asking you who *you* are since my men found *you* trespassing in my house!"

Kabar shrugged. "So ask."

Caspian frowned. "Who are you?"

"Kabar of El Hazzar."

"El Hazzar?" Caspian laughed. "Barbaric hellhole of a country."

Kabar sat unflinching. Caspian's opinions meant nothing to him.

"Why were you abducting my guest?"

Kabar laughed. "Your guest? More like your prisoner. I was sent to return the princess to Korbesh."

"Damn that Dorhling!"

"He does not take the abduction and intended sacrifice of his daughter well," Kabar said with a smile.

This time Caspian laughed. "The king of Korbesh should have chosen a better champion then."

A soldier bent his head to Caspian's and whispered. Caspian's eyes widened in surprise. "You are sure of this?"

The soldier nodded. Kabar couldn't hear what the man said.

A thin smile crept across Caspian's lips. "My man tells me that you are a known thief and mercenary, a murderer."

Kabar said nothing.

"Have you nothing to say?"

"Who am I to say what other men say?" Kabar shrugged again.

"My man also tells me that you are a great fighter. That you once fought in the arena of the King of Medina."

"Your man speaks truth."

"It seems I *have* caught a prize then," Caspian's face glowed with happiness. He began to pace, thinking, his arms crossed, his chin resting on his thumb. He stopped and stared at Kabar, and then began to pace again. "Have you royal blood?"

"As much as you have," Kabar said with a wicked grin. Caspian was a bastard of a soldier. His soldier father had usurped the throne of Sardiel and through him Caspian had inherited the kingdom.

Caspian frowned. "I should cut out your tongue."

Kabar smiled and leaned his head against the wall as if he were bored with Caspian's questioning.

"I suppose the lack of royal blood could be forgiven considering what a great warrior you are. A champion. That should be very appeasing."

"Do you have wives that need servicing?" Kabar asked.

Caspian's eyes squinted in anger. "The only women you will see are the guardians of the Cherufe and the princess as she meets her death."

Kabar leaned forward. "You speak in riddles, man."

"I will sacrifice you along with Dorhling's brat tomorrow at sunrise. The Cherufe will be doubly pleased with my offering this year!" Caspian laughed wickedly and waved an arm, ushering the soldiers from the cell. "We shall see you on the morrow, Kabar of El Hazzar."

Kabar could hear his laughter echoing down the corridor.

The soldiers came with the morning, their marching feet stopping in front of his cell. The warden unlocked the door and bound Kabar's hands and feet with strong ropes. Then they led him out of the dungeon and into the bright light of a courtyard. Before him stood a wagon with wooden sides and iron bars for railings. The princess already sat within it, tied to the bars.

"Kabar!" she shouted, fear heavy in her voice.

He was roughly thrust into the wagon and fell hard against the splintery wood. Kabar wiggled his way upright until he could see over the ledge and watched as they were driven outside the palace walls and through the city streets.

"Can you see where we are?" Laraine asked.

"Yes. They are taking us through the city and to the volcano."

"Caspian told me as much," the princess said, shouting over the noisy wagon. Each uneven patch of road jolted them and sent Kabar careening around the wagon bed. Laraine at least was tied to the bars and had something to hold onto.

"If I can just stand up, I can hold onto these damn bars," Kabar said. Gritting his teeth, he waited for the next large bump. When it came, he used the shock of its momentum to launch himself onto his feet. With both hands tied behind him he backed toward the bars and grabbed one, clutching it tightly.

Laraine watched him. "What do you think will happen?"

"They will tie us to something. A pole of some type. Close enough for the Cherufe to reach us easily. And then Caspian and his soldiers will leave."

"Would the Cherufe destroy them if they remained?"

"Most probably. In any case, they won't take the risk." Kabar watched the city shrink behind them as the wagon made its way up a steep path that grew rockier as they traveled. He noted where they were going and how they were getting there. Looking about, he saw Caspian upon a fine black steed, horseback soldiers surrounding him and the wagon.

"I am frightened," Laraine said, tears streaming down her cheeks.

"Do you have any gods?"

"Yes, a few."

"You should pray to them then while you have the chance." They neared a plateau. Kabar saw that the wagon could go no further and knew they would be forced to walk the rest of the way. He looked at the silk slippers on Laraine's feet and frowned. The sharp pumice surrounding the volcano would shred her shoes to rags in a few short steps.

The wagon came to an abrupt halt, slinging Kabar to its far side and jerking Laraine's arms sharply over her head. Two soldiers unhitched the back of the wagon and yanked the two captives onto the rocky ground. Laraine reeled, her knees weak, and one of the soldiers steadied her with a firm hand. She thanked the young man whose face appeared stricken with shame.

"Take them to the mouth," Caspian commanded and started his own hike up to the volcano top. One soldier reached down and sliced the rope that bound Kabar's ankles. Even as he did so, half a dozen spears were aimed in Kabar's direction. He frowned and began trudging up the mountain.

It wasn't long until he heard the sniffling. At the first muffled whimper he turned to look behind him. Laraine's silk slippers were crimson with blood, her feet cut to ribbons on the rock.

"Let me carry her," Kabar said to the soldier that held his arm.

The soldier looked to another who shrugged. "Go ahead," the man said.

Kabar walked to the failing princess and stopped in front of her. "My hands are bound. Will someone lift her onto my shoulders?"

The young soldier who had steadied Laraine lifted the lithe girl and laid her across Kabar's shoulders like a stole. She looped her bound arms around his neck and held on. Kabar continued up the volcano without a word.

Caspian sat waiting at the top of the volcano, drinking deeply from a waterskin and sweating profusely due to the sauna-like steam that spewed from the crater of the volcano.

"Tie them up," he said, without even looking at the captives.

Soldiers lifted Laraine from Kabar's shoulders and tied her to an iron stake. They dragged Kabar to another stake directly behind her and shoved him against the cold iron, his back to the princess. Kabar inhaled and flexed every muscle in his torso as the ropes were drawn tight around him, hoping Caspian's men didn't notice. To complete the illusion, he brought his arms forward until the ropes cut into his flesh.

Seeing his captives were securely tied, Caspian smiled. "The Cherufe will be very pleased. Farewell, Kabar of El Hazzar," he mocked, and walked toward the crater's rim. He held his hand over the edge and cut the palm with a jeweled dagger. Kabar watched Caspian's blood drip into the steaming volcano, one drop at a time.

After a moment, Caspian withdrew his hand and a soldier rushed forward and bandaged the wound.

"It is done. The Cherufe comes, let us go." Caspian began a fast descent followed by his soldiers. Kabar watched them depart, then looked over his shoulder at the princess who hung limply from her stake, sobbing.

Once the soldiers were gone, he relaxed his muscles. Because he had flexed to his fullest extent while being lashed to the pole, the ropes now went slack with the pressure removed. Two of the ropes slid down around his waist; one rope still constricted his elbows. His hands remained tied.

"Laraine?"

"What?" she said, anguish evident in her choking sobs.

"Do you have a pin, a broach, something sharp on you?"

Laraine sniffed and stopped crying. "Yes, I have an emerald pin on my cape."

"Can you reach it?"

Laraine was silent for a few moments. "I don't know. Let me try."

He heard her grunting and panting.

"Got the cape, I'm pulling it down toward my hands."

"Good girl."

"I feel it!" she said. "Wait, almost." She grunted again and he heard fabric ripping. "I have it!"

"Hold the broach in one hand and with your other reach behind you until you meet mine." Kabar strained to feel her hand. Her soft flesh touched his. "Now, pass the broach into your other hand, and into mine."

A few panting breaths later Kabar had the pin. The edge was thin, but its point was sharp. Holding it tightly he picked at the fibers on the rope around his hands. Every so often he stopped and strained against the ropes. He felt them weakening. At last, the snap of the fibrous bindings could be heard.

He broke the rope around his midsection and jumped free from the stake.

"Thank the gods!" Laraine said, reverence in her voice. "Untie me! Quick!"

Kabar shook his head. "No. I know you are afraid and I know you do not understand, but I don't have time to explain. You will see." Kabar ran toward the rocky piles that dotted the volcano top and began tossing sharp shards of pumice around.

"Kabar! Release me!" she commanded. Kabar ignored her demands and continued searching for the Singing Sword of Varquest.

Pile after pile of stone he searched until he began to suspect Moya had betrayed his trust. Instead of hiding the sword as Kabar had commanded, the thief had made off with the jeweled sword. Kabar cursed.

"Kabar?" Laraine's voice sounded small, terror-stricken.

"What is it?" he said with an impatient snap in his voice.

"Someone is coming."

Kabar looked toward the crater expectantly but saw nothing there. "The Cherufe has not fully awakened yet, princess."

"It's not the Cherufe."

Kabar swung around, surveying the volcano top. Out of the steam walked two women warriors, their defined muscles armored with leather and rivets of steel. Each woman was at least his height if not taller and each stern visage confirmed its owner's anger.

"Damn guardians!" Kabar said, spitting. "Always guardians!" His voice was full of disgust.

The women approached brandishing massive swords. No wonder Caspian had only tied him with rope and left no guards. The Cherufe had its own guardians who would ensure the sacrifices left behind were delivered to their master.

Kabar looked to his right and left, searching for a large rock to utilize as a weapon. It would be no match for two swords, but something was better than his bare hands. He reached for a fragment of pumice when he spotted a glint of silver. The Singing Sword!

Sprinting past one of the women, he slung the stones away and seized the jeweled hilt. Moya had not betrayed him after all!

Turning, he swung the sword in a mighty arc, catching the first warrior off guard. She fought back, but his element of surprise was enough for him to gain an early advantage and he clipped her arm, then hamstrung her as she turned to flee.

She went down hard onto the gray stone, her flesh filleted by the glass-sharp rocks. Battered and bleeding, she lay twitching, moaning.

The other warrior lunged for Kabar with a war cry that shattered the hissing and sizzling stillness surrounding them. She fought wildly, swinging, slicing, cutting – but in the end, she too fell beneath Kabar's sword. Just in time, too.

The stone beneath his feet began to quake and quiver. Large gusts of ash spewed from the crater and the heat emanating from it grew more intense.

Laraine screamed.

Out of the thick fog-like steam, rose a wall of crimson lava – bubbling and waving like an ocean wave – reaching toward them like a fluid hand. Kabar could make out two black eyes and a gaping mouth that bubbled black with some foul poison.

Kabar reacted quickly. Shoving the sword into his belt, he ripped fabric from his breaches and stuffed two wads of it into his ears. Then he ran to the screaming princess and, gripping her head firmly in one hand, wadded up two more balls of fabric and crammed them into her ears.

The Cherufe grew taller, rising from the crater in a rippling plume of molten lava. Sweat rolled from Kabar's flesh. His clothing stuck to his body and his hair matted to his face and head. He held the sword before him.

Deep booming laughter trembled the stone around them, cascading showers of pumice and dust down the volcano's sides. The taller the Cherufe grew, the lower it bowed its fiery head until its gaping mouth loomed over them menacingly, hungrily.

Kabar waited. Then – when the Cherufe hung just feet over their heads, red-hot, roasting waves of heat engulfing them with choking fumes – Kabar planted his feet wide apart and drew the Singing Sword of Varquest from his belt. He looked up at the monstrosity and, remembering the secret words shared by Dorhling, shouted into the scorching gusts above him: "Sing Sword! Sing!"

The sword quivered and danced in his hand, enraptured by a power all its own. The jeweled hilt glowed and warmed, even to his sweltering flesh. The steel blade vibrated like a tuning fork and Kabar could feel something emanating from it – but he heard nothing through the fabric in his ears.

Kabar and Laraine watched, he in wonder and she in wide-eyed horror, as the Cherufe recoiled from the awesome blade. The black cavern of the lava beast's mouth spasmed open and shut and its swollen lumpy appendages thrashed in agony. They saw it suddenly stiffen then bend its head to peer into the depths of the crater.

Warrior and princess craned their heads to see what it looked at, or for. Creeping from the depths of the crater, from lower than their eyes could see, the lava of the Cherufe began to change – began to harden and solidify. They watched as solid gray rock slowly ascended the creature's body. The monster whipped its molten head about in a desperate frenzy but it could not escape the transformation spreading through its vile being. The wave of ashy gray moved toward its mouth, then over its eyes and onward until the entire Cherufe was solid rock.

It moved no more.

The sword lay still in Kabar's hands. Sensing the danger passed, he yanked the fabric from his ears and turned toward Laraine. He dug the fabric from her ears as well and used the sword to cut her ropes. She fell into his arms, sobbing tears of relief and joy.

"Now do you understand?" he asked.

She smiled up at him. "I do. Thank you, oh, thank you!" He held her in a tight embrace and smoothed her sweaty hair from her black-streaked face.

"Let us get home to your father."

Laraine beamed. "You are such a good friend!"

"Friend? Ha! I did this for the gold!"

Laraine smirked but didn't say anything. Kabar lifted the princess into his arms and trudged down the steep volcano. When they reached the rocky bottom, they distinctly heard a horse whinny.

"Is that a horse?" Laraine asked, fearful the soldiers were nearby.

A thin man emerged from behind a rocky ledge. It was Moya, pulling two horses behind him.

"Moya, my friend! I thought you would be eating grapes from the pink fingers of a dancing girl in Korbesh by now!" Kabar boomed.

"I know you, Kabar. Trouble always follows you, and usually where there is trouble, there is need for a good horse." He handed Kabar the reins.

Kabar laughed loudly. He stroked the mane of his horse, then lifted Laraine into the saddle. He climbed on behind her.

"Aren't you going to take the other horse?" Moya asked, confused.

"But then, how would you get to Korbesh?" Kabar asked, a clever smile spreading across his face.

Moya laughed and mounted the horse.

"Let's get this princess home!" Kabar said and turned his horse toward Korbesh, Moya following close behind.

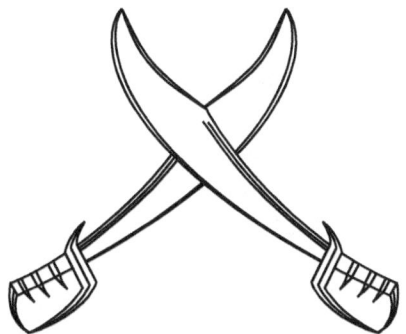

Rogue Blades
ENTERTAINMENT

Humor, when artfully used, can be delectable. Especially when cleverly combined with classic elements of Sword and Sorcery and utilizing Russian myth to deliver an interesting look into character and motivation. What follows is a rather fun examination of lust and the obsession thereof.

Robert Rhodes is a husband, father, attorney and writer who believes in the Good, the Beautiful, and the True. He thoroughly enjoys well-written Sword and Sorcery and has accepted the challenge to write some of it himself. Along the way and with his unusual affinity for Russian settings, he hopes to enlighten and entertain readers. Rob's story "Devotion" will soon appear in a forthcoming issue of Black Gate *magazine. You can learn more about Robert at http://rrhodes-writer.blogspot.com/.*

To Be A Man

by Robert Rhodes

When I heard the howling, I began to pray for two things. Second, that the Lord of the Balances would declare the crimes I had *not* committed outweighed all the ones I had. And first, that the wolves of the White Forest would show mercy and ravage my throat before my more sensitive parts.

I have always been a practical man.

And being such I continued, even in prayer, to struggle against the chains that bound my wrists and ankles to the cold slab of rock in the moonlit glade. To no avail, of course. The tsar's men had inspected each lock before galloping away in laughter; even if they hadn't, it would have mattered little. I have always been a diminutive man, crafted more for speed and quickness than stamina and power. Except, as Titania would remark, where it mattered most.

For a moment, I ceased struggling and focused solely on prayer. Thoughts of that woman could only bring anger, like a rash on the soul, and my soul needed to become as unblemished as it could. Quickly too, for the howls were growing louder.

Slowly I released my breath and watched the midsummer moon, haloed by its light in a glade of clouds. It was beautiful, silent and pure, and in a moment I felt no fear.

"I am sorry," I told the world above, "for the many wrongs I –"

Something rustled outside the glade. I craned my neck to look and saw, instead of wolves, a magnificent warhorse, an enormous black stallion with white forelegs and a blazon on its brow. At once my soul grew warm and irritated. I knew that horse.

That is, I knew its mistress. The stallion walked forward into the moonlight, and the massive shadow on its back became Titania – Titania and a man seated in front of her. His head lolled, chin upon chest, and one of her powerful arms encircled his waist. She guided the horse forward till it stood beside me, then vaulted down. The man swayed and fell. Titania watched him strike the damp earth with a thump; she gave a snort of laughter then came and towered over me. Her wild reddish mane, black in the darkness, eclipsed the moon, and I willed all thought and passion from my face. Except, I hoped, a measure of quiet dignity.

"A fair evening, Titania."

She scoffed. "Vasili, you worm. Why the hell are you still here?"

I lifted a hand and let it fall. Metal clattered on the stone, and the word *chains* escaped my teeth.

"Bah, those are not chains – they are threads of iron. And even if a runt like you cannot break them, you could pick the locks." She shook her head at my helplessness, then stopped as she looked upon my naked genitals; her eyes narrowed as she realized no shadow should fall just so.

She stepped from beside my head to my waist and leaned down. "What the hell is this?"

I sighed and turned my eyes to the moon. In the distance one chilling howl answered another, and her horse tossed his head, his large soft nostrils flaring.

"Sauce," I told her. "For the wolves."

She leaned lower and sniffed before extending a long-nailed finger. This she raked lightly but fiercely across my skin. My back was still arched and prickling as from ice and fire as she suckled her finger and smacked her lips.

"Mmmm . . . roasted lamb – from the tsar's own kitchen, no? It needs salt, but the herbs are good. Do not wash it off, you hear me?" she demanded as her fingers caressed my thigh.

I nodded stupidly. Naked and cold, chained and covered with lamb drippings in a wolf-filled forest, my ignorant body still succumbed to her touch. She noticed while teasing a lock pick from her hair and laughed.

"So the worm becomes a dragon," she chuckled, sliding the pick suggestively into one of the ankle locks. "But even dragon fire can be . . . quenched." The manacle clicked open, and she grinned.

I was watching the dark wave of her tongue flow across her teeth when two, then three, wolves howled almost as one, and my fear – and anger – returned.

"What are you *doing*?"

"Freeing you, idiot." She began working, less suggestively, on the second ankle lock.

"Good, since I'm only here because of you. How could you just ride off – with the diamond! – and let them take me?"

She shrugged as the second manacle clicked open. "It was all as I planned. If you prefer I leave . . ."

"No! Hurry! Please?" Her grin brushed my soul like a branch of poison oak. Only by staring at the moon did I not scream. "What do you mean *as you planned*?"

She went to the lock around my left wrist. "As of tonight, you are a dead idiot. Therefore, everyone will think at least one of the thieves has been punished. As for the diamond, I sold it. I kept half of the gems and sent the rest to the tsar with a letter naming the buyer. So you see, any pursuit of me will hardly be wholehearted. Once again, Titania has won."

I stared even as the third manacle opened, and my mouth with it, for I did see. By my capture and sentence of death, the tsar had received a measure of justice and would lose little pride. Moreover, with Titania's letter, he could recover his precious Egg of the Firebird, and he gained a choice. If he chose to purchase it or barter, he'd already received much of the price. On the other hand, if he chose to recover it through less diplomatic and less costly means, such as two or three members of the Brotherhood of Midnight Frost or his own elite guardsmen . . .

"Good gods. That's the largest gift to the treasury in centuries, no?" She nodded, almost smiling, but kept her eyes on the last lock. Wolves howled, and I glanced at the body on the ground.

"Who is that?" I asked.

"You, you idiot. I would stay and skin some pelts for the winter, but you are supposed to die helplessly." The fourth manacle clicked. "As you were before I came."

"I understand that. I meant, *who* is he?" I sat up, rubbing my wrists, and my skin tightened to gooseflesh at their metallic chill and Titania's glare.

"Why the hell do you care? A man who looks like you – not a simple thing to find so fast. Hurry and take his clothes." She lifted her chin and sniffed the air. "Huh, they come."

I turned the body over and saw a face that might have been my older brother's, twice pale in death and moonlight. He wore a peasant's clothes – woolen vest and homespun shirt, trousers patched at the knees, rope-belted, and low oiled boots. The mark of Titania's garrote ran deep and dark across his throat, and I had to borrow one of her knives to cut the shirt from his stony limbs. It smelled of sweat and wood-smoke, and my stomach writhed as I slipped it on.

While I dressed, Titania chained the body to the Howling Stone, as the tsar's court so wittily called it, and poured a skin of blood on the face, throat, and genitals. As she shook out the last droplets, I began a silent prayer for the man's soul.

"Vasili! Do not stand there like a priest's cock – get on!" She shoved me toward the stallion, which was stamping his black and white hooves, snorting and glaring wild-eyed into the forest. But he held still enough as I climbed onto his muscular rump, and an instant later Titania landed in front of me.

"There," she said with a glancing-back grin, "is it not better with a man between your legs?"

I shook my head and forced an indulgent smile. "A fair evening, A Man," I said, patting the stallion's flank. This had always been one of her favorite jests. To further its use, she'd renamed the horse the very hour its owner – a tattooed captain of Ivarian freeriders – gaped in disbelief as she wrestled his green-and-azure arm to, then through, a tavern table in Brinsk. It had been a cold autumn night, almost two years ago, and the captain's entrails had steamed like boiled sausages on the dirt beside the stables, after he tried to ambush Titania there.

Almost two years. My hand lingered on the stallion's flank. I could hardly believe he'd been with us so long. Titania's black boots pinched his sides, and he galloped from the glade. I put my arms around her waist and held on as she guided A Man between the shadows of the birch trees, beneath the shadows of their leaves and, behind us, a sky trembling with the sound of wolves.

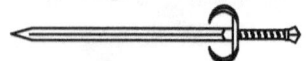

I do not quite remember how I met Titania Brashnova. Three years ago, I found myself at The Dancing Bear in Gravloz with only a few coppers in my purse. That summer, the streets were swarming with thieves of all persuasions – swindlers, false beggars, cutpurses, looters, pickpockets, robbers, charlatans, burglars, and even a pair of black-nailed ghouls – all drawn like crows to war by the new sapphire mine nearby. Though I was among the most skilled, the competition was brutal, and my recent efforts had borne little fruit. That night at the Bear, I had to choose meat or drink and, having a small man's appetite and need for laughter, chose drink. My stomach was empty; the vodka was clear and good. I remember nothing else.

When I woke the next morning, my wrists and ankles were bound to a ransacked bed, and for the first time – that I remember – I saw Titania.

She was standing over me, as imposing as Mount Voros and no less bare. I couldn't believe my eyes – nor could my rampant body, though it thanked my eyes profusely. She was the tallest woman I'd ever seen, the strongest and biggest-breasted, yet she had no bulges of fat and seemed to have all her teeth. These were sharp and white; above them her eyes were the blue of deep water, almost black yet gleaming.

"A fair morning, little one," she told me, "and to you, mighty stallion." She flicked my manhood, smiled and pounced, crushing the air from my lungs. Those were, for seeming hours, our last coherent words. At last, after she flicked my nose and vaulted down, I asked her name and learned I'd fallen in with the most notorious woman in the North, if not the nation entire. It was truly a memorable morning.

For even then, in the dawn of her travels, rumors of Titania abounded. She was, according to the most common, a barbarian warlord cursed into woman's form. She was Baba Yaza's granddaughter or great-niece. She was a twin who had devoured her brother in the womb and become a werewolf or vampire. She was a sword-witch who cavorted with goats, demons and hounds, or a succubus whose loins drained men of their heated souls and seed at once.

To my knowledge none were true, though the last I never quite discounted, especially in the nights following my rescue from the Howling Stone.

For three days we rode north through the White Forest, and each night, each morning, each meal, Titania – having gone eight days without riding her two-legged stallion – was ravenous. In hindsight, we didn't travel very far. Nonetheless, I was soon exhausted and bruised and, as we rode, lingered in a jolted, dreamlike trance, drifting between life and oblivion. Time and again I saw the dead man's face, the dark rut across his throat, and the blood Titania poured upon his skin. Sometimes the smell of his clothing would waft up, and I'd feel as though my heart had stopped and I were trapped inside a sarcophagus of stone-cold flesh. Only the heaving of my stomach and the warm, oily musk of Titania's mane reassured me I was alive.

On the other hand, I *was* alive – and without a smidgeon of the tsar's sauce to be found. Nonetheless, as we approached the port of Rhiev, I realized my soul was burdened, most heavily, with chains of shame and guilt. Titania had killed for us so often that death had become a part of our travels as much as emptied goblets and ransacked beds. There were the three cutpurses in Brinsk, nine bandits in the Misted Pass, a frothing lunatic in Gravloz, four outriders of the tsar's army, guardsmen too numerous to recall, a drunken barbarian who desired me for his bed, six or seven bounty hunters, and Nikolai the dwarf-assassin and his magnificent wolfhound. To say nothing of those whose wounds may have festered later, though few of Titania's attacks caused such wounds. Most killed outright.

As we rode for Rhiev, I remembered each of these deaths and escapes, and suddenly I understood. Titania had killed for me, often and well, but never before had she *murdered.* And now, because of her, some peasant had become wolf dung, and his soul was free and shining in the heavens. Because of Titania, my body was free, but what of my soul?

Suddenly my skin rushed hot, then cold, and I knew I had to do something, anything, or go running mad – a reeking, moss-bearded howler in rags, pounding on temple doors for a locksmith and invisible keys. But what could I do to bring atonement? Because of Titania, what could I possibly do?

Just then, she halted A Man in a grove of wind-swayed aspens, four or five versts from Rhiev and the glittering sea. She raised her chin and took two long draughts of the salt-kissed air; she arched her back, running her fingers upward through her hair, and glanced back at me, her lips moist and upcurved. At that moment, I knew precisely what I would do . . . anything in the world she commanded.

"Get off. Go into the city and buy some new clothes. If we are seen together, word might get out that you are alive, and it is too soon for that. Here," she said, tossing three heavy coins at my face (I caught them), "shave your head, too. You will be a wayward monk from Vosland – my spiritual advisor, hah! And a mute, too, so say nothing once you change. I will ride in with the evening bells. Await me at the western gate."

"But Titania—"

"Hush. When you are done, little father, find us a room. The usual kind—"

"Wide bed, strong floor, thin walls," I recited. "Of course, Titania, but—"

"Silence, mute – and fear not. By midnight, you will be screaming the twelve names of their god. Hah! Everyone will call it a miracle. Now go."

So I went, all but hearing a hiss of dragging links, like enormous serpents, at my heels.

After my days in the tsar's dungeons and then the wilderness, the city appeared as a riot of colors and voices, a feast of smells and wonders. But for the first time, I took no joy in such bustling. By the time I entered the merchants' quarter, I was sweating, and my mouth was dry as char. Suddenly a band of guardsmen rounded a corner, and I found myself crouching in an alleyway, shivering like a snow-blind mouse. In the shadows I trembled, and my eyes filled with tears.

I had never been so lost.

Whether the time was long or short, I do not know, but I dried my face and considered my paths. Fleeing from Titania forever, running through cities and forests, across deserts and seas, through the clear light of summer or the black cavern of winter's night, was utterly impossible. Even if I fled beyond the thrice-ninth land to the thirtieth kingdom, she had the skill to hunt me down, and more than the desire. For even in the beginning, on our first morning in Gravloz before she unbound me, she warned me of her only law.

You will do, but understand. If you leave me, I will have your life or your balls in return. Men do not leave Titania's bed for another.

Titania never spoke openly of my two or three predecessors. But from her remembrances – both sober and not – I supposed they, for whatever reasons, had tried to leave her, for they were dead. No, I couldn't run, and I could only fight her as a goose's neck could fight an axe.

Whether I liked it or not, evening was drawing near. I roused myself and stood, resolving to become the most tolerable, shaven, mute, and wayward monk in all the world, bearing my guilt as long as I could – ever hoping to dissolve it in vast, oblivion-bringing doses of vodka and Titania. I returned to the street to look for a barber's sign.

Suddenly I saw the moon. A white and gray half-pearl, it hung beyond the lifted fingertips of my right hand, rising in a sky as pale and brightly blue as the enameled falcon-helm I once spirited from a boyar's tent. It was light and shadow, imperfect yet shining, and then it was not the moon at all.

It was my soul.

The peace of the Howling Stone returned, so close my fingertips tingled. On my left, the sun sank toward the jagged rooftops. As if I were someone else approaching in the street, I saw myself clearly: a small man before a crossroad in his life, between day and night, sun and moon, between the rising road to freedom and oblivion's muddy slope. I wavered between the two, fish-legged and unbalanced, and closed my eyes so as not to fall. When I opened them, my right hand was touching the moon.

I stood petrified and biting my lip. "The morning is wiser than the evening," my grandmother would say before smiling and singing me to sleep; but for thieves, whose sun is the moon, the evening *is* the morning. I closed my eyes again and called not upon my grandmother's wisdom, but the wisdom gleaned after her death: the secrets of the night, of mist and shadows and bare feet on silent stone, of the well-placed word and the wolfish ear, of the just-cracked door, the persuaded lock, and the pleasant sigh of the golden coffer, teased open by a gentle hand.

And then it came, like a finger of cool black silk on my brow, and I was off like the stallion of Koshchéi Without-Death. Within an hour my head was shaved, and I'd burned the dead man's garments, purchased new ones, and acquired an obsidian-hilted knife, a clay jug of vodka, and a freshly skinned boar. I took a room at an especially sordid inn near the docks, gave the boar to the inn's cook, and hefted the vodka to the western gate. Had I chosen to speak during these errands, I might have arrived even sooner. As it was, I sat beside a fountain for three glorious minutes, with the ebbing sunlight like a mask of warm gold upon my face and gulls wheeling in the seaward sky. Then the evening bells began to toll, and the watchmen cursed with an earthy blend of wonder, fear, and lust as Titania and A Man thundered into Rhiev.

I stood to greet her with a silent, most holy gesture and presented her with the jug. That night, after the jug was empty, the boar stripped to bones, and the knife gleaming amidst her other twelve, I went to work. Leaving one candle to burn, I attacked with a zeal borne of purest desperation. I held, stroked, caressed, fondled, kissed, cooed, rubbed, nibbled, nipped, pinched, teased, licked, suckled, whispered, bit, praised, purred, thrust, teased, thrust, worshipped, bounced, gasped, rolled, panted, screamed, slid, teased, licked, teased, thrust, and *thrust* until the bed shuddered, the floor creaked, and the walls around us quaked from the fists of the envious and tired. Though some may have cheered – I could not be sure. For good measure, I bellowed the twelve names of the Voslandian god and the seven names of his invincible axe.

And then I did it all again.

Thereafter, as I lay with her arm around me and my head pillowed upon her bosom, I whispered, "Thank you for rescuing me, beautiful tsaritsa. Your bed is much finer than the Stone." She grunted and smiled, but her eyelids did not even twitch. The vodka, boar and I had done our work exceedingly well.

When her bosom and my head began to rise and fall more slowly, I murmured, "But wherever in the world did you find a man as handsome as this one?" I listened as if each low word were a guardsman's footfall and, when they crumbled into soft snoring, said, "Huh. I'm going for another jug. I'll be right back."

If the hearer does not hear the words, do the words create a lie? I considered this as I spurred A Man south toward Gravloz, but more often, I simply looked over my shoulder and prayed.

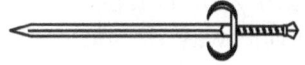

Two nights later, I knelt before the hearth in the dead man's home and listened to the soft breathing of his wife and daughters. He had been a miller, and the cool air tasted like grain and flour. I filled my lungs with the honest scent and emptied my belt pouches before the coals. Soon a mound of jewels glimmered darkly in the ember-light, like a hill of glass reflecting the summer stars. Sapphires, emeralds, diamonds – half of our remaining payment for the Egg of the Firebird. If the women were wise, they would be rich beyond their dreams, as would the daughters of their daughters and their own. I prayed they would be wise.

Afterward, I traced a heart in the ashes around the glimmering pile and beside it the Balances of Truth, tilted to the side of goodness. I wanted them to know their husband and father was indeed dead and had not abandoned them or become lost, as Titania's flawless abduction must have suggested. I wanted them to believe he was laughing in the country of endless summer, where a man might gather gemstones from a crystalline brook and leave them for his loved ones in the night. I wanted to believe it, too.

I left through a window by the mill-wheel, just as I'd come, and slept beneath a birch tree, fitfully and not long, for I dreamt the earth trembled with Titania's footsteps and a lightning of knives flashed in the sky. In the afternoon I rode into Gravloz and tethered A Man by an apothecary's shop. Inside, my old, fat friend was leaning over his work table, oozing sweat in the city's heat as he powdered green and black leaves with his mortar and pestle. He saw me and bellowed in surprise.

"Vasili! Gods! How have you been, lad?" He peered over my shoulder, patting his beard dry with a kerchief, and frowned. "But what happened to your hair? And where is . . . ?" he whispered, cupping his hands before his chest as if to cradle two monstrous pumpkins.

"I left her, Boris. She—"

"You *whaaaat*?" He squeezed his burdens in horror. "That is not thinking with your cock! Even if you shave your head to look like it, I tell you it is not the same. Are you mad? Sick?" His eyes narrowed craftily. "If not . . . do you know how she feels about fat men?"

"Boris, she would kill you. You don't—"

"A man has to die one way or another, and being crushed beneath those onion-domes would be a glorious one, worthy of song!

I tell you, lad, if that woman were the angel of death, no man would care to reach his fifteenth year."

"Yes, and if she finds me, I will never reach my twenty-sixth. I need your help. *Now*."

He shrugged. "I'll do what I can for you, lad, as long as she doesn't find out. And if you give me your blessing to bed the wench one day – more than one day if she's kind."

The gleaming of his eyes told me from which organ these words had come. I simply nodded. "If you can find a bed, or a floor, to hold the two of you, I wish you well." I patted his doughy shoulder and guided him toward the back of the shop.

"Now go find some vodka to soothe your nerves," I told him, "and sharpen your finest knife."

I sighed and shook my head. "You're not going to approve of this either."

When all was done, I bid Boris farewell. My destination lay on a green and rocky hill, a day's ride to the east: an ancient, bone-colored chapel from the days of the first believing tsar. I gave its white-bearded priest a handful of coins, promised to guard the reliquary for seven days, and sent him to visit his great-nephew in the city. After he left I sat, as comfortably as I could, beside the rough-carved wooden altar, with a flask from Boris's shop and the priest's copper lantern close at hand.

Then I waited. During the first night, a thunderstorm boiled over the hilltop. Lightning flashed through the narrowly arched windows, and across the flaking murals, the golden haloes of martyrs and prophets burned silver then black. A Man began neighing in the small stable behind the chapel, pawing at its door. I thought to bring him inside, but suddenly I heard the stable door bang open, his whicker of recognition . . . and a vast and terrible calm.

Quickly a cold sweat seeped from my skin. I jerked the stopper from the flask and gulped the bittersweet brew, shutting both within the reliquary the instant I was done. I hurried to the altar and slid carefully to my knees. Lightning flashed again, followed by harsh thunder and then a thunder that was not thunder but the door of the chapel crashing to the floor and the horror of my name in Titania's scream.

"Vasili!"

High upon A Man, she thundered across the fallen door and vaulted from his back. Even before she landed, she was spinning two knives in her hands.

"Sanctuary!" I yelled. "Sanctuary! L-listen, Titania—"

She pointed with one of her knives, and – I swear to this – her eyes flared with crimson fire. The priest's lantern exploded. Shards of glass tinkled on the stones, and the temple fell dark.

"Cockroach! Shit-dwelling worm! Did you really hope to steal from Baba Yaza's granddaughter and *live*?" She seized one of the knives in her teeth and with one hand grabbed my tunic and hurled me onto the altar. The knife between her teeth was the one I'd given her in Rhiev; I could see its hilt by the pale glowing of her other, her finest, the curved and enchanted one she called My Cock. She pressed that one's tip into my skin, just below my breastbone. I dared not move except to lick my lips and summon my last bit of courage.

"I–I didn't mean to steal from you! Just to leave! I forgot about the gems until I had gone. I wasn't going to keep A Man! I swear it! I was—"

Her brows narrowed, and she spat out the other knife, catching it with her open hand. My Cock edged closer to my heart. "What the hell is wrong with your voice? You sound like a damned fishwife."

"You–you said I had a choice, remember? Our first morning. If I left you, my life or my balls. Here. *Here*," I said, slipping a pouch from my tunic and laying it on the altar. "They're yours."

For a mere instant, her mouth fell open. Then she stared into my eyes and gave a snort of contempt and disbelief. Her knives disappeared into their sheaths, and but for the chaotic flashes of lightning, all was dark. I heard her open the pouch and sniff deeply and long.

"I went to an apothecary," I told her, "or someone who called himself one, and—"

"That friend of yours? The turd in heat?"

"Him? Boris? Gods no, he cuts nothing well but farts. No, some pockmarked bastard in the Low Quarter, a hole in an alley – gods, I should have known better. He—"

"Hush. Get down and take off your clothes."

"He took some of the gems, you know, just after he finished. A Man and I chased him – I tried to catch him, Titania. I did, but—"

"Take off your clothes."

I had no answer to that voice. In a moment I wore nothing but bandages and stood before her in the glow of her knife. "If I take these off, the wound will fester," I whined. "I have committed many crimes, Titania, but I've never defiled a temple, and I won't now. You'll have to kill me first."

She laughed and tossed the pouch on the altar. "Poor Vasili, poor idiot," she purred as her long fingers unlaced her bodice. "You should know that *seeing* you is not the proof I need."

And so began the trial of my life. I'd been desperately praying that, when at last it came, Titania would trust her fingers before her eyes. And she did. Still, I'd surely have died that night if I hadn't quaffed all of Boris's flesh-numbing potion and not just half, as he promised would be enough. Without it, as I knew from countless days and nights near Titania's body, my own body would have betrayed me – betrayed itself – through its quick and ignorant lust.

As it was, as Titania danced half-naked around the altar, her breasts magnificent, achingly glimpsed in flashes of lightning, her lips parted and whispering filth, her fingers and tongue darting out of the darkness to kindle my nipples and thighs, my flesh might as well have been frosted stone. Except, of course, where it mattered most.

So complete was my body's sluggishness that, when the final testing came, Titania's hand closed upon my bandages for only a moment – and recoiled. I felt her stare in the darkness. At last she scoffed, "You must be the greatest fool in the thrice-ninth lands." But there was no fury in her voice. It was done.

She sent me out to sleep in the leaking stable, while she and the stallion remained inside. It mattered not; the potion had left me drowsy enough to sleep on the chapel's dome. In the morning, I stood before the trampled door as she mounted A Man and bid me farewell. She promised to tell all who would listen how she'd wearied of me and how I'd castrated myself in despair. I promised, in return, never to say otherwise. Titania nodded and made A Man rear up; she mockingly licked the pouch I'd given her.

Then she was gone.

Thereafter, I had many long hours to repair the chapel door and sweep up the shattered lantern, to think, and to pray. I sought guidance for the future and mercy for my singular act of ghoulishness, for robbing a fresh grave in Gravloz and having Boris castrate its occupant to procure Titania's gift. True, it had been a great necessity – Titania never believing I might repay her with the same coin by which she'd rescued me from the Stone – but as my grandmother often said, "Need does not excuse all."

And need does not. It does not indeed, though in the endlessly silent nights of the chapel, I struggled to believe that atonement and mercy do. I still pray that they do.

The old priest returned on the afternoon of the seventh day. We shared bread and salt, and I inquired of his visit and he of my meditations, and I promised to bring him a new lantern as soon as I could return. It had broken during the storm, I meekly told him – a true statement, word for word. He walked with me to the door, squinting at the hinges but saying nothing, and laid his blessing upon my shoulders as the sun reddened in the West.

I carried the warmth and silence of his hands as I descended the hill, following my last vision of Titania upon A Man and remembering how powerfully, how gracefully he carried her, his black and white legs flowing down the sunlit grass – but in the direction and pace she chose, entirely at her command. For three years I had been like him, with two legs instead of four. But no longer. I closed my eyes, and when I opened them, my vision of her was gone. I was free of my chains. I was whole. And I resolved never again to be A Man.

E.E. Knight is the author of ten published novels (as of December 2007), the winner of the Compton Crook, Darrell, and Dal Coger Memorial Hall of Fame awards, and the occasional teacher of genre fiction writing at William Rainey Harper College in Palatine, Illinois. Discover Eric's novels on his author's site at http://vampjac.com and be sure to follow the link to his terrific blog Bohemian Word Werks to find further writing advice. To our great benefit, Eric happens to be a friend of Howard Andrew Jones, one of the founders of the original *Flashing Swords* magazine and currently Managing Editor of *Black Gate* magazine. Howard kindly agreed to pen the following introduction.

Eric Knight and I met after we were printed in Fraser Ronald's late, lamented e-zine, Sword's Edge. *I'd read Eric's tale and been impressed, so I wrote him. It turned out that he kind of liked my story too, and we struck up a correspondence. We've become close friends in the years since, and I'm one of the ones privileged enough to be able to say "I knew him when" for I was there to see his first* Vampire Earth *book launch with Roc, and sell well; the second and third followed quickly and within a few years his fiction occupied almost half a bookshelf in every store in the major chains. Before long his dragons took wing in the* Age of Fire *series, capturing a whole new readership. Both series are still going strong, and knowing him as I do, I'm sure that there's a whole lot more we'll yet see from him, whole new worlds and characters.*

Eric is immensely giving of his time and his energy and donates both to help other writers, me among them. He's devoted considerable brainpower (from a considerable brain) over the years to the process of writing. Here's a distillation of some of his most considered advice on the craft of writing. Study and remember – he knows what he's talking about.

Storytelling

by E.E. Knight

Storytelling is as old as human society. It goes back to our hunter-gather ancestors telling how they flushed the bear out of the cave, or outwitted the lions. How did they do it, I wonder? Did they act out the movements of the encounter? Did they shriek out imitations of the beastly cries and display scars or gory trophies? Of course today everything is comfortable and complex and storytellers get categorized into singers and dancers and actors and journalists and playwrights and screenwriters and novelists according to whichever muse guides your tastes.

I'm in the last group, novelists.

It's an honorable trade. Tell people you write stories for a living and suddenly your scraggy hair, cockeyed eyeglasses and uneven sideburns are the mark of an intellectual rather than a slob. At least that's my experience.

I chose the word *trade* carefully. Writing is a trade, not a profession. No degree can make you a novelist. Only learning and then honing the craft of storytelling will get you to a point where someone will cut a check for your work. Editors don't care what school you went to, where you live, or who you know.

I meet a lot of people who want to be novelists. They've got odd ideas about the lifestyle, because the only authors they tend to see in the media are the extremely successful ones. I meet considerably fewer people who want to be storytellers.

Forget the trappings, forget the art and the imprints and the editors and bestseller lists and going on Oprah. The storyteller is at heart a yarn-spinner, an organizer of people, places, and things who relates a tale in an interesting and lively manner. A storyteller takes the audience by the hand and guides them down a path, pointing out interesting sights along the way and possibly dropping a hint or two about what it all means.

If that's what you love to do – and if you enjoy the unique music of a supple sentence – you've got a good chance of seeing yourself in print.

But back to my trade talk. In a trade, the apprentice starts out learning from someone more experienced. That's why I'm writing this piece, to offer what I know about the craft to others, just as more experienced writers helped me. There's a strong *pay it forward* ethic among speculative fiction writers; it's one of the finest parts of this field.

Priorities

So, you want to take up the word processor and learn the trade? As Lawrence Block suggested to someone who said the same thing, go lie down until the impulse fades.

If that doesn't work, there's nothing to do but sit down and hammer out a few pages. Eventually you'll run out of enthusiasm and ideas. You'll come to your senses and go give the dog a bath. He really needs it. There's also expiring milk and you're about out of fresh vegetables, so a trip to the store is in order.

You've learned your first lesson, newbie writer. Take care of life. Eating, exercise, confabs with friends and family, taking a good walk, listening to music, having sex, bathing, having sex while bathing, having sex while bathing and listening to music, these are the things life is made of, and being of and in the world helps your writing. Believe me. About everything other than putting the boom box next to the tub when you're having sex.

Anyway, if you're using writing as an excuse not to do these things, something's wrong. Writing, even getting published, won't fix it. As the wonderful Anne Lamott said, being published will just make your "current level of obsession and doubt and self-loathing look like the Good Old Days. Honest."

So see to nutrition, rest, hygiene, and relationships.

Unless you're on a deadline, but that's for later.

But then, having lived well that day, suppose you're in bed or the tub or feeding the cats in the pre-dawn or pushing the remains of your lunch around on the plate and you just can't get the story out of your head. What your characters might be saying to each other keeps echoing in the Eustachian tubes of your imagination, and you think you'd better get up and jot down a few ideas while they're clear.

Now you're really in trouble. You probably have a story in there trying to get out.

But maybe you've just got this one little idea, based on one of your deepest fears. Thanks to a missed detour sign you're lost far from home and damn, you screw up while looking at the map and crash the car. No cell towers around, and you don't have OnStar, and to top it all off you've got a bloody nose and a painfully cut lip. But the idea pretty much ends there.

From such tiny acorns grow mighty oaks of stories. You've got your three basic elements a storyteller needs. There's a person, you, and that's a character. There's a problem with the car. That's plot. "The middle of nowhere and a long way from where you want to be" is what we in the drama game call setting. That's all writing a story is, is deciding when and how to tell about characters, plot, and setting.

The Iron Triangle of Storytelling

Plot, character, and setting are corners joining an iron triangle of story. Each must be connected to the other two. Setting will effect your plot and characters. Your characters will move the plot and alter the setting. Requirements of plot will provoke the characters to take further action and possibly change setting. The stronger and more compelling these connections and interactions, the better your story.

I usually tell new writers to work hardest on their plots. If you've got enough action in your story, readers won't mind that your characters aren't making them forget about Faulkner or that you can't depict a landscape like Willa Cather. They're too busy worrying about the bomb that the heroine doesn't know she has in her trunk going off.

Plot

So I'm going to talk plot first. A plot has three pieces: Setup, Complication, and Resolution.

I've got some more good news for you – your idea there is a Setup. You've got a person with a problem in a location. "Begin at the first sign of trouble" is a watchword in storytelling.

With Setup done, you move on to Complication. Complication is simple. I know it sounds like a tautology but it's true. You just need to figure out ways to make things worse. In fact, that's all plotting is, making things worse for your character.

The process of plotting consists of creating problems and introducing them to your characters. Problem, meet character; character, meet problem. You're not going to get along.

Your character is going to do something about the problem. Beat it, solve it, try and get away from it. Just make sure your character acts! Ideally, she'll act in an interesting and unexpected manner. But the key is to do something. Readers don't like stories about people who are passively blown through life by events. If Rose had been a good daughter and did exactly as her mother said, Titanic wouldn't have made two billion dollars.

You've got to decide what happens in the character's effort to solve the problem, which will probably lead to all new problems. Repeat until you write "The End." It's a bit like Marxist historiography. Thesis and antithesis meet and form a synthesis. Then the synthesis becomes a new thesis to meet a new antithesis.

So let's go all Marxist on Titanic, since I brought it up. It's a story partly about class distinctions, after all.

Rose is a girl from a society family. Her problem is she doesn't like the path in life that's set for her: rich husband, life of endless parties, balls, dinners and cotillions.

We should all have it so hard. But I digress.

Rose decides to solve the problem in the ultimate expression of teenage drama – a half-hearted suicide attempt. But she meets Jack, who talks her down from the rail.

Problem solved, right?

No. Things just got worse. The initial problem is still there, she's just no longer about to kill herself over it. Furthermore, she's gained a new problem. She falls for Jack. He's an artist and a wanderer, two things she's interested in. But her fiancé finds out. Now it's not just Rose being upset with herself, Rose's mother and her fiancé are involved. Rose tries to solve the problem by giving up Jack, but realizes her mistake and goes back to him. She solves her problems by breaking up with her fiancé in a rather spectacular, though private, fashion. She has Jack draw a nude sketch of her wearing a fabulous diamond. She and Jack run off and make love.

Problem solved, right? Happily ever after?

No. Things just get worse. Several problems hit Rose within a few minutes. The ship hits an iceberg. Rose's fiancé frames Jack for theft of the diamond. Jack ends up handcuffed on the lower decks, and Rose is on a sinking ship with lifeboats for less than half the passengers and crew.

Now she's got problems.

Notice how the problems got bigger and more serious as the story moved along? We went from a problem between Rose and herself, to Rose and her family and fiancé, to an entire ship full of people, including Rose and the two men in her life, in peril. At least half are automatically doomed, given the lifeboat situation. Aristotle noted this too, that as the story went along, the drama grew, and nowadays we call it his incline.

Plotting reminds me of a schoolyard game I used to play with my gross-minded little chums, sort of a cross between Billy Crystal's *SNL* "Oy, I hate when that happens" shtick and imaginative whatiffery. Mostly it involved painful objects being used as catheters.

"Wouldn't it suck if ____?"

Fill in the rest.

You can break down a lot of famous storylines using my freshly-patented "Wouldn't it Suck if _____?" analysis:

> Wouldn't it suck if I finally met an ideal man, but hated him at first because he pricked my vanity. De-

> spite this I grew to appreciate him and fell in love at last. Then just when I think things are going to quit sucking, my stupid spoiled whore sister runs off with ideal man's most hated enemy, shaming my family and possibly destroying my social position.

or

> Wouldn't it suck if the charming, handsome man I thought I married turned out to be penniless, or worse, an embezzler, or worse, a murderer. A murderer who decides to off his wife! The suck!

or

> Wouldn't it suck if I was an English naval captain during the Napoleonic Wars and took my ship to the other side of the freakin' world to help a Central American madman launch a revolt against Spain, only to find out once the revolt got started that Spain had become England's ally while I was out of touch with land? And the Spanish and my superiors expect me to fix the mess I created just by doing a great job of following orders?
>
> Wouldn't it suck if every bird in creation decided to get together and attack people?
>
> Wouldn't it suck if an unstoppable robot from the future came back to terminate me to keep me from giving birth to a post-apocalypse resistance leader?
>
> Wouldn't it suck if I was a dragon, and all the sword-swinging heroes of elfdom and dwarfdom were trying to kill me?

Okay, the last one is kind of lame. But you get the idea.

To recap, a story will have three basic parts. Getting your characters together and making them realize the world of suck that's descending on them is called the Setup. We've talked about that for a while now. More worse suck happens, and that's called Complication. You saw that with Rose and the way her problems got thornier and more deadly. Then the characters are either overwhelmed by the suck or they figure out a way to mitigate, deal with, or eliminate the suck, and that's the Resolution.

Resolution is easy compared to the rest of your jobs. You've just got to sort out the winners and losers and give a hint or two about what comes after. How have the characters and how they view their settings been changed by what they've been through? Is Kansas "no place like home?" Does Rose survive, and if so, how is she changed by events?

Most of your storytelling will be spent on the more worse suck. That's been the trend in publishing for a while, shorter setups and resolutions (nothing makes an editor happier than a fairly complete setup on the first page) in favor of a long, riveting complication.

However you decide to make the "worse suck" complication happen, try not to make it the first thing that pops into your head, or too much like anything you've seen in a book or movie unless you're playing it for laughs. What bad thing happens in the average R-rated horror movie to women with broken-down cars in the middle of nowhere? Serial killers stop by to help, of course. Sometimes they're charming, sometimes they're creepy and off-putting, but they're definitely serial killers. Or the Children of the Corn wander out of the fields.

Even if you want to have a serial killer show up, you've got to figure out a way to switch things around. Maybe have an off-putting guy pull up and help, but just as she accepts his offer of a ride she notices something frightening: he's got rubber gloves on his dashboard, and a big discarded syringe lying in the pickup bed. What looks like dried blood is caked around the edges of his fingernails. As the heroine sweats out not getting into the truck after all, the county sheriff comes driving down the road. The sheriff gives her a ride into town, explaining that the local vet is a lot better with animals than with people, especially when he's been up all night with a tough calving.

But then the sheriff doesn't take her into town. Or to a phone, or a garage. He takes her to his "spread" – which is even more in the middle of nowhere.

Or if you think your audience will see right through that, make your woman with the broken-down car the serial killer.

Pacing

However you decide to complicate matters, you can't unload the dump truck of despair all at once. Making things worse for the character in your story has to be done right. Like the apocryphal frog in the boiling water, you need to turn up the heat slowly. You don't want to put the worst suck up front. A stripper spends way more time shimmying behind the pom-poms of her cheerleader costume than removing her g-string, so take a hint from the stripper and save the best for last.

Like Nigel Tufnel's amp, you save going to eleven for the end, when you need that little extra push. I know Nigel would never start at 1-3, but your story can, then it should move up to 4-6, then toward the end progress right through 7-10. Each time you amp it up the readers need to be shaking their heads saying, *Wow, and I thought Eloise Q. Heroine had problems before!*

Remember how things went from poor to bad to worse for Rose? Cameron's answer for amping it up to eleven was to have Rose and Jack go into the freezing North Atlantic water, far from the lifeboats.

This is called pacing.

Personally, I like giving the readers a good jolt right at the beginning, cranking it to seven or seven point five. It worked for the James Bond franchise for better than twenty movies, why not for me?

But there's another element to pacing you have to keep in mind. Your reading audience is a lot like a rat dropped into a swimming pool. If he just gets chucked in, he'll swim for a while and then give up and drown. But if you give him a board to sit on for a while before forcing him to swim again, he'll swim a lot longer before giving up and drowning. Rats need hope. And cruelty-free animal testing, but I digress.

Readers need that hope too, so they'll keep swimming through the hardships in your story. A big part of pacing is deciding when to give the readers a break and let something good happen. Allow your characters (both the good guys and the bad guys. Be fair now!) some pleasure – hey, Rose gets her steampunk groove on in good old backseat-of-the-car fashion – some slow, quiet moments in safety (even if it later turns out to be illusory), a victory against the odds here and there. Most people rejoice when your hero sticks the landing.

Things have to go well for the bad guys throughout the story too, otherwise they look ineffectual and unthreatening.

Letting the villains win and putting the screws to your heroes is liberating – you get to get in touch with your Inner Wicked Witch and unleash the flying monkeys on your characters. But one of the jobs of the writer is to make your audience like and be interested in the heroes so they will rejoice if and when they triumph; otherwise they want the flying monkeys to win so they can stop reading. So you have to figure out a way for the audience to like the heroes and dislike your villains. Even if you find the bad guys charming and more fun to write than the hero. Make the bad folks into people the audience wishes to either get far, far away from or destroy.

Best way to do that is through character.

Character

So it's time to talk character, the second corner in your storytelling triad. Because I'm not particularly original and too lazy to dream up names I'll use the conventions of Hollywood and categorize characters into groups: actors, supporting actors, minors, and extras. This is your cast.

How big your cast is depends on you. You don't have a budget, so you can hire as many as you like, but in my experience, the newer the writer the smaller the cast should be.

Hopefully you've got some idea for your actors. These are the main heroes and villains of your story: Luke, Leia, Han, and Vader. What they decide to do, and whether they succeed or not is going to move your story along.

Your supporting actors are going to get a lot less time in your story than the main cast. Maybe they'll be there to give the audience a good laugh, or a good scare, or a nice warm fuzzy feeling of emotional support. They can still be key. After all, who's the most memorable personage from *Silence of the Lambs*? To continue my Star Wars analogy, Obi-Wan, C3PO, R2, Chewie, and Grand Moff Tarkin are supporting actors.

Here's a little author trick: Sometimes it's better to let your supporting cast completely steal the scene. Let them ham it up, even if they make your protagonist seem a little bland by comparison. It allows the reader to imagine themselves as the hero or heroine meeting these interesting folks.

Finally, there are the minors, who get a scene or two at most. These are Luke's relatives, various imperial officers, red and gold leaders, Biggs, Wedge, the nasty fellows in the cantina, and of course the garbage monster. They exist to temporarily create a problem or add interest.

Of course you can stick extras in, even if they don't say anything. They add color and action and verisimilitude and sometimes they blow up real good.

With your actors, the first thing you're going to find out is what they want out of your story, and why they want it. Thou shalt give thy characters reason for acting the way they do, sayeth the writing gods. Motivation, in other words. Of course, what they want at the beginning need not be what they want at the end. See *Casablanca*. Twice.

But wait. Wants aren't the same thing as needs. I think I remember the prof talking about that distinction in Psych 101, right? Something to do with Maslow? Margaret Mitchell became rich and world-famous distinguishing those two.

On the other hand, there's something to be said for consistency of motivation, especially with your villains; otherwise *Moby Dick* wouldn't be a whale of a tale.

Where am I going with all this? It all boils down to your characters needing a reason to act the way they do. They're a combination of wants (what they need or think they need) and aptitudes and attitudes (how they get what they want). Frodo and Saruman each have their own idea of how the Shire should be, but they're going to go about putting their ideas into effect in very different styles.

Figuring out what the hero is willing to do to get what he wants must be part of your conception of the character, and it can be a fascinating part of your story. How about the villain? Again, this is flexible. As events spiral out of control, what the hero decides he's willing to do may change, viz *The Untouchables*. Or maybe the hero won't change until either he breaks or his code does, like Lancelot.

Crossing the chasm between wants/needs and moral limits is the actor's capabilities. Once again, this is not written in stone. Luke's not ready to do much but whine and bull's-eye womp-rats at the beginning of his Star Wars story, but thanks to Kenobi and later Yoda, he grows in stature. Your characters can also grow in ability, given time and training and experience, if your story covers that kind of time frame.

Another important commandment to practice until you can preach it is Steven King's maxim that every character is the hero of their own life. It's the rare person who consciously plans what they consider to be evil. In *Casablanca* the Nazi officer probably saw himself spreading the benefits of German culture and efficiency around the world as he attempted to rein in a vile Czech propagandist.

Beware the Mary Sue

Don't make things easy for your characters. If you've got someone who is always the smartest, most beautiful, most athletic person in the room who triumphs because she's just so darn good at everything and everybody likes her and she's got a Barbie dream house only for real and an ideal boyfriend who never leaves the seat up what you're writing about is a "Mary Sue." Create one and editors will gleefully put a bullet between the eyes of your publication hopes.

So put in a few flaws and shortcomings and don't make it too easy for 'em.

Characterizing your Characters

But there's more to a person than just a set of motivations and abilities and flaws. That describes a robot, not a human being. Everyone has a personality that colors how they move through life. Giving your actor or supporting actor or minor character a personality is called characterization. Maybe your characters will be vivid colors and easy-to-read labels, Robert E. Howard style, or maybe they'll be soft rain-washed pastels with their personalities described in tiny gestures and words, Anne Lamott style. It's up to you and your tastes as a writer.

So your first job is to come up with a personality to describe. You've got to decide what the character is like. Cocky? Gregarious? Shy? Vain? Easygoing? Miserly? Vengeful? Pretentious? Wounded? Dippy? Organized?

All of the above?

Well, pick one, or at most a couple. Then think about it. How is this personality type a good thing? What are the unpleasant side effects? Might any of this move your plot forward?

Let's say you're going to introduce a new character in your broken down car scenario, a rural guy in a pickup truck who stops by to help. You decide you'd like him to be cocky. Characterization is just a matter of making him act, talk, and look cocky. How does a cocky guy look? Maybe he cuts the sleeves off all his shirts, like Chachi. Or maybe he walks with a bit of a swagger, and stands so you see the rodeo champion belt buckle. How does a cocky guy talk? Does he roll down the window, holler that it helps if you face forward when driving, and call the accident victim "darlin'" and "beautiful" despite the cut lip? How does a cocky guy act? By gunning his engine and winking before he uses his powerful pickup to pull her car out of the ditch? Your job in describing this character as the book moves along is to reveal his cockiness. Get to the truth. How deep does his cockiness go? When things get serious does he puff up even more, like a rooster getting set for a fight, or does he wilt and pee himself?

I repeat: Get to the truth. That's part of the appeal of writing. You get to tell your truth about life and what makes people tick.

The third corner of the storytelling triangle is your setting.

Setting

Setting is comprised of two elements: time and place.

You need to nail down both elements as quickly as possible. Moviemakers have a term for it: the "establishing shot." This can be as simple as heading your chapters with a time and place, or putting a sentence such as

> "With the evening rush over, Chicago's financial district falls into small-town quiet."

We know we're in Chicago's financial district and it's the evening after the rush. That's enough to start the reader off. You can talk about what color the streetlights make people's skin and the rats in the dumpsters behind the restaurants later.

Your world building should read like a liberal arts curriculum: geography, history, anthropology, sociology, psychology. You don't have to go into extreme detail for any of this, just give little snapshots that hint at the larger story behind.

The thing to remember about world building is to make your world alive. Cultures, institutions, religions, they all are born, grow, thrive, dwindle, and die. An organic world will have elements from all parts of the life cycle. The world will lay down paths for the characters to follow, traditions for them to keep or break, expectations for behavior. The more world-building you do, the more you'll find there are built-in plots and character backstory, which will make the rest of your storytelling easier and (bonus!) authentic.

The world will push the plot at times. Screw with the world too much and it strikes back.

One of my favorite bits of world building is from the movie *Firefox*, where Clint Eastwood is in Soviet Russia attempting to steal an advanced fighter. Another character warns him that the KGB is like a great sleeping dragon. You can tiptoe past the dragon, and if you're careful, it will sniff you but keep sleeping. Cause any trouble, blunder, or otherwise awaken it and you don't stand a chance. That line was simple, evocative, and then proved out in the story, where the dragon sniffs at Eastwood's character and is later awakened.

A good story often has several worlds – look at all the worlds in *Gone With The Wind* – the Old South, the Reconstruction South, the way women's and men's worlds are divided, the world of the soldiers, the world of the slaves/freedmen.

One of the greatest examples of multiple world building I've ever read is in the novel *Watership Down*. It's our world, yet it's not. It's a quiet English countryside, only seen through the eyes of rabbits. Something as simple as real estate development is an apocalypse to the rabbits. A dog running loose in the woods can alter history. The rabbits have their own set of values (food and safety related), their own gods, traditions, beliefs and so on designed to match rather timid creatures whose only defense against their thousand enemies is flight or a safe hole. We visit three fully realized rabbit worlds, the typical one of the home warren, and a sick rabbit world where the rabbits have made an unvoiced, Faustian bargain with a farmer who sets snares, and even a totalitarian warren ruled by a brooding, violent General.

Rabbit habits of feeding and safety are different in each. The rabbits in the sick warren never speak of the snares or those rabbits lost to snares. The rabbits in the totalitarian warren are strictly regimented, organized by scars given at birth, and have a militaristic hierarchy that trains them to be aggressive.

Then there's the new world the rabbits who escape the doomed warren are trying to build.

Setting boils down to values. What is valued in a particular world and how are you expected to go about getting it? What is allowed, what is encouraged, what is forbidden, what is winked at? You can build entire stories around people who go against the flow, or figure out a way to rechannel the flow itself.

Outlines

Hopefully by now you've got a plot, some characters, and a setting, or better, several settings. I think it helps to put all your ideas down in the form of an outline, so you can see your setup, complication, and resolution on paper, along with the key characters and some setting notes. It will allow you to question your work and may save you a lot of rewriting later. You'll also be able to judge the scale of the problems. Does the story go to 11 at the end, or is it more of a 6, overshadowed by that big 10 in the middle?

Of course things change. As you write, it's a hell of a lot easier to change your outline than to go back and rewrite big sections of text. Measure twice, cut once.

There are dozens of ways to write outlines. My personal method is to try and summarize the story into a page or two. I've read excellent outlines that go scene-by-scene with key dialogue.

But some people like to write by the seat of their pants. More power to you if you can get it done that way. But don't say you weren't warned.

Okay, you've got your characters, plots, and settings, either in an outline or swimming around in your head, trying to get out. Time to write that first word. Then the second.

Here's where the real work begins.

One Word at a Time

Stephen King, when asked how he produces so many stories, answers "One word at a time, man."

While it sounds like a quip, there's a core of truth to his reply. Writing a story is a tremendous amount of work, it's like sitting down to eat an elephant. You're going to devour this elephant one bite at a time.

So the first thing you're going to do is choose a word. There are several types of words.

Nouns – Schoolhouse Rock defines a noun as a person, place, or thing, and that's good enough for us. Stories are about nouns and how they act on each other. The key to using nouns well is precision in choice of noun. A vehicle can be anything from a bike (itself a pretty vague noun, do you mean a motorcycle or a bicycle?) to a space shuttle to the Spirit of St. Louis. Being incorrect or imprecise, for example saying "boat" when the characters are on a "ship" will annoy much of your audience and make you look like an idiot.

Precision! as Tevya shouts in *Fiddler On The Roof.* Wait, it was Tradition? Well, pretend he sang precision. Preci-sion. Precision!

Precise nouns mean more to the audience. They allow the reader to draw from their own experiences as they follow the story. They're not just painting pictures in their heads, they're smelling what's cooking in the kitchen or what's decomposing under the breezeway. They're feeling the jungle humidity or gasping in the thin air on the mountainside. You can say your character ate a piece of fruit, but "fruit" doesn't create a very solid image in the mind of the reader, does it? Is there a particular color or taste or texture to the word "fruit"? You need more information. Apple or orange or grape? Say that the character ate an unripe banana and all sorts of associations get in the readers head, the sharp taste, the firmer texture, the fainter smell . . . and help them along with reminders.

There's a subset of nouns called **pronouns** "he/she/it" and so on that are quick and easy words to use in place of our noun. They're handy but they're the very devil, they'll trip you up and leave your sentences unclear. Whenever you use one, be sure that it's absolutely clear who or what the pronoun refers to.

Verbs – verbs are the action in your story. Once again, the more precise you can get, the easier it is for the reader to experience. "Dick assaulted Jane" may be perfectly true, but it doesn't allow the reader to paint as precise a picture as "Dick stabbed Jane."

Dick kissed Jane lets you know that he kissed her. Dick pecked Jane has different implications. Dick frenched Jane has different implications still, as did Dick air-kissed Jane. A kiss is not just a kiss. All these variations in verb tell you something about Dick and his feelings for Jane at that moment in your story. He might love her deeply, but he's preoccupied. He might be feeling guilty. He might be feeling randy. All these things could change the verb you might use to depict the kiss.

Sometimes a verb just can't tell the whole story. You can help it out with an **adverb**. Adverbs modify verbs to let you know how the action was carried out. Dick passionately kissed Jane tells a different story than Dick absently kissed Jane. But you've got to watch adverbs – they're a handy and perfectly valid tool, in fact they're such an easy-to-use tool that they can lead to laziness and wordy writing.

Let's say Dick is walking down the street. You want to show him in a rush. So you could say

> "Dick walked rapidly down the street."

But that's having two words do the work of one.

> "Dick hurried down the street"

is better in a lot of ways, because it tells you Dick is in a hurry; it tells you something about Dick's state of mind.

Verbs give you fantastic opportunities to let the reader know a characters mood, state of mind, or habits.

> "Dick marched down the street"

tells you something about Dick – he's determined, right? He's going to take care of business when he reaches wherever he's going. Or maybe Dick does everything in life with military snap-to. If Dick ambles down the street he's in a different mindset entirely, right? What about if Dick wanders down the street? What if he floats down the street? Assuming the street isn't flooded, he's in a full-blown Gene Kelly-on-roller-skates wonderful mood.

Your last type of word is **adjectives**. Just like adverbs modify verbs, adjectives modify nouns. I'm way less strict when it comes to adjectives, they add color and life to nouns when used properly. I love color and life. Just make sure you're not using them unnecessarily because you haven't used a precise noun. "Jane ate a yellow oblong curved fruit" is a clumsy way of saying "Jane ate a banana."

You're Ready to Write a Sentence

Words are the building blocks of sentences. There are all sorts of sentences, short, long, simple, complex, compound . . . you had this in grade school. I hope. The basic thing to remember about sentences is to make them clear by choosing precise words (see above) and presenting them in a readable style.

It also helps to vary them. Mix up short and long, simple and complex.

Sentences can also be used to set a tempo for your action. Longer sentences slow things down a little, giving the reader time to savor and reflect on all the detail you're presenting. They give the reader more to absorb. Short pops.

When depicting fast-moving action, a fight or a chase or whatever, it's best to keep your sentences short and vivid. Pay particular attention to your verbs in action scenes.

A good sentence has clarity and precise meaning, regardless of length. A sentence might mean something to your brain, your eyes, your ears, and even your nose by evoking smells. Work lots of sensory detail into your sentences. It puts readers in the story. Dick shouldn't just grab a beer from the fridge, he should grab a cold beer from the fridge, and it should instantly go wet in Dick's hand in his hot apartment kitchen. Tell us how it tastes to Dick after his exhausting encounter with Jane and all those trips down that same sorry street.

Try to avoid passive voice when writing your sentences. Passive voice is when you make the object of the sentence the subject, as in the classic politico-speak "mistakes were made."

You want to describe who is doing what, not what is happening to whom. It's better to say "rain fell on the trees" than "the trees were wetted by rain." You're adding extra verbs and needlessly complicating things.

There's nothing absolutely wrong with passive voice. It's grammatically correct and has its place. There are times when you might want to use the passive voice, when you want to slow things down in your story, show time passing, paint a picture artfully. But they'll be rare, and you're almost always better off using the active, just for clarity's sake.

Precision! Sing it with me. Snap your fingers and dance, because now you're getting it.

The Art of the Paragraph

Sentences are the building blocks of paragraphs. While sentences are all about clarity and meaning, paragraphs are all about organization. The paragraph is the most basic tool for presenting your story in an interesting and lively manner.

A paragraph is simply a collection of related sentences. A paragraph can be as short as a one-word line of dialogue. I've read paragraphs running for pages. Not a pleasant experience.

How you organize paragraphs is an important part of your writing. It allows you to add weight and emphasis. Shorter paragraphs, like shorter sentences, speed things up and stand out.

Let's say Jane gets the drop on Dick. She draws a revolver from her purse, points it at Dick, and even pulls back the hammer so she can fire in a split second.

> Crying and trembling, she reached into her purse as Dick felt for his handkerchief. She pulled a chrome revolver and pointed it at him with a newly steady hand. The hammer clicked as she cocked it.
>
> Even from across the desk Dick felt the barrel of the gun, a phantom finger pressing just above his heart.

All these actions describing Jane pulling the gun are related, so they can be put in a paragraph together. I started a new paragraph with Dick's reaction to the appearance of the gun, though there's no real rule that says I have to, it just feels right to my taste.

Let's say I wanted to give particular emphasis to cocking the gun, to highlight to the reader that she probably means to shoot, or she's expecting some kind of reaction from Dick and wants to be ready to kill him in a split-second. I'd give that its own paragraph, to let the reader know that detail is extra-important.

> Crying and trembling, she reached into her purse as Dick felt for his handkerchief. She pulled a chrome revolver and pointed it at him with a newly steady hand.
>
> The hammer clicked as she cocked it.

> Even from across the desk, Dick felt the barrel of the gun, a phantom finger pressing just above his heart.

A few guidelines for paragraphs:

> * For clarity's sake, whenever someone new speaks, start a new paragraph.
> * Whatever you're describing in the first sentence of a paragraph should be supported by the rest of the paragraph. I wouldn't write about Jane pulling a gun on Dick and then spend the rest of the paragraph talking about what the cat on top of the file cabinet is doing, unless its diving out of the way at the sight of the gun.
> * Longer paragraphs usually require a more skilled reader.

Scenes and Sensibility

Paragraphs are the building blocks of scenes. If sentences are all about clarity and paragraphs are organization, a scene is where you show off your storytelling.

A scene is a little mini-story within a story. They will usually have their own setup, complication, and sometimes resolution. For reasons of suspense, you might decide to leave off the resolution of the scene to make the reader breathless to move on to the next scene or chapter, but be wary, the effect can get tiresome when used repeatedly.

A scene needs to have a reason for being in your story. It should either advance the plot, develop a character, or depict some important element of your setting. Ideally, it should do two or even three of these things in the interest of economy.

This is not to say that you need to present the reason for the scene's existence with twinkling Broadway lights saying THIS IS THE POINT I WANT YOU TO GET. Sometimes you'll hide an important detail or factoid in other business that seems more important at the time. This is what makes the really good mystery writers the marvels that they are. I said before writers are kind of like strippers. They're also Three-card Monte operators at times.

Scenes should always contain some element of conflict or change. Conflict and change are interesting. If a scene has neither, either yank it or put some in. Sow doubt or clear things up, add a new character or reveal a change in an old one…think of each scene as a conveyor belt in a Buggs Bunny cartoon, where Daffy goes in one end of the machine looking like a duck and comes out pressed and trimmed into a saxophone. A scene has to develop your overall story in some way.

When you approach writing a scene there's always some business you have to get out of the way at the beginning of each scene. You've got to let the reader know if time has passed or location has shifted since the conclusion of your previous scene. A lot of thriller writers like to do this in the simplest manner possible, by giving the time and place of each scene, like a wire service header:

Warsaw, June 12, 3pm

While I don't do this myself, I like the simplicity of this approach.

Scenes are the building block of stories. You'll write scene after scene after scene until you've finished your resolution and it's time to write those wonderful words THE END.

The feeling of accomplishment is worth all the effort, believe me.

Notice I left out chapters. Chapters are certainly important, but where you put chapter breaks is very much a matter of your own personal style so I'm hesitant to give rules. Or even advice. I think if you've got multiple point of view characters in your story, you should probably separate points of view by chapter, unless you really want the action moving fast and furious, but even then you should insert a line break when shifting your POV. You can let everyone know you absolutely want a line break by typing

#

in a line of its own.

POV

Which brings me to point of view. If I want to leave you with one piece of advice as a writer, it's to pay particular attention to point of view.

Point of view is one of the biggest decisions you'll make in telling your story. Through whose eyes will we see this story?

Limit those pairs of eyeballs.

I don't have anything against multiple point of view stories, there are many wonderful examples out there. I love Thomas Harris's structure in *Red Dragon*, where after a good deal of time seeing the effects of Francis Dolarhyde's actions through the investigator studying the case (and a quick bounce into Hannibal Lecter's POV as he seeks revenge against that same investigator) he spends a few chapters in Dolarhyde's POV so we can see how the monster was made. It's chilling and heart-rending.

POV and its uses are worth a whole article, if not their own book. But let me just say this: when you're in a point of view, really get into it. Show us what that character feels, hears, tastes, touches. Give me sensations! I want to feel the sweaty palms of a man with a knife to his throat, the electric fear running up from the adrenals of a woman who realizes she's being stalked as she crosses a parking garage, the painfully cracked lips of a man dying in a desert. They don't all have to be bad, of course. I don't mind reading what a salty margarita tastes like as I look out on a Pacific sunset on a Costa Rica beach one bit.

But remember, no two characters will experience that margarita and that sunset in quite the same way. Keep that in mind when you're changing to a different character's point of view. E.E. Knight, author, likes a good margarita. Someone else might consider it the devil's poison, and someone else will just be reminded of an ex-husband, and someone else might need the tequila to face what's going to appear once that sun goes down . . .

Honestly, I don't have the experience in writing multiple point of views to be of much help. Generally, though, if you're going to skip around between people keep it clear and organized (George R.R. Martin names his chapters after whoever they're depicting). I think it's best to write in the POV of the principal actor in the scene or chapter, or from the POV of whoever has the most to lose from the scene's outcome.

There's a reason Peter Benchly opens *Jaws* with Chrissy's POV as she takes her ill-fated moonlight swim off Amity Island. And it makes a hell of a setup.

Like our hunter-gatherer ancestors I mentioned at the beginning of this piece, Benchly told a tale of the human community dealing with a threat. He told us that we can face our fears and triumph. The hunter-gatherers would have nodded to each other across the cooking-fire in appreciation.

I might as well admit this right from the start: There isn't a single sword drawn in this tale. I know, I know, this is a Sword and Sorcery Heroic Adventure anthology entitled Return of the Sword. *So how can this be? Readers familiar with Morlock will know that the man can match heroic attitude with any barbarian sword-slinger out there while his cleverness out-matches many of them. The cantankerous old bastard may carry the world's largest chip upon his shoulder and pretend he doesn't matter, but he's still able to find every fight, female, and frothy mug of ale out there.*

James Enge started writing Sword and Sorcery because he wanted to read more of the stuff he enjoyed – like Zelazny's original Amber *books and Leiber's Fafhrd and the Gray Mouser tales. Combining this desire with the knowledge of his day-job (teaching Latin, Greek and mythology in a public university), James created Morlock, a talented but embittered fellow suffering the mother-of-all-midlife crisis. As James says, though Morlock thinks he's done with life, he's wrong – and life is not yet done with him. Read more about Morlock at jamesenge.com – or in his novel* Blood of Ambrose, *to be published by Pyr in 2009.*

The Red Worm's Way

A Tale of Morlock Ambrosius

by James Enge

Fair of face, full of pride,
Sit ye down by a dead man's side.
Ye sang songs a' the day:
Sit down at night in the red worm's way.

—Swinburne, *A Lyke-Wake Song*

Morlock was sober when the coin winked at him, but that wasn't his fault. Towns were scattered thinly through the masterless lands east of the Narrow Sea, and he'd been walking and sleeping in the open air for weeks since he'd had his last drink. The town he finally arrived at looked promising. All the shops were shut down; all the people were in the streets wearing wreaths; the whole town seemed to be gearing up for a party. *If you can't get a drink in a place like this*, Morlock reasoned keenly with himself, *why the hell not?*

It was what he was still asking himself more than an hour after hitting town. If there were any taverns in the place they were locked up, the same as the rest of the shops. He ended up wandering after a crowd singing various slightly discordant songs, and following them out to a large field that seemed to serve as a sort of fairground. Here Morlock hoped he would find some agreeable person with a cask, selling or giving away strong drink of some type – wine, or beer, or hard cider at least.

But there wasn't. There were a number of more or less amateur performances; there were clowns and jugglers and singers; there were farm animals of various remarkable sizes or abilities; there were vendors selling a surprising variety of foodstuffs conveniently impaled on sticks. But Morlock, wandering among the singing, laughing crowd, concluded that, whatever was elevating their spirits, it wasn't liquor of any sort he could recognize.

"What good are you, then?" he muttered to the town as a whole, and made his way through the field with the intention of getting as far away as he could just as fast as he was able. A town with no drinking was no town for him.

"Sir!" a woman cried as he shouldered past. "You are a stranger here!"

"Yes," he said, and would have gone on, but she grabbed him by the arm.

"You can help me!" she said urgently.

"Maybe," he conceded gruffly. "I probably won't, though."

"My husband has just died."

Morlock turned to look at her for the first time. She wore a wreath, like her fellow-townsmen, but it was black and trailed widow's weeds. Her face was stained with fresh tears and the tracks of old ones. Morlock had recently lost his own wife, although not by any process as benign and peaceful as death, which was one of many reasons he currently preferred drinking to thinking. This widow's apparent grief at the loss of her husband angered him obscurely. But it also caught his attention.

"So?" he said.

"There is no one to sit the wake with him tonight. Our town Loukios, as you see, is on holiday. If you could—"

"Sit it yourself. Or cremate him: that way you won't have to worry about burying him alive."

"Please, sir. *Please*. He is dead. That is not in doubt. And I cannot sit the wake, or I surely would. His body must lie one night in state before it is buried, and someone must sit with it to protect it from . . . someone must sit with it."

"To protect it from Strigae?" Morlock said coolly "You have a cult of corpse-eating witches hereabouts, is that it? In that case, if I were you, I would get the body underground before dark."

"Our laws do not permit that."

"Change them. Or break them."

"Please," she said desperately. "Please. I can pay you! I can pay you with gold, with good solid gold!" And she held out a fistful of gold coins.

Morlock's interest in gold was slight indeed; he made it by the boxful whenever he needed some, which was not often. But, as a maker of things, he had once had some interest in coins. He glanced instinctively at the discs in her hands.

They were of a type new to him. Each design was different, and some were horrible – he could see headless corpses and hanged men on a few of the gold cartwheels she held out to him. The coins might be solid and perhaps they were gold, but he doubted they were *good* in any generally accepted meaning of the word. They stank of evil magic.

He was about to say as much when one of the coins, showing what appeared to be a crow or raven wearing a crown, winked at him. It could have been a trick of the light, but he didn't think so.

"What will you take for that one?" he asked, pointing at the crow-coin.

Guile entered the eyes of the grieving woman. "That is an especially valuable one, sir. They say the Crow King will do any service for the person who holds this coin."

Morlock grunted skeptically and said, "How much for it?"

"I am not selling these coins, sir. I'm offering them to pay for a service. You cannot buy this coin; you may earn it."

"By keeping the Strigae from chewing up your husband's corpse tonight."

"Please do not speak so disrespectfully of the Sisters of the Red Worm (I summon them not!). But that is the general idea."

Morlock thought idly about knocking her down, taking the coin and running away with it. But his conversation with the woman had drawn a crowd of interested listeners; he doubted he would get away clean. Besides, stealing magical gold often had unintended consequences. On the other hand, he could just say *No* and walk away. But it occurred to him that he wasn't going to do that.

"All right," he said. "Keep the others; I just want that coin with the crow."

"I will give it to you tomorrow morning."

"If I keep your husband's corpse intact."

"Oh no. Not at all. If you stay on watch through the night I will give you the coin, even if the Unnamed Ones violate poor Thelyphron. But . . ."

"But?"

"Our law says that whatever parts are missing from a dead body after a vigil must be made up by the watcher."

"So if poor Thelyphron's nose is missing in the morning, he will be buried with mine? Likewise liver or testicles?"

"Yes. That is only fair, wouldn't you say?"

Morlock considered the question briefly. "No. Where do I stand, or sit, this wake?"

There was a brief patter of applause as those who had been watching with disinterested interest turned away. Morlock felt almost as if he had been performing in a playlet for the entertainment of the fairgoers. He hoped the feeling was mistaken. The widow led him through the crowd to a small hut set in the field a little distance away from the fairgrounds. There were still plenty of people around, though, laughing and singing.

"How late does your festival last?" Morlock asked.

"Oh, all night. Until noon tomorrow, in fact."

Morlock felt relieved, and it must have shown, because the widow said earnestly, "You must not think that."

"What?"

"That the Sisters of the Red Worm would be ... repelled by ... by the festival." Some of the nearby townspeople turned to look at them with obvious and not obviously friendly interest. "Quick, let us go in," she said and hurried through the low door into the corpse-house.

Inside the corpse-house there was, of course, a corpse, lying in fine garments atop a stone table.

"The dearly departed Thelyphron, I guess?" Morlock said.

"Yes," the widow replied gently, averting her eyes.

Morlock glanced at her and said, a little less roughly, "I am sorry. To me this is a different sort of problem, but I will try not to offend your grief."

She nodded, her face still averted. "I am glad to treat this as a... problem. Something that needs, and has, a solution."

As opposed to grief and death, Morlock supposed, which had none. He nodded.

"I was going to say ..."

"About the Strigae," he prompted.

"About the Blessed Sisterhood (I name them not!). They . . . There are many of them among the townspeople."

"Oh?"

"Yes. In the day, they walk even as we do. In the night... They will surely come tonight, in some numbers. The people nearby—"

"Will be Strigae themselves."

"They *may* be those whom we do not name. They may not be. But we do not . . . we do not . . ."

"No one will intervene against the Strigae."

"It is too dangerous. The Gentle Sisters (who hear me not; who see me not) will not harm us if we let them be. And they are so powerful, we could not stop them even if we tried."

Morlock grunted. "You could leave. Strigae tend to be pretty territorial."

The widow nodded slowly. "But this is my home. It is the only place I know."

Morlock knew many places, but he could never go again to the place he considered home. He shrugged his crooked shoulders and turned away to inspect the walls, floor and ceiling of the corpse-house. There were many cracks in the mortar that had been hastily patched. Several sections of roof were loose; Morlock could swing them back like shutters on a skylight. There were brown streaky stains on the wall that were probably blood. The floor was beaten earth with a definite slope from north to south; several rat holes had been plugged with plaster. The place stank like the devil, but that's what you'd expect from a corpse-house.

"You don't think I will make it, do you?" he said to the widow.

"I hope you will," she said earnestly. "If, during the night, you have to flee the . . . flee here, I will understand."

"Will you understand so far as to pay me the crow-coin?"

Her jaw tightened. "No. I'm sorry."

"Me, too." He shook his head. "I will need a couple of barrels of water."

"What?"

"I'll need a couple of barrels of water."

"You—"

"Need a couple of barrels of water. Soon, if both Thelyphron and I are to make it through the night intact."

"It's just – I thought you were going to say something else, I suppose. I will get you what you need. I doubt you will want to eat in here, but do you want anything to drink, besides water? A mug of beer or wine?"

Morlock shrugged. If someone had had the decency to offer him a drink an hour or two ago, he'd be well on his way to oblivion by now. And likely to wake up with his nose and ears chewed off by a Striga. "No," he said. "I never drink while I am working."

"You are a man of principle."

"Hmph," Morlock said doubly dryly, and turned back to inspect the wall.

Morlock was almost done digging his channel around the walls of the corpse-house when the widow returned with two barrels of water. The barrels were carried in, one at a time, by a burly young man the widow introduced as her son, Zatchlas.

"I am called Myrrhina," the widow added, and glanced significantly at Morlock.

He didn't like the way she'd put that. It was almost as if her real name was something else, and she had reason to keep it secret. Sorcerers did that sometimes. "My name is Morlock," he said flatly.

"Oh," Myrrhina said distantly. "What in the world is that you are working on?"

"A ditch," Morlock said, descending to technicality. He nodded at the barrels being lugged into the corpse-house by the sweating, rather softly muscled Zatchlas. "Strigae cannot cross running water, you know."

"Er, yes. But surely the water will not run uphill?"

Morlock shrugged and said, "Can you get me a lantern or some candles? There is nothing here and I will need light for my watch."

"Of course. Zatchlas will bring them, won't you, dear?"

From the expression on his heavy features, Zatchlas seemed aggrieved rather than grieving, and he rolled his eyes at his mother's request. But he gruffly admitted he'd be passing that way later.

"Good luck to you, Morlock," Myrrhina whispered as they left.

"Do not spend that coin," he replied, and turned back to his digging. By the time Zatchlas returned, perhaps a half hour before sunset, the channel was complete, mirror-gates were set at the high and low points of the stream, and Morlock was pouring in the water from one of the barrels.

He felt Zatchlas' heavy presence behind him as he poured, but said nothing until Zatchlas said, "You really think that will work?"

"It might," Morlock replied, and stood the barrel upright.

The water ran down the channel and through the mirror gate. From there it turned upward, along the square lines of the corpse-house, until it reached the upper mirror-gate. When it passed through that it turned downward once more. The corpse-house was now a fortress against Strigae, defended by its odd rectangular river-moat.

"Magic!" Zatchlas whispered.

Morlock shrugged. He never knew what to say to that. "Anyone can do it, if they know how," he said this time. "That's the trick; knowing how."

"How is it done?" Zatchlas asked.

"The mirror convinces the water that gravity works differently on either side of the gate; the water behaves accordingly."

"You can't convince soulless matter of something that is not true."

Morlock shrugged. "Water is not quite soulless, not the way a rock is (and even then it depends on the rock). Water is also quite gullible, in small amounts."

"I can't believe it!"

"You I am not trying to convince. Did you bring the lamp?"

"Eh? Oh, I have a bundle of candles here. Wax candles, not tallow. Mother said you would know why."

Morlock did. Tallow candles were made from the fat of dead animals, and were relatively easy to infect with hostile magic. He'd have felt better if his employer were unaware of this.

"And this," Zatchlas said with some relish, handing over the candles, and a large covered mug.

"What's 'this'?" Morlock demanded.

"A long drink of wine. It will be a pretty cold night; mother thought it might help."

Morlock snorted, but accepted both the candles and the wine cup.

"I will stop by sometime after dark," Zatchlas added. "Not as a relief, you understand."

"Yes."

"Just to see how you are doing."

"Thanks."

Zatchlas left and Morlock was left glaring at the wine cup.

Morlock hadn't always been a drunk – everybody has to start somewhere. But by now he was a fairly experienced one. He didn't think a single cup of wine, no matter how tall, was going to incapacitate him. But he knew that something started when he began to drink; he switched from one mind, almost, to another. That, of course, was the point: his undrunk mind was a burden to him and drink was an escape. But undrunk Morlock, as annoying as he was in some ways, was a more reliable person than drunk Morlock. Drunk Morlock forgot things; drunk Morlock wandered away from tasks; drunk Morlock reacted to potential dangers too slowly and ineffectively. If he was going to do what he had set out to do, he would have to remain sober.

On the other hand, did he have to do what he'd set out to do? He'd come into this town for a drink. Now he had one. Why not drink it and go? The widow had even said she'd understand if he didn't stay through the night. She might even understand if he didn't stay until nightfall. And if she didn't, so what? He need never come this way again.

He wouldn't get the crow-coin, though, unless he successfully completed the corpse-watch. And to do that, he'd have to be sober.

On the other hand, one drink of wine wouldn't knock him flat. Really, it would just settle his mind. The thing was distracting him; he never should have accepted it. But since he had, he might as well drink it down and get it over with. The sooner he did it, the sooner the effects would pass. If he wanted to be sober through the night, he really should drink it now. Now. *Right now.*

Morlock reached toward the wine cup and deliberately knocked it off its perch on the corner of the corpse table. It sprayed its contents on the packed-earth floor and rolled under the corpse table.

"So much for that," he said, "and," he added to drunk Morlock, "so much for you."

In fact, drunk Morlock and undrunk Morlock hated each other. *Someday one of them will destroy the other*, Morlock reflected. He wondered which one would win.

By then the sun had set. He lit the first of many candles, putting it on the end of the empty overturned water barrel, and settled down to wait for what the night would bring.

The red light of torches and bonfires wounded the darkness beyond the corpse-house door. Morlock often heard laughter and voices, not so very far away. He could never catch what anyone was saying, but it all sounded merry enough.

Morlock found it easy to stay alert, though. There was an odd tension in the air, as if someone had spoken, paused, and soon would speak again.

There were rats scuttling around the corpse-house. Morlock kept circling around the corpse table, prepared to catch them if he could. But they were wary, and he couldn't even seem to find where their hole was. But as long as none of them got to the body, he supposed he didn't care.

Glancing up from his rat hunt, he saw the red worms.

They were coming through the patchy walls of the corpse-house – hundreds of them on every side except the wall with the door. Morlock watched without doing anything. Strigae must be pressed up all around the outside walls of the corpse-house; they far outnumbered him. His precautions would work or they wouldn't; if not, he needed to know now so that he could get out soon.

The worms were a grayish red, the color of a rather unhealthy human tongue. But they were long and thin, and each one terminated in a little tongueless mouth with needle-sharp teeth. They wove their way through cracks in the wall, and extended into the empty air beyond the wall . . . and were foiled. When they came to the air over the little channel of running water they began to twitch and shudder. They could go no further. One by one they withdrew; the water had defeated them.

Morlock saluted his departing enemies with a rude gesture, but he didn't imagine this was the end of his troubles. He continued with his rat patrol, kicking away any of the vermin that seemed to be trying to climb the sheer legs of the corpse table.

Eventually he heard a thumping on the ragged roof. It was what he had expected – Strigae could not cross running water, but they could use a bridge to cross above it. The wood of the roof would shield them from the effects of the purifying stream. Perhaps he should have pulled the roof off the corpse-house, as he had thought of doing. But the roof served as protection against arrows or spears or rocks – or any other kind of throwing weapon. Just because the Strigae could use magic didn't mean they had to and, once he was dead or unconscious, they could figure out a way to defeat the stream. It would be easy enough just to slap a board across it; crossing over so close to the running water might prove difficult but, with a corpse to chew on the other side, they would no doubt find a way to do it.

Morlock got up on the corpse table, crouching under the low roof, with one foot planted on either side of the dead man. He waited until something thumped gently on a loose patch of the roof, just over his head. He punched it solidly; the patch flew up and whatever was on it flew squawking away and thumped, less gently, on another part of the roof.

"Get off there!" he shouted. "If you don't get off the roof, I'll pull it down, and you with it. Then you will be in here. Within the sacred boundary of the stream. With *me*."

The thumping hastily retreated to the edge of the roof. There was the sound of whispering outside the corpse-house for a while, and then silence. When Morlock was fairly confident they were gone, he got down from the corpse table and resumed his rat patrol.

Morlock was lighting a new candle from the sputtering corpse of an old one when he felt someone looking at him. He glanced up and saw Zatchlas standing in the open doorway.

"Good evening," Morlock said, oddly relieved. "I would offer you some wine, but I didn't save any."

Zatchlas gave him an unreadable look, then said, "Well, I am not much of a drinker. It is a good evening for you, anyway. I saw a cloud of Strigae around the place and thought you were done for. But now they all seem to have gone."

"They will be back, I suppose."

"Almost certainly. But it is amazing you have lasted this long."

"Thanks."

"Nothing personal. Many of us are rooting for you, you know."

"Not enough to intervene and help me, I suppose?"

"Not directly," Zatchlas said, a little shamefacedly.

Morlock shrugged; he wasn't surprised.

"Besides, it would spoil the bets."

"You're betting on whether I make it through the night?" Morlock asked, intrigued.

"Some of us are," Zatchlas said. "So we could not interfere, even if we dared, you see? The bets would be off."

"Don't worry about it," Morlock said. It embarrassed him to see the bulky young man justifying himself.

"But . . . well, a few of us. We thought we might walk by here a few times, when the Strigae are not about. Just to see how you are doing."

"Thanks."

"It's all right. I'm sorry we cannot do more."

Morlock shrugged his crooked shoulders again. He hadn't expected anything, so he wasn't disappointed.

"It's just . . . I thought you should know." Zatchlas seemed to be having trouble coming to the point.

"What is it?"

"I think the Strigae left something behind them. It's propped up against that wall, and it seems to be moving. I didn't want to get too close to it . . ."

"Wise choice."

"But I thought you should know about it," Zatchlas concluded.

"Thanks." This sounded bad, Morlock reflected. If they had left some sort of device to topple the wall inward, he'd have to do something about it. The fallen wall might serve as a bridge for the Strigae to cross the stream – quite apart from what falling stones might do to his skull, if he was caught in the collapse. "I'll have a look at it," he decided.

Zatchlas stood away from the doorway to allow Morlock through. As Morlock stepped across the stream, Zatchlas drew himself up in alarm and glanced around, gesturing at Morlock to stop.

The gesture turned into a fist and hit Morlock in the face. The dark world grew a little darker for a while. When Morlock came to, he lay across the stream with his head almost under the corpse table. Looming large, like actors on a stage, were three rats eating another lying in the pool of wine beneath the overturned mug. Their sleeping comrade whined and snored but did not otherwise protest as his mates fed upon him.

A great weight encumbered Morlock. His ribs grated on each other and creaked. Whistling voices spoke words he didn't understand, then he heard Zatchlas say, "I *am* being careful."

The weight oppressing Morlock shifted, and shifted again. Morlock sluggishly realized Zatchlas was using his fallen body as a bridge to cross the stream. That meant Zatchlas was a Striga, or at the least an ally of the Strigae.

Zatchlas grunted and the weight on Morlock's body increased. Zatchlas now carried the dead body of Thelyphron – straight out of the blessed boundary of the stream, where the Strigae could feast on it in peace.

Morlock seized the fallen wine cup as the only available weapon, and surged to his feet, throwing Zatchlas a sprawl on the ground outside the corpse-house, the dead body of his father atop him. With surprising lightness, Zatchlas leapt to his feet and ran off, hauling the body with him toward the lights and laughter of the fair.

Morlock ran after him into the carnival night.

Zatchlas was burdened with the dead body, but Morlock had been knocked unconscious. Zatchlas almost reached the fairground before Morlock caught up with him. Several groups of people stood nearby, talking and laughing in apparent indifference to what was happening before them. Morlock likewise ignored them and punched the bulky young man savagely on the right side of his fat sweating neck. Zatchlas went down.

Morlock bent and seized the dead body with one hand, tossing it across his shoulder (Fortunately, the dear departed Thelyphron had been rather elderly, and had died after some wasting disease had left his frame frail and thin). Morlock turned to run back to the corpse-house, but Zatchlas managed to grasp him by an ankle, and this time it was Morlock who hit the earth with a corpse atop him.

He pushed the body away and kicked up with both feet as Zatchlas' silhouette, dark and featureless against the nearby fair lights, approached. Morlock's double kick made contact with something under Zatchlas' loose robe that issued a tiny scream; Zatchlas screamed, too, an instant later, in eerie harmony. Morlock leapt to his feet and smashed the wine-cup across Zatchlas' face. Amazingly, there was still some wine in it; Morlock saw the spray. Zatchlas screamed again, staggering back, clutching at his eyes.

His robe fell open and Morlock saw the man was naked. Mostly. Things were attached to his pale sweaty skin: dark things with glittering green eyes. They had toothy mouths, each of them issuing dozens of grayish tongues, like the red worms. Strigae. Dozens of Strigae hung by their tongues from Zatchlas' body.

Morlock felt rather than saw the approach of more townsmen. He looked up to see groups from the fair converging on him. They talked and laughed, yet he still could not understand them. Then he saw why. There were no heads on their shoulders. Each of their necks ended abruptly in a pair of dry soft protuberances vaguely like lips. These moved as air passed through the open neck, producing indistinct word-like murmurs that were not words. Their hands clenched and unclenched as they murmured and laughed and advanced on Morlock.

He scooped up dead Thelyphron's frail body and ran back to the corpse-house as fast as he could. Morlock threw the body through the doorway, where it sprawled across the corpse table, and leaped over the protecting stream.

The water level was low – no doubt much of it splashing out when he fell into it. The wine cup had proven a useful tool in need, so Morlock carefully set it down on the overturned empty barrel, next to the lit candle and the stubs of its dead predecessors. Then, from the full barrel, he dumped water into the stream until it ran full again.

He shouted out the open doorway: "Morlock, three; Strigae, zero. Try it again, you corpse-chewing bastards!"

He figured they would try again and that he stood a better chance of repelling it if they acted hastily and recklessly. He straightened Thelyphron's body on the corpse table. *If that jaunt didn't wake Thelyphron up*, he reflected, *nothing would.*

"I'd like a drink," he reflected aloud, and glanced ruefully at the wine cup.

Amazingly, miraculously, magically it was full. His impulses betrayed him; Morlock had the cup in his hands and was drinking before he'd decided to do so.

The wine was gone in an instant. Strong, not very good, with an oddly bitter metallic taste to it. That didn't matter. Morlock wasn't a connoisseur of wines; he was a drunk. He drank it all, and didn't waste a drop.

At least there is only one cup, he thought as he lowered it from his wet lips and set it down next to the candle. He studied it and saw the cup was full again. He reached for it, then stopped.

All right, there it was. Myrrhina had sent him a magical cup that would refill whenever it was set down. A generous thing to do; she probably hadn't realized he was a drunk. It did mean she knew a little magic, but he had already suspected as much. The night was already well advanced – perhaps the Strigae were discouraged and wouldn't attack any more . . .

He drank the cup dry again, then set it down and watched it re-fill.

Morlock was not yet drunk; unquestionably, he would be soon. Drunk Morlock very nearly had the upper hand, and there didn't seem to be anything to be done about that now.

He decided he would do a rat patrol, one circuit of the corpse table for every drink. That would slow down the process some, and perhaps he and Thelyphron would make it to sunrise relatively in-tact.

Morlock took a quick trip around the corpse table in record time; there didn't seem to be any rats trying to climb the table. Per-haps they were all asleep, or discouraged. Or drunk. Morlock chuckled a bit at that thought as he drank his third cup, wasting some of the wine. He supposed he could get used to the brackish metallic aftertaste.

Morlock's trip around the corpse table went a little slower this time. He found it odd there still were no rats; he remembered see-ing them earlier.

He peered under the table and found some there, the same rats he had seen after Zatchlas had struck him. The one who had been sleeping was now dead, great troughs of raw flesh opened up in his sides. Beside him lay his three comrades, asleep, their bloodstained mouths yawning open, their snores making their whiskers quiver. It was really almost touching, the three rats wearily resting beside their fallen comrade. It would have been, of course, if they hadn't eaten him alive, but still . . .

Morlock wondered why they were tired, so very tired – almost as tired as he was. As if they were really discouraged. Or drunk.

Or drugged.

Morlock swore violently and staggered to the doorway. He shoved a finger into the back corner of his mouth and leaned forward. Soon he was vomiting like a fountain, striving not to drip anything that would defile it into the protective stream. Striving successfully, too: he was an experienced vomiter.

With his belly emptied of the drugged wine, Morlock leaned wearily against the doorpost and wiped his mouth with his sleeve.

He had no idea what was in the drugged wine, but it had to be pretty potent: the cannibal rats must have passed out simply from eating their drugged comrade. He didn't think the drug itself would be fatal to him, as no doubt the Strigae looked forward to chewing his flesh in addition to Thelyphron's. But he had to come to grips with the fact that he might pass out soon. Indeed, he already felt it might be more than he could do to stand away from the doorpost.

They were watching him of course; they had watched him from the start. Perhaps Myrrhina was one of them; perhaps she wasn't. It suddenly occurred to him that Zatchlas had brought the wine. Perhaps she had not sent it at all. In any case, they had seen him drink it; they had seen him vomit. When he passed out they would see that, too, and come for Thelyphron. And for him.

Unless they *couldn't* see. He nodded, then regretted doing that – his head felt half-full of some warm dark fluid, and moving it made the fluid slosh about. He nearly passed out then, but pulled himself together.

Morlock pushed the doorpost away and stood as straight as he could. Unhurriedly, trying to make it look less labored than it was, he crossed to where the candle burned on the upended barrel.

He stared at it and tried to think clearly. He might not have much time, perhaps not more than a few seconds. The top of the upended barrel was full of melted wax and wick-stumps. If he failed to snuff the candle properly, if he just tipped it over, it might burn for hours, giving the Strigae ample opportunity to see him.

Morlock picked the candle up, turned around, and tossed it out the open doorway. Then his legs gave way and he collapsed by the upended barrel in the darkness.

Morlock first became aware he had closed his eyes from the sensation of faint light falling upon his lids. His eyes gaped open. *Morning? Am I intact? Is there anything of me left?*

It didn't seem to be morning. The light flickered, dim and bluish, unlike dawn or torches. Through the fitful light, he saw a cloud of red worms descending from the ceiling toward Thelyphron's corpse.

Morlock surged to his feet, screaming, "Get out! I'm still in here, corpse-chewers!" He leaped onto the corpse table and, although a wave of darkness passed before his eyes, managed to keep both his footing and his consciousness. He pounded on the ceiling and shouted wordlessly.

The red worms withdrew slowly. But nothing moved up on the roof. He heard faint whispers. They but waited. They knew he couldn't last much longer.

Morlock glanced desperately out the doorway, hoping to see some sign of approaching dawn. He didn't, but what he did see caught his full interest.

His vomit was burning.

Morlock carefully stepped down from the corpse table and walked to the door. He had not been mistaken. The candle he had thrown out had landed at the edge of the pool of vomit on the path outside, and now a flickering blue flame ran across the top of the greasy fluid.

Morlock knew what it was to concentrate the spirit of wine many times, to make a more intoxicating – and flammable – beverage. Perhaps that was what had been done to the wine from the magic cup. Or perhaps the drug in the wine was itself highly flammable. *If it is strong enough to make my vomit burn, how much will it burn without being diluted?*

And he had an unlimited supply of it.

Morlock staggered to the barrel to get a fresh candle and the magic wine cup. He staggered back to the doorway and stooped to light his candle from the flickering blue flame. He climbed back up on the corpse table and, holding the wine cup and candle in one hand, he punched a hole through the roof with his other.

Morlock stood upright, his head and arms passing through the hole in the roof to the open air. The light of the candle revealed the Strigae scattered about the patchy roof. They looked like owls, with great wing-like folds of gray hair on either side of their bodies. But rather than raptor claws, each had a single soft foot, like a snail. And no heads. Instead, two greenish eyes glowed near the top of each body and wide toothy mouths grimaced mid-torso, the multi-branched red worms of their tongues hissing like snakes. The Strigae retreated out of his reach, but no farther.

"Good night, ladies," cried Morlock, "good night, good night." He doused the roof and the nearer Strigae with cupfuls of drugged wine – then he touched it off with the candle.

Flame leapt into the cloudy sky. The Strigae screamed like screech owls and fled from the roof and from his sight.

The wet wood of the roof burned for an hour before caving in. By that time the edge of the sky was gray with dawn.

The world was full of dim gray light when Myrrhina appeared, running from the fairgrounds to the corpse-house, her lips and face as gray as the sky.

She saw Morlock standing by the door and paused.

"I'm all right," he said, answering her unasked question.

"And my Thelyphron?" she whispered.

He nodded toward the corpse-house door. Glancing in, she saw the corpse was intact and gasped. "But the roof is gone!" she said. "You must have—"

"It was a rough night," he said. "Over now. I'll take the crow-coin."

"I do not have it with me," she admitted shamefaced, looking oddly like her son.

"Oh?" he said. But it was the way he said it.

"I will pay you, though. Indeed I will, Sir Morlock! I'll swear any binding oath you ask."

"I'm just asking for the coin."

"I can't get it for you now. The funeral will be soon. The procession is on its way. Will you come to my house after the funeral?"

He looked at her for a few moments. Finally he nodded. "I will give you until then."

She flushed and bowed her head gratefully. "Thank you, Sir Morlock! And now, if you wouldn't mind, the procession will be here shortly, and I would like a few last moments alone with Thelyphron."

Morlock shrugged his crooked shoulders and nodded indifferently. He'd pulled the mirror-gates at dawn, and the stream was settling into a muddy puddle. He helped the fastidious Myrrhina across the threshold and turned away to give her privacy. He wandered off for a few steps and kept his back toward the corpse-house. Presently he heard her come out.

He turned in time to see her smiling at him with her red mouth. Then she turned away and hurried toward the fairground, where the funeral procession was already forming up.

He stared after her thoughtfully. A few moments with Thelyphron had certainly put the roses back into her lips. Her cheeks had seemed fuller, too.

A dark suspicion stabbed him through the heart. He rushed into the corpse-house.

Thelyphron's nose had been eaten away, along with large stretches of his cheeks and chin. The red cavities of gnawed flesh glared at Morlock in stark contrast with the waxy white flesh around them.

Myrrhina, Morlock realized, *but why? Why go through this rigmarole if she was a Striga herself? Or had it been a Striga disguised as Myrrhina?*

It didn't matter. They had won. He thought he could hear the funeral procession approaching. If they caught him here they would mutilate him, as Thelyphron had been mutilated. And if he ran, Myrrhina would never pay him the crow-coin, and it would all be for nothing.

He slumped down in despair by the overturned barrel, where the last of his candles was guttering in a pool of its own white wax.

Morlock waited on the steps of Myrrhina's house at noon when she and Zatchlas returned from Thelyphron's funeral. Zatchlas drew up short when he saw him, but Myrrhina did not seem surprised.

"Sir Morlock, good day," she caroled. "I suppose you have come for your coin."

"Yes."

"Zatchlas, perhaps you have something to do around town? Sir Morlock and I have a few things to discuss."

Zatchlas turned on his heel and walked away.

"Poor boy," said Myrrhina warmly, reaching into a pocket for her house key. Morlock, glancing down, saw her pocket held a number of interesting things, including Thelyphron's nose. "You set him back badly with the Sisterhood last night."

"You are both Strigae," Morlock said flatly.

"Well," Myrrhina said, as she unlocked the door and led the way in, "I am, and he aspires to be. We are mostly Strigae in this town. We fly at night and walk during the day, you see."

"I don't," Morlock said, following her. "If you are a Striga, why didn't you just bite Thelyphron's nose off yesterday and have done with it?"

"Oh! That would be against the rules. Family of the dead are not allowed until at least a night has passed after the death."

"Hm."

"Oh, it may seem cruel," Myrrhina continued, leading Morlock into an inner room with a strongbox. "But, otherwise, as soon as a family member died, his own family would chew him down to the bone and no one else would ever get a mouthful. So this is really fairer. Don't you see?"

"No," Morlock admitted. "Yesterday you seemed genuinely concerned about Thelyphron."

"I was. I am. We meant a great deal to each other. But he's dead. And you cannot imagine how useful a dead man's nose is in certain kinds of binding magic. Or how rare it is around here. I thought I would risk biting it off, since you gave me the opportunity. It was a bit of a wrench, of course. I would have been the first widow in fifty years to bury her husband intact. What a mark of status that is in the Sisterhood! Although, as far as anyone else in town knows, that is exactly what happened." She put a brown hand over her red mouth to hide a slightly hysterical laugh. When she had calmed herself, she lowered the hand and said, "Morlock, may I ask you a question?"

"You have not paid me my coin yet."

She opened the strongbox with her door key, reached inside and drew out the crow-coin. She flipped it over to Morlock who snapped it out of the air and tucked it into his own pocket.

"Your question?"

"*How* did you do it? I sat through the entire funeral, staring at Thelyphron's nose on his face and fingering it in my pocket. No one else realized, I think. Of course, they knew *they* had not mutilated him. If I hadn't bitten his nose off personally, I would have been sure Thelyphron's corpse was intact. How did you do it?"

"Wax."

"Wax?"

"Candle wax. I happened to notice the wax of the candles was exactly the same color as Thelyphron's skin. I had a good deal of it from all the candles I burned. So I modeled patches for Thelyphron's face out of the melted candle wax."

"It is a good thing we buried him before the sun got warm, then. Still, the likeness was superb, and you could not have had much time. You really are a gifted maker of things, Morlock."

"Thanks."

"You do not like me much, do you?"

"Not today. Yesterday you were all right, I guess."

"Well, I am still most grateful. I could do a good deal for you, besides just giving you that coin."

Morlock shrugged his crooked shoulders.

"Of course, the Crow King will give you a wish," she said earnestly. "But only one, and he will do his best to cheat you. I would never cheat you, Morlock."

"You want me to watch your corpse after your death, is that it?"

She laughed harshly. "I am afraid it wouldn't do much good." She pulled her nose off and showed it to Morlock. "When I was a teenager, my best friend died. I could not bear the thought of her being mutilated, so I agreed to sit the vigil. They got more of me than my nose . . . But I've shocked you," the noseless woman said gently.

Morlock shrugged impatiently. "I see that you are good at seeming. It goes with the life you lead. As for me, I am what I am."

"Goodbye, then, Morlock."

Morlock turned away and left the house. He took the shortest road out of the town. When he had come to open country, he took the coin out of his pocket.

The crow-like bird with the crown on its head still adorned the golden coin. Its eye looked expectantly at Morlock.

Glancing around, he saw the fields about him were black with crows. Hundreds of crows, thousands.

Morlock took the coin in both hands and said a word known to those-who-know. He cracked the coin like an egg and out of it flew a full-sized (in fact, rather large) black crow.

The golden shell faded until it resembled the fingernails of a dead man. Morlock dropped it and ground it into the dust.

Looking up he saw the great black bird he had released standing in the field before him. It wore no crown, yet there was no mistaking its regal quality. The other crows stood around their king in ragged concentric circles: murder upon murder of crows in attendance to their newly released king.

Morlock met the king's black inquisitive eye and said, "Still here? I'd think you would want to stretch your wings."

The Crow King cawed a question.

"No, I don't want anything," Morlock said. "A crow did me a favor once; now he's dead. This is my repayment."

The Crow King cawed again, more imperiously.

"That's up to you," said Morlock dismissively.

The great crow looked at him for a few moments, then hopped up into the air and flew off. The air was full of crow wings for a while, and then they were all gone, the murders flying in different directions, dark clouds disappearing in distant skies.

Morlock walked off into the empty lands. He thought alone, but many eyes – Striga-green and crow-black – watched him as he went his way.

To love someone enough to kill for them is one thing. To do it for hundreds of years and still claim some shred of humanity is quite another. To display that shred is most impressive of all. Then to go even further, to grant consideration when none is merited and to offer salvation when none is expected – these are things unfathomable, things unbelievable. What better things are there to write of in tales of heroic endeavor?

Michael Ehart is just a guy who writes speculative fiction. He writes because his head is full of stories demanding to be told. The Servant of the Manthycore is one of his favorite characters to write. Because her life is so blighted and dreadful, adding a single ingredient (in this case a tiny bit of compassion with a dash of indignation) makes it stand out in stark relief and allows Michael to examine the change from any interesting angle he chooses. Read more of Ninshi and Miri's adventures in the recently released The Servant of the Manthycore *(published by DEP and available through your favorite bookseller) and visit Michael's blog at http://mehart.blogspot.com/ to find out what he's up to.*

To Destroy All Flesh

A Tale of The Servant of the Manthycore

by Michael Ehart

The screams seemed to come from so very far away, though Miri knew they were all around her and some of them must be hers. She could see very little. What was not obscured by the dust that swirled around the fight was hidden by the bulk of her dying horse which lay atop her.

Her arms were free, but the pain in her legs made her weak, and every time the horse gave a feeble kick or twitch things would go speckled black for a moment. In between waves of dizziness Miri caught glimpses of her mother, whirling and leaping as she fought. The stub of a broken arrow jutted from her mother's side.

Miri tried to reach her dagger, but her belt had twisted around when her horse fell and it was underneath her hip. Here in the mountain passes they had dressed in heavy furs, and their bulk and the weight of the horse made it impossible for her to get her hand under her body.

She blinked away dust and looked up to see the hulking form of a man standing over her, grinning with blackened and broken teeth. Half of a broken shield hung from his left arm. His right held a spear, poised to thrust at her chest. Miri coughed out a cry, and twisted to the side. The spear thumped flat against her chest, the bandit's severed hand still grasping its shaft. The bandit was thrown to the side by her mother's shoulder to his middle and he fell. The fountain of blood from the stump of his wrist painted a crimson arc against the gray afternoon sky. Some of it pattered into Miri's face, and she blinked and spat, gagging at the coppery taste. It burned salty in her eyes.

Much of the screaming had stopped. Blinded by pain, dust and bandit's blood, Miri had trouble at first making out what was around her. The bandit who had tried to stab her lay facing her, dead, pale eyes open and still. Two arrows had buried themselves in the side of her horse; she had seen that before it fell on her. Somewhere behind her a camel bellowed, whether in rage or pain she couldn't tell.

Someone coughed behind her, deep and rasping. It ended in choking and a retch. The cougher spat, and Miri started at the callused hand that stretched into her view. She watched grasping fingers find the dead horse's lead rope, clench tight upon it and haul their owner alongside her. It was her mother.

"Ninshi," Miri whispered in horror. Her mother's face was battered and covered with blood, and her breath was ragged and unsteady.

"Child," she croaked. Her teeth were red-stained, and her words sprayed blood in a fine mist from her mouth. "Are you—" Ninshi doubled in a bubbling series of hacks that left her gasping and pale beneath the dirt and gore.

"Ninshi, I cannot get from under my horse. I think there is something wrong with my legs."

Ninshi nodded. "I will need your help. If I do not draw this arrow, I will soon die. If we can do that, then we will see what we must do to free you." She pulled herself closer, the pain etching her scarred face. "Remember, swift and hard, or it will tear."

The arrow thrust from just beneath her mother's left arm, the jagged shaft less than a hand's width long. It was enough to grip, but it was slippery. Miri took a deep breath then pulled hard. Ninshi screamed, and Miri's hand slipped from the blood-slicked shaft.

Miri choked on her fear. Her mother lie unmoving, the broken arrow still in place, pointing in accusation. Miri sobbed then angrily dashed the tears from her eyes. She twisted, ignoring the jolt of pain from her legs, and wiped her hands on the shirt of the dead bandit on her other side. She ripped a piece of the shirt free, and twisted back. She used the bit of cloth to wipe the arrow then wrapped it around the shaft. She took a deep breath, and pulled hard and fast. The arrow came free, its square bronze head covered in the same deep red as the ebb of blood that followed from the wound. Miri threw the arrow over the side of her dead horse then collapsed weeping against the still-warm hair of its back.

"Good . . ." Ninshi rasped beside her, then coughed and spat. "Good. I will rest then we will see about using that spear to pry you free."

Miri smeared her tears away with the back of her hand. "What about the bandits? Will they come back?"

"I doubt it. Those that live fled with most of our goods. There is nothing more here for them."

"I have tended her legs, and she will walk again. They were not broken, merely very badly bruised. But she may not travel for a few days." The hugely obese priest frowned at Ninshi through his matted hair and beard. "Your wounds seem to have largely healed themselves."

"Yes."

There was a long pause as the priest Dingir waited for an explanation he would never get. Ninshi was very old, kept alive for many lifetimes of men by the broken-tooth talisman which hung on the leather strap about her neck. The talisman bestowed rapid healing from anything that did not outright kill her and it protected her from any sorcery save its own. The symbol of her bondage to the great evil beast she served, it was also the means by which she summoned it to its ghastly feasts of its favored meat – the flesh of men. For over forty mortal lifetimes she had sought to be free of the Manthycore and the long centuries of murder, until she had given up hope. Then, just a few summers before, she had learned of seven great herbs, used to command the beasts after the deluge. In exchange for finding the ancient rubies known as the Tears of Ishtar, the goddess of drunkards had told her of the location of the herbs. One of the herbs was to be found here, in the far north.

The priest cleared his throat, and tried again. "How is it you come to this place?"

"We are seeking an herb, one of the *Shappattu* given as a gift to Utnapishtim, whom some know as Noach. It is said to grow only here."

The priest nodded. "This is known to us. We can provide this to you. But none of our gifts are without price. What do you bring to us in exchange?"

Ninshi shook her head. "All that we had was stolen by the bandits who gave us these wounds, save for the camel I brought her on. I have gold, but I am told that has little value here at the top of the world."

"The mountains are a perilous place for a woman to travel, especially with this child to protect. I am surprised they let you live." The priest pondered for a moment. "I will take your camel, though they do not thrive here, as it is all that you can offer in payment for the care we have given to the girl. But you must provide a service for anything more. You are far from comely and the girl is of an age forbidden to those of our brotherhood, so we must find other than the obvious ways for you to serve. Have you any skills?"

Ninshi sighed. "I have only one real skill, that of slaying men. We traveled with four others, fierce warriors from the north but only we survived and those who ambushed us paid dearly."

The priest peered at her through one piggish eye, shaded by a massive, shaggy brow. "We have had trouble of late with these bandits. I would disbelieve that a woman of your stature would be able to stand against them, but here you are, and really, it is unimportant. They are troublesome though, stealing from us the occasional shipment of wine to which we owe our survival. Know that this is the very valley in which grapes were first made into wine, and still the wine which our brotherhood makes is the finest in the world. Yearly we send a tribute of our wine to the king of Ikizepe, the great Ashkish, who provides us with protection against the other of the fifty Cities of the North."

"Your news is old," said Ninshi. "Ashkish is dead, these four years or more. The king is now Jermaish."

The giant priest shrugged. "No matter. Kings live their time, then are gone. Our brotherhood endures, having been here since the Deluge. Even cities pass. Izizepe lies at the mouth of the mountain pass, and so is nearest, but I suspect someday it too will fall, and we will pay tribute to yet another." He turned to the door of the turf-walled hut where they had carried Miri to be examined.

The light from the smoke-hole in the center lit his matted hair into a dark-brown halo. "Your camel will be payment enough, I suppose, for a ten-day's guesting, but no more. If you are able to recover your goods from the bandits, we will tell you of the herb you seek. Or, if you find that your goods are gone or consumed, it would not displease me to learn of the bandits' elimination."

"Where is their camp?" Ninshi asked.

"That I will tell you freely, as you would learn it anyway simply by asking. They live in the next valley up the mountain, where they have made a fortress of the Great Vessel. A formidable assault, but if you are so very fierce, as you say, then a task of little account, I trust." He pushed out through the leather door flap and was gone.

Miri watched her mother in the gloom of the hut. "What is the Great Vessel?" she asked.

Ninshi shook her head. "I do not know. I will have to find out, I suppose, so I will be traveling to the next valley up the mountain. I will try stealth, if I can, to recover our goods. I do not care for this brotherhood of priests, so take care while I am gone. Sleep as I have shown you with—"

"With my knife at hand," Miri smiled. "Yes, Ninshi. I will trust no one except you." Miri thought for a moment. "Will you kill them then, if you cannot steal back what was stolen?"

Ninshi was quiet for a moment. "Bandits sometimes are a different thing from what you are used to, traveling as we do on the great caravan roads. In a place like this, they are often simply the men of a poor village, forced to banditry not by wickedness or greed, but by starvation. This valley is fertile, from years of cultivation and by nature of the steaming water which flows from its mountainsides. I do not imagine the next valley up will be prosperous at all. The men who ambushed us were ill-fed and no great warriors. Had they known their business, they would have stayed in the rocks above and filled us with arrows. Perhaps they had no more to shoot."

"But they still tried to kill us."

"Yes, and they stole our goods, though at great cost. A poor village cannot afford the death of six men. I fear they may lose still more before we are done. Still, it does not please me to kill poor men who are driven by the starvation of their children, even after all the centuries of murder I have done."

Miri reached across the cot in which she rested and patted her mother's arm. "You will do what is needed, and what is wise."

Ninshi shook her head. "I suspect I am not wise," she said. "Just very old."

Ninshi was gone for four days. Miri had not quite gotten to the point of worry. She was kept busy by the wonders of the Valley of Vines. As Ninshi had said, it was warmed by the steaming water that flowed from the side of the mountain. The lush green valley floor was an amazing contrast to the stark gray and white of the surrounding mountains. An enormous variety of plants grew there. The fat young priest who brought her meals and helped her to walk claimed the plants were descendants of all the seeds of the world that were gathered by Noach in preparation for the Deluge.

Miri did not know many priests, but she was beginning to suspect they were all fond of gossip. This one certainly was. He spent each day's mandatory walk regaling her with all the village infidelities. They had just finished her fourth such walk through the small turf-hut village which served the greater temple and winery in the center of the valley when Miri recognized her mother's figure descending the path which wound down the side of the mountain. She interrupted the priest in the middle of his latest story to point her out.

He helped her back to the leaning board in front of the hut. She could walk by herself, now, though it was painful still. She stretched her legs out in front of her, and brushed away the tiny fragrant leaves of the low-growing bushes that lined the path through the village. Her soft boots and her linen leggings were stained green by them.

Seeing he was ignored, the young priest took his leave, and waddled back to the temple.

"Young admirer?" Ninshi asked when she drew near.

Miri laughed. "I have only seen thirteen summers, and already I am much less ignorant than that smug little man will be if he lives to be eighty. His whole world is this valley, wine, and village gossip." She wrinkled her nose. "I do not care for his hair and beard. These priests do not believe in grooming of any sort."

Ninshi snorted. "When will you be able to travel?"

"I feel much better, thank you for not asking. I can walk now, though not far. The young priest tells me I will be fit enough for farm work in a handful of days. You are not leading our other camel."

"By now our bandits should have just finished eating her. It is most likely the first meat they have had for many days. Their village is little more than an encampment in front of a large, strange building that grows out of the ice-covered side of the mountain. They fled into it when I approached, leaving our camel roasting over a fire. Their tents are very ragged, and if they posses any treasure it is kept inside their refuge."

"And our goods?"

"The pepper I found trampled along the trail. I suspect they did not know the bag was holed. The rugs they may have taken with them into the building. It must be very cold in there, as it barely protrudes from the hard ice and seems to go back a ways into it."

"Could you burn them out?"

Ninshi shook her head. "The wood is quite ancient, hard as stone and frozen through with old ice. It would take a mountain of timber to ignite it. There are no trees in that valley, only the same gorse I see rubbed into your leggings and a sad little garden that cannot yield much. As long as they are inside with the door barred they are safe. We could starve them out, but I do not know how long that would take and if we are not ourselves going to spend the winter here, we need to be gone before the first snow."

"What shall we do then?"

"I think we will wait a day or so until you are better able to travel, then make our way back to the valley above. It may be we can set our own ambush or catch them out in some fashion. They are two fewer again, as they had lookouts posted at the mouth of the valley. Those I took unaware. There cannot be very many of them left. I would guess less than a dozen women, a few children and no more than four or five remaining men."

The lookouts had not been replaced. Miri and Ninshi made cold camp where the men should have been. From the small hill they could see down into the valley. It was trough-shaped and narrow. Early snow coated its hillsides. Thin lines of smoke rose into the cold air from the far end, where Miri could make out the faded colors of tents, pitched in the shelter of a large black object which protruded from the icy wall of the mountain. It was squared-off, blocky, and for it to be so clear from so far it had to be enormous.

The priests had given them travel food, but begrudgingly. It may have been simply a desire to see them go. Miri had told the young priest a little about her mother, and it may be that the tales had awakened a memory in one of them of the caravan song about the Betrayer:

What has been destroyed belongs now to no one.
No one is able to take it away.
What will be destroyed belongs to the Servant
Who comes for the mother's fruit and takes it away.
She is a destroyer, a slayer of men.
Men who would do ill, men who have done ill,
But justice does not broaden her breast
Neither does vengeance, though claim it she may.
Love is the slayer, love the betrayer
Love the blood drinker, slayer of men.
Freedom she seeks, from the binder of youth,
Freedom she seeks, so then binds men in death.

"Have they seen us, even without a fire?" asked Miri.

"They have seen us."

When it was fully dark, they moved to the large rocks at the top of the hill. Miri's legs were still not as strong as they might be. Ninshi helped her up, then handed Miri her bow. Ninshi scrambled up the neighboring boulder and they both stretched out flat, facing the lookout camp where they had left their packs rolled up in blankets.

Miri regretted leaving those blankets almost immediately. The constant mountain wind had swept the boulders on which they perched clean of snow, but the stone seemed even colder. She cupped her hands over her mouth and breathed through her fingers, as her mother had shown her. She would have nimble hands, and it was nice they at least were warm, but the rest of her seemed like it was nearly frozen. The wind cut through even the heavy mountain furs. Worse yet, the cold made her injured legs ache.

She did not look over at her mother. She knew even if she could see her, Ninshi would be perfectly still, as if grown to the rock. Miri concentrated on not shivering, and on not letting her teeth chatter. She hated the cold. She was born and spent her first eight summers in the Twin Kingdoms, where the great river ran north past the pyramids of the ancient kings.

After an eternity of frozen misery, the moon rose from behind the far side of the hill and cast its pale light across the snow. It revealed the lookout camp and their bundled packs lying undisturbed below them. "A fire might make it a little easier to see them when they come to kill us in our sleep, but might also make them suspect a trap. That they are poor at the craft of banditry does not make them stupid," Ninshi had explained. "And if it comes to close fighting, if we have been staring at a fire, we will be at a disadvantage."

Though Miri hated the cold, she found herself dazzled by the moonlight as it sparkled its way over the snow. The wind blew small gusts of snow like tiny diamond whirlwinds, dashed them against a rock or higher mound then swept up another. The wind, the snow and the moonlight danced together in endless variation as Miri watched, cold, miserable and fascinated.

Dark figures moved to the right, from below, and formed in the darkness into the shapes of men, bent and careful as they crept to the camp. Miri sensed rather than saw her mother shift her bow. There were four silent stalkers. They spread two to a side around the camp. Miri carefully rose and drew back her bow, the arrow already nocked. The two nearest were hers, and left to right was the rule. Years of practice had made her quite capable with the bow. Having a teacher who had centuries to perfect her skill helped.

Miri heard her mothers bow sing, and she too let fly. The bowstring popped against her fur covered sleeve. A man cried out, but Miri ignored him. She plucked another arrow from under her knee, drew and fired. Her first target still stood, so she put a second arrow into him and he fell.

Both of Ninshi's targets were down. One of them, the farthest away, struggled up for a moment then fell back. Miri could hear him sobbing and coughing. Sometimes he managed to push himself up and crawl, only to collapse again in a spasm of coughing.

"Lungs," whispered Ninshi. "Probably both."

The night was no longer beautiful, just cold. The moon had nearly set before the man grew silent and still, his sobs silenced by the cold and loss of blood.

Miri felt the sting of her tears as they froze on her cheeks. Ninshi always cried when she fought. Miri thought she knew why. All of the songs about heroes and glory were only to hide the ugliness of killing. Traveling with Nin-Sinnus, the Lady of the Song, had made Miri witness to the truth behind the caravan song.

She must have slept, because the morning light surprised her. They had stayed on the rocks in case a few of the bandits held back or came looking for their companions. Finally they had, but not just a few. Perhaps thirty people, women and children, stood in an arc a hundred paces below the hilltop. In front of them were two bound men, kneeling.

Ninshi stood on the rock and Miri followed suit, fighting the cramps in her legs. Ninshi pulled her heavy-tipped sword from its wolf-hide scabbard and held it at an angle across her body, point down. The morning snow dazzle reflected brightly from the bronze of its blade. Miri lowered her bow and pulled the knife from her belt.

"Mistress," called a woman from below. "We do not know how you wish to be addressed."

"I do not wish to be addressed," answered Ninshi. "And I am mistress of no one." She sighed. "Call me whatever you wish."

"We have brought you the last two of our men, who took from you that which you have slain for. I told them who you must be, but they were fools, as men are, and thought they could make war against a goddess."

Ninshi shook her head. "I am no goddess. Come closer, you."

The woman walked slowly up the hill. Her hands were empty, and she wore layers of clothing. Her topmost coat contrasted brightly with the worn and weathered layers that peeked out below. It was heavy, made of a rug. As she drew close there was visible a talisman about her neck, made of carved bone in the shape of a large, broken tooth. There was only one city where that could come from.

Ninshi grunted in annoyance. "How fares Jermaish?"

The woman knelt in the snow in front of the rock. "Your son the Great King is well, and his city prospers."

"My son?" Ninshi choked.

"Yes, Mistr—my lady. Jermaish, Strangler of Lions, Son of Goddess and King, ruler of Ikizepe, whom no man can stand against. He has built a temple to you, and once a year there is a festival held to celebrate Jermaish's rescue of you, his mother, from the clutches of the usurper Ashkish."

Miri had seen her mother weep and once had even seen her laugh, but usually there was nothing to be read from her scarred and weathered visage. Now Miri was stunned to see Ninshi's face grow slowly darker, until it was a deep, purplish red, the color of pomegranate juice. It must have terrified the woman before her, because she fell on her face and the women and children behind her dropped to their knees, moaning and quietly sobbing.

"Get up, get up!" Miri cried, waving her hands. Ninshi's head snapped around, the force of her glare nearly knocking Miri from her perch. She stumbled and slipped, half-jumping, half-sliding down the side of the rock. Miri hit the ground hard and her right leg collapsed under her. She gasped in pain, but struggled forward to grasp the sleeve of the woman who lay face down in the snow and tug her to her feet.

"You must not kneel to her. Get up, get up." Enslaved as Ninshi was to the horrible beast, she still refused to kneel to it. She would not abide another kneeling to her.

"Miri." Her mother's voice was flat, even harsher than usual. "Gather these . . . people. Leave the men bound, but free their legs. They will follow us to their village. We will see what is left of our goods. If it is enough to purchase the knowledge we need, then we will spare them."

Ninshi stalked down the hill, her heavy greased braid swinging like the tail of a wet cat, not looking at anyone. Miri, with the help of the woman who had spoken to them, was able to start the people down the hill only a few hundred steps behind the small angry form of her mother.

Miri had heard of Jermaish. Her mother had described him as a young fool whom she had met on the road. He had convinced her his uncle was the greatest warrior of the age. Miri wasn't sure how, but in the end the uncle was dead, Jermaish was king of his small city, and in gratitude he had told Ninshi of the wise man who had started them on their quest for the ancient herbs. She had said nothing of his being her son, and Miri was pretty sure that Ninshi would have mentioned that, if true. She was used to the legends and songs being wrong about her mother, but it was astounding that a story could have changed so much in living memory. She suspected that if Ninshi and Jermaish ever met again, it would not be a peaceful meeting.

The village was a disappointment. The clarified butter, or *ghee*, pepper and carpets they had carried to exchange for the knowledge of the ancient herb known by the priests of the Valley of the Vine were no more. The pepper had been lost, and the near-starving bandits and their families had consumed the *ghee* with greedy relish. When it was gone, they had even cut the leather bags it was carried in into strips and chewed them to glean the last bit of precious fat they could.

Inside the Great Vessel there were several sacks of old grain and a few stunted and scrawny goats. It too was a disappointment. Ninshi made a torch of tent cloth and camel grease, and she and Miri searched every corner they could, which wasn't much. Sometime in the distant past the ice had crushed the structure and filled it to less than forty steps from the front. It was huge, solid and ancient, but shallow.

Ninshi and Miri came from the dark and deeply musty interior into the dim light of day, to find their prisoners waiting tensely. In the full day, with them all assembled, it was clear that every one of the trade rugs had been cut up and made into crude coats.

"There is nothing to trade to the Brotherhood, is there?" Miri said.

"No," grunted Ninshi. Her color was nearer normal.

"Will you kill them, then?"

Ninshi was still for several heartbeats. Then her head rose, and she whipped the still burning torch into a drift of snow. "Not today. Have them gather what they can carry. Make certain they bring what food they have. We are returning to the Valley of Vines."

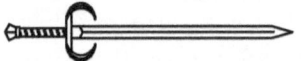

"I have been informed of who you are. The evil you carry is not welcome here." Dingir the head priest stood in the middle of the road. Behind him waited forty of his order, none as fat as he, but all of great size, and all armed with shovels, pruning hooks or hoes.

"I have come to trade," replied Ninshi. "You have knowledge of the herb I seek."

"I see no goods, unless that rabble behind you are slaves. They are ill-fed, though, so will not have much value."

"They are all that remains of the bandits who troubled you. They will trouble you no more. I will take them to Ikizepe. I have done what I have said I would do. Now you must do the same."

The giant old priest rocked back and forth, pondering for a moment. Then he nodded. "It is a true exchange, I think. I did say eliminate, did I not? Very well." He bent over and grasped a handful of leaves from the low bushes that lined the path through the valley.

"This is your herb," he said. "Now go."

Ninshi was very still. Miri held her breath, and even the children of the former bandits seemed to know to be silent. Slowly Ninshi's hand crept up to the talisman on the thong about her neck. It rested there a moment then she lowered it.

"Speak you the truth? Is this the *Shappatu*?" Her normally harsh voice was low, nearly a whisper.

The old priest nodded, his wild matted mane bobbing up and down. "It is the *Iten Shappatu Enkash*, the third great herb of the deluge. It has mild healing powers, and it is said when combined with the other six *Shappatu,* none of which are known to us, could do great things, though just what exactly those things were are long ago lost."

"A roadside weed." Ninshi gritted.

"A roadside weed, unless one has the knowledge to discern. Take what you want, and go. Never return."

Ninshi raised her hand, and her prisoners shambled past, each woman or child carrying a large bag, the two men bent double under bags of grain. The Brotherhood cleared a path for them to pass.

They walked in silence until they were atop the last hill and the pass to Ikizepe lay before them.

"We will camp here. In three days we will be in Ikizepe." Miri related Ninshi's instructions to the woman who had first spoken to her.

Miri walked with the woman as she gave orders and arranged the camp. "What is your name?" Miri asked.

"Aina. I was a brothel slave in Ikizepe. Running off with a bandit seemed . . . romantic."

Miri nodded. "I too was a slave, before Ninshi found me, though too young for the brothels. I suspect I would have ended up there. Even starving freedom is better, I suppose."

Aina helped a younger woman with a baby settle her strip of rug against a low boulder to make a makeshift shelter. The tents had been too heavy to carry without pack animals. “Yes,” she agreed. “Though I suppose returning to slavery is better than being fed to a beast.”

Miri shook her head. “She will not sell you. When we get to Ikizepe you will be free.”

“Free?” Aina exclaimed. “But we tried to kill her. We destroyed her goods. Is it because some of us are of her cult?”

“I think it would be best if you made no mention of any cult. No, it is that she gathers these herbs to compel the great beast she serves to end her slavery; I think after perhaps forty lifetimes in bondage she will not have another serve her or any other but themselves.”

Miri looked across the road to where her mother stood, absently sniffing a handful of the *Iten Shappatu Enkash* as she stared into the slowly dimming sky.

“Yes,” Miri said, softly. “Perhaps soon you will be free.”

Does the pursuit of a thing allow one to engage in its opposite to obtain it? Is it acceptable to be unjust in attempts to establish justice? 'Tis a fine line between pursuing ideals universal and personal; between the knowing and the doing of what is right and best for all – or for one. There are those who believe the ends do justify the means, regardless of damages, losses or compromised ethics. Others deem a momentary lapse in morals under the stress of do-or-die situations defensible. Yet some don't allow for even that. This tale grapples with such demons, inner and otherwise. One demon is Rage, and while Rage can get one out of a jam, it will consume a part of one's soul in the process . . .

Thomas MacKay uses the process of story crafting to explore the nature of compassion, conflict, growth and the consequences of one's actions – basically, what it means to be human. Thomas uses his protagonist to personify the continual struggle to remain human and in pursuit of what is right and good while living in a world desensitized to evil. The following tale became the prologue to Shieldbreaker *– his novel-length examination of the risk of allowing our own anger and frustration at injustice to tempt us into perpetrating even further injustice. February 11th, 2008, Thomas began serializing the novel with the first of a projected 20 installments online at http://www.myspace.com/tmmackay.*

Guardian of Rage

A Tale of Jack Spryte

by Thomas M. MacKay

Jack's hand slipped on the slime-covered wall for the thousandth time. He wondered why he always seemed to wind up ankle deep in the muck beneath the streets of Dalarda's capitol city, chased by an outlawed demon cult, and carrying what he suspected was the key to their demon-lord's summoning in a box whose carven runes had writhed strangely in the flickering lamplight while the glow-beetles had lasted. Alright, this situation was rather unique, but Jack found himself in strange circumstances far too often for coincidence. *My ancestors must enjoy toying with me,* he thought disgustedly.

A tired whimper at his side broke Jack's self-pity. The small hand in his was limp and cold. Jack squatted on his heels, ignoring the chill of fresh sewage seeping through the seat of his pants.

"Just a little longer, sweetheart," he whispered as he gathered her slight form to him. Weary arms went around his neck as the little girl leaned against him. Jack peered around for someplace to rest, doubting she believed him any longer. He picked her up and set her down upon a pile of rubble that seemed somewhat drier than the rest of the tunnel floor. "We can rest here a bit," he said quietly. She nodded solemnly. He guessed her age at six or seven, but she'd refused to speak since her mother died. Jack could tell she couldn't go much farther; soon he'd have to carry her. And that was dangerous, as they had discovered the first time the cultists found them.

Jack had barely been quick enough to thrust her to the side and block the attack. The cultists had learned, though, that two of them were not enough. The second time there had been more, and Jack had fled. The third time they had been found, it was by nothing human. An obscene, tentacled horror from mankind's nightmares had unfurled its glistening, ropy lengths at Jack and the girl. It had been driven off by a lucky bolt from Jack's *qaal*, though the device's crystal had cracked and he'd discarded it. That creature scared Jack in a way the cultists couldn't, and he fervently hoped it would not venture this near the surface world.

Jack forced himself to think. Daylight came in a couple of hours, and they needed to be somewhere safer by then. Clan Bevyar would be looking for Jack with all their considerable resources, but they'd have to be circumspect no matter how much they wanted the demon box. They wouldn't want the other Great Clans to find out what they were seeking. Even the outclans and demi-humans would turn on the Bevyar for consorting with demons. Jack's skin crawled at the feel of the box – greasy dark wood the size of a large book – held against his back by a sling contrived from strips of cloth torn from Jack's tunic. He didn't dare leave it behind; some instinct told him it would enable the use of powers Jack couldn't counter.

Jack's trousers squished as he sat gingerly down and the girl leaned against his shoulder. He had a room at an inn, but the Bevyar were probably already watching all of the inns. He had the curved dagger and short sword of a blooded warrior, and he was a second-level adept in the Teinne Doigh, that form of unarmed fighting that teaches the control and use of the *sean-aoidh*, the life energy wizards called mana and used for their spells. He also had contacts among the Paz'yan, the desert nomads to the east. If they could reach the sands, they would be safe. But they had to get out of these damned sewers.

That was the problem, of course. Weak golden moonlight filtered through grates in the street above where waste would be dumped, but there were no ladders up to the grates. That bit of moonlight faintly illuminated the sewer tunnel, but second moonset was approaching and the light was beginning to weaken. Jack had been hoping the larger tunnels would lead eventually to the river, but he wasn't exactly sure what direction they were headed any more. The girl was shivering as inactivity allowed the cold to gnaw at them, so Jack forced himself to his feet and reached down for her hand.

A faint splash came from one of the side tunnels ahead as Jack pulled the girl reluctantly to her feet, and they both froze. The girl looked at Jack in a wide-eyed combination of fear and trust. He made a quick decision and silently urged the girl forward as he pulled his sword. Jack kept himself between the girl and the side tunnel as they moved as quietly as possible through the sludge toward that black opening. They heard no other sounds, but some sense was lifting the hair on Jack's neck in a warning he could not ignore.

Jack looked around the corner, curved sword at the ready. A hundred feet down, there was a faint spot of light from a grate to the street above. Jack peered through the darkness, willing himself to see through sheer determination. He focused on that spot of light, could see movement in the mud below it. Jack started uneasily across the tunnel opening, pulling the girl behind him. He kept his gaze turned toward that faint patch of light, and he saw something large and dark move into it. Amber moonlight glanced off of slimy black skin as though repulsed by its touch. Jack cursed. He now knew what had been moving in the mud, and could almost sense those twisting, wormlike lengths wriggling along the walls as well.

Gagging sounds behind Jack shook him from his horrified daze. "Look away," he instructed the girl as he tried to control his own rebelling stomach. Unable to obey his own advice as they moved past the opening, Jack knew when the thing saw them. A sudden squirming knot of tentacles filled the tunnel as it strained forward and Jack flinched, though it was still too far away. It placed gelid fingers against the wall and began to pull itself toward them with terrifying speed.

"Run!" Jack shouted to the girl as he shoved her in the back. She stumbled and fell, and Jack dragged her back to her feet. "Run, damn it!" This time he obeyed his own commands. They fled as fast as they could, but as he heard the beast come around the corner Jack knew with sick despair there was no way they could outrun it in the sucking mud.

"Keep running!" Jack shouted to the girl as he sloshed to a halt. She looked back at him in alarm. "I'll catch up to you," he lied breathlessly. She slowed, then kept running as the thing came closer at a speed that should have been impossible. It was huge, nearly filling the wider tunnel as it dragged itself forward along the walls. Jack pulled the knife from his belt and backed slowly up to one of the feeble patches of moonlight. He didn't think there was any way he could really hurt this thing, but he hoped to delay it so that the girl might get away.

Jack balanced himself gingerly on the mud, and tried to empty his mind of thought. Deep, even breaths slowed his racing heartbeat as Jack began to exercise the mental disciplines that were the Teinne Doigh. He let go of hope, and felt the fear drain away. He let go of need, and desire fled. He let go of hate, and anger lost its hold on him. He forgot the future and the past, and living and dying lost their meanings. Jack embraced *an-aigneadh*, "no mind," the void where intention and action were as one. He felt the *sean-aoidh* rise within him, a golden glowing core of heat and light that coiled in waiting stillness.

The beast slowed as it got closer, and Jack examined it carefully for any sort of weakness. Undulating black skin slid in greasy ripples across a twisting, knotted body. Thick snakelike tentacles squirmed along the tunnel floor and waved blindly through the air toward the walls. Whatever those slithering appendages touched was embraced, and pulled toward the thing. A long boneless fleshy tube ended in a bundle of finer whip-like ropes of skin and muscle, which tore through the air with an angry violence. Any object brought close was caressed by those slender ebon tongues, and then dropped to be lost beneath the bulk of the body as it slid soundlessly forward.

Jack didn't see any vital organs, nothing that looked like a head. He slid his left foot back, and raised the short curved sword parallel to the ground. No eyes glistened in the moon-cast shadows, so he didn't even know what kind of perceptions the thing had. Outside the stillness of *sean-aoidh* meditation, Jack's mind rebelled from further contemplation of the beast, and he let thought drain away rather than lose his center.

The first dripping tentacle whipped toward him, and he lifted his sword to meet it. An appalling strength was evident in the thing as he fended it away. Worse still, the sword's razor edge met that rubbery appendage full on – scraping along it for several feet as it twisted away – and left not a scratch in the creature's skin. Jack fended off the next few attacks, waiting for the beast to get closer, realizing he would not get close enough to strike a telling blow.

In moments, Jack's world narrowed to shadowy snakelike forms glistening in the fading moonlight. Tentacles crept past him along the walls and the floor, gripping to pull the creature close. Soon he was surrounded by the crawling flesh, until it seemed the tunnel had become the gullet of the beast, and Jack swallowed within it. Still he danced, the sucking filth gentle beneath his feet; hands, arms, and body all moving in the curious rhythms of the Teinne Doigh, somehow keeping the beast from grasping him. He was forced back along the tunnel, until he had passed through the darkness and again into the failing light from a grate above.

The beast's fleshy tube flailed angrily through the air, and an uncanny and repetitive susurrant sound issued from somewhere within the creature's body. The nature of the attacks changed, became less grasping and more whip-like, left slimy, painful welts that burned to the bone. Nothing human could withstand that attack. Dozens of sinewy ropes whistled through the air, and no amount of skill could keep Jack from being struck. At last, the beast caught him full in the chest.

The force of the blow lifted Jack from his feet and hurled him violently against the stone wall of the sewer. The impact flung the short sword from his hand and robbed him of breath. It also loosened the haphazard ties that had bound the stolen demon box to Jack's back, and as he dropped gasping to the sodden floor the box fell next to him. More alarming than the loss of his sword was the fact the box had fallen open and sickly green light spilt into the tunnel. Jack scrambled away, certain he didn't want that light falling upon any part of him.

The beast had stilled as the box dropped, but now its eerie hissing chant began again. Tentacles crawled over the mud to gently and carefully gather up the box, lifting it almost reverently from the floor. The box was fully open now, staining the tunnel with a green glow, making it seem more like one of the nether hells than any place on the honest earth. All of the creature's tentacles swayed in time to the inhuman chanting, in a rhythm almost hypnotic. It began to raise its body, lifting its corpulent mass toward the ceiling, holding the box before its bulk. As the greenish glow fell upon the thing's belly, Jack recoiled against the wall. There, nestled among the folds of skin and mud, surrounded by hundreds of tiny wormlike fingers, was a human face! Jack held on to *an-aigneadh* with difficulty. The golden fire that was his *sean-aoidh* flickered and dimmed as his mind struggled to comprehend the horror of that image. The eyes and mouth dripped with filth, but the thing blinked the mud away and gazed with mad wonder upon the demon box.

Deep breaths. Jack regained the stillness of the void, and his *sean-aoidh* rose within him. From that place where intention is action, he moved. As he pulled his hand back behind his head, *sean-aoidh* fire flowed through his body into his arm. His hand flew forward, all that glowing power pooled within it taking flight with the half-forgotten dagger he threw toward the beast. Jack could almost see the golden energy whirl through the air as the dagger spun unerringly toward its target. Whatever sound it might have made as it hit was lost in the beast's song, and the curved blade sank up to its hilt in the left eye of the beast's human face.

The box snapped closed and fell to the floor, and Jack would swear it did so of its own volition the moment his dagger struck. Seconds later the beast began to shudder. He covered his ears as the creature let out a hiss that shook the stones. Convulsions and tremors shook the beast's body, and tentacles whipped with awesome force against the sides of the tunnel. Jack pressed painfully back against the tunnel wall as the thing toppled forward and smacked squirming into the mud. Finally it was still, and he slowly pulled himself to his feet.

That dagger was somewhere beneath the beast, and Jack wasn't about to try to recover it – or do anything else that might make him touch the dreadful thing. His short sword had landed a few paces away, and Jack felt a little better once he had it in his hand, though he realized it was a false sense of security. From the blaze of pain in his side, Jack could tell he had at least two cracked ribs. He would have a hard time catching up to the girl, much less fighting.

Jack turned to start down the tunnel, but hesitated. That ancestor-cursed box. More than ever he didn't want to touch it, but he still didn't dare leave it behind. Jack picked his way over and around the flaccid coils of the beast's unmoving tentacles. Had he seen even a twitch, he'd have left the box where it lay, but the beast was truly dead and he reached the place where the box rested lightly on the mud. Its dark surface was undamaged and without a single splatter of mud, as if even the fetid soil of the sewers fled from the box's touch.

Jack made himself pick up the box and tuck it beneath his arm to make his way out of the tangle of flesh. The last golden rays of moonlight were barely enough to illuminate the little girl's tracks, so Jack forced himself to move more quickly. He had to find her before the light faded completely. It would be easy to lose her in this maze of tunnels.

Ten minutes later the light had waned noticeably, and Jack began to worry. If he didn't find her soon, he never would. A piercing scream from ahead relieved him of that fear, but only at the cost of a more immediate one. Jack broke into a run, which he knew he'd pay for later.

Around the corner, and straight into the waiting arms of two men. Jack's reflexes had been honed razor fine by the nights events, and the sword slashed across the belly of one man and thrust into the chest of the second without a wasted motion. As the sword slid home into the second man's chest, he grabbed Jack's wrist in a grip of iron. There was light here, though Jack didn't note the fact until later, and he looked into lifeless eyes.

This was one of the two men who had attacked Jack the first time in the catacombs. The cut across his throat gleamed wetly, and his face was pale and blue. No breath stirred in his lungs, and the hand about Jack's wrist was cold. He'd left this man lying dead on the stone hours ago. Jack's sword jutted obscenely from the corpse's chest as it tightened its grip on Jack. Moments later Jack was held fast in the grasp of two dead men. He heard cruel laughter in the background.

Jack's state of mind made him first think his ancestors were laughing at him. But the shock passed and Jack took a look around. It was, of course, the Bevyar lord. There were six other cult members huddled back against the walls of the candlelit chamber as if afraid to draw their master's attention. The little girl was clutched in the grasp of one of those cult members, who flinched as he met Jack's gaze. Jack didn't know what the cultist saw in his face, but it seemed to escape Garryn Bevyar as he stalked triumphantly toward Jack.

"You cannot kill a man twice," Garryn said between chuckles as he approached Jack. "If you could only see your face."

"You are a pig, Bevyar," Jack retorted with very little energy. The pain in his side had grown to the point where he was having difficulty breathing.

Garryn smiled. "That may be, Jack, but I'm a powerful pig." The smile faded from his face as he took the demon box from Jack. "You should not take things that don't belong to you, you know." His hands caressed the dark wood and his face flushed as he gazed at the writhing runes.

"Why not? You take lives that don't belong to you!" Jack responded scornfully.

Garryn smirked at Jack, then his gaze was drawn back to the demon box and he said almost absently, "I took nothing that was not already mine."

Jack looked over his shoulder at the little girl and recognized the Bevyar features on her face. His heart clenched as he realized Garryn planned to sacrifice his own daughter. Turning away from Jack, the Bevyar lord took the box to the center of the room and placed it on a carved wooden table there. He turned back to Jack as if something had just occurred to him. "How did you escape the guardian?" he asked curiously.

"You mean the black beast?" Jack asked. Garryn nodded. "I did not escape it," Jack said with a nasty grin. "I killed it." This news caused a stir of fear amongst the cult members. Garryn just shrugged. Then his lips twitched and his eyes took on a gleam Jack didn't like at all.

"Ah, Jack," Garryn said companionably, as he turned away from his old enemy. "You know, there must be a guardian." He positioned the box with careful precision off-center on the table according to some rule that was not apparent. Garryn turned back to Jack. "And since you killed it," he continued casually, "it seems only fair you be the one to replace it." He watched Jack avidly, waiting to see the impact of his words.

Several things fell into place, things Jack had been avoiding thinking about. That horrible human face on the belly of the beast and the fear of the cultists at learning the beast was dead. Garryn's implication was clear: the guardian had once been human, warped by demon power into the foul shape Jack had fought. No wonder the cultists were afraid; they didn't know who might become the next guardian. With frenetic strength, Jack renewed his fight against the two dead men that the Bevyar lord had raised. Garryn watched with almost a lover's intensity, as the unholy strength in those dead hands held Jack easily. At last Jack subsided, helpless against the cold grip of the dead.

Garryn sighed in utter satisfaction as Jack sagged in defeat. With a flushed face and parted lips, Garryn turned back to the ominous waiting blackness that was the box. It seemed to anticipate what was to come, and the runes danced in the flickering candlelight. The Bevyar lord began an oddly familiar chant. Jack's stomach lurched again on recognizing the chant as the one which had issued forth from the beast when it gazed upon the box.

It seemed no matter what he did this night, Jack was doomed to failure. Helpless in the clutches of the dead, and facing a fate worse than death, he nearly sobbed in frustration. Horror upon horror, fear on fear, pain over pain, only to come to this. Jack watched as Garryn tenderly opened the box, and nacreous green light spilled out, staining everything with its unholy hue. Something broke, deep inside Jack, in that moment.

Jack grew still and calm. Not the calm of *sean-aoidh* meditation; something else. He had always thought of anger as something hot, burning, and wild; a human thing that led to mistakes. What he felt now was not hot. Frost and cold issued from that broken place, numbing parts of Jack's mind. The parts that felt fear and concerned themselves with consequences, fairness, and compassion; all were numbed beneath the deep coating of ice that now wrapped his soul. Not hot, no. So cold, and quiet, and calm. This was Rage, and there was nothing human in it.

Escape was irrelevant now, as Rage said to itself, I will hurt him the most he can hurt. I will take away everything with meaning to him. I will see his dreams in ashes, his body rotting in the grave, his Clan in ruins.

Jack's Rage didn't consider impossibility as it coldly considered option after option, and it was inhumanly patient. Jack had grown so still and cold as he thought even the dead holding him noticed, though Garryn Bevyar was still wrapped in his chanting.

The corpses gripping Jack became restive, though he never moved. As if the cold within him disturbed them, they began changing their grips every few seconds.

Garryn finished his chanting and reached gently into the box. As he withdrew his hand that unclean glow clung to it, dancing around his fingertips in a primitive and unsettling rhythm. His eyes reflected that green light as he turned and began toward Jack.

Jack's Rage waited.

"Now, Jack," Garryn whispered with hoarse triumph. "Now you will serve the Old One for eternity." His eyes gleamed with a madness hidden before, and he reached toward Jack.

Still waiting.

One of the dead began to shift his grip as Garryn's glowing fingers neared Jack's chest. Waiting ended.

A twist, and Jack's arm was free. A kick shattered the knee of the corpse holding his other arm. Garryn's eyes widened and he thrust his hand desperately at Jack. Rage spread Jack's lips in a grin as he caught the Bevyar lord's wrist and spun to place his body between Jack and the dead. Jack's other hand grabbed Garryn's shirt and pulled him close. They struggled, Garryn's glowing hand held between them like a poisonous dagger. Jack shattered Garryn's nose with a head butt, and as Garryn reeled back, Jack twisted his wrist. Shining fingertips barely brushed a straining chest and the green glow blinked out. Garryn and Jack broke apart. The dead were between them now, and Garryn laughed in mad victory. Blood from his nose coated the lower half of his face as he looked at Jack expectantly, fairly jiggling with anticipation.

Jack's Rage smiled a cold smile and he shook his head slowly. "Not me, Garryn Bevyar. Your demon lord has chosen another for his guardian."

Garryn seemed puzzled as the dead hesitated, then fear crossed his face as he held his hands up before him. A faint echo of green radiance shone from his skin. It was all over his body now, even his face was glowing. He screamed in denial as the truth hit him. The dead faltered, and fell to the floor. The skin on Garryn's fingers split apart and twisting ribbons of boneless black flesh slid out of his hands to begin whipping about in frenzy. He shuddered in horror at the tentacles that had supplanted his fingers.

Garryn looked at the cultists who had been frozen in terror since Jack first moved. "Help me!" he screamed. "Don't just stand there, you idiots!" He stumbled forward, and Jack moved casually out of his way. The cultists backed away, which only served to make Garryn angry. "I'll make you suffer for this!" he promised. Seconds later, he screamed in pain. The skin on his back split open and black blood spilled toward the ground. A cacophony of unearthly sounds poured from the demon box, an eerie counterpoint to the Bevyar lord's screams. Ten – twelve – twenty foot tentacles slid forth, their weight driving Garryn to his knees. Rage smiled in icy satisfaction. Garryn's screaming choked off as his chest cracked wide, spilling forth still more tentacles. One coiling appendage snapped against the leg of the table, sending it spilling over. The demon box fell to the floor, still singing that otherworldly chorus. That was it for the cultists, and they broke and ran. The one holding the little girl hesitated, but Rage looked through Jack's eyes at him, and he released her and fled.

The two corpses Garryn had raised began to bubble and steam, and ichor ran from their wounds to mingle with the slime from Garryn's continuing change coating the floor. Its ends accomplished, Rage released its grip upon Jack, and returned to the pits of his soul. *Another time, Jack,* it promised as he sagged in sudden weariness.

This seemed like a good time for them to leave, as well. The dead men were puddles of sludge, and Garryn Bevyar' body lay twisting on the floor in the grip of the change being wrought by his demon lord. Jack slipped past aimlessly flopping tentacles to where the box lay. Stepping up behind it, he kicked it closed. The shrieking song cut off abruptly. The only sounds were the wet tears coming from Garryn's body as his flesh was molded into something inhuman by the powers he had summoned.

The little girl ran to Jack and threw her arms around his waist. Tears soaked what was left of Jack's tunic as he knelt to pick her up. He could ignore the pain in his ribs long enough to get them out of there. This time, he knew which way to go. He'd just follow the cultists. There was no courage left in them to oppose him.

They sat on the bank of the river and watched the sun rise over the golden spires and emerald stones of Dalarda. There were decisions to make; what to do with the girl and the demon box, how to get out of Dalarda, what to tell his own lords once Jack returned to

Freehaven. For now it was enough to feel the sunlight warm on their faces. But there was a new place inside Jack where the warmth no longer reached, where an echoing voice whispered in the silence. For Jack, it seemed, Rage had come to stay.

Can one become too civilized for one's good? Can becoming civilized destroy the innocence of a far-removed culture that knows nothing but war and domination and survival of the fittest – a society where death is expected and the reaving of it normal, where there is no such concepts as 'theft' and 'sin,' where deeds determine leaders, and leaders have right to all? Of course it can, for civilization carries with it a most fearsome double-edged gift named Guilt.

Christopher Heath lives in Indiana and has written tales of fantasy for over a decade, either as an official Dungeons and Dragons role-playing game designer or penning works set in his Azieran fantasy world. His prolific writings have been published in dozens of venues. This particular work is a stab at the heart of Sword and Sorcery – a direct conflict between barbarian and sorcerer. It is part of an examination of how a barbarian who has been exposed to culture would relate to his people upon returning to them. To further follow the exploits of the barbarian Brom, watch for his continuing tales in Flashing Swords magazine!

Claimed by Birthright

A Tale of Azieran

by Christopher Heath

Wyvgrin, exalted Wyvgrin, thin and frail, held secrets beyond the mortal cast of common flesh and bone, beyond the entire mundane existence of barbarians that plagued his doorstep and held sorcery in utter disdain. Yet there it lay across his lap, a fabulous sword of mirror blade that was the famed birthright of a savage clan-king. *Such hypocrisy*, he thought, reflecting upon how barbarians used certain gramarye such as this rune-pocked weapon but rebuked other forms. *And what of their shamans?*

Regardless, the sword was a grand and wondrous trophy, and the wizard pondered how it might best be used to his advantage. The mage-lord savored quaffs from a golden chalice of platinum filigree overlay and concocted his plan. In time, he collected upon a past favor.

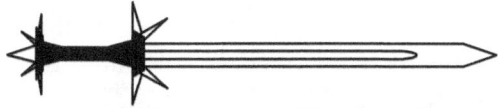

"Why have you called upon me?" asked Kahzvax, his inflection hinting of boredom. He stood before emaciated Wyvgrin, scorn for the pallid-complected arch mage blatant in his bearing. The silver-haired elder sat upon his elevated throne as always, no staff evident, but instead sipping his bubbling emerald ambrosia from the gold and platinum chalice.

"To settle a score you rightly owe me." Wyvgrin stared down upon the other mage's shaved pate. "Recall 'The Scourge that Plagued the Seventh Son'?" His voice resounded across the nearly barren stone chamber.

"Speak not so loudly!" Kahzvax hissed. "We both know I am indebted, and the reason should ever be our secret."

Wyvgrin hid the elation he felt watching the other man squirm at mention of the old atrocity. "My apologies."

Kahzvax lowered his voice. "Accepted. Now . . . what service may I perform to be relinquished from your hold?"

Wyvgrin smirked, and brought the chalice to his lips, imbibing a modicum of elixir before answering. "Often the philosophers have debated regarding which is superior – the savagery of muscle and steel, or the art of sorcery. I intend to answer this question by pitting a most capable mage, that being yourself, against the famed brutality of one of Fohktouhl's most revered savages – King Brom of the Ar'uuk Clan."

The mage lord silently laughed as Kahzvax failed to hide his sudden anxiety, his desperate search for excuses betrayed by the subtle widening of his eyes. Eventually, he responded. "I think your motive is to rid The Broken Kingdom of a powerful barbarian king, rather than answer the question of philosophers."

"I would not need to orchestrate a duel if I merely wished to rid the land of its most infamous clan-king. I want his defeat to be legendary; I want all to know the sheer strength of even the mightiest brute is no match for the sorcery within the ancient halls of Holbard. It has been reported that some of our subjects have been consorting with barbaric clans in plotting our downfall – I want to send a message to our people. We will put an end to this rash of disloyalty by instilling despair into their hearts and persecuting a few key instigators."

"Even if I agreed to such a base act, stooping to duel as a gladiator for the amusement of our subjects, how do you propose to capture Brom or persuade him to cooperate?"

Old Wyvgrin stood and moved to the side of his throne. He pulled forth a formidable blade from behind the ornate oaken frame. Strange runes ran the length of its polished steel, runes that harkened back to the ancient kings of frigid Bjorsek. Its quillons and hilt cast of cross-latticed steel, the bands conformed beneath the rain guard into a skeletal hand that clutched a diamond the size of a horse's eye. That diamond shone with the crimson light of a captured eldritch soul; some whispered it belonged to the ancient, long-vanquished queen of the dracul. The arch mage felt the power in his hands and yearned to unlock its secrets. They would come in time.

"Behold, Avva'rin, *Shard of Ice*." Wyvgrin enjoyed his theatrics.

"Gods! How did you . . ."

"Never mind how I came by it," Wyvgrin snapped. "Fortune has landed the blade in my lap, and I know Brom will come to reclaim it, risking life and limb as would be expected of a mindless brute."

"And will he be permitted to wield it in the duel?"

"No, of course not," Wyvgrin sneered, his mouth forming a rictus snarl as he furrowed his brow. "That would defeat the purpose of our exercise, would it not? No, he will face you with nothing but common weaponry and brute strength. Rest assured, even so, you will be tested. This is not the drinking of blood from newborn babes, or the disemboweling of helpless prisoners for your perverse amusement. This is a barbarian king with muscle of steel and will of iron coming to claim his birthright!

"Is your sorcery powerful enough to keep him from his prize, or will your greatest art seem mere parlor trickery to one such as he?"

"If Brom is to be denied all magic, including Avva'rin, then I will agree to the duel . . . if I may claim the sword as my own in victory."

"Ha! You overstep your bounds as always, Kahzvax. I keep the blade. However, you will be relinquished from the debt already held over your head, and I shall even offer one-quarter of all coin raised in the event."

"One-third."

"Now we have ourselves a bargain."

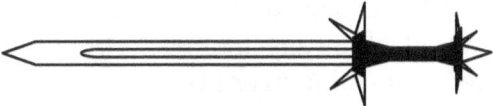

Wyvgrin smiled when he first heard the news that Brom agreed to challenge Kahzvax in vying to regain his lost birthright. He laughed with glee when he learned that the clan-king had braved the swamplands and entered the ruined city of Holbard alone. And now, he tittered with elation to hear that Brom was in the castle, awaiting further instruction. The arch mage sipped from his chalice as he swiftly navigated the fourth level where he held jurisdiction as overlord. He was expected to speak with Brom personally, so made no secret of his journey through the serpentine halls of crumbling walls and cracked ceilings.

Dregs and riff raff – outcasts from other societies – filled the corridors. The air, heavy with pungent odors, carried aloft their foul words that inevitably ended abruptly as they cowered at first sight of the tyrant mage. After some quarter-hour of walking, Wyvgrin came to the remote but well guarded holding chamber.

Dismissing the guards and ensuring their departure, the mage-lord unbarred the door and entered, expecting to see a muscular savage. Wyvgrin's mind reeled; his heart raced as it never had before, prompted solely by the presence of Brom. The brute was what he expected to see, but far more so. The barbarian's frame seemed gargantuan and posed a blatant threat simply by its mere proximity. Wyvgrin was reminded of being a boy who, despite having some impression as to the size and strength of a horse, had been both surprised and overwhelmed by the sheer massiveness of the animal when finally standing next to it. Such was the case, here. The barbarian's gaze, an abysmal, Cimmerian well, set the arch mage even further on edge. For the first time in a very long time, Wyvgrin felt fear in the depths of his heart.

Clad in leathers and furs that included a bearskin cape, Brom appeared a hulking beast, towering at six-and-a-half feet in height. A wild mane of deepest black framed a face that scowled with utmost contempt while his eyes – a moment ago a vacant well – now burned with intense hatred. Six long, tightly woven braids adorned his head, each ending in a grinning bat skull dusted with ash. Wyvgrin knew what they represented, and he swallowed dry while considering each denoted a dracul – a powerful, vampire-like creature – slain by the barbarian's hand. The tiny grinning skulls hanging on their thin strands seemed overtly sinister, as if they could spring to life and attack at any moment. Brom's corded muscles rippled and flexed, tightening over his massive body in response to the mage's scrutiny; a wary panther preparing to spring and attack at any sudden movement.

Wyvgrin eventually found his resolve and spoke. "I am pleased you have come to reclaim your birthright, Clan-king Brom. You are alone as ordered, and made the journey without magic upon your person?"

"Of course, as you have requested." The words were not thickly accented with a bastardized Bjorsekian inflection, as the mage would have thought, but rung with the air of one schooled in majestic and civilized Moongoth. This, too, rattled Wyvgrin.

"I must give fair warning; I arranged this duel as a trap – but with no intention to deceive you. I wish to ensnare your opponent and end his life. You see, he is a powerful mage, lord of the third tier of this castle, and he rivals my own talents in the art of sorcery."

Wyvgrin waited for some form of response. The barbarian only regarded him coldly.

"I wish you to slay him for me, and in return you may reclaim your precious Avva'rin. I cannot unlock its secrets, so it is of no use to me. Also, there are certain . . . political ramifications if I was to succeed in killing the mage Kazhvax myself. There is some honor among practitioners of the dark arts, you see – at least between nobles. I think we shall both find this arrangement beneficial."

A tell-tale nostril flare animated the barbarian's otherwise stoic features, indicating he knew these statements to be coiled in falsehood. Again, Wyvgrin paused, but Brom did not present any of his thoughts. He only stood in stark, intimidating silence.

"I offer you this," the wizard proffered, holding out his hand to reveal one thin, crisp wafer of bread, many exotic herbs and seasonings coating its surface. "It is not magic in and of itself, but this combination of certain potent extracts will repress sorcerous art and give you an edge. Strike swiftly, however, for it can be used only once."

"Then give me more."

Wyvgrin hesitated, startled at the sudden order, the cadence of Brom's voice intimating he was familiar with issuing commands and rarely left wanting. The arch mage quickly regained his composure and could but smile at the warrior's audacity. "I only have the one. It should do the trick. And with Kahzvax dead, you will have your sword, and I will have the third tier under my thumb and be well on my way to controlling all of Holbard."

"How do I know the wafer is not poisoned?"

"To what avail? If I simply wanted you dead I could have had you killed when you entered the city."

Brom held out his hand and accepted the gift, his mind obviously now heavy with thought, his calculations shining clearly through otherwise dark and savage eyes. Again, Wyvgrin grew disturbed.

"Another point to consider," the mage-lord warned. "Kahzvax will likely be warded against metal. He will be a difficult kill."

A thousand and more spectators – dregs and degenerates, perverts and liars, slaves and cannibals, cheats and thieves, murderers and rapists – filled the dilapidated underground coliseum and cheered. Kahzvax stood menacingly in a high collared crimson robe, waving a camphor staff overhead, the wood lathed in many bands and sporting rune-etched, iron-shod ends. Sweat already beaded his bald head as he anticipated the duel to come.

The mage's eyes widened as the rusty gate creaked, slowly rising, and Brom, king of the Ar'uuk clan, stepped forward, out beneath the fractured concave ceiling high overhead. The crowd was stunned to silence at the sight of the mammoth form of the barbarian clad heavily in furs. A sword with leather-wrapped hilt strapped to his waist proved to be his only discernible weapon.

Brom seemed to his opponent the embodiment of primal brutality and savagery. The hairs of the barbarian bristled as he studied his foe who suddenly ceased pandering to the masses. Brom then became aware of his prized blade, Avva'rin, displayed down a tunnel on the far side of the arena. Inspired by the sight of the weapon fixed to the wall, he wasted no time and charged. The crowd roared, enthused by the barbarian warrior's sudden attack.

Kahzvax hurriedly uttered an incantation, calling into creation a misty green tentacle that slithered forward to strike with a viper's speed and grace. Brom dodged the attack with a diving roll to his right, then arose instantly and continued the charge, the mystic feeler chasing after him.

The crowd grew silent as Brom closed the distance between himself and the sorcerer, even as Kahzvax uttered another incantation. Brom tossed a throwing dagger to disrupt the art, but the metal blade ricocheted off the invisible weirding armor that surrounded the sorcerer. Kahzvax smirked as he continued his spell-chant.

Brom reared back to strike, a small weapon hidden in his raised fist, but a second mist-like tentacle appeared, instantly springing forth to grip his wrist and hold the arm at bay. Despite appearances, the appendage offered solid resistance and felt heavy as a thick metal cord. The other tentacle raced up behind Brom and slithered around his chest; it began constricting, crushing the air from his body.

The clan-king recalled being entangled by the giant constrictor Ah-zuu Mah'tul deep in the heart of Vornwood, and knew from experience to hold his breath. He fought with a beggar's greed to retain every morsel of air in his lungs, for when he exhaled, the clan-king knew the tentacle would further tighten and prevent a second breath. The smoky appendage around his torso slithered up to coil his left arm with supernatural strength, holding the upright limb in check. Kahzvax laughed a wicked laugh, stepped forward and slapped Brom in the face, degrading the savage king in his final moments while simultaneously whipping the crowd into excitation.

Kahzvax leaned in, stared the barbarian in the eyes and laughed again, deep and hollow. The brute stared back, sweat dripping down his face in thick beads as he struggled to be free. Brom refused to submit, and this gave the mage even more cause to revel in his triumph as he stared on, sure of his victory, certain his opponent would face a merciless death by arts tempered and proven through centuries of use.

The clan-king looked past the offending mage-lord, down the far tunnel where his enruned blade from the old lands of Bjorsek hung waiting to be reclaimed by rightful hands. He found solace in his birthright and resilience in spirit as he directed his massive thews to strain with all the might of an indomitable will spurred by the promise of blissful reunion.

Brom struggled, shifting his fist back and forth, mere inches at first, but realizing the tendril had difficulty reacting to counter his movements when he shifted the direction of his efforts. Kahzvax, arrogant and amused, leaned forth to slap the barbarian king once again. Brom seethed as he forced his hand backward, anticipating the slightly delayed reaction of the tentacle's adjustment to restrain him. Before the tentacle could fully react, he shifted directions again; with a sudden burst of strength summoned by all the might of his iron will and oaken limb, Brom thrust toward the mage. His fist plunged down upon Kahzvax with just enough force to send the wooden stake it clenched stabbing deep into his neck.

The sorcerer screamed, dropped his staff and fell to his knees. The sudden lethal wound and ensuing mental discord caused the misty appendages to vaporize. With trembling effort, Kahzvax pulled the stake free, releasing a grotesque fount of blood. He began to weakly utter an incantation, his head sagging as he clamped a hand over the wound in a vain attempt to staunch the bleeding. His eyes suddenly widened as Brom's broad shadow fell over him like that of a hawk's diving upon its prey.

The barbarian roughly grabbed the shaved head of the mage-lord, thrusting aside the man's scrabbling fingers. Warm blood pumped across Brom's hands with each panicked beat of the man's heart. Brom clasped the mage's jaw in a vice-like grip and in one quick motion snapped his neck. Knowing the lifeless thaumaturge no longer remained warded from metal in death, the clan-king unsheathed the heavy bastard sword and arced the blade downward. He flashed a taunting grin toward the crowd as he picked up the wizard's severed head and cradled it in his arm like a helpless babe. This silenced the spectators only for a moment.

Brom wasted no time sprinting across the arena as the crowd erupted in frenzied hatred, throwing all manner of objects including poorly aimed weapons. He disappeared down the low-ceilinged hall to reclaim his prize.

High above in the luxury of sectioned seating, Wyvgrin smiled, knowing the tunnel held no exit and that he had spent an entire night on a most complicated invocation to place a ward around Avva'rin – a ward that would slay any who attempted to remove the blade from its perch. The mage-lord stared down onto the headless corpse of Kahzvax and was pleased. His plan had worked to perfection.

Wyvgrin leaned over and commanded his guards to retrieve the body of Brom from the hall, and drag it out for the people to see, so they might further jeer the barbarian's lifeless body and cheer his death. During the interim, the old mage mentally reviewed the speech he would deliver to dregs and rabble-nobles alike. He began to fantasize about how he would come to control the remainder of Holbard.

His attention turned to more urgent matters, however, when the guards exited the tunnel shrugging their shoulders with confused looks upon their faces – and without the body of Brom. Wyvgrin arose, hurriedly descending an aisle as the crowd turned deathly silent. The mage-lord exploded into the arena and ran for the corridor, past his guards. His heart pounded and he cursed to see no sign of the barbarian or the sword. Instead, Kahzvax's pallid head stared blankly, open-mouthed, mocking him from where Avva'rin once hung. As Wyvgrin approached the tunnel's end, he no longer sensed his ward to be present – it indeed had been activated. But if that was the case, Brom should be dead.

For the moment, these events mystified Wyvgrin. The mage hated himself for concocting too complicated a plan. The barbarian could have been dealt with in a simpler manner after slaying Kahzvax, but that would not have proven to all of Holbard that Wyvgrin's gramarye could slay the barbarian king when Kazhvax's could not. It would not have proven that, ultimately, the savages plaguing The Broken Kingdom were but thorns in the sides of the true masters of Fohktouhl.

It was on the eve of that day, after reports were delivered that no sign of the barbarian could be found in the treacherous surroundings of Storcven Swamp, that Wyvgrin, mighty Wyvgrin, finally calmed enough to set his mind to unraveling what might have occurred. As he examined the events, he was astounded at the implications, astonished he had so sorely underestimated the savage despite noting the overt signs that it was no ordinary barbarian intellect with which he dueled.

The first summation Wyvgrin had to concede was that Brom did not use the wafer to dampen Kahzvax's magic and defeat him. The clan-king defeated Kahzvax by sheer will and strength alone! Second, Wyvgrin surmised Brom must have smelled the trap, known a double-cross had been planned and that magic would likely play a part. And so he had saved the wafer as insurance, eventually using it to counter the death ward surrounding Avva'rin. Wyvgrin's final conclusion was that Brom must have garnered at least some knowledge of the strange sword over the years, and used its runic power to transport him far away, across planar space, to safety.

Wyvgrin, sour Wyvgrin, sat sipping emerald ambrosia from his gold and platinum chalice, enraged at the loss of Avva'rin and the lost opportunity to slay The Broken Kingdom's mightiest clan-king. Still, he had gained much in the death of Kahzvax. He continued brooding the remainder of the star-strewn evening, coming to terms with the reality that the brawn and cunning and unrelenting will of a barbarian king had not only conquered the sorcery of Kahzvax, but the sorcery of Wyvgrin as well. This was certainly not the message he had hoped to send those of his oppressed subjects who plotted rebellion. The actions of Brom had crushed the maxims regarding barbarian culture as mere brutish and dumb. That did not bode well for Wyvgrin's future prospects.

As the mage-lord fell toward what was sure to be a deep, intoxicated sleep, he admitted to himself he had been played for a fool, and perhaps even erred in eliminating Kahzvax. If rebellion and war with the barbarians did occur, powerful sorcerers would be needed in the times to come. Again, Brom had out-maneuvered his opponents. Despite these major setbacks, Wyvgrin vowed to have his revenge. The mage's fleeting thoughts soon sank to the ephemeral depths of dream, never registering the broad shadow which loomed over him – the shadow of a hawk diving upon its prey.

Is there anything nastier than betrayal? Or cooler than an all-out battle to the death between armored warriors? One of the more aggressive tales in the anthology, this is a vivid exploration of the sundering of Loyalty. Darkness hides in the soul of every person . . . whispers in the ears of many . . . couples with Ambition to birth a shattering of Trust in more than a few . . .

Nathan Meyer writes for money – and because he's rather positive he could do nothing else, even if he tried. Fortunately for him, Nathan writes as a contract author for Harlequin Imprint Gold Eagle under the names Don Pendleton and James Axler and isn't relying on sales such as this one to take his family of five out to dinner. Unless it's to a fast food dollar menu. Fortunately for us, he enjoys writing action-packed tales of low fantasy. Read some of the past issues of Flashing Swords *magazine for a taste of what else he has to offer. Otherwise, you can find Nathan posting under his own name at the SFReader forum.*

The Hand that Holds the Crown

by Nathan Meyer

I have grown old here, thought Conn Morrison.

He turned away toward the window. With eyes that kept their own counsel, the Lord of Loch Dwyer watched the shinning, golden disk of the sun rising at the edge of a desert he had come to hate with every fiber of his being.

Exile to the sun blasted land had left him unmoved at first. Now, he hated every stark line and harsh, open space. He had come even to hate the people who dwelled here because they loved the bittersweet wasteland. Sadly, Conn had grown to realize, his growing dissatisfaction had even extended to the native woman sleeping so blissfully in the bed behind him.

I am leaving you, he though silently from his perch at the windowsill.

The message had come yesterday, brought by a caravan master who'd taken it from a merchant ship's captain. The seal of Conn's royal family, of Dwyer Deep, was prominent and unbroken upon the parchment. The seal of Clan Morrison. The message had been simple and Conn still felt surprise that so few words could carry so much meaning.

> *Your father is dead.*
> *All is forgiven.*
> *Come home,*
> *Carsk*

Forgiven? For duty? He only wished he'd discovered the treachery before the birth of that bastard of a pretender. A pretender now grown to manhood. No, it was not right that another should wear the crown. Between he and the bastard there was no contest. Of course there was another, but he would waste no more thoughts on the ridiculous.

Conn put the parchment down as he heard the woman stirring on the bedding. There were many things in this place bittersweet besides the land. He did not hate this hot-tempered consort who shared his bed. He loved her. Naked, sun streaming in rays of brilliance around his body, Conn Morrison, kin-slayer and woman-killer, moved back toward the bed to say his good-bye.

I am leaving you, he thought.

"He will come." Carsk said.

Garrett, Prince-Regent of Dwyer Deep, stood with his back to his chief man-at-arms and cousin. He stood watching a sun of hard, golden brilliance rise above the tops of mountains never untouched by the blanket of snow. His arms were folded and his feet planted in the dew-wet grass of the churchyard. He looked down at the grave of his father Auric, Duke of Dywer Deep. Beside it lay that of the Duke's lover Morgan, who had been the wife of another man and Queen to this land.

"Then let him come." Garrett answered simply. "Once he is gone none will question my rule."

"There is—" Carsk began.

Garrett frowned.

From the doorway of the chapel the hooded figure charged with keeping the mountain cemetery watched the two warriors who walked among the headstones and Celtic crosses. Carsk watched the lean figure and wondered if they had been overheard, and if so, what that one thought. Even as he looked on the chapel warder withdrew into the shadow and silence of the building.

Spring mist hung like clouds amid the hidden valleys of the mountains. In the early morning it was damp, a cold shroud clinging to the glade. Ribbon-like, a stream of snowmelt cut through it. The water was neither deep nor swift, but cold and pure. It snaked into the woods and then ran gurgling for six miles before leaking into that bottomless, highland lake, Dwyer Deep.

On one side of the mountain meadow stood the chapel and its charge, the little churchyard filled with the graves of Clan royalty from generations past. Across from the chapel lay the ruined foundations of the watchtower that had stood beside the mountain road. In the middle a sturdy wooden bridge crossed the stream.

Unattended by vassal or squire Conn Morrison sat atop his great warhorse. The mount was a stallion and high tempered. He wore full link piece-armor of unfinished black and his shield bore no device. He wore a great Heaume helm over his chain mail coif. His hands were steady upon the haft of his lance.

Motionless, Garrett sat on his own, snowy, charger. The horse, a gelding, was not frantic in anticipation but waited calmly for his master's rein. The Prince-Regent looked down to Carsk.

"I hope to take him in the first pass, he was always an indifferent jouster."

Carsk nodded, face set. A heavy crossbow hung from his saddle. A longsword hung from his belt.

"True, but make sure you hurt him, his sword arm is strong." Carsk said.

"Oh yes, the sword arm that slew my mother and father."

"That slew *his* mother as well, cousin." Carsk answered.

Garrett said nothing, jogged his spurs into the charger's flanks and rode forward.

Conn saw Garrett coming at a steady pace across the meadow, the point of his lance in the air. In answer he urged his stallion toward the bridge. Each knight halted on either side of it.

"Brother."

"Brother."

"For twelve generations this bridge has been the symbolic entrance to the land of our fathers, Dwyer Deep." Garrett began.

"You've no father in common with me, Pretender." Conn spat.

"Aye, nor mother either since she was butchered by your hand, kin-slayer."

"Say no more, Pretender." Conn said. "I found her betraying my father, your lord, on her very knees like some Frankish harlot."

Garrett's face flushed, the veins of his temple stood out.

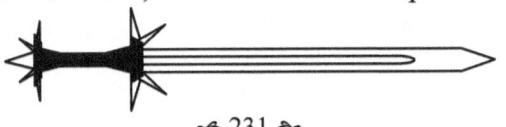

Carsk began to walk his horse slowly toward the shouting men. Behind him the hooded chapel warder followed.

"Some would say," the robed figure said softly to the kingdom's Knight-Captain, "it is not fit for brothers to fight, even over a kingdom."

"Half-brothers." Carsk corrected, gently. "Besides, you know better."

"Yes," nodded the other. "And the kingdom goes to the hand that holds the crown."

On the hilt of his longsword Carsk's grip turned white-knuckled. He walked forward, the chapel warder a step behind.

Garrett sat straight in his saddle.

"I say again, woman-slayer, this is my land now. By right of law, renegade, you shall not cross."

"You are the bastard child of a whore and a traitor. I will rule in Dwyer Deep."

"To the hand that holds the crown!" Garret shouted and wheeled his charger.

Likewise Conn turned his stallion on its hind, and galloped away. Armed and armored, each knight again turned his steed. They lowered their lances and gave wild cries as they charged. Above them the rays of the morning sun shown with brilliance hard as diamonds.

The hammering of hooves across the flat was like the early rumbles of an earthquake. The warhorses were huge specimens, heavily muscled and bred for aggression. Closer still they raced and louder came the drumming of hooves. It echoed inside of both riders' helms until it swallowed all other sound.

Sweat slicked the padded vests beneath the breastplates of their link armor. Eyes narrowed behind faceplate visors. Each man knew only total focus on their point of aim would save them. Each knew the other's lance raced nearer.

Both brothers were screaming when they struck. They met in the middle of the bridge with a clap of thunder. On the bank of the stream Carsk saw Garrett drive his point low to ensure he'd unseat the older Conn. He saw as well how Conn unerringly guided his lance point over the lip of Garret's tear-shaped kite-shield and straight into the other man's visor.

Conn sat astride a war saddle, not the high backed saddle designed for tournament jousting. When the lance struck him his forward momentum was so great Garret's lance bowed and snapped. Conn was thrown bodily backwards, massive armor pulling him hard to the thick wooden planks of the bridge.

At the last moment Garret tried to turn his head aside. He refused to move his eyes off his target, ensuring a strike. The metal tip of the black armored outlaw's lance drove straight into his helm. The metal crumpled under the impact and his cheekbone shattered. He felt the salty sting of blood across his eyes and tasted its copper-tang in his mouth. Blinded, he felt his world spin and his helm fly off as he hit the bridge.

The chapel warder gasped aloud at the mask of blood that was now Prince Garrett's face. Carsk seemed mesmerized as if by a glamour. His eyes were bulging, locked to the scene he witnessed. He saw Conn's magnificent black stallion beat the white charger to the rear, forelegs churning air.

Coming down with all its weight there was a sound like hammer on anvil as the white charger's linked piece armor gave way beneath the assault. The white horse sagged under the weight of the falling blows. It tried to turn but the bridge was too narrow. In desperation the animal sought again to rear in its own defense, but the stallion was already there.

With the sharp crack of hoof hitting bone the charger crumpled. Still the stallion reared and brought hooves raining down. The beast seemed enraged, blood mad, its snorts and whinnies frantic, its eyes rolling white.

Garrett came up over the brutalized corpse of his charger and drove the haft of his splintered lance deep between the massive columns of muscle that made up the stallion's chest. He sank the wood hard. The stallion's shrieks sounded like a woman's screams.

Helm still in place, his bottom rib cracked in half, Conn hurtled from Garrett's periphery and struck him at a dead run, driving the other man before his onslaught. They hit the guardrail of the bridge fighting, Conn trying to drive home blows from his heavy gauntlets into Garrett's unprotected head.

Garret was driven backward across the rail, spine bending painfully. His grip locked at Conn's helm and he twisted with every ounce of his strength.

"Woden's eye, they are going over." Carsk said.

The inevitable happened; Conn's wild punches overextended him as Garret gave his strongest twist and jerk. Suddenly, the Prince-Regent felt his enemy's momentum change and the warrior was jerked up off his feet and half-across Garrett's chest.

Arms windmilling, they tumbled over the rail and fell like stones six feet to the shallow water of the stream.

The splash was loud as the mailed knights hit the knee-deep water, driving through and onto the gravel bed. Carsk dismounted from his steed in an eager motion. He threw his reins at the startled chapel warder and stepped to the stream bank.

Both warriors came up grasping for swords and gasping for air. Each was exhausted from the brutal strain. Each possessed enough energy to kill the other. Conn tore his loosened helm from in front of his eyes, tossing water in an arc. He turned, dazed. Hunting for his nemesis he ripped his sword loose. Spinning, he saw a brilliant dazzle of sunlight flashing down the length of Garrett's blade.

Conn brought his sword up as Garrett's came cutting down. Steel rang clear on steel as the two men struggled. They fought not in the manner of duelists but with all the desperation of the battlefield. Bone against bone, muscle straining hard against muscle.

They broke and Garrett brought his blade down again. Again Conn stopped the wild cut, catching it on his crossguard. He was driven to one knee under the force of the blow and the wild light in his eyes was suddenly tempered with something other than bloodlust.

Blood.

The stream was pink with snaking tendrils of their blood. Above them the bridge was flooded with great black-red pools of horse blood amid the cast off weapons and bits of broken armor. Each warrior's lungs burned, screaming for air. Their hearts bounded in the cages of their chests while their hands ran slick with fear-sweat inside their gauntlets.

Conn let Garrett's blade slide off his and answered with a wild slash. It came fast, forcing Garrett back and giving Conn time to rise. As soon as he reached his feet Conn parried another chopping slash. He could feel his strength ebbing and he knew if he did nothing to come off the defensive he would soon falter and die on the other's blade.

It was then that he saw it: the crown.

Garrett had worn it under his great helm. The war-band of Dwyer Deep. A flat band of hammered steel inset with the rune of command. There was a palace crown as well, to be sure. It sat in palace vaults encrusted with jewels and formed from the thinnest crafted gold. But that crown had come after, later.

No, it was the war-band that had united the clans and calmed the kin killing. It was the war-band that had made scattered tribes into one people. It was the only crown that those people would now swear fealty too. The only crown the kingdom needed. And to the hand that held the crown would that kingdom go.

Prince Garrett screamed one, long cry of rage and fear. His silver shield reflected sunlight and Conn blinked back the glare. His eyes focused again only to realize the shield itself flew toward him.

He brought his mailed forearm up in answer and felt the heavy disc rebound off, staggering him. Conn lowered his arm and saw Garrett's rushing figure half a heartbeat away before the heavily armored warrior crashed into him with the force of an avalanche.

Sword spinning from his grip, Conn was barreled over and driven straight down onto his back. Cold mountain water closed over his pain twisted face and rushed down into his armor. The exiled prince struggled hard but his efforts were useless, uncoordinated flailing. Garret sat astride him like a rider does a horse, the combined weight of their armor serving to pin Conn further to the streambed.

Pushing down hard on Conn's head, Garrett held him under. Conn looked up at a world distorted by water like a window with too many panes of glass. Darkness was taking the periphery of his vision and within the black pinpoint flashes of light popped and burst like dying suns. Conn's throat no longer burned from the asphyxiation. A strange peace took him.

Death greeted him kindly, arms open.

He thought of dark eyes laughing under a desert sun and felt a pang. The pang became a memory of fierce desert warriors who rejected a knight's heavy mail in favor of speed and how they had filled the long, hot days showing him to wield their whirling scimitars and how to fight a heavily armored man such as himself.

Conn's eyes snapped wide open and he pulled a hand free of its armored gauntlet. Running his hand across his waist to the buckle of his sword belt, he jerked the palm knife free. Shaped like a T, the haft ran lengthwise across his palm while the slim blade jutted from his fist like a steel thorn.

Conn struck, punching his point up under Garrett's armpit and through the simple leather covering. It sliced straight into soft, vulnerable flesh. When the blade was home, close to the pounding organ of life and the numerous, tangled vessels, Conn twisted.

Like the breaking water of a birthing woman blood rushed out, staining the side of Garrett's armor a sudden scarlet. The Prince-Regnant arched his back like a jumping fish and Conn easily unseated him. Garrett pushed aside, Conn's face again broke the surface of the water.

Sweet breath flooded Conn's lungs and he took in huge gulps of it. Unsteadily he rolled and pushed himself to his feet, the palm knife still naked in his fist. Dazed, he cast it away, then stooped to retrieve his sword. If he had worn plate armor he would have drowned, unable to rise.

Garret lay against the dirt bank, legs still in the water. Behind him the meadow grass was a verdant green in sharp contrast to the steadily flowing crimson that leaked so readily from him and down the stream.

Coming straight up from his knees, Conn brought his longsword around. Gripping it overhand, he grasped the cross-guards. Looming above the Prince-Regent, he lunged forward.

Garrett weakly held up a hand, strength draining from his limbs as rapidly as his blood pouring into the stream.

Screaming, Conn brought down his blade. It was a choked sound, mixing pain and rage and something else even more primal. The sword caught the helpless man where he sat folded at the waist, just above his cuisses. Though Garrett's piece armor was of the finest quality, nothing could have stayed the descending assault of Conn's blade.

The point slid home, sinking into Garrett's entrails with the sound of ripping flesh. The young warrior-prince spasmed once, leaning forward over the weapon. Then the blade drove through him, out his back and deep into the stream bank.

Conn's face was less than a foot from Garrett's. His gaze narrowed as he watched the light in Garrett's eyes slowly fading. Garrett made as if to speak and a bubble of blood formed. Then it burst and ran out over his beard.

"Bastard," he whispered. Then he died.

Sickened, but insanely elated, Conn pushed himself to his feet. His euphoria was limitless. He reached down without ceremony and pulled the war-crown free from his half-brother's head. In possessive triumph he held it aloft. By blood and sinew he'd reclaimed his birthright. He had known no happier moment in his life. His laughter echoed through the meadow.

"To the hand that holds the—"

There was a sound like a mis-plucked harp string.

Conn jerked with the impact of the quarrel. He teetered for a second and put his foot out to catch his balance. His limbs refused to work for him and Conn sagged heavily to his knees. The pain between his shoulder blades bore straight through to his sternum. Looking down, he saw nothing.

He cast about him in stupid confusion. He saw Carsk drop the heavy crossbow that had hung on his saddle.

"No." Conn said. "It's *mine*."

He sagged forward, an arm coming out to catch his fall. With his other hand he held tightly to the crown. Conn tore his eyes away from the approaching Carsk and looked down at the gray iron war-band.

"Mine. I hold it."

Carsk pulled his longsword from its sheath. Behind him the chapel warder held the reins of his horse. Approaching the crumpled Conn, Carsk's face was grim mask.

"Damn you, cousin." Conn said.

Conn swung his arm out wildly, his vision blurring. He swung the crown like a weapon only to overextend himself. With a splash he fell forward into the water again. Limbs unbelievably heavy, Conn struggled to push himself back up.

Carsk's foot came down across the back of Conn's neck. The man-at-arms pushed down hard with his weight. Conn struggled weakly under the usurper's foot.

From a great distance, rushing ever closer, Conn saw a pair of soft brown eyes, eyes filled with sadness. Then he saw only darkness.

Carsk bent down and eased the iron crown up from Conn's limp fingers. He spat down at the dead man and then watched the sun's brilliance sparkling off the centerpiece. He closed his hand tightly around the war-band of Dwyer Deep.

The hand that held the crown.

He was king, for who else but—

Lost in the reverie of the moment he heard the horse too late. Surprise clear on his face, Carsk spun.

The chapel warder drove the horse hard into the water and down upon the stunned Carsk. A Lucerne hammer, once secreted beneath clerical robes, rose above the rider's head, poised to strike.

"Lass, no!" Carsk screamed.

Carsk, veteran of a hundred battles, was a naive babe to treachery born in the bedchamber. His horror slowed him. The big charger, his own mount, ploughed hard into him, sent him spinning like a rag doll.

Helene, daughter of Morgan, whom Conn had named 'the Whore of Dwyer Deep,' fell upon her lover and cousin, the final obstacle between her and the crown. The wicked hammer fell and rose and fell again. Standing in the stirrups, she clubbed him to death like harvesting a seal pup out on the ice.

Then it was over.

The ruler of Dwyer Deep surveyed the culmination of her machinations. Her raven hair fluttered in a tattered banner behind her. A tight smile froze her full lips in rictus.

Three mighty men-at-arms, legendary warriors of the realm, lay dead and bloody in the snow-melt waters winding their way down the mountain to feed Dwyer Deep.

She dismounted and bent, snatching the war-band of the Clan free from the dead hand of Carsk, last male of the blood line. The crown was splattered with his blood where it had sprayed under each merciless blow. Tearing away her drab robes, jubilation filled Helene's breast.

She was the mirror of her mother at her age, with a generous and inviting figure. Face and eyes set in cold beauty. A beauty men had wagered kingdoms for. A beauty now accentuated by the slender iron war-band on her brow. She swung easily onto Carsk's horse.

When she appeared in the courtyard of the ancient keep in the crown of her mother the people would greet her on bended knee, as they always had. As they would always bow before the hand that held the crown.

Readers of Flashing Swords *magazine are long familiar with Dermanassian's quest to avenge his people. We're aware of the trials of deception and double-cross that have dogged every step of the last desert elf. This story continues the pattern, but while delivering more of the same pensive writing we've come to anticipate, this one cuts deeper than ever before. Continuing our study of betrayal begun in the last tale, we have discovered something nastier: unknowingly being used to contribute to our own betrayal.*

S.C. Bryce crafts some of the best introspective storytelling I've read. Each of her tales leaves a reader with something to ponder. She says she's recently been developing stories from simple phrases she finds interesting – in this case, the title. Fortunately (for all of us), she had Dermanassian waiting around for another adventure. S.C. has been a lifelong junkie of fantasy books and documentaries and she likes the challenge of thinking up different spins on the same ol' tropes. Visit her website at http://scbryce.com to find one of the most interesting author websites out there.

The Dawn Tree

A Tale of Dermanassian, Last of the Desert Elves

by S.C. Bryce

Dermanassian crouched in the merchant's walled garden, watching the little tree in its center. The tree's rough bark reflected the thin moonlight. Its sheer ancientness was beautiful in itself, with none of the manufactured perfection of the surrounding plants that smelled of orange and ginger. He could understand the fascination the Ulumi had with the Dawn Tree, even though they did not know what it truly was.

The clouds parted briefly and moonlight streamed down. He sunk into a patch of shadow, watching the red-tiled rooftops again for signs of Bhetheri i'Bhet's guards. But the jaded guards did not bother to walk the inner walls; they relied heavily upon Bhetheri's well-earned notoriety. Thus, there were none to see the desert elf hidden in the cool dark. He shifted the blue lotus sword's sheath, freeing it from the folds of his gray cloak to lie more comfortably at his back.

Above him, the white dragonet that had become his constant companion hid behind the broad, waxy leaves of a fruit tree. Its onyx eyes blinked nervously as it stretched its long neck around to watch. Though it desperately wanted to perch upon Dermanassian's shoulder and chitter its disapproval, it had learned the wiser course was to stay put. It dug its talons into the bark of its perch and ground its icicle-shaped teeth, waiting.

When Dermanassian turned back to the Dawn Tree, a tiny figure stood beside it. Despite the night chill, she was clad in a sheer, multi-colored gown from which peeked bare legs. Her auburn hair hung loose to her waist and her skin was vaguely luminescent. She stretched in the moonlight with a deep sigh before swinging into the tree gracefully to inspect each long bud and hum in satisfaction. She unwrapped each corner, peeked inside, and then lovingly re-rolled the blooms – each fully as large as she was.

"Pae," Dermanassian whispered, stepping into the moonlight.

Almost inaudibly, she gasped as her large green eyes widened and her hand flew to her mouth. In an instant, she vanished, leaving only the aroma of flowers.

Dermanassian crept to the Dawn Tree, almost placing his bronze hand upon its bark before remembering such an act might well be greeted with poisonous barbs.

"Lady Pae," he whispered urgently. "I have been sent for you."

Cold silence emanated from the tree. He pleaded for hours, but as the first glow of day appeared in the sky, he could risk no more time. The merchant's reputation promised that any intruder caught would be greeted with the most arcane of punishments rather than turned over to city authority. Dermanassian knew that any confrontation would result in the blue lotus sword slick with the blood of guards simply trying to earn their pay.

With a sigh of impatience, the last of the desert elves and his dragonet melted away with the night.

Dermanassian squinted. Both the sun and his stomach agreed that it was an hour past noon.

He munched spiced meat pastries and purple-skinned fruit at the edge of the lavish market, leaning against the corner of one of the brightly painted brick-and-stucco buildings. For the heat of the day, his gray sleeves were rolled to his elbows. The dragonet nestled in a folded cloak within Dermanassian's travel pack, for the little creature was not fond of heat or sunlight and appreciated the refuge of the fabric cave. Its own belly stretched by a careless mouse, the dragonet snored softly.

His gaze turned to the hills surrounding the port. On the seventh of the seven hills, his eyes lingered. Nestled among the red-tiled estates of the city's mercantile elite, was Bhetheri i'Bhet's wide mansion.

He had not expected reluctance from Lady Pae. When sending him here, his foster brother had suggested replanting the tree was a simple matter of making the request of its guardian. Dermanassian agreed to do it because of his pact with his foster brother. Dermanassian would aid him in his self-proclaimed war on Fate; in return, the former monk would aid Dermanassian's objectives.

At any rate, the desert elf knew he would be back in the walled garden when night fell.

And so, as the distant gongs noted the hour after midnight, Dermanassian slid down a thin rope. Soundlessly, he dropped to the ground. After pausing briefly to assure himself that he had not been detected, he crept over to the tree.

"I am here for you," he murmured to the tree, its whiteness stark in the cold night.

After long minutes, came Pae's disembodied answer. "Why?" she softly puzzled.

"Lady, your tree must be replanted."

"Why?" she asked again with disinterest. "The steppe changes around us, but still we bloom. I care for nothing else. Be gone."

"Lady, I know little of your lore or those forces that rule the Dawn Tree. But I am told that the tree must leave the steppes of Mera and be replanted."

The tiny voice was curious, but steely, its thick accent difficult to place. It was deeper and more melodic than he expected. "Who makes these claims?"

"One you do not know – Desmarais."

"Ah, Desmarais." Lady Pae appeared, nodding in sudden and grave understanding. Her face was touched with cold irony.

Dermanassian frowned. Desmarais had failed to mention that he had any relationship with Pae. It seemed that even as his foster brother took him into his confidence, he withheld information. He muttered to himself, "His list of acquaintances grows."

"So he has finally begun his war on Fate, has he? And he wishes me to play my small part." She placed slight hands upon slim hips and stared with piercing, inscrutable eyes. "I thought he might soon call on me. The stars twinkle with ill-defined and ill-omened change, and Desmarais is ever observant."

"Lady," Dermanassian nearly pleaded. He watched the walls for guards, well aware that first light approached while he stood exposed in the courtyard. He did not want to discuss his foster brother's esoteric war. When aiding Desmarais to achieve his arcane goals increased Dermanassian's chances of succeeding in his own, he was willing. And Desmarais had assured him that replanting the Dawn Tree would aid them both. "I know only that the Dawn Tree must be replanted."

"Is that so?" She raised an arched, auburn eyebrow. Murmuring, she stroked one of the curled buds, her face softening, tinged with sadness. "Perhaps. The buds grow with an urgency that suggests what you say is true. I have seen the barest hints of it in the rustle of the leaves, the crooked lines running through the bark, the slow growth of the roots." She paused and cocked her head as if listening to sounds beyond Dermanassian's keen hearing. Suddenly she smiled and nodded to herself. "It is time."

"How do we move the Dawn Tree?" he asked. "What is your counsel as its caretaker?"

She waved away his concerns. "We do not need the tree. Only this," she plucked a hidden seed. It was reddish and smooth, and enormous in her little hand. She showed it to him with a wink before she hid it in the folds of her robe.

Then she transformed into a tall woman of long, black hair and dark, angular features that matched Dermanassian's own. The furled flowers of the Dawn Tree decorated a thin circlet on her brow that held her crown of hair from her face. Her luminescence turned to warm bronze skin like his, though she was clad in the same blossom-gown and her feet stayed bare. The startling green of her eyes and the sweet scent of flowers remained.

Dermanassian could not avoid her heavily lashed eyes and she noted his strange expression. "Does this disturb you?" she asked.

"No," he said, but he lowered his gaze nonetheless. It had been many decades since he had seen another desert elf. "Let us go," he said, his voice rough.

He turned to the white bark of the tree. With Pae separated from it, it was a ghostly husk. Dermanassian was struck with the sudden premonition that the tree would be dead in days.

In the morning, they purchased supplies for several weeks and two small mares of local stock, bred in the mountains and as accustomed to hard living as they were rough terrain. As they exited the city, Dermanassian guided his horse eastward toward the great expanse of the Mera steppe.

Pae halted her rangy mount. "Where are you going?" Seeing his confusion, she asked, "What do you know of the Dawn Tree?" She smiled gently, as a tutor questioning a favored pupil.

"Little," he admitted. For him, the Dawn Tree had been only a vague legend until his foster brother asked him to go to Pae. Even then, Desmarais, as was his habit, said little about the tree – a bit of history, nothing more. Dermanassian's attempts to gather more information were fruitless.

Pae patted the rough coat of her bay. The dragonet, perched upon the pommel of her saddle, chirped irritably until she patted it as well.

Dermanassian frowned away the odd jealousy that crept into his gut.

"The Dawn Tree has been replanted more than once," she said. "The tree aging in the merchant's mansion was the fourth. The first Dawn Tree grew in the garden of Te and Ai. Do you know them?"

"No." Distracted, Dermanassian answered too quickly. He reconsidered. "Yes. They are the progenitors of Desmarais's people, the Children of TeAi?"

"Yes."

She spoke patiently. "I learned that the Dawn Tree must be replanted. So I took a seed to the kelp beds of the Hairy Sea. The first Dawn Tree became the Dusk Tree as I planted the seed and the second Dawn Tree sprang from the sands, heralding a new epoch. Then I learned that the Dawn Tree must be replanted. So I took a seed to the Bog of the Lost Cavalry and the second Dawn Tree became the Dusk Tree. The next seed, I took to Mera's barren steppe. And now you come and tell me that the Dawn Tree must be replanted once again. So the tree in Bhetheri i'Bhet's courtyard will become the Dusk Tree as the fifth Dawn Tree springs from the soil."

"And where will you bear the seed this time?" Dermanassian asked, laying a hand on his mare's coarse mane to quiet her as she shuffled her feet.

"I do not know." She smiled. "The world is new to me, for I fully wake only when the tree blooms and I move about only to replant the tree." She stretched and breathed deeply, and to Dermanassian it seemed that she breathed in more than just the spring air, but the afternoon sun and the breeze and the trees and all besides. She smiled again, her large eyes half-closed and hidden in her lashes. "I will see where the wind and this mare can take me. When I find the place, I will know it. The seed will tell me."

"Then I will go with you," he said with sudden, enthusiastic gallantry, "to see the new Dawn Tree rise."

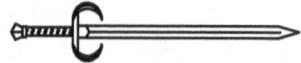

They ran their horses until the tough mares foamed in the setting sun and Ulum-ka was far behind them.

Two weeks later, Dermanassian laughed. He could not remember the last time he did so; more than likely it was as a youth, centuries past. Until that moment, he did not realize how much of the weight upon his spirit had lifted. The blue lotus sword dangled carelessly from his mare's saddle and Dermanassian imagined a world in which he would never wield the blade again.

As their horses noisily cropped, Dermanassian and Pae lay upon a woolen blanket in the willowy steppe grass. Their hands and black hair were interwoven. The dragonet curled in sleep in the crook of Pae's arm, contented curls of smoke drifting from its tiny red nostrils. Above, clouds flowed smoothly across the vast blueness like white petals carried by a swift and infinite river.

Pae plaited an intricate ring from blades of yellow grass. With a small smile, she placed it upon the index finger of his left hand where it shone like gold. Warmed by their hands and the sun, it felt as eternal.

"Perhaps I will not let you plant the new Dawn Tree! I may keep you for myself rather than share you with a shrub," he joked. He brought her perfumed hand to his lips. He had succumbed completely to his feelings for her; all else seemed a faint memory of dark times. He could think of nothing beyond his certainty that his centuries of loneliness were at last ended.

"You mustn't tease about that," she scolded him.

Dermanassian was surprised to see that she was quite serious. "Why?" he asked.

"The Dawn Tree is terribly important. Why, without it—" she frowned.

"What?" he prompted.

She shrugged. "The world would stay at it is, locked in a single epoch, always. It would not be able to grow, mature, to fulfill its nature. It would remain as a child, forever."

"Would that be such a terrible thing?" he laughed again.

"I think most would disagree. And you," she smiled tensely, "would not like to be in the company of those who did agree."

"I would gladly prevent the world from progressing beyond this one moment," he said lightly.

"Be serious."

"I am. Let us forget this business about dawning trees and dawning epochs. Let us forget Desmarais and Fate and war and vengeances and divinities. Let us forget that anything exists except ourselves. We shall lose ourselves in this tall grass of gold," he tickled her, "or return to Glorious Tehare and do our best to repopulate the world with desert elves."

Abruptly, he sat up. "I thought I heard—"

Suddenly, the little mares pricked and swiveled their ears, their haunches taut as if to bolt. Dermanassian jumped to his feet and gathered their dangling reins. The taller mare jerked and snorted; the bay stomped nervously, whinnying.

The sound was at the very edge of his hearing, but it chilled his blood: a high-pitched wailing reminding him of a gust through an iron keyhole. Dermanassian winced.

Then Pae gasped and clutched her stomach, curling over in the grass. She seemed to be in such great pain that no further sound came from her. Her mouth hung and twitched in agony and her green eyes glazed.

The dragonet chittered with terror.

Dermanassian rushed to her, yanking the horses with him for fear they would flee from the menacing whispers in the air. He grasped her shoulder tightly with one hand, the leather reins firmly gathered in the other.

"Pae—"

"It cannot be," she forced the barely audible words through unwilling lips.

"What is it?" he asked hurriedly, torn between concern for her and whatever approached.

"It is destroyed."

"What?" he urged, at the same time pulling her to her feet so she could mount the snorting mare.

To the west, wisps of darkness churning in the distance like a great flock of innumerable birds or the beginnings of a tornado.

"The Dawn Tree. They have abused its vulnerability during the transition, exploited my absence. It has been cast from the ground by Terrat and set ablaze by Kulkameht," she whispered in disbelief as her pain subsided.

He shook his head. "The Earth Elemental and the Fire Elemental? What reason have they to harm the Dawn Tree?"

The horses reared, nearly pulling him from his feet.

Pae's hand clutched at the secret pocket in her multi-hued robe. She stared into the distance as if seeing for the first time the unknown danger approaching. She frowned, trying to understand. "They are powerful in this epoch. Perhaps they fear that they will lessen in the next." She shook her head uncertainly.

"Whatever their reason, they search for the seed now," she continued fearfully. "They will destroy it if they find it and then the line of the Dawn Tree will be ended. For without the Dusk Tree, I cannot obtain another seed. Surely the disturbance approaching was the work of Hyalenee of Air. If the Elementals have united, then Marseanu of Water cannot be far behind." She pulled the reins of her bay mare from Dermanassian's fist and, tears streaking her face, she mounted the skittish little horse. "We must go."

Dermanassian knew they would not survive the onslaught of one enraged Elemental, much less the combined might of the Four Sisters, if indeed the quartet of Elementals were leagued against the seed. He jumped upon his own steed in agreement.

The horses needed no encouragement to leap into a full gallop; their riders simply gave them rein and the mares took the iron bits between their teeth and sprinted through the grassland. Above, the white dragonet streaked through the sky, its long tail lashing.

Above their abandoned blanket, a patch of air shimmered. Desmarais appeared, his blue monk's robes flapping around him. He stared hard at the fleeing horses. A twitch of impatience flashed across his face before his countenance returned to its typical, mask-like rigidity.

The dragonet dared a glance over its shoulder; Desmarais was already gone.

The air grew cold, for they had reached parts of Mera barely touched by the warm fingers of spring. Less heat during the day aided their flight, allowing the sturdy horses to travel longer. At night, Dermanassian huddled in his gray cloak, although Pae was unbothered. He dared not risk a fire, despite her assurances that the Fire Elemental would not be capable of using it to discover the seed. He longed for the blanket left behind.

On the twelfth morning he woke in a domed shelter conjured from the soil by Pae. Tendrils of plant life had curled from the sleeping earth at Pae's gentle coaxing and weaved themselves into a crude structure that reminded Dermanassian of an acorn turned upside-down. He crawled outside to stretch and rub the soreness from his limbs, and found the horses shaking off a thin layer of frost and stomping their hooves in the hard-packed ground. Even the rising sun seemed unable to inject its array of colors into the uninviting gray.

They rode for hours in a snowy twilight that drained Dermanassian's strength and spirit. Pae ceased attempts to engage him in conversation. The only sounds were the crunching of ground beneath plodding hooves and the heaving of tired flanks.

His face, like hers, was thin and pale with fatigue; the heads of their mares hung low. Days ago, the white dragonet had disappeared into the relative comfort of Dermanassian's pack. Even Pae was unable to get the creature to leave it except for the most pressing necessities, which it did with a great show of bitterness. Though mere weeks had passed since leaving Bhetheri i'Bhet's compound, they felt they had roamed the whole face of the world waiting for the seed to alert its caretaker, all the while subjected to cutting wind, land tremors, rain, and flashes of lightning.

"How is it that the Elementals keep passing us? Will they not find us?" he suddenly asked, slowing his exhausted mare to a walk. "We breathe in the air, our bodies are made of water, our feet touch the earth."

Pae considered, for the questions plagued her as well. She offered the only explanation she had. "They are not looking for us. They are looking for the seed. As long as it is not exposed, neither are we." She shook her head, and long black hair shifted loose from her crown of blossoms. "Their search spirals out from the

Dawn Tree. Hyalenee would have felt the seed touch the air when I removed it from the tree, if she had been watching. Certainly they knew I had left the Dawn Tree. But since then, the seed has been hidden and protected. The Four Sisters can only circle out from the merchant's courtyard and search for the seed as a pack of hounds casts for the scent of its prey."

Dermanassian was not comforted.

They had few options. Pae felt strongly that she could do nothing other than keep the seed hidden and wander until it told her where to plant it. Dermanassian's skills included rudimentary dreamcreeping, and he would have liked to use the refuge of the dreamworld for transporting the seed there. Surely, he reasoned, it would be safe hidden in that gray monoscape. But hiding it in the dreamworld was not feasible, for Pae and the seed were inextricably tied to this world and could not be removed from it no matter how many times Dermanassian tried.

"Can you not simply plant the seed and be done with it?" he asked yet again. "The Elementals will have little reason to harm you or the Dawn Tree once the seed is planted. The new epoch may see their power increased or unchanged, both of which will satisfy them. And should the new epoch see them diminished, then they will not wish to harm the Dawn Tree and remain in that age forever. Likely, the opposite would be true: they would wish it to change as soon as possible and do anything they could to nurture the production of another seed."

Pae shook her head insistently, having gone through this logic with Dermanassian several times. "The place where the seed is planted influences the epoch that arises. I must find the proper location. The seed will let me know when I have found it."

Yet the seed gave her no indication other than the general direction north, seeming content to lie within the protective folds of its caretaker's multi-colored gown. It was not filled with the concerns harassing Dermanassian and Pae: that they would be discovered and crushed or that Desmarais's simple request had turned into a harried chase which might well end with its defenders torn asunder by the Four Sisters.

"I do not know how much longer we can wait, Pae."

"Nevertheless," she murmured. "I will wait for the seed's command."

"We cannot run for eternity. In a few more days, our mares will collapse beneath us and our only sustenance will be melted snow, if we even dare a campfire to melt it. We – and the seed – will be stranded in this frozen nowhere."

He reached out, feeling the first drops of frigid rain. The skies to the west were quickly churning into a fast-moving storm. He looked hopelessly about the unbroken tundra. "We will need to find shelter. If we are wet through—"

"Yes," she agreed mechanically. "The water will eventually soak my robe or the wind will work a path through the fabric. Either might touch the seed and bring our doom."

Yet the steppe offered no shelter that might withstand the fury of the approaching storm. Not a tree or hill dotted the wasteland.

Sheet lightening flashed.

Dermanassian brushed a bit of wet hair from his eyes as the rain fell more and more heavily. His skin stung, for the air had become so cold that the rain felt like ice biting into his flesh. His gray cloak offered little protection, flapping about his frame like a flag being wrenched from its pole. He was drenched to the marrow of his bones.

Pae's robe was soaked also, its many colors darkened into a kaleidoscope of browns. Her green eyes were worried; they both knew the moment they most feared was at hand.

The rainwater touched the hidden seed.

The dragonet chirped a warning.

Shrieks filled the distant air. A tornado came as if from nowhere. Gut-shivering howls sent the little mountain horses twisting, their spirits renewed by dread. Their shaggy tails whipped about them and their hooves slipped on the tundra as the crust of snow mixed with the rain into slush.

Dermanassian and Pae exchanged a brief look. They could not outrun this storm. Their mares were nearly spent. The horses twitched with exhaustion and terror, but they had little left to give. Their desperate whinnies were nearly lost in the approach of disembodied screeching. The air churned, driven by the Four Sisters.

"The Chaner-jobi," Pae said, her voice flat with fatalism and her long-fingered hands tightening on the reins until her knuckles paled.

"You know what circles towards us," he said, his voice carrying more accusation than he intended as he fought for control over his mare.

"Yes," she admitted. "And it seems this time we will not evade them."

The dark, roiling mass grew stronger as it bore down. It would be upon them soon; the clouds boiled and the thin, frozen topsoil was ripped into swirling dust. The piercing cries were hungry and Dermanassian's keen eyes began to make out whirling, ghostly shapes within the maelstrom. They were uncountable.

"There was a time when they stayed upon the mist-covered mountains of Donabi-jar, guarding the shifting cloud palace of the Air Elemental from fortune-seekers and worse," Pae continued, barely heard above the screams. "And now, they have found the seed."

"And now they will kill us."

She turned her great green eyes upon him sadly. "Turn back to Ulum-ka, my dear. They may spare you, for their mission is the destruction of the seed. But they will kill me, for I will defend the seed unto my death."

"Then they will kill me as well," he pledged, "for I can defend you with no less vigor." He yanked the blue lotus sword from its sheath and turned his terrified mare into the wind. "Let us hope, my lady, that the Chaner-jobi can be slain." He knew they would be dead in moments regardless, for the army of Chaner-jobi would overwhelm the pair almost instantly. They would be helpless before the number of tornado-borne specters.

The rain and bluster intensified, tearing his black hair from its cording so that it bit into his frozen face. He winced from the desolate yowls of the Chaner-jobi. But he squinted and clamped his legs tightly about the rugged mare as she struggled against him. He held his sword ready, its faint blue glow muted against the dark rain clouds, and wondered whether the sword would have any effect on the hounds of Hyalenee.

Suddenly the full power of the storm hit them.

Dermanassian's long fingers flailed about the black pommel of the blade as his mare reared and he nearly lost his seat. But he forced himself back into the saddle, yelling and whirling his sword above his head as the first of the Chaner-jobi streaked down upon him.

He had no time to be horrified by the ragged claws upon its six-fingered, double-jointed hands. He did not flinch from the over-sized jaw gaping with a lolling tongue and needle-like teeth, or from the huge, glassy eyes burning with single-minded hunger. Instead, he brought the sword down, cleaving the howling specter in half. It shivered for an instant as if in shock before melting into the swirling air around it.

Beside him, Pae also fought both her mount and the phantoms. She thrust out her palm as if to stop an apparition threatening her. Dozens of tiny barbs shot from her bare palm, peppering the phantom. Dermanassian gasped as the barbs passed through, seemingly without effect. But as he moved to aid her, wide holes opened in the ghost as the poison of the barbs ate into it. Thrashing in the air, it disintegrated, as did all those ghosts in the barbs' path.

Dermanassian returned his attention to his own foes. It was all he could to stay in the saddle. The wails of the Chaner-jobi seemed to eat into his mind and as he fought for his life, he fought for his sanity as well.

Near crazed, he swung the sword about him and where his blue blade slashed, the forms of the Chaner-jobi dissolved into the wild storm. But for each of the groaning specters that was dispelled, more howled into existence.

Dimly, he saw Pae's mare collapsing in a jumble of hooves and squeals. The flesh of the horse's throat flapped loose, gushing steamy blood into the tundra. Covered in muddy slush, Pae dragged herself clear. Bloodied skin peeked through the tears in her robe where claws had raked her stomach. On her knees, her green eyes flashed and she flung a hail of barbs at the specters.

A single thought stabbed through the chaos in Dermanassian's brain. *In moments, we will be dead unless—*

"Plant the seed, Pae," he yelled, hoarse from exertion.

She shook her head at his heresy, struggling to regain her footing while the whirlwind concentrated above her. Dermanassian kicked his mare to her side, thinking to shield her. But the small horse's body provided scant protection from the swarming apparitions.

Beneath Dermanassian and Pae, the ground softened. The change was near imperceptible at first. Yet as they slashed desperately at the innumerable phantoms, the slush of the tundra grew deeper and deeper. Dermanassian realized this was more than just the rain turning the ground to sludge; the Earth Elemental was transforming the frozen tundra into quicksand that sucked at foot and hoof alike and threatened to immobilize them.

Dermanassian's mare stumbled, her hooves sunk to the fetlocks. He wrapped his fingers hand into her coarse mane to keep from falling over her neck. Her eyes rolled with fear and foamed dripped from her chest and flanks.

Worse, the ground now heaved and rumbled.

Before them, tundra split, opening a black gash in the earth. From it, a band of stony golems slowly emerged. Even stooped over with the weight of their huge, dragging arms, they stood two stories tall. Their mouths were grinding, toothless slits and their eyes glittered like sapphires. A score of the Earth Elemental's fabled warriors prepared to join the battle. They lumbered stiffly forward, each footfall shaking the ground.

As Dermanassian's mind struggled to grasp what he saw, the rain itself transformed into yet another threat. The drops thickened, congealing into a dozen of the hunched, tentacled forms of the Water Elemental's elite guard. Fed by the stinging rain, the hunched giants grew in size and mass until they dwarfed even the stone golems. Their tentacles writhed and shuddered as the monstrosities came to life.

"Choose, Pae," Dermanassian screamed. "Plant the seed! Or we – and the line of the Dawn Tree – die now!"

Pae chose.

She scraped at the cold muck, her elegant fingers bent into frantic claws, her hair a wild, black halo. Falling to her knees, she tore the last seed of the Dawn Tree from her torn robe and slammed it into the muddy shallow.

The liquefying earth suddenly bubbled beneath her. She flattened her palms over it, pressing down all her weight atop the seed to prevent the gurgling mud from spewing it into the storm. Her arms sank nearly to her elbows, her dress splattered with mud and heavy with rain.

In an instant, the reddish seed sprouted and rooted. The combatants recoiled and fell silent.

The polished bark of the new Dawn Tree erupted from the flat, unassuming seed. Its trunk thickened and widened, and branches prickled from its wood. Already, it appeared gnarled with age. Curved, oval leaves unfurled and their serrated edges fluttered in the maelstrom as if tickled by an autumn breeze. Though the new tree stood but knee high, its presence was that of a colossus.

As if commanded by a distant general, the storm suddenly abated. With a single, jagged flash of lightening, it retreated. The tentacled forms fell apart, the water falling into the soaked tundra in a series of plops. The rock golems sighed and crawled back into the earth. The Chaner-jobi swarmed around them once, before streaking away in the direction from which they'd come.

In moments, they were alone.

Dermanassian's sword fell heavily into the turf, for his fingers no longer had the strength to grasp the hilt. He dismounted from his trembling horse to kneel beside Pae.

From his pack, still attached to the hooks of his saddle, a long white snout peeked out with flaring nostrils, then withdrew in a puff of smoke.

For long minutes, Dermanassian and Pae remained in silence, too tired to think of the cold and wet as they knelt in the hushed tundra. The marks of their flight into the north and their battle with the soldiers of the elements were clear. The sickly scrub grasses were scarred by foot and hoof. It was a sodden, black stain that would only disappear beneath the next snow.

Dermanassian's muscles twitched and cramped; he barely held onto consciousness.

"A good choice, I think," he finally whispered. His voice grated in his damaged ears and he winced.

"We will see." Her green eyes were troubled with doubt, uncertain of the consequences of her action.

"Surely it is better than the alternative. Your mission is to preserve the Dawn Tree. You fulfilled it."

He brushed the black hair from her angular face. Smiling thinly, she pulled his bronze hand to her mouth and kissed the braided ring on his finger. He would have gladly knelt in the icy mud for eternity to be beside her, but already the lovely form of the desert elf that Pae adopted began to shimmer. She would soon return to the tree and sleep until the fifth Dawn Tree bloomed. With a last kiss, she transformed. Once again, she was the tiny, luminescent figure with remarkable auburn hair.

Curled at the foot of the new Dawn Tree, she yawned. "Come back when the tree blooms," she said, her voice heavy with impending sleep. She closed her eyes and vanished into the tree.

Dermanassian clutched the plaited ring. He forced himself to his feet. Then he cast spherical wards around the new Dawn Tree in five disciplines of sorcery. It was all he could do for her. With the last of his energy, he stiffly mounted his little horse. Jerking the reins, he turned the mare away and sent her limping across the vast white emptiness, grateful to the fatigue numbing his mind from awareness he was alone again.

Unseen, Desmarais watched Dermanassian retreat, the little mare kicking bits of snow into the air as she trudged into the pink horizon. When the pair was no more than a dark smudge against the tundra, Desmarais fully materialized. The former monk gathered his faded blue robes about his legs and walked to the edge of the warded sphere, his sandals squishing in the slush as he approached the shimmering dome.

Thus far his plans had gone well, even if slower than he wished.

He had been plagued by concerns and forced into actions he would rather have avoided. But he worked too hard at engineering these events to stand aside and let them be undone by chance or incompetence. It was delicate work pushing the Elementals and Pae toward this confrontation. Too easily, his plans might have gone awry.

First, the Elementals so inexpertly searched for the seed he worried it would decide upon a new site and alert its caretaker to plant it before the Elementals found it. He was obliged to conjure the storm to soak the seed, ensuring it was discovered by the Chaner-jobi. Then, as the battle joined, he worried the Four Sisters would actually destroy the seed before it could be planted. Again he was compelled to intervene. He used Dermanassian to present Pae with her momentous choice and, almost too late, she made it.

In doing so, Pae influenced the fifth epoch much more than she feared. By planting the seed independently of its command, she unwittingly ushered in an age of autonomy – the very thing Desmarais worked this risky scheme to achieve. It was a crippling blow in his war against Fate. He would not squander it, not matter who or what must be sacrificed.

He raised his hand to break Dermanassian's wards. They flickered briefly before winking out of existence.

Pae appeared beside the tree, her figure tiny and translucent. "Desmarais," she greeted him, her words thick with sleep and distress. "The Dawn Tree is replanted, though not without trouble. The Elementals destroyed the Dusk Tree and nearly the seed. And I worry that I have made a terrible mistake." She paused, placing a tiny finger to the corner of her mouth as if deciding whether to continue. "I should tell you, that mistake may foul your would-be war. I planted the seed, Desmarais. I planted it without its command. Can you think of any greater crime?" Her green eyes glittered with tears. "Few are more learned than you in mysticism and metaphysics, Desmarais. Tell me, what repercussions might my blasphemy have?"

Desmarais did not answer. Pae would understand his decision, he told himself. He curled his hand into a bony fist.

The Dawn Tree contracted, stretched, and twisted. Its contortions shuddered through the universe, though there were few able to feel it.

"Des—," she gasped in surprise, her face reflecting the torture and betrayal of the Dawn Tree. Her agonized eyes flashed with the realization he was destroying the fifth and final Dawn Tree. "You would not dare—"

But Desmarais gritted his teeth in determination, tightening his fist. Then the Dawn Tree shuddered and Pae screamed as her minute body was sucked back into the convulsing tree. The Dawn Tree collapsed into itself as it was squeezed out of existence. A furious tremor ran through the body of the earth, radiating from the heart of the battlefield's black stain in the snow.

Desmarais's hands sweated and shook from the effort. He wiped his palms against his faded blue robe with distaste, brushing away guilt along with sweat. He did not – would not – think of himself as a murderer. He was a liberator taking a necessary step in a necessary war.

The Epoch of Freewill was here at last. Now it would stay.

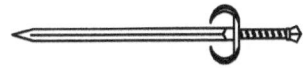

Good ol' tales of fun adventure do still exist – and here's one of them to prove it! Once again, betrayal rears its ugly mug, but this time . . . but I'm getting ahead of myself. There's always something to be observed about human nature in the tales of heroic deeds, and it is nice to make such observation with a smile now and again.

Allen B. Lloyd and William Clunie are a couple of old college buddies who write fantasy and horror stories over dinner and drinks. They have written one novel and twenty or so short stories in the years they've been collaborating. This story, the first in a projected series, was conceived over steamed dim sum at the House of Louie.

An Uneasy Truce in Ulam-Bator

A Tale of Gerhard and Ez-Arod

by Allen B. Lloyd & William Clunie

Soon after dawn Gerhard found an obelisk of bleached skulls. Bound by a flesh-colored substance hard as stone, it stood a good nine feet in the center of a shallow basin ringed by crumbling blood shale. *If you discover an edifice of bones*, his employer had warned, *the silth's lair will be nearby. No one knows why silth fashion the ghastly pillars. Boredom I suppose. Be vigilant.*

Gerhard unsheathed Cragmar, his longsword, and scanned his surroundings.

Dunes stretched endlessly, hissing in the stifling morning breeze. A nimbus of grit bit at his eyes, worked its way inside his tunic, scoured the skin beneath his heavy armor. This was thirsty work. It was too hot. There was no ale. And the fool's poultice, alleged to ward against silth enchantments, stank like a chamber pot.

"Close-fisted fop!" The young wizard's offer of two silver talins for a silth's head was not enough.

Gerhard scowled and fingered the amulet he had purchased in Ulam-Bator.

Fashioned in the likeness of the goddess Mynestra's single eye, it appeared to be nothing more than a thing of paste and tin when closely examined. But the amulet was purported to have great protective powers – purported, at any rate, by the ancient merchant who had sold it to him.

"Do not be fooled by its appearance. Everyone is wearing one," the merchant had wheezed. "What greater testimony to its efficacy can there be?"

Something laughed behind him. As Gerhard turned, gripping his sword tightly, a dark, sinuous shape slammed into him, knocking him against a dune. Stunned, the warrior shook his head and cursed. Cragmar lay before a serpentine beast, well out of his reach. The silth, coiling and writhing without pause, lifted Cragmar with a splayed tail and licked it.

The creature's face was beautiful, like masterwork jewelry: unblinking eyes of jade set in finely carved alabaster, crowned golden, sneering lips. The serpent's tongue flicked at the blade again. Gerhard stood and braced himself.

"Take," the creature said and flung Cragmar at the warrior's feet. "Fight," it hissed. "Die."

It lunged.

Gerhard rolled to his left, dodging the beast. He snatched Cragmar from the sand and swung it at the swaying thing. The blade slashed nothing but air. The snake behind him laughed.

"You're a quick bastard," Gerhard muttered, "and easily amused it seems." He spun to face it, swinging his sword. The silth's tail streaked forward, crashing against the arcing blade; green, viscous liquid splattered from a gashed coil, and the silth screeched. The giant serpent slithered backward, its head swaying. Gerhard stepped toward it, a slight mist of sand blowing against his leather boots. Hot perfume burned his lungs, soft trilling filled his ears. Gerhard froze. The wizard's poultice had failed spectacularly, as had the amulet. The silth's magical breath and song rooted him to the shifting dune.

Cragmar hung limply from locked fingers.

The silth circled and taunted, speaking in its strange, sibilant tongue. Gerhard cast a prayer to the gods who gambled with the lives of men and prepared to die. Then, as the creature rose from the sand, arching its great spine, fanged jaws stretching for the kill over Gerhard's head, a great desert sirocco engulfed the giant serpent in a cloud of sand and dust, and the beast sneezed.

The charm broke. Cragmar swung up and around in a mighty arc and the silth's head fell at the warrior's feet. Gerhard collapsed, breathing hard, but the sand beneath him boiled, discouraged lingering. He stood and retrieved the silth's lovely head, placing it in his burlap war bag and slinging both over his shoulder. Ulam-Bator was a day's march away. Best to be moving before the sun cooked the living and the dead.

"Aye," Gerhard muttered as he crested his first dune, "the wizard will compensate me for his flummery, and I will drink an ale to my victory."

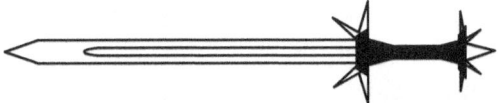

"The subject is closed," his mother said, her small eyes glaring in the folds of her powdered face. "I will hear no more of it." She turned then, slowly, her great weight shifting beneath her gown. The thud of her footsteps echoed down the stairway from the rooftop garden, growing fainter.

Her perfumed stench of jasmine and sweet wine remained behind, competing with the strong smell of oranges that wafted from the trees in the courtyard below. Ez-Arod Rashere clenched the marble banister tightly and stared out at the courtyard that rightfully belonged to him – soon, in fact, would, despite what his mother said. The sun lowered in the sky, melting slowly into the dark blue sea beyond the city's ports. *Your sun shall set as well, brother*, Ez-Arod thought, *and mine shall ascend.*

He cursed the politics of lineage, those archaic laws of Ulam-Bator, outdated edicts that granted all monies and estates upon the firstborn son, leaving the second born nothing but a nobleman's name and a sycophant's job. Older brother Jamal had, upon their father's recent death, inherited all the great estates of the Rashere family, while he, Ez-Arod, had nothing.

Listening to his mother's reasons why Jamal deserved all the inheritance – save for a small grove of stark fig trees – had prompted Ez-Arod to argue with her, to demand a greater portion of their vast riches. But contradicting Mother was pointless and unnecessary. If all went well, he would soon have everything.

Ez-Arod wandered to the other side of the garden and raised a brass telescope, searching the mountains to the east for a sign of his hireling's arrival. If the large, ill-tempered barbarian succeeded, Ez-Arod would soon possess the final component of the spell that would catapult him to prominence. The Spell of Immaculate Enthrallment, learned from a moldering tome, was purported to place its subject under the will of the caster. Once ensorcelled by the charm, his brother would seek religious enlightenment, suddenly embracing a life of cloistered celibacy and horsehair tunics, while resigning his wealth and lands to his beloved Ez-Arod.

Numerous figures milled about beyond the gates of Ulam-Bator, none of them resembling the hulking northerner. Ez-Arod hoped he had not erred in hiring the fair-haired lout. He had spent half a day combing the bars and brothels of the city's dank, dangerous port streets, looking for a fighter of sufficient stature to retrieve the head of the eldritch desert silth.

The brute had been holding court in a seedy inn, regaling brigands and harlots with tales of his mighty deeds.

Squinting through the smoky dimness of the Wasted Hyena, Ez-Arod had approached the barbarian, not only due to his braggartly tales, but to the impressive girth of his well-muscled frame. His light hair, bleached by sun and wind, bore testimony of an outdoor existence, and his rough clothing and scarred armor bespoke a life spent fighting for his wages. A deal had been struck; a few coins and a Poultice of Protection changed hands; instructions followed.

Now, two days later, Ez-Arod wondered if his coins had been spent in vain. He wondered if the poultice's potency had expired. He wondered if he would ever see the barbarian again.

And he wondered why his manservant was clearing his throat behind him.

"Sir, a gentleman of dubious character is waiting at the gates."

Ez-Arod turned. "A foreigner?"

"Yes, sir."

"Rather large?"

"Yes."

"Let him in. Show him to my study."

A stinking cloud assailed Gerhard as he entered the room. His eyes stung from the layer of churning yellow haze. The young wizard stood over a smoking cauldron, his back to the barbarian. The minion who ushered him in coughed politely. "Sir. Your guest."

Ez-Arod raised his hand and gestured ambiguously. "Enter, northerner. Try not to break anything."

The minion left. Gerhard stood in the center of the room. He waited for a moment, letting his gaze wander. Ez-Arod's study was filled with the accouterments of the spell caster: vials, jars, mixing bowls; thick tomes, brittle scrolls, fading parchments. On a delicately inlaid table near the cauldron sat a glinting amulet, an Eye of Mynestra. Gerhard's fingers strayed to the worthless Eye that hung about his neck. The light in the room highlighted the obviously superior value of the other.

He tired of waiting and dropped the bag containing the silth's head to the floor. It hit with a moist thud.

"The deed is done, young mage. I am here to collect my due."

Ez-Arod turned, a frown upon his delicate features. "Your due? Oh, yes. Your fee." He reached into a small velvet purse at his waist and removed a pair of coins.

"As per our agreement," he said, rubbing the silver talins between his fingers. Gerhard did not reach for the coins.

"Two silver talins would not cover my payment into the afterworld, Rashere."

"Your point being?"

"I was almost killed fighting that beast."

"How unfortunate."

"Your poultice was worthless."

"Ah, well. You apparently managed." The sorcerer bent to pick up the bag containing the desert creature's head. Gerhard pinned the bag to the floor with a booted heel.

"I need greater compensation," he said. "At least ten more talins."

Ez-Arod straightened and flicked nervously at the front of his silken robe. "Don't be ridiculous. We agreed upon this amount, and it shall be no more or less." He tossed the pair of coins to Gerhard's feet and turned, harrumphing loudly. Gerhard suppressed the urge to unsheathe Cragmar; lopping off this nobleman's head would result in the loss of his own. *Soft cur*, he thought. He glanced at the valuable amulet on the work stand. With swift, well-practiced fingers he snatched it up and replaced it with the gimcrack from around his neck.

"You are a canny businessman, Rashere." Gerhard stooped and picked up the coins. "I will take my pay and leave."

"Do that," the sorcerer muttered.

The Eye of Mynestra sank quickly to the bottom of the cauldron, followed by the head of the silth. Ez-Arod stirred the thickening brew with a copper ladle and intoned the enthrallment spell he had spent days studying. The brew sputtered and sparked; the smoke above it congealed into the shape of a miniature desert silth that seductively swayed and danced; then it dissipated with a hiss. A heady feeling of empowerment engulfed the sorcerer: the spell was complete.

Ez-Arod chortled and raised his hands imperiously:

"Brother Jamal – come to me!"

Time passed. Jamal did not appear. Ez-Arod knew his brother was in the house; he had spoken to him just that morning, learning his itinerary for the day. Surely, the spell had worked. "Jamal, hie thee hence!"

Ez-Arod sat and leafed through a magical tome, impatient for his brother's appearance. Had he made an error? Impossible. The broth's base had been proportionately correct. The catalyst – the desert silth's enchanted head – had been added as prescribed. The most important ingredient – a possession of the one to be enthralled, Jamal's *Eye of Mynestra* – had completed the enchanted soup.

Still Jamal did not appear.

Perhaps the power the spell granted him was limited by distance. That must surely be the answer. The ancient masters were ambiguous on many points.

Closing the tome and slapping it decisively down on the table next to him, Ez-Arod stood, straightened his robes, and walked briskly from the room.

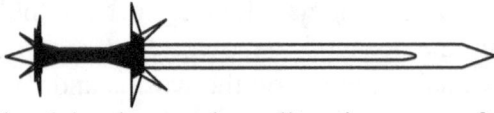

Jamal reclined in the garden, directing one of his many mechanical servants, a brass-and-iron gardener pruning a hedge. Jamal twirled his well-oiled mustachios and said, "Clip at a vertical slant, lack wit. Not horizontally!"

He turned to a trio of sycophants who hovered about him. "I do enjoy gardening, but good help is so hard to design." The henchmen chuckled uniformly.

Ez-Arod approached and commanded, "Pour me some tea, brother." He waved his hands in what he hoped was a mesmerizing fashion.

Jamal laughed and waved his hands in return. "Pour your own tea, brother."

Was the spell still not working? "I would speak with you alone, Jamal. Have your flatterers leave us."

"You are rather imperious in your tone, Ez-Arod. What you have to say can be heard by my companions."

"Never mind," Ez-Arod said in a huff and left the garden. He overheard Jamal's laconic chuckle. "Ta-ta, fair brother." The sycophants giggled.

The spell should have worked. He had done everything correctly. But something was wrong. As Ez-Arod stormed into his study, he reflected that now was the time to speak with his familiar.

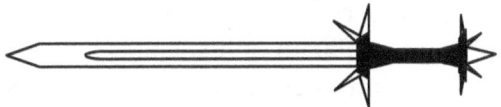

He had purchased the djinn from a traveling purveyor of Arcanum and had received quite a good deal.

"A djinn for the novice, really," the golden-skinned easterner told him. "Excellent for beginners, and seasoned practitioners in a pinch. It doesn't do much, but what it does do, it does quite well. Excellent at solving conundrums and puzzles of the more fantastical sort."

Ez-Arod certainly had a conundrum on his hands. He fetched a stoppered crystal bottle and uncorked it with a pop. Greasy smoke rose from the bottle, coalescing into a greenish homunculus.

"Yes, Master?"

"I require your assistance," Ez-Arod said, "concerning a spell I have recently attempted." He explained the events, omitting nothing.

The djinn stroked its tiny chin, then floated toward Ez-Arod's cauldron. He sniffed it once. "Ah. Yes. I see."

"Well?"

"The spell worked perfectly. It is not, however, affecting your brother."

"Then it is surely not working perfectly."

"Ah, but it is. You have enthralled another. Your hireling."

"My hireling?"

"The northerner."

"Gerhard."

"Yes."

"Damn," Ez-Arod muttered. "How?"

"There are many forms of sleight-of-hand," said the djinn, and vanished.

Candlelight flickered from a dozen tables in the smoky confines of the Wasted Hyena, sporadically illuminating the denizens of the shabby inn. A table of drunken harvesters, sooty and maudlin, sang wistfully of their mines to the west; a slender, one-eyed Aldoni warrior played mumblety-peg with a vicious stiletto, swearing softly all the while; the tavern's mascot hound rooted at the floor like a pig. In the center of it all sat Gerhard, a brace of wenches on his lap and a flagon in his hand.

"Give us a kiss!" implored one of the maidens, and Gerhard complied.

"What about me?" chimed the other.

"Of course, lass," Gerhard said, kissing her as well. Leaning back in his seat, he reached out, stroked the silky maid's cheek, and produced a silver talin, which he dropped into her bodice.

The maiden squealed with delight.

Ah, there was nothing finer than a purse full of coins and a fine town to spend them in; the gods' dice were good to him this day. Gerhard had received a fair amount from the amulet he had pilfered from the mage-child Ez-Arod Rashere, enough money to last a frugal man several months. Or enough to last a lusty northerner a week.

One of the maidens began to do something rather interesting with her tongue when the door to the tavern burst open, admitting a stream of magical light. All eyes turned to survey the grandiose entrance. As the brilliance abated, in its midst appeared the youthful mage himself.

"Northerner," Rashere called, "I would have words with you."

"Sorry, busy at the moment."

"Outside, I command you!"

"Hah! You dare command me?" Gerhard pushed the pair of damsels from his lap and stood. "I cannot be made to jape and prance like one of your play-things!"

"Oh, really," said Rashere. He pointed to Gerhard's flagon. "Pour that drink upon the floor."

"What? This is fine Illyrian mead!" But he obeyed the command – he could not fathom why – quickly pouring out the sweet, expensive brew as he walked toward the door.

"Who do you think you are?" he shouted, then realized he was outside the inn.

"Evidently, your master," smirked Rashere.

Gerhard reached for Cragmar; the sorcerer raised a hand and said, "Do not pull that sword." Gerhard's hand froze over the hilt. He cleared his throat.

"What enchantment is this?"

"One that was meant for my brother, but, because of your larcenous ways, has ensnared you, instead."

"Free me now, or I will—"

"You will what?"

Gerhard raised a clenched fist, but found he could not strike the young mage.

"Barbarian," Rashere said, "show that husky traveler your fist."

Reeling toward them was a drunken Rathdal, a huge, misshapen representative of that race born in the unseemly breeding chambers of the Hanth wizards.

Gerhard generally avoided offending such daunting creatures. His fist, however, had no such compunction. It slammed upward against the Rathdal's craggy chin.

The Rathdal stumbled back half a step. "What you do that for?"

"I really could not say," Gerhard muttered. Stepping forward, the Rathdal slowly pulled his arm back.

"Stand your ground, warrior!" Rashere commanded. "Let your playmate strike you!"

As the gargantuan fist approached him, Gerhard cursed his sudden immobility.

A second later, he was flying through the air, crashing backward against the wall of the Wasted Hyena. He reeled, but did not fall. The Rathdal pushed past him into the inn. "I thirsty now. I kill you later."

Gerhard worked his jaw with his hands. His neck cracked. His temples throbbed. When his vision cleared, he saw Ez-Arod Rashere sprawled out in the mire of the street, unconscious.

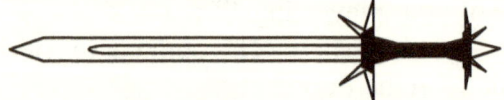

With trembling hands, Ez-Arod mixed the headache potion.

"What exactly is going on here, Rashere?"

"Please, warrior," the mage mumbled, "not now. Give me a few more moments."

Ez-Arod drank the vile brew, and instantly the pain in his head subsided. His jaw, however, continued to throb. He rubbed the side of his face and grimaced at the barbarian. "We are more than bound to one another, northerner."

"What do you mean by that?"

"Apparently, the spell contained features I did not anticipate. Although you must follow my commands, whatever pains you suffer, I will also suffer."

"Oh, really."

"Quite. Very inconvenient."

Abruptly, the warrior pulled his dagger from his belt and pricked his forefinger.

"Ow! Damn! What are you doing, Gerhard?"

"Testing."

"Stop!"

"One more thing," the barbarian said. He reached out and slapped Ez-Arod across the face, jumping with surprise as soon as the blow landed.

"That hurt," Gerhard laughed.

"Idiot! I command you to sit down. Do not speak until I say otherwise!"

Gerhard sat in a chair across from Ez-Arod and said nothing.

"Much better. Now, what we must do is find a way to dispel this mishap."

Ez-Arod reached for the djinn bottle and opened it. The creature popped out and sat cross-legged in mid-air. "Yes?"

"I have a problem that requires your assistance."

It sniffed at Ez-Arod. "The enchantment. Ah. My. You do have a problem."

"How does one revoke it?"

"Oh, the counter-spell is quite simple, I understand."

"Really?"

"Certainly."

"What is the counter-spell?"

"That I do not know. But I do know precisely where it is located."

Ez-Arod smiled for the first time in hours. "Excellent. Do tell where."

"To the east. Several hundred leagues."

Ez-Arod felt his smile slough away. "That is quite a ways."

"Well, distance is relative. Regardless, it is located in the Temple of Ordo in the wizard's city of Cath-Car."

The warrior cleared his throat and gestured at his mouth.

"Yes?" Ez-Arod sighed. "Oh, feel free to speak."

"I know of this Cath-Car," Gerhard said. "I have been there, long ago in my youth. It is very difficult to reach, and most dangerous once there."

"Wonderful," Ez-Arod muttered.

"I might add," the djinn said, "that the far-flung city is only safely accessible in the company of a heavily armed caravan. Quite difficult to find one this time of year, unless you had the fiscal wherewithal to hire your own. Which can be most expensive."

"How expensive?" Ez-Arod asked.

"Very," said the imp.

Ez-Arod threw his hands up in disgust. "I don't have any money! Certainly not enough to pay for a caravan."

"If I may make a suggestion, sir," said the djinn. "There is quite a bit of money right under this roof."

"What?" Ez-Arod said.

"You could always rob your mother."

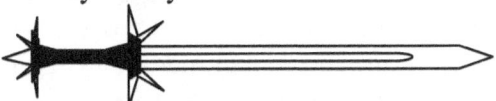

Sundry traps and devices designed to bar the common thief safeguarded the path to the subterranean treasure room. Gerhard had already disabled a dozen miniature ballistae and avoided their poisoned darts. Now he faced the massive stone door to the treasure room itself, which, according to the hastily scrawled map Ez-Arod gave him, could be opened only by correctly pressing a series of runes in the proper sequence. One mistake and the floor would drop away beneath him.

"I'm not sure what is down there," Ez-Arod had said, "but I think its spears and vipers. Or is it spears and tigers? Anyway, once inside the room, the jewels are for the taking."

By the light of his flickering torch Gerhard carefully studied the instructions, then pressed first one rune-stone then another, following Ez-Arod's sequence. A series of clicks preceded the sound of a bar sliding free. Gerhard pushed open the heavy door and slipped inside.

His jaw slackened. The blaze from his torch rebounded through a cavernous treasure room. It was a thief's paradise. Every gem imaginable – and many more he had never imagined – sparkled in the light of his torch, gold coins spilled from chests forged of ivory and silver, and jewels enough to finance a small kingdom lay in great heaps on the marble floor, beckoning to him.

Gerhard stepped forward, not knowing quite where to begin. He grinned. The most impressive spoil of them all stood on the far side of the vast room, a gigantic warrior clutching two magnificent, gem-encrusted scimitars as long as war-spears. It appeared to be made of gold, and Gerhard wished for a band of thieves that he might haul off this huge trophy. *Perhaps another time*, he thought, and bent to practical matters.

Thrusting his hands into a great heap of gold coins, Gerhard began to fill his sack, stuffing handfuls of wealth within. Enough loot to frequent taverns and brothels for the rest of his days. Enough, he amended, to *own* as many taverns and brothels as he might wish.

"By all the world's gods," he laughed, "this is a fine day indeed."

A grinding din and an ominous hiss froze his hand mid-grab. The door to the treasure room slammed shut behind him. On the other side of the chamber the golden warrior's head turned, glaring at him with fiery crystalline eyes. Steam wheezed from vents inlayed along its massive frame. Its scimitars began to swing back and forth. It took a ponderous stride.

And then another.

Gerhard dropped the torch and scuttled backward, drawing Cragmar. He crouched, studying the glittering giant as it moved toward him, marveling at how a thing of metal could move with such grace. Gerhard pulled one of his throwing daggers and cast it at the construct's ominous face.

The blade struck and clattered worthlessly to the floor. The thing moved inexorably forward, more quickly now, heedless of the treasure in its path, kicking it aside or crushing it beneath its incredible weight. Gerhard continued his retreat, grabbing at everything he could find and hurling it at the treasure room guard. *Idiot wizard*, he thought, *how could you not know of this monstrosity?*

Glittering blades arced toward his head. He felt the cold wall behind him.

He ducked. Steel cracked lightning-loud against stone. Tumbling forward, Gerhard slipped around the giant and slashed Cragmar against a metal leg.

The blade rebounded. The monster began to pivot. Gerhard retreated, searching for a chink in this relentless tower of armor. He spied the hissing cylinder covered with hoses and valves riding high on its back. Gerhard thrust upward. Sparks flew as Cragmar skipped across the mechanical dervish. The thing turned. Gerhard skittered sideways trying to stay behind it. The blur of the guard's blades careened like twin comets through the treasure room. One struck a pillar and marble dust exploded.

Gerhard swung his sword, a wide loping arc aimed at one of the hoses snaking from the cylinder and missed. "Metal bastard!" he cursed, and threw himself at its back, clambering up it. The hot, oily body bucked beneath him and an elbow flashed back, slamming against Gerhard's chest, hurling him to the floor. The giant clanked toward him. Gerhard scuttled back against a sea of coins and gems and pulled himself to his feet. As a sword swung at him yet again, he attempted a parry – foolishly, for the strength of the guard was far too great, and Cragmar was knocked from his grip.

Red rage engulfed Gerhard, a mighty berserker onslaught. He shouted such curses as might come from the lips of a warrior god and threw himself forward, dodging blades, tumbling and rolling, coming to his feet behind the thing, a throwing dagger in his hand. He threw quickly, aiming without thought. One of the hoses exploded, writhing and spewing steam and oil.

Still the thing's arms flailed, and still its blades spun, but slower now, no longer whirlwinds. It turned.

Lurching, Gerhard sidled quickly to stay behind the clanking, wheezing device. Its arms lowered, and after several long moments it grew still.

"I weary of you," Gerhard muttered, and thrust a foot against its backside.

The thing wavered, then fell, crashing loudly into the mounds of treasure.

Gerhard spied his sword and stumbled toward it. Retrieving it, he sat on a chest and planted the blade like a stanchion in a mound of coins, his head resting heavily against its pommel. He closed his eyes.

From somewhere in the room came the sound of stone grinding against stone.

Gerhard jerked his head up, his eyes darting. One of the walls slid heavily aside, revealing an enormous, angry, and sumptuously dressed woman surrounded by archers, their bows drawn. A dozen arrows pointed at him.

Silence reigned in the treasure room. Gerhard cleared his throat at last and said, "Good evening. Am I graced with the presence of Madame Rashere?"

"I hate thieves," the woman responded, her voice booming. "Give me one good reason why I should not kill you immediately."

Gerhard smiled. "I think I can do that."

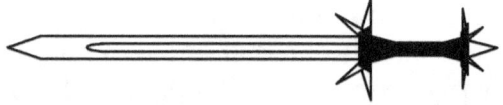

His mother and his brother sat on a dais above him, scowling. Ez-Arod lowered his head, ashamed to meet his mother's penetrating gaze. Next to him stood Gerhard, looking strangely unconcerned. Guards flanked them.

"I am most disappointed in you, childling," his mother said, shaking her head sternly, her several jowls shifting from side to side. "I thought your father and I raised you better. This petty attempt to make your brother your thrall was most unbecoming. I can only hope the other noble families of Ulam-Bator do not learn of this." She glared at the guards in the room, ensuring their silence. "You have greatly displeased your brother and me."

"Yes," said Jamal, "my prized automaton can never be replaced!"

Ez-Arod said nothing.

"And I must say," Jamal added, delicately enjoying a pinch of snuff, "this entire scheme of yours was quite common. A monastery? Really . . ."

"Do you have anything to say for yourself?" his mother asked.

"I felt I was treated inequitably after father's death. To receive nothing – it pained me, Mother, and interfered with my plans."

"You were treated according to the laws of primogeniture, child. You were granted a fig grove in the north, and a stipend which would allow you to live comfortably. You are too young to have plans."

Ez-Arod chewed his lip. "Yes, madam. Figs."

"And now you must be punished."

"As you wish, Mother."

The corpulent matriarch gestured to the barbarian at his side.

"Your creature has informed us of the end result of your magical bumbling. It is my understanding that the sundering of the ensorcellment can be found in the far-off city of Cath-Car. I decree that you shall be banished from this realm for no less than two years, during which time you may travel thence to seek your freedom from your own inept machinations." She paused and drank deeply from a goblet. "The only assistance I shall grant you will be the sparing of your lives. Now be off from this house which you have disgraced."

"Noble mother," Ez-Arod said, "may I be granted an hour to collect some of my personal possessions?"

"I grant you only your wits and the clothes upon your back," she responded.

"The barbarian may keep his sturdy sword, as I suspect you shall not live long without its assistance. Now begone."

Ez-Arod looked up at his mother for what might be the last time, then turned and walked slowly from the room.

"Ta-ta," came his brother's singsong farewell. "Be safe."

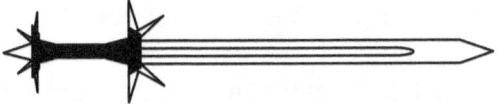

"I cannot believe she let you keep your sword," Ez-Arod said. "Me, her own son, she gives nothing."

"She gave us our lives, lad. A man has little more than that at any time."

"It seems unreasonable."

"You tried to rob her and depose your brother. She had a right to our heads."

They stood before the grand house that had been Ez-Arod's home. The young sorcerer slumped against its door, looking as though he might start pounding on it, begging for admittance.

"Come along now. We have a long journey to make."

"With nothing! No money, no food, no horses. No Arcanum! We are doomed . . . Why are you so cheerful?"

"Our circumstances are a bit difficult, I admit, but we are far from our graves. And," Gerhard added, "we are not without some resources."

Ez-Arod looked up at him. "What do you mean?"

"You of all people appreciate a bit of magic, don't you?" Gerhard reached with a flourish behind Ez-Arod's ear and plucked forth the crystal bottle containing the mage's djinn.

"How did you get that?" Ez-Arod said, snatching it from the barbarian's hands.

"Trade secret." Gerhard grinned. "But wait." He reached again behind the sorcerer's head, and produced a leather purse. He opened it and poured the contents into his hand: several large and lustrous gemstones. "From your mother's treasure room, lad. More than enough to outfit ourselves for a journey east."

"I'll take those," Ez-Arod commanded.

"Hold on, I stole these fair and square –"

"You forget, northerner, that you are in my thrall. My wish is your command."

"That is so," Gerhard glared, "but I assure you I will make a poor puppet. It seems to me that we would be best served by an equitable relationship. Slavery is impractical, particularly when the slave would sooner die than be abused." Gerhard extended a hand to Ez-Arod. "I offer you a bond stronger than magic, Rashere."

"I do not give my hand lightly, barbarian."

"Nor I," said Gerhard. "But we shall both be better served by comradeship than struggle."

Ez-Arod thought for a moment, then sighed. "Very well. We shall travel as companions."

Their hands met and shook, briefly but firmly.

"It will be a long and dangerous journey," Ez-Arod muttered.

"Aye."

"Do you think we will succeed?"

"Who can say, wizard," Gerhard said, slapping him on the back. "The gods play with us as men might play at dice. Anything can happen."

"That is small comfort."

"Then let us sell these gems and find ourselves a bit more comfort for the night. It is remarkable what a flagon of ale and a buxom tavern wench can do for a man's spirits."

Wrapping his arm around Ez-Arod's narrow shoulders, Gerhard led him away from his glittering home – the young man looking back once in sorrow – and into a bustling, muddy street where gods – and men – played with loaded dice.

Vengeance? Or Redemption. Which defines the spontaneous swearing of awful vows and the bloody fulfillment of them? Vows taken to avenge a man, an ideal . . . or to redeem a name, a future. Honor. Duty. Lust. All provide motivation enough; combined, they've driven most all of heroic fiction. It's what is sought that turns the tale. Does our protagonist seek to take or to buy back?

Steve Goble is a fan of Godzilla and of beer. Most of all, he is a staunch fan of Sword and Sorcery short fiction. This is the guy who gave us Calthus, after all. Though this anthology does not include a new Slaughter Lord of Thaal tale, it does contain this story of the origination of the Faceless Sons. These guys are intense. Their series of stories offers Steve and readers a three-way exploration of the concepts of duty, honor, heritage, societal expectations, and heroism. Visit http://stevegoble.com/blog to learn more.

The Mask Oath

A Tale of The Faceless Sons

by Steve Goble

One mask, white as bone,
another bloody red,
a third as black as midnight's own
– and seven demons dead.

—from *Song of the Faceless Sons*

Dried flesh and brittle bone crackled as the Faceless Son drove the demon's skull upon the blackened stake.

The man in the bloodstained white mask contemplated the impaled head. It stood in a row with three others, ghastly trophies mounted before the great fortress city.

The dead quartet stared at him as he hefted his massive warhammer to his shoulder. Scaly, petrified flesh clung stubbornly to the skulls, for not even crows would eat this foul meat.

From the walls of Brythane, soldiers and clerics and whores and laborers peered at him. Above them, from a balcony, his king and queen looked down with grave countenances. All of Brythane wished to see whenever one of the Faceless Sons returned. They watched in hushed awe; Gharan's sons had been the first to take the mask oath in centuries. The mask was a symbol of dedication, of a vow made kneeling before the gods. Those who wore the oath mask renounced much of what was enjoyable in life and declared themselves willing to die in pursuit of their quests. Such mighty oaths were seldom made in these days of peace and plenty, but the Faceless Sons belonged to an ancient and noble house where the old ways were kept. Or had been, once.

They would see those days revived.

This Son gave in to an urge to seek out one face in particular among the throng on the wall. Aloyssa. He saw her, pale beauty itself in her dark mourning gown. She would wear the black gown as long as he wore the mask . . . and perhaps longer.

She belonged with the nobility, yet stood with the rabble on Brythane's outer wall. She did not beckon him, nor did she call. He watched, and soon learned why. Her slim hand stretched out – then dropped a pale cloth that fluttered on the wind before suddenly finding a direction and heading straight toward him. His gaze followed the descent to the ground at his feet. When he again raised his eyes to the wall, Aloyssa had vanished within the silent crowd.

The Faceless Son knelt and picked up the fallen cloth. It was a clean, pale mask to replace the blood-smeared and claw-ripped one that now covered all but his eyes.

He yearned to follow her, to caress again the dark hair beneath her veil, but he would not enter Brythane this day. He would never enter the royal city until his mission was done, nor show his face to god or man. Nor woman. For despite the buzz of flies and the stench of death, three naked spikes yet awaited their grim trophies.

He rode south along the Miscalan foothills, as chill wind shoved mighty gray clouds overhead. In the distance, the towering heights brought to mind the Temple Fastness of Orn, where he'd taken the oath.

The demons had scattered far and wide within moments of slaying Gharan, the wizard who had summoned them. The monsters fled more out of fear of one another than of anything men might do. The Faceless Sons had spent years gathering their trophies and continued hunting the remainder. If tales were true, this Faceless Son now sought the demon said to haunt the towering Miscalan heights.

"Die, demon hunter!" The scream cut the chill air as an attacker charged from the heavy brush. The man's eyes were wide, and spittle dripped on his chin. His hair hung limp and dull upon a tattered shirt. The interloper's spear aimed at the horse's ribs.

The Faceless Son whirled his steed about. The spear missed its mark, but grazed the mount's flank. Long had the Faceless Son trained with his hammer, and even from horseback, he wielded it expertly. The great weapon swooshed through the air; ribs cracked like kindling and the man fell in silent shock.

The Faceless Son spun his horse in a tight circle, for he knew there could be more assailants. A second man, eyes as wild as the first attacker's, drew close. He was creeping forth, thinking to catch the Son from behind. The masked man dropped from the saddle and brandished the hammer.

He had seen such deranged men before. They worshipped the demon out of fear, and the demon used them to spread terror and chaos. The Son roared at the man, hoped his foe's addled mind could grasp the words. "Where is Durgord?"

His answer was a crazed laugh and a spear thrust. The Son's parry shattered the spear haft, and his riposte smashed the man's skull in a rain of gore.

The Son walked toward the first man, who writhed in agony and clutched his ribs. He knew there was no hope of purging the demon taint in this man; the eyes told him this one was beyond questioning. So he killed the wretch as quickly as he could. Then he scowled at the waste, and rode on.

No one had commanded the brothers to seek out the demons. Neither had King Wendik seen reason to send his armies to slay demons who ravaged lands beyond his own.

Gharan's sons had seen things differently.

The Faceless Son spurred his mount into a trot. He had been the one to suggest the oath, once his father's remains had been gathered and burned. He recalled now the pride that rose in him when his younger brothers, both with shocks of red hair like his that marked them as wizard's offspring, agreed without a moment's pause.

Together, they'd bathed in the River Orn to wash away the privileged lives they had lived. Together, they'd emerged naked and nameless. Together, they'd knelt before Orn and sworn to hunt down the seven terrors their father had foolishly unleashed.

"Your devotion will inspire men," the head priest had told them. "It will remind men of the glories that come only through Orn, only through deeds dedicated to Orn."

And so they had left, disciples of a kind of honor men had forgotten. Living embodiments of strength and purpose, wearing the masks so all Orn's people would know honor yet lived.

He wondered now how his brothers fared; he had not seen them in years. He knew they had met with success, for there were now four demon heads mounted before Brythane's gate and he had slain but two. But he had seen neither of his brothers since the day the three Faceless Sons rode forth from Brythane.

He gazed up at the moon, pale and featureless as his mask, and wished his brothers well.

"You are one of the wizard's sons," a voice behind him said.

He replaced the ladle in its crook at the well, and lowered his mask again. Once his face was hidden from sight, he turned toward the woman who had emerged from the huddle of villagers. Her simple clothing marked her as a peasant. Pale blue eyes that seemed to have never known sadness looked at him and her smile teased. Beautiful, a single finger twisting dark hair in a way he recognized. But she was not Aloyssa.

"I've heard the tales. You hunt demons," she said. "And you hide your face." Her eyes traveled quickly up and down his frame. "You certainly are built to do deeds."

"I do not speak of it," he said. Indeed, the rules of the mask oath forbade it.

She seemed to regard that as a challenge, and moved closer. Beyond, villagers whispered. Her presumptuous behavior would have earned her a slap from many a noble, and likely would earn her punishment later from these commoners. He had seen women behave so before. The mask, designed to inspire, also intrigued.

She spoke softly, with a musical lilt. "The demons slew your father, they say. Tell me, strange one, is revenge for your father's death worth giving up your own life . . . and pleasure?" Again, the flirtatious smile.

So like Aloyssa . . . It had been a long time...

He thrust the thought aside.

"They say living well is the best vengeance," she said. "Your quest will not bring your father back. What compels you to seek death so?"

He could not explain, but he could try to give her a sense of it. He breathed deeply, and her scent filled his mind. "Once a man named Tryddan Gost did a great deed," the Son said. "In a war long ago, against Surland invaders. The battle raged for many hours, and King Lor joined the fight, Tryddan beside him. The sides were nearly even and many died from both armies. Then the frenzy tilted in the enemy's favor. Tryddan saw a spear leveled at his king, saw a sword cut the standard bearer's throat – and Tryddan leapt. His gut took the spear that would have skewered the king and ended Brythane's hope, and, though sorely wounded, his hand caught the standard before it fell and raised it high. Though his lifeblood leaked onto the ground, they say Tryddan Gost's triumphant roar carried the length and breadth of that bloody field.

"The king's men rallied and held, and won the day. Tryddan's name has been hallowed ever since, and his descendants share in his honor."

The woman looked puzzled. "What does that have to do with your impossible quest?"

The Faceless Son almost whispered now. "Tryddan died slowly, and talked much before he was gone. He was no hero, he said. His father would have taken the spear, his grandfather would have done it, and so he had done it. He had done only what he must. He was a nobleman of Brythane, a servant of Orn."

"I still don't see what that has to do with you hunting down your father's demons."

"It has everything to do with it." He climbed into the saddle and rode away, swiftly.

The body was twisted, bloated, scarcely recognizable as something that once had lived.

The Faceless Son found it by its stench. It had been dead for days, hung on briars yards from the road. And the crows had been at it.

The Faceless Son had heard of an attack in the night, a wagon toppled, people slain. Broken timber, bones and bloodstained rock told the tale.

The survivors had retrieved their dead, short a single man. The demon had thrown this one, judging by its awkward position and distance from the battle scene. The corpse dangled, upside down, and blood had soaked the ground below it. Entrails mingled with briars, and crimson stained the leaves. Demons fed on fear and sowed its seeds with such grisly slayings.

The Faceless Son clasped his hands in prayer. Soon, he would find a stable for the horse, climb the mountains and avenge this man. For now, he gathered wood for a pyre.

He clung to the ledge and pulled himself up, tearing his knee as he did so. Another hole to let in the cold through his breeches, more blood to freeze on his skin.

The Miscalans towered above him, their heights lost in gray clouds that hurled sleet in savage gusts. The wind scraped him with icy grit that rimmed the eyeholes in his mask.

The mask no longer carried Aloyssa's perfumed scent, and for that he was both saddened and grateful. Her scent was a distraction, a reminder of what he'd given up – what he yet might lose forever. He needed all his heart and soul for the task at hand.

Still, thoughts of her came unbidden, until he quietly moved them aside.

The wind howled like the demon he sought: Durgord, most cunning of the seven.

The Faceless Son climbed. Bits of armor and his weapon hung in a leather sack strapped about him. The hammer's weight sought to tear him from the wall and hurl him to his death, but he needed the weapon. His father, once the realm's mightiest mage, had created it. Gharan had used the powerful head of that hammer to forge celebrated blades for kings and lords, and the hammer carried a trace of magic from every one of those forgings. Twice already, the hammer had crushed bones few other weapons could harm. When he found Durgord, it would do so again.

Chill wind clawed at him, and tired muscles protested. But whenever he thought he could endure no more, he had only to call the hated images into his mind. His father, torn asunder by the very demons he'd thought to use as pawns in his bid for Brythane's throne. The seven unleashed horrors. The vacant eyes of those whose loved ones the demons had consumed.

Aloyssa, garbed in black and tears.

The Faceless Son walked now, across a broad and naked bluff. Mountains rose to his left, and sun fire rose behind them. Ice and snow draped them in white. To his right, a steep drop led to lands hidden by the veil of gray clouds through which he'd climbed. He'd spent four days in these mountains, with nothing to eat but what he could uproot or kill.

A snap warned him.

Wild men rose behind concealing boulders, spears aimed at his chest – a dozen of them at least. The men wore untanned hides and carried crude weapons, and stared at the Faceless Son as though he were a phantasm.

He lowered the hammer, and held out a hand. "I bring no trouble," he said. "I am hunting."

If they understood, they did not show it. They barked words at one another, unintelligible grunts that left the Faceless Son bewildered. With waves of spear tips and nods of their shaggy heads, they indicated a direction. He took it, and they fell in behind him. Two retrieved a slain ram, trussed on a pole, and carried it on their shoulders. The chilled mist of their breath hovered about them.

The hike took several hours, during which his captors' nervous fears seemed to increase. They led him, finally, to a cliff face dotted with yawning caverns and lit by late-morning bonfires. Spitted rams cooked, their aroma jolting his snarling stomach. He pointed at the meat, and one of the shaggy spearmen tore a hunk off for him.

The Faceless Son lowered his head and lifted the mask only far enough to allow him to eat. Not even savages such as these would look upon his face until he had seen his quest done.

A woman, as hairy as the men, came forth. He could see the shaggy captors held her in reverence. Pustules poked out among the hairs that dotted her face, and she hunched forward on spindly legs. Her eyes, one gone milk-pale, stared at him. She uttered words he supposed to be questions, and he shook his head. Then, kneeling, he plucked a burning stick from the fire and scraped a crude drawing onto the dead rock. A dragon face, framed by long horns curling downward. Narrow eyes. Forked tongue.

Durgord.

He saw recognition in the woman's eye, detected madness in the commands she spat. All around him, spears leveled once again.

He took up his hammer and stood, pointing first at his chest, then at his weapon. Then he dropped the maul's massive head squarely onto the demonic face he'd drawn. Great cracks snaked from the impact, sparks flew in sizzling streaks and the mountains rang with thunderous echoes.

Spearmen cried out and the woman gazed at him in horror. The sharp spear tips pointed at him with renewed menace and moved closer.

He'd hoped they'd seen the demon Durgord. He'd hoped they'd lead him to it. He'd supposed wrong.

The haft of his hammer was longer than that of a typical smith's instrument, for it had been made as both weapon and tool. Still, the spears were longer and his foes had the advantages of reach and numbers. They pressed him quickly, and confidence crowded fear from their eyes.

He thought to run, to avoid battle entirely, but gave up the notion. The spears, although crude, were lethal enough – and they could be thrown. Attempt escape, and many would lance his back.

So the Son sought to shock them into retreat. His hammer spun around him, shattering spear tips that exploded into sharp, lethal missiles. His attackers leapt backward, but did not relent. They hurled their spears, too many for him to dodge or block. The armor on his shoulders stopped some, as did the greaves on his thighs. Spears broke against his hammer, and many sailed over his head, but one ripped open his lower leg and another tore a red gash along his ribs.

He had no choice, for he would not fall now and leave his quest undone. He thought of his father, and of Aloyssa. He thought of his great ancestor, Tryddan Gost. These mountain men had chosen battle, and this Faceless Son would give it to them in full.

In the lands far below, people spoke of the Faceless Sons in hushed, reverent tones. But these mountain savages had never heard the young legends, else they'd never have attacked him. Those who swore a mask oath gave up much – human contact, the pleasures of life, even their place in the glory halls after death – to devote themselves to a single great purpose. A hard choice, but the oath-takers gained somewhat in return. There was power in the mask oath; prowess and fortitude granted by gods.

The Faceless Son showed them that power now.

The hammer whipped about, crushed skulls, broke ribs, shattered legs. Cries and howls of pain echoed in the mountains. Bodies bounced across the cliff face and toppled into the cook fires. Flames crackled and snapped as they consumed the corpses, the scent of burning flesh clogging the air. Blood rained on the naked rock.

Those who did not fall crippled or dead ran howling into their caves. The Faceless Son did not relent until there were none left before him but the hag. She stared at him with her milky eye as though he had emerged from the fiery depths of the damned.

He looked at the carnage around him and silently begged forgiveness from his gods. He had come to kill a demon, not foolish savages. It consoled him little they had left him no choice.

The Son stood before the hag silently and pointed at what was left of the demon sketch, now awash in blood. Crying out, she pointed beyond the obscuring smoke of a fire. He stepped aside and saw a deep fissure in the cliff. Odd runes, painted in dark smears that could only be blood, surrounded it. Above the runes, surrounded by a crimson circle, stared a familiar face. It was a crude, amateurish painting, similar to the one he'd drawn. The Faceless Son realized now why the mountain men had assaulted him.

They'd seen his demon, and made it their god.

He closed his eyes, and wondered how many the demon had killed here, how much it had fattened on the fear and worship of these mountain people. *How much bigger is Durgord now?* He clenched his jaws to choke back a curse.

The cleft seemed to open a path deep into the rock. He fashioned a torch from a chunk of wood and a dead man's garb. Then he lowered the warhammer onto his broad shoulder, ignored his stinging wounds and conjured again the memories, precious and hated.

The Faceless Son strode into the cleft.

Hammer poised before him and torch raised high, the Son crept slowly down the passage. The light he brought did little to fend off the dark. The visible world extended only a few feet from him; beyond that, all was darkness. The cleft had been narrow at the entrance, but now he could not be sure of its width. He knew only that the right-hand wall was within reach of his torchlight; the left-hand wall vanished in the dark beyond.

Acrid smoke from his makeshift torch stung his eyes and curled beneath the ceiling just a few feet above him – destroying any hope of detecting his enemy's scent. The floor was rock, strewn with grit, and his boots crunched noisily with each cautious step.

A shape ahead, a dark oblong, caught his eye. He approached cautiously and discovered a shaped stone set in the midst of the passage. Sinew cords dangled from it in many places, looping beneath smoothed edges. An altar, white at the base, dark above. He looked closer, saw how the darkness ran downward in streaks to a pool of dried blood.

Sacrifices. Durgord has feasted well, indeed. The beast has not even left bones. The Faceless Son wondered how much stronger the demon had become.

He went on, nonetheless.

There, in the dark, his memories returned. His father, mad drunk with unholy powers he'd thought to control. Frenzied with the idea he should rule by right of the powers he alone commanded – or thought he commanded until his summonings turned upon him. Gharan's sons had heard the mad howls and run to their father's aid. But they had been too late.

Had they known what he was attempting, the sons would have stopped Gharan. Only his demented scribblings, read after his death, revealed the wizard's aims. They'd had no warning but Gharan’s cries of agony.

They had watched the demons rend Gharan, tear and toss his limbs aside as a storm wind threw weak branches. The Faceless Son grit his teeth and closed his eyes tightly. He dug into his mind for another image, one of honor.

He pictured Aloyssa, tear-streaked face lifted high and brave smile beaming as he rode from the gate of Brythane for what might be the last time. Aloyssa understood honor, understood why he had taken the oath – for that more than anything else, he loved her.

Decorum demanded she wear mourning garb, for the oath had made him as lost to her as though he were dead. But there had been vibrant life in her words. Her voice rang now in his ears.

'Do what you must. It is what makes you the man you are. I will do what I must, and so will await your return.'

'And if I do not return?'

'You will,' she had said. 'For you have made the oath, and I know you will show yourself worthy. The gods will honor that. Have no doubt, my love.'

The Faceless Son returned to the present, smiled, and moved on into the dark.

Teeth and yellow eyes pounced at him from the blackness before his hammer thwarted the attack in a shower of blood. The thing that had leapt at him fell aside, but another came behind it. Its hot breath misted the warrior's mask. Fangs clamped onto his shoulder, denting armor, as a whip-tail wrapped around his leg and claws dug into his clothing and flesh. He could not bring the hammer to bear, for the creature's weight pinned his weapon arm against his torso.

Stumbling, the Faceless Son wielded the torch like a club, and the beast yowled in pain as flames sizzled on its scaly back. It dropped from him, and a backhanded blow from the warhammer sent teeth and scales hurtling to clatter against the stone wall.

A third beast hit his chest like a battering ram. The tail of the dead thing, still wrapped about the Son's leg, tripped him, and he fell back with the living, snarling enemy upon him. He lost the torch, and the hammer.

The jaws opened and teeth gleamed moistly around a tongue that licked at his mask. The tongue coiled around his throat, and it began to pull his head toward the dripping maw.

His fingers clamped on the beast's slender neck, and his nails dug into the rough hide. Claws tore at his belly and scraped against the armor on his thighs.

He thought of his father. He thought of Tryddan. He thought of Aloyssa.

The Faceless Son rolled, tumbling himself and the beast over the torch. A hiss and a yelp told him the monster had been burned, and he seized the moment to grasp his dagger. He gasped for air, a frightful sound that reverberated in the darkness. He plunged the blade into the thing's gut, and tore it open until the dagger ripped free from its throat. The serpent tongue writhed obscenely, and the cold monster grew colder still, and died.

Sweat and blood drenched him, and he had to dig deep within himself to find his way past the pain. He caught his breath, stood, and looked upon the corpses. Lizards they were, the size of hunting hounds but with outsized claws and teeth. He wondered if they were natural creatures, or things summoned from some netherworld by the demon he sought. No matter. If there were more, he would deal with them as well. He gathered his torch and hammer and proceeded slowly through the darkness.

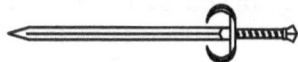

He could not see beyond the circle of light thrown by his torch, but air swirled slowly around him, told him he had entered a larger passage, perhaps a chamber. The tunnel had been cool, but now the air chilled him with a deeper cold and sharp crystals formed on the mask as his breath froze.

The Son had felt such cold before once – the night of his father's death.

Durgord stepped out of shadows cast by the torchlight: towering, leering, licking the lips of its obscene black snout. Eyes of pure malice reflected torchlight and turned it blue. Wet teeth glistened with venom, and claws tapped a bizarre, quiet rhythm on the great horns that hung from its head.

"Wizard's son," Durgord said softly. The voice echoed in the cavern and seemed to come from everywhere, its quiet tone at odds with the fiend's horrid visage.

"Aye," the Faceless Son said. He brandished the warhammer. "And a wizard's weapon."

Durgord's eyes narrowed. "The hammer will not avail you," it said. "It has brought you this far, but it will carry you no further."

The Faceless Son felt his legs become icy stalagmites and realized he could no longer move. He closed his eyes to better conjure the memories that spurred him. He remembered the day of the mask oath, sought the fire that had driven him and his brothers to that decision – and willed himself to step forward.

The demon ended the odd, soft tapping on its horns. Its eyes widened with surprise, and it clawed at a gold medallion suspended about its serpentine neck. Tiny black runes encircled the shining disk, and dark stars were embossed upon it.

The demon growled. "You are mighty, it seems, but you would do well to turn around and go home, wizard's son. Gharan your father thought he could control us, and he was wrong. You think you can destroy me, yet you know even less than your fool father did."

The Faceless Son kept approaching, staring at the demon's amulet.

"Do you recognize it, masked man? I took it from your father when I ripped his ugly head from his shoulders." Durgord hissed and licked its teeth. "A protection he made for himself, to guard against the enemies his power games would create. Its magic turns vengeance back upon the avenger."

The demon shivered with the delight of victory.

"I smell the magic in your weapon. Come, strike me with your mighty hammer, wizard's son! It will be your own bones that break, thanks to your father's trinket!"

Durgord stepped forward slowly on mighty legs. One hand tapped the amulet, the other aimed claws at the Faceless Son. The snakelike tongue danced in wet circles.

The Faceless Son stood dauntless before the nightmare that menaced him. He knew the demon could not see the masked smile that played upon his lips.

"I will slay you," the Faceless Son said.

"I will eat you raw, wizard's son."

"You know the depths of magic, demon," the man said tersely. "But you do not know the depths of a man."

The torch fell as the hammer arced. Its massive head shattered a horn, ripped through the demon's jaw with a wet sound and threw blood across the floor as Durgord's head snapped backward like the lid of a chest suddenly thrown open.

The beast fell backward, its own blood raining upon it, and its eyes clamped on the warrior who loomed above him. The hammer dropped once more, and a leg thick as an elm trunk snapped with a crack like an iceberg breaking in spring. The demon's scream buried the echoes of that blow.

"Vengeance?" The Faceless Son crushed the demon's other leg. "Did you think vengeance pushed me up that mountain, pulled me into your lair?"

A hammer strike to the demon's gut forced venom and blood-moistened air to gush from the snakelike snout. Crimson drops clung to the gleaming ivory spears of its teeth.

"Had you and your obscene brood not torn my father to bits, I'd have done so myself!" Bile rose in the Faceless Son's throat. "Ours was a noble house! My forefathers fought beside kings, swore allegiances in blood, took vows that my mad, greedy father trampled beneath his feet!

"I swore no oath of vengeance, you brainless hell-spawn. I swore a mask oath to erase the stain of my father's shame. And so I shall!"

He thought of his father, then of Aloyssa, and lifted the hammer high to drop the killing blow.

It never dropped.

Durgord roared, and the demon's maw erupted with flame that streaked toward the Faceless Son, blinding him with its brilliance. The Son twisted and dove, escaping the flame but not the searing heat that raised blisters upon his back. He rolled as another spear of fire blackened the floor where he had fallen.

The demon had grown stronger indeed.

The Faceless Son rolled into an unsteady crouch and faced his enemy. A lunge now, before another burst of demonic flame, could bring him within striking reach.

But no, Durgord was still too distant, despite crawling toward him on powerful arms, dragging his broken legs behind him and holding his head high. "It seems knowledge of the depths of magic will suffice to win the day," Durgord growled. Each dagger-tooth in the demon's face formed a menacing silhouette against the furnace raging in the beast's throat.

The Faceless Son dove again, into the darkness beyond the light of the dropped torch, where his shoulder slammed painfully into an unseen boulder. He scrambled over the rock as another wave of flame broke upon it. He closed his eyes and mind against the heat, and covered his ears against the demon's roar.

He had but one chance, though an unlikely one. He steeled himself, drawing upon the power of the mask oath for the sharpness of mind and strength of spirit to do what he must. It was the only option remaining him – and failure meant certain death.

Durgord's roar silenced and flames vanished as the monstrous demon inhaled deeply for another blast. Its dead legs scraped across the grit of the coffin-cold floor as it approached, and the Son stiffened at the bone-scrabbling sound of the demon's claws.

The Faceless Son had come near death before. In his last fight with a demon, he'd been battered and hurled aside like a child's doll. But that furious, frantic battle had left him no time to consider death, to smell it coming, to see it leering.

This time, he felt death's chill breath on his brow.

The Son tried to call upon the images that had sustained and driven him thus far. His father's treachery. The valiant Tryddan Gost. Sweet Aloyssa.

Then, steel in his heart, he rose in that pause between hellish blasts and hurled the warhammer with every ounce of might within him. The enchanted weapon flew with an arrow's accuracy and Durgord's forehead exploded in bloody pulp.

And the Faceless Son realized only one image had filled his mind in that moment between life and death.

Once more outside the gates of Brythane, he had hoped to find only one naked spike so this final trophy would end the quest.

But three spikes yet stood unadorned.

The Son dismounted and dumped the contents of the bloody sack onto the ground. Watchers gathered in silence along the wall to witness the impalement of Durgord's head. He heard that silence turn to gasps when he finished and strode toward the gate.

He commanded the guards atop the wall. "Open it!" They hesitated only a moment, then great hinges groaned and chains clattered loudly as the massive doors opened. In the courtyard beyond, the giant bronze image of Tryddan Gost stood, holding Brythane's standard – and staring at the Faceless Son.

City guardsmen gaped at him blankly. He addressed them without stepping into the city. "I would speak with the Lady Aloyssa."

The statue seemed to study him while he awaited her. The Son held his breath when he saw her, the pale skin of her slender neck showing beneath the dark gossamer veil. Time and worry had crinkled her face a bit, but neither had touched her beauty.

She walked steadily, and came in the company of Orn's priests. One walked on each side of her, and she gently shrugged their hands away when they sought to slow her pace.

The priests, robed in red, looked at the Faceless Son gravely. "Have you forsaken the oath you took before Orn?"

"He has not!" Aloyssa whirled upon them in fury, her mourning gown swirling a small storm of dust from the ground. Her back was to him now, but he could see the way the priests retreated from her wrath. The Faceless Son could well imagine the blue fire in her eyes, burning through the veil. Her instant, unquestioning defense of him ignited his pride.

The priests stopped, frozen by her scorn. She turned to face him. "He will do what he swore to do, and would do so whether he wore Orn's mask or not."

"I would walk with you, Aloyssa," the Faceless Son said.

She joined him and they walked toward the River Orn. She did not look back to see if the priests approved, and neither did he.

"I will continue hunting the demons," he said, after they had rounded a bend and were beyond sight of Brythane's gawkers.

"I know," she said.

The Temple Fastness rose in the heights across the swift waters, too distant for their words to be heard there.

Aloyssa glanced toward the temple. "Let them watch, if they wish," he told her. "I do not care whether they approve of my acts or not. They are unimportant."

She nodded, and looked upon him.

They faced one another as Orn's waters hummed. "I had much time to think as I rode home. Much time to ponder."

She touched his cheek, and he could almost feel her fingertips through the cloth.

"Many times," he said softly, "when I might have given up, I focused on my family's honor, my father's crimes, my intended life with you. Such visions reminded me of my oath, what I fought for, and helped me to go on."

She did not interrupt, but he could see her eyes through the veil, and they asked many questions.

He swallowed, for he knew leaving would be more difficult this time. "I was nurtured on tales of Tryddan's deeds, on nobility, on sermons from Orn's priests. I knew little else, really. But I have learned much since then."

The Faceless Son took a deep breath. "I swore a rash oath, Aloyssa, because I thought honor demanded it." He could almost feel the relief in her, the easing of tension. She sobbed. "Oh, my love . . ."

His finger on her lips, beneath her veil, quieted her. "And I will keep that oath. At least, I will keep that part of it that matters. I will go on with this quest, because my brothers are out there somewhere and I will face the dangers I led them into. I must stand with them. And we will kill the last of the demons. I swear it."

"I know," she whispered.

He found it difficult to look into her questioning eyes. "But I was wrong, Aloyssa, to hide away from the world . . . from you. Without you, without us . . . what matters honor?"

His eyes implored her to understand, and her brave smile told him she did.

"I do not have to revive the family honor my father spat upon. Tryddan Gost was a great and brave man," the Faceless Son said. "My father's crime did not change that. Nor can anything I do add to or diminish Tryddan's deed."

"True," she whispered. "Others see that, always saw it, although you could not."

"Nor do my father's crimes stain me."

"True again." Her hand touched his chest, and the warmth of it filled him. "Magic drove Gharan mad, spurred him to traitorous evils, but the shame is his, not yours. It was never yours. I prayed you would come to realize this."

Their eyes met. Tears streamed from hers; he could see their tracks through the veil.

"I will go on, Aloyssa. I will kill the fiends. But not for family honor, and not for the priests. I will do it to make the world safer for you, and for my brothers who are out there hunting now. I had a moment of true clarity, Aloyssa. The diamond-hard, knife-sharp clarity that only imminent death can bring. And in that moment, when I knew myself to be unutterably mortal, I did not see Tryddan's legacy, nor my father's crimes, nor Orn and his priests glaring at me. I saw you. Only you. And that alone sustained me, Aloyssa. That alone let me live. For I had to see you once again, and I had to tell you something. I may die in this quest, but not without telling you that. And showing you."

His chest swelled as he lifted the mask. "I am Trevor Gost, and I love you."

Their embrace held all in the world that truly mattered to them. Pale mask and dark veil fell together into Orn's swirling waters.

The common soldier can offer some of the best observations on life. Maybe it comes from always looking up at everyone else. From always getting dumped on and finding a way out from under. Surviving means far more than just living another day. And what soldiers survive for – yes, live and fight for – isn't always what kings and rulers say it is. It's not that they seek to deceive; they simply don't know. While ideals of God and country and freedom and equality most often do exist at the onset of hostilities, by mid-battle none of those matter any more. No, what matters only is the soldier on either side. The comrades stuck in the same thick of things. Right then and there, the last two beings on earth standing beside one are more important than any words lost on the winds.

Bruce Durham has spent his lifetime reading and watching anything related to science fiction and fantasy. He is of an age where he's probably seen close to every idea under the sun – and now he has an idea or ten. He's been working double-time on sharing all those yarns rattling around in his noggin. This story was meant for bigger things – until an asteroid struck his hard drive and melted everything but these 5,000 words. Check out Bruce's newly created website at http://brucedurham.ca.

Valley of Bones

A Tale of Mortlock

by Bruce Durham

A boot to the ass stirred me. I opened my eyes to the grizzled mug of Sergeant Clantalion looming like an apparition from one of the Three Hells. His square jaw and scarred face thrust near mine. I mustered a crack about his breath. It came out as a grunt.

He grunted in return. His voice was gravel. "Get up, Mortlock. Time to die."

I swallowed and tried again. This time I managed to sound coherent. "Already Sarge? I was dreaming."

"Me and your wife again?" he countered, moving to kick the next person, a friend of mine called Fearson.

I moved my legs, stretching full length. Cartilage cracked. I shifted. Pain shot across the lower back, a grim reminder of yesterday's march over rugged terrain.

Fearson turned to face me. Calloused fingers wiped at his sleep matted eyes. His weary voice echoed my pain. "I hurt."

I sat up, clearing my throat to spit. "Might be that slab of ground we slept on." I looked around. A handful of shapes lurched zombie-like in the glow of the full moon. I stood to a symphony of pops and snaps.

“Simple agreement would have sufficed, Mortlock,” Fearson replied, standing beside me.

The morning air was damp and chill. My nostrils caught a familiar scent. Food. Some kind soul had stoked last nights’ fire. Over it an iron pot boiled feverishly, filled to the brim with a pungent smelling broth.

Stomach grumbling, I sauntered over and sat on a log, stealing warmth from the crackling flames. I helped myself to breakfast.

Sergeant Clantalion, the hulking, square jawed veteran with the active boot, wandered past as we ate. Someone offered him a spot. He took it. Another offered him a plate. He took that.

In the distance I saw the first light of false dawn.

Chewing noisily, Clantalion asked, "Daydreaming Mortlock?"

My reply was eloquent. "Yep."

He chuckled, a sound like grinding rocks. "Well, you'll have plenty of time for that, son. We’ve a distance to cover today." He swallowed a last mouthful and returned the plate and spoon with a nod of thanks. "Don’t tarry, boys. We’ll be moving soon."

A pikeman with gangly limbs and bobbing Adam's apple asked, "How far today, Sergeant?"

"Not sure, Gyvens. There's an old valley several leagues from here. Why? That stick you call a body not up to it? Does Coranthe’s finest need more sleep?"

"Sleep, Sergeant? You mean I’m awake?"

A steady march brought us to the Greatbough Forest, a looming wall of ancient, majestic trees. Dwarfed by their thick, knotted trunks, we approached a trail, a dark opening flanked with dense undergrowth and dangling vines. Somewhere a tinny horn sounded, and the light cavalry raced ahead to enter two abreast. Their racket sent hundreds of birds screeching in anger.

I shared pained looks with Gyvens to my right and Fearson on my left. “Nothing like warning the enemy,” I cracked.

Slowly the forest swallowed our infantry, its canopy of branches obscuring the sunlight and casting everyone into eerie gloom. Pine needles carpeted the ground and muffled our footsteps. My left boot sunk into something soft and sticky. I looked and cursed. It was a gift from the cavalry. How I detested horses. Somewhere, someone else cursed.

The forest grew increasingly oppressive, and my tunic became soaked with sweat; the pike resting against my shoulder was slick and awkward to grip.

Suddenly the ground rumbled. It felt like an oncoming thunderstorm. Cavalry. The sergeants reacted, cursing and edging our column aside to clear a path. Moments later King Agyis raced past, flanked by his Generals and escort. The King was bareheaded, his sandy hair blowing back to reveal a youthful, strongly featured profile. We gave up a cheer.

Heartened by his appearance, the next few leagues passed quickly. Soon we noticed the immense trees thinning out. Slivers of light gradually brightened the trail until it emptied onto a field of short, sparse grass. Beyond it lay a row of hills topped by elements of our light cavalry.

Gratefully we spilled from the forest, and were shortly ordered to halt. Men from the supply train distributed water skins. I passed one to Fearson and idly turned to watch the yellow ribbon of the morning sun peer over the horizon.

Our infantry commander, General Calion, rode before us surrounded by his Captains and Lieutenants. He was old, his once strong frame now hunched painfully over his mount. But we loved the man and cheered. The General smiled thinly and raised a hand in acknowledgement. The command staff dismounted and stood around him. The sergeants joined. Their meeting was short, but animated. No doubt King Agyis had already devised his battle plan, and the Generals were merely passing along instructions. When they dispersed, the sergeants strode toward us with purpose. They bellowed orders to form infantry squares.

A sack of butterflies erupted in my stomach.

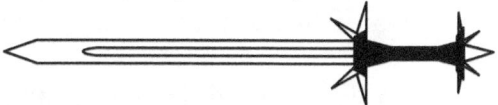

I was among the first to hear the telltale sound of an army on the move. It was distant but unmistakable: the clash of metal on metal, jingling livery, the rumble of several thousand feet.

I looked at Gyvens. "We have company."

He wasn't pleased.

The musketeers attached to our regiment appeared on my left, each man clutching a heavy gun and forked stake. They trotted to the front of our formation before turning sharply right and forming into five lines.

General Calion appeared on the summit of a neighboring hill. He drew his sword and waved. Horns blared and our Lieutenant sprang to action, giving the order to advance. The army lurched forward, pikes upright, a slow rolling wave on an ocean of grass.

Sergeant Clantalion stalked our formation, halberd horizontal, ensuring our lines remained steady. Then he backed, watching our progress, growling at us to keep step. We reached the base of the hill and began a gentle ascent. At its summit we were ordered to halt. The order was repeated the length of the army.

My throat tightened. We occupied a hill overlooking an uneven valley, but what swarmed on its opposite slope had snatched my attention.

The enemy, the Khatan.

In stark contrast to our disciplined squares, the Khatana infantry was little more than organized rabble. They were equipped with spears, short swords and oblong shields. Some had armor of quilted leather and conical bronze helmets. A few wore chain or banded mail.

The valley floor separating us was rocky and uneven. A good sign. It neutralized Khatan's major strength – the horse archer. The feared bowmen were their most dangerous weapon: mobile, quick, and deadly in the open. But with ground like this they were practically ineffective. King Agyis had chosen well.

But we were still outnumbered. The Khatana army lay stretched like a blanket of flesh across the opposing hills. Their leaders gathered around a commanding position and carefully studied our formations. They pointed vehemently, angrily. Spies may have given them word of our newly acquired muskets, but the sight of our disciplined squares had definitely caught them with their leggings down.

I chuckled. "It's not like the old days, you maggots. Not anymore. We have the weapons, and the training."

Gyvens looked at me, not entirely confident.

Sharp orders to the musketeers had them take position on the forward slope and pound their forked stakes into the soft earth.

I closed my eyes to concentrate on the sound of shifting armor, jingling weapons and the thud of hammers on wood. I inhaled the conflicting aromas of morning dew and the acrid scent of well-oiled chain mail. My thoughts turned to Helyna, my wife, and Katlyn, our three-year-old daughter. I wanted to hold them, and I prayed to every god that I'd survive the day.

Fearson leaned close. "This should be easy, Mortlock. Look at them. No discipline."

I glared, but stifled my retort. My attention was elsewhere.

The morning sun was still low on the horizon. But it had become an ochre orb, its dull glow bathing the armies in a yellow-brown haze. My neck hairs tingled. This wasn't right.

Men shouted with alarm. I faced the valley. A salmon-colored mist curled lazily off the irregular surface. Slowly it thickened, twisting and swirling like a live thing, spreading along the valley floor toward our position. The cool morning air grew sticky and oppressive.

Someone cried, "Magic!"

The horrifying word spread fast. The mood of the men changed. Most had never witnessed magic, save for healing spells or festival tricks. Fewer still had faced magic designed to kill.

Sudden terror clawed my spine. My mouth turned dry. I swallowed and asked, "Magic? Theirs or ours?" I glanced over both shoulders, searching out our magicians. They were here, somewhere.

"Steady boys! Steady!" Sergeant Clantalion said in his best motherly voice. He prowled our ranks, working to counter our growing panic. A hasty glance to the valley betrayed his unease.

We watched the mist reach the base of the hill. It swirled momentarily, gathered, and crept upward. I looked at the sun. It was blood red.

The magic wasn't ours.

The rumble was barely perceptible at first, like a distant cavalry charge. The ground shifted; men cried out. I looked at Gyvens and Fearson. The sun had bathed their worried faces in a ghastly light.

The mist churned at my feet now, the musketeers on the forward slope standing waist deep. The Khatana were a faint mass along the distant hills.

The rumbling continued. The valley, now thick with fog, shifted and swirled in violent reaction to some unseen disturbance. The sound was like wet ground tearing asunder. It suddenly ended, and became deathly quiet.

But the silence was short, and the noise started again. It began as a gentle tapping, hollow and muted, like bone on bone. The men shifted uneasily. They sensed something approach, unseen.

A trumpet blared, the shrill note desperate. Sergeants sprang to action.

"Pikes!" roared Clantalion. Gone was the motherly voice, back was the deep bellow we knew and loved. I hoisted my pike shoulder high and let it ease until the iron tip extended beyond the two ranks before me.

"Musketeers!"

The front rank responded, nestling their heavy guns into the crook of the previously placed stakes. Freshly lit serpentine wicks smoldered bright red. The remaining four ranks stood ready.

The tapping now echoed the length and breadth of the veiled valley. My gut twisted at the sight, and then lurched violently in response to a sudden discharge of musket fire. The sputtering retort was an uneven series of muted pops. Men screamed. I craned my neck for a better look, saw a block of pikes bobbing and dipping. Sergeants urgently called for calm, men cried out in return. Another sporadic round of gunfire erupted, closer now. More screams. Formations wavered. My bowels tensed.

"What in the Three Hells is going on?" Fearson cried; his voice edged with panic.

Sergeant Clantalion growled, "Steady! Steady! Remember your training!"

It happened swiftly. Several musketeers shrieked and collapsed, disappearing into the mist. Their muffled cries reached out from the ochre haze. Weapons discharged at unseen targets; flashpans flared, their flames swallowed by the encroaching fog.

The first rank of pike reacted. Men were yanked from their feet, drawn screaming down the slope and out of sight. The second rank reacted. They pointed, stamping the ground with heavy boots or slamming pike butts repeatedly.

I stood with the third rank trying to burn a hole through the mist to the grassy surface. The film was low, barely ankle-high.

Something slid past. Something else brushed my boot. It felt rough and bony. I stomped hard with my boot and heard a hollow crunch.

The draft from my action caused the wispy tendrils to swirl, revealing my assailant. It was the skeleton of a snake. One of our unseen invaders. My victim was small, no more than a foot in length. The broken bones rattled as they refused to release the magic powering them. I shuddered to think what had stolen the men from the slope.

I stammered, "They—they're skeletons!"

The Khatana magicians had brought the long dead and buried back to animated life.

A creature charged from the mist to my left and launched itself at the adjacent square. There was no time to react, and the formation buckled as men backed in fear. It vaguely resembled a giant bear, its earth-clotted bones oozing earthworms and maggots. The thing crashed among them.

Men died under its powerful assault, torn limb from limb by ancient claws and long, jagged teeth. It rampaged until tangling among the soldier's pikes. Slowly the men applied leverage to the thick shafts, snapping the horror bone by bone.

Fearson shouted, "Where's our bloody magicians?"

Sergeant Clantalion brought his halberd down on something unseen and cried, "Hold steady! Hold! The bastards die!"

Someone snapped, "They're already dead!"

I grinned in spite of myself. *Good one!* I sensed the sky grow brighter and glanced at the sun. It was no longer blood red, but a deep yellow.

My humor was short lived. A monstrously large creature emerged from the haze, a massive skeleton on four thickly boned legs. Two impossibly long tusks protruded from its fearsome skull. It vaguely resembled an elephant, a beast I'd seen years past with a traveling circus. It was large, deadly, and it walked. Tufts of earth flew from its skeleton with each lumbering footfall. It rumbled directly toward me.

A thunderclap exploded from behind, the concussion stinging my ears. Another thunderclap exploded, overhead this time. A series of rumbles followed, cumulating with yet another blast, closer to the enemy.

The musketeers broke and ran, muscling through our ranks, their eyes white with terror. Sergeant Clantalion shouted in a vain attempt to rally them. But musket balls had little effect against animated bone. He gave up and roared, "Form up! Brace pikes!"

I planted the butt-end of my pike in the earth and stayed it with my boot. I screamed prayers to every god I knew.

The abomination crashed into us with a thunderous crunch of bone on metal. Brushed aside like toys, the men were powerless against the long dead behemoth. Pikes slipped and skittered along its mammoth legs, doing little damage as it plowed forward.

The beast dipped its massive head and speared Fearson through the belly. It reared; Fearson impaled like a rag on the ancient tusk. He clawed feebly at the sharp length, his life draining.

Another stride and it would be upon me. I closed my eyes.

A thunderclap wrenched the air from my lungs. I dropped to my knees and gasped for breath. My head cleared and I blinked away tears. I should have been dead – gored by the beast.

But I laughed; a short bark of relief. The mammoth had crumbled scant feet before me, collapsing into a giant mound of bones. Only Fearson, hanging limply from its tusk, served as a grisly reminder of the unnatural magic that had powered it. I looked away from the gruesome loss of my friend. I would deal with it later.

The good news was our magicians had come through.

The mist receded to reveal a hillside covered in creatures long dead. Some I recognized; others were too ancient to tell. Uncounted men lay among them, torn and shredded by curved and jagged claws, or pierced with sickle-like fangs.

Scattered moans drifted from the mass of bodies. A few twitched in death throes; others crawled painfully, pleading for help. A handful climbed to shaky feet to stagger into the arms of relieved comrades.

A sudden breeze swept away the last vestiges of mist, leaving the enemy visible on the opposite hill.

They began to chant, a rhythmic battle cry that carried across the valley of bones. The ritual mantra lasted minutes, growing into a crescendo before ending with a shout of defiance. Horns blasted and they swarmed down the hill toward us.

Our sergeants screamed orders. Many regiments remained scattered and disordered. The musketeers lurked somewhere behind our lines.

I watched the Khatana charge with curious detachment. The magic-driven horrors I had faced were defeated. I had confronted the reanimated mammoth and lived. And now I faced ordinary men. A fury gripped me, filling me with anger. They had tried to kill me with magic, and now they dared insult me with mere weapons.

I gripped my pike and advanced to the forward slope. I planted it in the ground and waited, challenging. Others took position around me.

The Khatana poured across the valley, but faltered when they entered the pile of debris churned from the depths. The vast amount of life that had lived and died over the centuries awed me, their existence long forgotten under layers of dirt and grass. Khatana magic had animated every dead creature, and now their countless bones lay spread like a jagged carpet.

And while the enemy magic had damaged us, the remains proved to be our salvation. The Khatana slowed while negotiating the obstacles, giving us precious moments to regroup.

Sergeant Clantalion appeared; halberd in hand. "Pikes!"

I raised mine overhead, tilting it to aim mid-body as taught.

He scanned our lines, cajoling those too slow to react. Satisfied, he slipped into the ranks to stand by my right. He caught my eye and mumbled, “Good man.”

We were ready when the Khatana cleared the valley and ascended our hill. They crashed against the massed line, their front ranks collapsing under the thrusting of our iron pikes. Row after row died, the bodies growing into a mound of pierced and torn flesh.

But they were relentless. In places sheer weight of numbers dislodged our pikes, breaching our lines, their curved swords wrecking havoc in close quarters. But our formations were deep, and another Coranthan was always poised to step forward, pike flashing and jabbing. Soon the gaps sealed, and the enemy was repulsed to lie dead and trampled.

The Khatana launched their spears in frustration. The man before me collapsed, an iron tipped shaft lodged deep in his belly. I stepped over him and jabbed at an exposed chest. The unwieldy pike wobbled and struck the face. The pike entered his mouth and split the jaw. I twisted and pulled free. I jabbed at another, twisted, pulled, and jabbed again.

The fury of their assault lost momentum and the Khatana backed slowly, defiantly waving weapons and screaming taunts. Some swore colorfully in heavily accented Coranthan.

I raised my hand in a shooing motion, stood my pike on end and leaned into it. Pushing back my helmet, I wiped sweat from my brow and reveled in the cool air that crossed my face.

The respite was short. A dozens horns sounded behind us. The order to advance.

The enemy continued to retreat in the face of our longer weapons as we pushed down the hill and across the valley. However, the bone covered ground soon fractured our formations, and the horns sounded a halt. We waited, using the lull to rest our weary arms while the sergeants dressed our ranks.

The Khatana used the opportunity to reform on the crest of the opposing hills. Their ranks were visibly depleted.

Someone pushed past me. It was a musketeer. The men with the clumsy weapons filtered through our lines to take position before us. We advanced again, marching slowly, picking our way carefully through the debris and bodies.

The Khatana watched and waited. Suddenly they roared and charged.

A horn sounded and the front rank of musketeers dropped to one knee. With no time to plant stakes, they braced the musket stock firmly against their boot and tilted the barrel at the approaching mass of bodies. The infantry shuffled forward, the two front rows of pike reaching over the musketeer's heads to provide limited protection.

“Fire!” The order echoed across the battlefield. Muskets flashed and belched. Some fizzled, producing an innocent puff of smoke. Others exploded, their owners screaming and clawing at burnt and blackened faces. The remainder let loose a hail of stone that sliced into the enemy, tearing holes through armor and body. The first rank retired to the rear and the second rank moved forward. There would be no time to reload.

"Fire!” Another ragged volley tore holes into the enemy. The third rank moved into position.

"Fire!” The enemy slowed, felled by the murderous shot. They stumbled and staggered in the debris-laden field, struggling to continue.

Our men began to taunt them.

But I was above such nonsense, of course. My luck I'd piss off the one guy who was their best archer.

"Fire!" Khatana resolve shattered.

"Fire!" They broke, casting away their weapons and madly fleeing.

The musketeers dropped back, their job complete. The air was thick with smoke now, its acrid odor stinging my eyes and irritating my lungs.

Horns blasted again and Sergeant Clantalion bellowed, "Pikes, advance!"

We marched carefully across the remaining stretch of valley and up the opposite slope. The enemy offered little opposition.

I reached the summit to see the remnants of the Khatana army scatter into the forest, fleeing south toward their homeland.

Sergeant Clantalion called a halt.

I dropped to the ground with the others, pike rolling from my hands to bounce once before settling. Reaching for my water skin, I drank deep, casually eyeing the ground we had fought so hard to take. It was no different from the ground we had come from.

A brilliant light flashed from beyond a nearby hill. A blast of thunder followed. We all looked. I thought I could hear war cries and the clash of steel. I decided to investigate.

The climb was steep, but at the crest I looked into a second valley. Scattered across the grassy floor Coranthan and Khatana cavalry struggled fiercely in battle.

Near the conflagration was a clearing, a circular area ringed with stone. At its center lay several bodies, many in painfully twisted shapes. Looking closer, I noticed three among them still lived. They sat on the ground cross-legged, motionless, hands joined.

The sky flashed again and cracked with thunder. A bolt of lightning ripped into a dozen Coranthans. Horses and men were pitched like so much wheat. I caught a whiff of charred flesh.

Realization dawned. The men in the circle were sorcerers! Khatan's sudden retreat had stranded them before they could be roused from their deep trance. And now they fought for their very existence with the aid of the Khatana cavalry. Alarmingly, their magic was tipping the balance, and judging by the scattered bodies of our men they were winning.

Then I saw the familiar helmet of our King. He was in the middle of the fight, surrounded by his guard, attempting to force a path to the ring of stones and the magic-users.

I drew my blade and looked back at the resting men. Some of the curious watched me. I waved in a *follow me* motion and then ran down the slope, straight for the stone circle. I prayed someone would follow.

The battlefield was chaotic, the blood-slick ground cluttered with the corpses of man and beast. I threaded my way through the preoccupied enemy, my blade thrusting and jabbing at exposed legs and arms.

A horse reared before me, the wild eyes of a Khatan soldier burning with triumph. He raised his sword, but I lunged forward to seize the bridle, forcing the beast's head into the Khatan's descending blade. Blood sprayed, the animal screamed and bucked. I slipped past the falling mount, slicing the man's heel with a turn of my wrist.

The circle of stones loomed before me.

The air exploded. I hit the ground hard, my mouth tasting blood. I rolled to my knees and grimaced in pain. The world was strangely silent, save for a ringing in my ears. Before me a cluster of broken bodies lay twisted and bloody. Their flesh smoldered. They had borne the brunt of a spell.

I stood; legs shaky. My sword hand throbbed. It was black and pink, the wrist oddly bent. I cast about. My blade lay near my feet, charred and cracked.

I wiped the tears from my eyes and looked to the circle. A gap had been created by the blast. The three sorcerers remained seated, their thin lips silently moving in preparation of another spell. The bodies of their comrades surrounded them, their features frozen in agony, blood seeping from ears, mouth and eyes. They had died horribly when their animation spell was shattered.

Pressing my ruined hand against my stomach, I dashed through the opening. My good hand fumbled for the knife in my belt. As I rolled the blade for a stabbing blow, a sharp pain lanced into my side, the impact twisting me about. An arrow was lodged in the flesh above my hip.

Biting back pain, I spotted a horse archer glaring in triumph, not twenty paces distant. He calmly notched another shaft and took careful aim.

A figure flew past him, his sword arm a blur. The Khatan's head leapt from his shoulders in a spray of blood. His torso slipped from the saddle.

The rider came sharply about, his horse rearing as he reined it in. It was King Agyis. He tipped his blade at me, and then pointed at the sorcerers.

I nodded.

The air crackled again with power. Their spell neared completion.

I lurched forward, ignoring the pain from the shaft. The last few feet became agony, but I clenched my teeth and brought the knife down hard into the neck of the nearest magic-user.

His face contorted, his mouth opening wide in a silent scream. I wrenched the blade free and reversed it, slicing his throat. Warm blood gushed across my hand. I pushed the body over.

The air ceased to crackle, and the remaining sorcerers stirred from their trance, dazed and fearful. I advanced, but they saw me and fled, straight into the waiting blade of King Agyis.

I stood swaying as he rode up. Spitting blood, my ears ringing, I managed a half-smile and cracked, "Thanks for the help."

The King smiled and replied. I couldn't hear him.

Other men arrived, including Gyvens. He offered me a shoulder to lean on.

I looked again at my King and managed to croak, "You wouldn't know a good physician, would you?"

I collapsed.

Rogue Blades Entertainment

Whenever possible, one should always ask the master of a subject to introduce it. In the case of Harold Lamb, none other than Howard Andrew Jones will do. Howard sells himself a bit short in the following introduction, completely omitting the fact that he is the sole reason Bison Books ever put out the four Lamb collections. He does correctly describe the man's writing, though. Lamb's historical biographies are wonders to read, and I was collecting his books long before I ever knew he wrote short fiction. I look forward to further collections and agree with Howard's imperative: find and read them yourself. This tale, courtesy of Bison Books, is a terrific introduction to Lamb's adventures for those new to Harold Lamb – a fun read for those familiar with his writings.

In the 1950s, almost anyone researching the history of Asia would have turned to the works of Harold Lamb, just as, a generation earlier, readers turned to his stories set in Asia – tales featuring Russians, Mongols, and Muslims – for swashbuckling, page-turning adventure. While Lamb's name is no longer as well known today, his reputation as both historian and storyteller is untarnished. He was one of the first adventure writers to craft tales with a modern, cinematic sense of pace, and wrote convincingly from the viewpoint of other cultures. His prose was moody, bloody, exotic, and riveting, and it's no small wonder that Robert E. Howard, best known as the creator of Conan of Cimmeria, named Lamb as one of his favorite writers.

Once Lamb's work was difficult to find; until 2006 his stories were sandwiched only in dusty library collections and moldering pulp magazines. You're in luck, though, because today his work is available again through several venues. The University of Nebraska press has recently reprinted a set of four books that collect all of Lamb's tales of adventurous Cossacks: Wolf of the Steppes, Warriors of the Steppes, Riders of the Steppes, *and* Swords of the Steppes. *Each volume features stories from Lamb's heroic Cossack cycle, although the final volume features almost a dozen standalone adventures. This short story is one of those. Mayhem, action, danger, surprise, exotic setting – it's all here. Best of all, Bison Books will shortly be printing more Lamb collections. If you like what you see in these pages, I hope you'll seek out the rest of his work. You won't be disappointed.*

Classic: Red Hands

A Tale of the Steppes

by Harold Lamb

Charny came to himself a little at a time. First he was aware that he sat in a saddle. Then he saw the familiar gray steppe grass and felt the wind on his head.

His head troubled him. It was wet with sweat and it had no lambskin kalpak on it. Inasmuch as most of his skull had been shaved a few days ago, it felt cold. A fiery thirst tormented him.

Besides, the level steppe behaved strangely. It rose dizzily and then dropped away from him, although his horse paced along steadily enough. Charny knew what this meant.

"I've been licking the pig," he thought.

He remembered singing a chorus with some fellow Cossacks in a town tavern. After that – night and the saddle and a rushing wind.

"Devil take it all," he muttered. "I've come far."

No town was visible on the swaying steppe. The Cossack bent over and looked down. He had no coat, but his wide leather breeches were there and his prized shagreen boots – he looked on each side to make sure. His shirt appeared torn and stained with tar. What mattered most, he still wore his sword. So, he had not drunk that up.

But the horse! After awhile he drew rein and dismounted, holding firmly to the saddle-horn. Streaked with sweat and dust, with burrs clouding its long tail, this black horse was certainly not his. A good horse, however, a wolf-chaser.

"How did I get you, *kounak*?"

Evidently after the drinking bout he had taken a horse from the stable and then raced off into the plain – naturally enough, after so many cups of brandy. It was afternoon now, the sun almost setting, and Charny saw no sign of a trail. Only the waving grass, clusters of dark oaks, the hazy sky – and the brown sail of a boat moving majestically over the grass, far off. The Cossack closed his eyes and looked again. The brown sail was still there.

Well, brandy played tricks like that. Worse than the *myzga*, the mirage. Charny tried to remember whether he had gone north, east, south, or west from the frontier town, but without success.

Leading the horse into the nearest shade he loosened the saddle girth slowly. He searched for a picket rope and found none. Letting out the rein, he slipped it over his shoulder and laid down, his head on his arms. He would sleep for a while and then let the horse find the way to water . . .

Instead, he woke with a start. The red glare of sunset filled the sky, and the wind had ceased. Along the ground he had heard the thudding of hooves on the hard clay. Instantly he leaped to his feet, his hand touching the sword hilt at his belt.

Then he relaxed. Only one rider had come up, a Cossack on a piebald horse – a broad Cossack with long arms, wearing a clean sheepskin coat, a black kalpak with a red crown, and polished boots. His was a brown, lined face, like a Tartar's, with tufted mustaches.

"*Tfu!*" grunted the rider.

"Draw that curved sword and I'll slap you in the snout."

Charny's head was clearing. The other man had saddle-bags, with a rolled-up bearskin and a jug behind the saddle – evidently a registered Cossack, on service. In that year of the Lord 1684 it was well to look twice at one who rode alone and armed in the eastern steppe. The towns and the Muscovite merchants lay under the sunset to the west, and the steppe here was at the edge of the frontier.

"What man are you?" Charny asked.

"They call me Vash. I patrol from the Zarit *stanitza*. The others turned back, but I kept your trail like a weasel."

Zarit, Charny remembered, was the hamlet where he had been drinking at the tavern. He looked at the man called Vash expectantly as the other dismounted.

"Seventy versts you rode between midnight and now," went on Vash. "Straight over the steppe to the east. Well, I'll take you back."

"Why take me back?"

"Don't you know? Last night you licked the pig – you were dancing the *hopak* in the Cossack's bed[1] when his Highness, the lieutenant of the Starosta, rode by. He said something, and you pulled him out of the saddle and used the whip on his hide until he danced. *Tfu!* There was a devil in you—"

"How did I find the horse?"

"It's his Highness's charger – a good one. The Starosta gave command to all of us on the border patrol to follow and bring you back. They are raging like bulls in a pen, the Starosta and his men. Come on, it's late."

Charny knew well enough what awaited him at Zarit: the stocks; the scourge; or his ears clipped off. They had his horse and

[1] The trampled earth in front of a tavern door where Cossacks were likely to be found asleep in the morning.

his silver, his *svitka* and his hat, while he had one of their best chargers. So, he had stolen nothing. Moreover, he was tired of the Russian settlements where a man could not even drink without being caged.

"My road is to the east," he decided. "To the devil take your Starosta and his commands."

Vash considered a moment, his slant eyes measuring the tall fugitive. Then he leaped at Charny, his powerful arms clutching. But Charny was in no mood for a fight. Stepping aside, he drew his curved sword swiftly.

"Steel to you!" shouted Vash, jerking out his own sword.

For a moment the two Cossacks circled warily, Vash half crouched, his muscles tense, while Charny sidestepped softly, waiting. Then Vash leaped again, his saber swinging over his head. Charny parried the slash at his ribs and drew back while the Zarit Cossack pressed him with cut after cut.

Suddenly the taller man stepped forward, twisting the curved blade of his saber around the other's sword until the hilts locked. Without warning he wrenched the blades toward him, and Vash's sword flashed into the air, falling to the ground behind Charny, who set his foot upon it.

"The devil's in you still!" Vash muttered, rubbing his hand. "Get into the saddle, and may the dogs bite me if I don't carve your ribs there. To fight on a horse – that's the best way. Only sheepherders fight on their feet."

A smile touched Charny's thin lips. With the red glow of sunset on his half-shaven head, his dark eyes seemed on fire.

"Well, what will you do?" Vash asked irritably. "Don't you see that I'm your prisoner? Do you want me to take grass in my teeth?"

"Do what you like." Charny picked up the other's sword and sheathed his own. "I'm not going back to Zarit to be strung up on a rope."

"Well, I can't go off into the steppe without a sword. Now listen, you aren't my captive any longer, that's clear. I won't try to take you back there." Vash's tufted mustache twitched in a grin. "Allah, they say his Highness the lieutenant howled when you kissed his hide with the whip. It's all one to me. Only give me back the sword."

He held out his hand.

"Faith of a Cossack. I pledge faith by all the Cossack brotherhood, alive or dead, out yonder." And he motioned to the north and east, to south and west.

He had served, that Vash, in the wars, and his oath was the oath of a Zaporoghian – of a free Cossack who had once belonged to the great war encampment of the Siech. If he gave his word as a Zaporoghian, it would be trusted.

Charny handed him back his sword.

"*Aya tak,*" he said, "Aye, so. Now give me water from that jug."

Vash sheathed his sword and stared.

"Water! Would I carry water with mother Volga flowing under my snout?"

And, remembering the brown boat's sail on the steppe, Charny laughed. Truly his head had been bitten. Ten minutes later the Cossacks and the horses were drinking at the bank of the wide gray river that flowed soundlessly between borders of high rushes. Charny thrust in his head, snorting, and wringing the water out of his scalp lock. The burning fire left his brain, and all at once he felt ravenously hungry. He found Vash sitting his horse on a sand mound that rose above the rushes. The Cossack of the patrol had barley cakes in his bags, but both of them felt the need of meat or gruel.

With experienced eyes Vash studied the river in the deepening twilight. Swallows flitted overhead; out in midstream a log raft drifted without lights, although the deep notes of a boatman's song came from it over the water. On the far side the gray banks were turning black. Upstream he made out the blur of some large islands. But he shook his head.

"Not a tavern; not a fishing boat. Nothing to eat here."

"Yonder's a fire," observed Charny. He knew nothing of the Volga, but he had been born in the steppe and he had noticed what the other had missed: the thin glow of firelight against trees upstream near the islands.

"Gypsies, it may be." Vash nodded. "Well, God gives."

As they rode north, keeping to the hard ground above the rushes, he explained that this portion of the steppe was deserted except for a few summer huts of *burlaki,* or river men. Gypsies sometimes followed the river trail. Farther north bands of river pirates haunted the shore, rowing out from inlets to board and capture cargo boats, killing the crews and setting the vessels afire after carrying off what they wanted. To the south near Astrakhan Tartars raided across the Volga in the winter, to seize cattle and slaves in the villages. Richly laden merchant vessels sailing down river, or carrying salt and fish and sealskins north again, passed this region without stopping.

"We only kill flies," grumbled Vash. There was no support for the Cossacks of the Zarit patrol, except to pick quarrels with the governor's militia. "And kiss the cow girls when there are any along the river."

It was almost dark by the time they approached the fire, and Vash drew rein with an exclamation. The place seemed to be a large encampment without tents or huts. Along the shore in the firelight some two-score men sat at meat around three smoking pots. Most of them were armed with short sword and pistol, while pikes were stacked in military fashion. A few of them, in fine clothes, looked like Russians. And Vash noticed these had no weapons, although there were two women in their number.

Among the crowd he made out Kalmuks in white felt hats and a scattering of *burlaki*.

"There's no wagon train, no horses," he muttered, spitting out the sunflower seeds he was chewing.

Charny, who was hungry, urged his horse forward. As they came down to the shore some of the men rose to meet them.

"Whose men are you?" demanded Vash.

The strangers made no answer. They stared at the horses, and one went to the top of the rise on which the fire had been built to peer into the darkness behind the Cossacks. Someone else threw a dish of grease on the flames, which soared up, hissing, lighting up the shore.

Vash noticed a figure in a priest's hat and veil seated by the women, who had bold painted faces and the physique of Amazons. At least three of their companions wore the fur-trimmed garments of boyars – noblemen. But these, although they looked curiously at the patrol rider, had nothing to say. Perhaps they spoke only Russian and did not know the Cossack speech.

"Well, people," Vash remarked, "is there no one to bid us to sit down to bread and salt?" The odor of mutton and garlic tickled his nostrils.

A tall man in a red Tartar *khalat* rose from his place and came over to the Cossacks. He had curly hair the color of wheat, and he bore himself as if accustomed to command. With his hands thrust in his girdle he inspected Vash and Charny without haste.

"What seek ye?" he asked curtly. He spoke in the fashion of the Muscovites, like a boyar.

"We are riders of the Zarit patrol—" Vash stretched and pointed to include Charny "and, by Allah, we want to set our fangs in meat."

"Well," said the tall boyar, "I am Kolmar, the lieutenant of Astrakhan and I have no meat for you thieving dogs." He spoke to one of his followers and turned back to the fire.

Vash glanced anxiously at Charny, who had horsewhipped the lieutenant of a smaller town after drinking brandy. It would not do, he thought, to try that game with this Kolmar. Cossacks would not have turned a hungry man away from such an abundance of food: but these chaps seemed to be Muscovites with a following picked up along the river.

Charny, however, was more interested than angry. Suddenly he reined his horse forward, passing Kolmar and halting to stare at the women and the priest.

"If you have no food for us of the steppe," he said slowly, "give us at least a blessing, little father."

Some of the men laughed, and the bearded priest turned his head as if troubled. Hastily he raised his hand and muttered something.

"Get out!" said the Lord Kolmar softly. "And if you show your head this night you will taste a bullet."

One of the women cried out shrilly but Charny wheeled his horse and trotted off. He headed straight away from the river, as Vash joined him, and kept on until he was beyond the last of the firelight. Then he halted and sat motionless.

"The ox tails – the stall cattle!" muttered Vash. "They had white bread and kegs of mead enough for a barrack. But then they're Muscovites, and God made them so they can't see beyond their whiskers."

"Kegs and chests they had," Charny observed thoughtfully.

His eyes by now were accustomed to the gloom. A half moon, low over the river, shed an elusive light. To Vash's surprise, he began to quarter the ground at a hand pace, bending down to inspect the light patches of sand between the clumps of dwarf oak and saxaul.

"There's no bread here," Vash remarked after he had grown tired of following his champion about.

"Nothing," Charny agreed. "Only the tracks of men who came out of the wood. No carts, no horses, and no tracks of many people."

For a moment a chill of dread touched the Cossack of the patrol, who had all the superstition of those who ride the steppe. Kolmar and his people had food chests and cakes with them, and they could not have carried such things on their shoulders. In fact, they did not seem to have passed over the surface of the steppe. And Vash had seen no sign of a boat. They were there on the shore, waiting by that fire, as if they were dead souls who haunted the river in the hours of darkness. He thought of the florid faces of the women, and the silent priest, and glanced over his shoulder uneasily. True, they were not like honest folk of flesh and blood.

But spirits did not boil mutton over a huge fire, nor did they slake their thirst with honey-mead. Moreover, Kolmar had been a true *boyar*, ready to blaze away with powder and ball. No, they must have landed from a riverboat, although why they should have done so on this deserted stretch of shore Vash did not know.

"The fire," Charny said softly. "Did you see where it was?"

Hastily Vash glanced over his shoulder, half expecting to find the fire moving away somewhere. But it still flared and smoked on the rise by the shore.

"Devil take it!" he grunted. "Haven't you ever seen a fire before?"

"Not like that."

Vash reflected that he himself would have built a fire in a hollow out of the wind, where it would not catch the eye of roving Tartars. Or, to cook meat, he would have made a small fire between rocks and let it die to embers. But these men made a blaze as if to signal down the river.

"Well, they're Muscovites," he responded. "And they have women to keep warm. Why shouldn't they kindle up?"

Then he started. They had been walking the horses slowly down river, when Charny's mount shied away from a clump of saxaul. Something slipped out of the shadowy thicket and sped away soundlessly.

Charny went after it in a minute, lashing his horse through the brush. By the time Vash caught up with him the Cossack had dismounted and was wrestling with a dark figure. A knife flickered in the moonlight as Charny caught the arm of his antagonist and jerked. Charny had muscles of pliant steel in the hundred and eighty pounds of him, and the figure went down on the sand.

Jumping from his saddle, Vash was going to kick the stranger in the head – because a knife in the dark is more to be feared than any sword. But Charny pulled him back and spoke to the stranger, who made answer in a whisper.

"It's a woman," muttered the Cossack of the patrol, bending down. "A girl. Eh, she's pretty, too. A dove. *Hi-hop!*" He began to twirl his long mustache.

"Shut up!" grunted Charny. "She's a Gypsy, and she can take us to some food."

"But—"

Charny took the reins of the black horse in one hand, and he twisted his other fist in the end of the Gypsy girl's long, loose hair. She was barefoot, with a sheepskin *chaban* over her slender shoulders, and she led them swiftly toward the river.

"But," whispered Vash, coming up, "look out for yourself. These Gypsies are witches. They know how to lay spells. They can cut your heart out of your body."

The Gypsy girl laughed softly, hearing this. She did not make any effort to escape from Charny until she scrambled down into the gloom of an oak grove, with a warning cry that sounded like a night bird's.

It was answered from below, and the Cossacks saw that they were at the river's edge, a long musket shot upstream from the fire of the Muscovites. Beneath them, a timber raft was tied to the shore. On the raft whispers sounded faintly and bare feet moved over the logs.

"My people," explained the girl. "They are honest folk, O my falcons."

Vash doubted this. It would bring bad luck, he thought, to follow this girl of the night. Charny, however, let go the girl and leaped down to the raft.

"I am Yamalian," a gruff voice greeted him. "What would you, Cossack?"

"I," Charny answered, "am a masterless man from Zarit with a stolen horse, and this comrade of mine is a fugitive who has kissed just one girl too many. Give us bread and salt."

A chuckle came out of the darkness.

"Be welcome."

The Tsigans – Gypsies – being horse traders and singers, were on good enough terms with the border Cossacks, who liked to hear the tales they brought up and down the river. They knew more, even, than the Yiddish traders, although how they got their tidings remained a mystery. They drifted over the steppe with their carts and strings of ponies, their hags and children; some of their girls, like Makara who had guided the Cossacks to the raft, were beautiful and fiery in spirit.

Yamalian had two of his sons on the raft. While the Cossacks ate hugely of his *kasha* and bread washed down with Vash's brandy, the old Gypsy explained they were on their way south to Astrakhan where they would sell their logs and spend the Winter months when the Volga was frozen. They had tied up to the bank for the night.

"Now tell the truth," Charny demanded. "What did you steal from the Muscovites down the shore?"

From the raft the mound with its blazing fire was in plain sight over the fringe of rushes at the shore. Most of Kolmar's men had disappeared, but the women with their boyars and the priest were still to be seen. The Gypsies had not even a lantern on the raft. The only light came from the moon piercing the branches of the oaks.

"Eh, from them – nothing." Yamalian sounded sincere enough and Makara laughed a little.

"How did they come?"

"By boat, in two *saiks*. This morning they passed the raft, O my falcon. Now the *saiks* are hidden in the rushes."

"As you were hiding in the shadow – why?"

"Because I am afraid."

"When was a Tsigan afraid of darkness? And when did nobles of the north journey with their women in open *saiks*? What kind of priest gives a blessing like a fisherman? Eh, tell."

"I'm afraid. The fate of every man is in God's hands."

"Of what are you afraid?"

The old Gypsy made no answer, but the girl, Makara, said defiantly—

"The red cock."

Charny only shook his head impatiently. Vash, who had been chewing sunflower seeds and spitting them out, leaned forward, startled.

"Eh, the red cock will crow?"

"Before the first light," assented the girl.

"Here?"

"At the fire."

"What is this red cock," demanded Charny, "and his crowing?"

Vash felt for the brandy jug and took a long swallow.

"River pirates," he whispered. "Red hands. After they have attacked and slain, and taken out what they wish, then they kindle up with fire, and the boat goes burning down the river. They say it is the red cock crowing. Allah, we would have had more than bread in our gullets if we had sat down with them."

Many things became clear to Charny – the two score armed men waiting on the shore, their boats concealed in the high rushes. He wondered why they should sit by a fire and why some of them wore the dress of noblemen.

"Red hands down from the north," muttered Vash. "But that Kolmar is a nobleman, devil take me if he isn't. What are the women for?"

Yamalian chuckled.

"Are you a Cossack, to ask?"

"But they're dressed up like peasants, and this Lord Kolmar of Astrakhan has on Tartar rags. Eh, why?"

Makara, who had been watching Charny, leaned forward impatiently.

"When the red hands work, keep your tongue between your teeth."

It did not please the stocky Cossack to be spoken to in this manner by a girl.

"Well," he snorted, "you were spying on them. What did you find out?"

But she shook her head. Charny, the one who had run her down and thrown her to the ground – who had stolen a horse fit for a prince – was the one she wished would look at her.

"What is that?" Charny demanded of Yamalian.

Far up the river a pin-point of light appeared. Presently it vanished, to reappear again.

"It's a boat, the *Kniaz*."

"May the dogs bite me!" Vash clutched at his head. "How do you know?"

Yamalian did not see fit to explain how tidings of the ship's approach had crept down the river ahead of it. He knew the talk of the river men, the whispers that passed up and down the broad river – and Makara had ears like a cat.

"A rich ship," Vash muttered to Charny. "The last one down before the ice closes up north – for Astrakhan at the Volga mouth, with gold and gear, powder and arms and merchants' goods. *Hi-hop!* The red hands know. They are waiting like wolves." He turned to the Gypsy. "Where's your skiff?"

In spite of the instant protest of the men on the raft, Vash searched until he found a small skiff tied to the logs.

"It's devil's work Kolmar and his lads are about," he explained. "There are honest folk on the *Kniaz*. I'm going to warn them."

"Nay, Falcon," Yamalian objected. "They have cannon, muskets. What harm to them?"

"The devil only knows." Vash considered and shook his head. "It's clear those red hands came to wait for them. Now I must go out on the water and tell them to keep away from the fire. Plague take Makara – if it wasn't for her I would not be able to go."

Charny entered the skiff with him, and a Gypsy took the oars. Yamalian had whispered to him to look out for the skiff. Just as they pushed off the girl jumped in beside Charny.

"See how she loves you," Vash grumbled. "But it's bad luck having her along on the water."

The girl, however, showed no inclination to be put back on the raft.

"*Na kon!*" Vash cried. "Make haste."

They met the *Kniaz* about a league up-river. First the patch of square sail, half furled, showed in the moonlight and then the blunt bow of the small bark – that was a large ship on the Volga. A great lantern on the break of the after-deck gave the light that Charny had seen at first. Little air was stirring, and the ship barely had steerage way in the current. A sailor in the bow took soundings steadily, for the shifting channel and submerged islands made the river treacherous.

"*Hai!*" Vash stood up to hail. "Who commands here?"

"Keep off, you swine!" retorted the leadsman.

Heads began to show along the rail. Light came from the ports of the after castle, and the light wail of a violin ceased. Someone shouted at the skiff in Russian, and a sailor repeated it.

"Have you a message?"

"Aye, so. There is danger down by the islands."

"Come over the side. The serene, mighty lord will speak to you."

At a word from Vash the Gypsy swung the boat in, and the Cossacks hauled themselves up by a rope to the shrouds.

They dropped over the rail and stopped, surprised. A seaman held a blazing pine torch close to their heads, and a half dozen soldiers in helmets and breastplates pointed long pistols at them. Behind these guards stood three officers – one the stout Muscovite ship's captain, another a young ensign in a green uniform, and the third a dry little man who held himself stiff as the gold-headed cane he carried.

"Halt!" he snapped, and put a round piece of glass in his eye to look at them. He said something they did not understand, and the green ensign translated.

"Tell your names, occupations, your master's name and your business upon the river. But first lay down your swords on the deck. It is forbidden to come over the side with small arms."

Instead Charny took a step forward.

"Allah! We have come to warn you."

The officer of the glass gave a second command, and the ensign explained:

"I should count four, and if at the count of four you have not laid down your weapons my men will shoot you. Come now, fear God! One. Two—"

The Cossacks exchanged glances. On land they could ever run for it, but here on the cramped deck with the water behind them they were helpless. With a mutter of anger Vash drew his saber and dropped it, while Charny laid his down silently. The ensign picked up the weapons, and the guards lowered their pistols.

It seemed to the Cossacks as if the men on the *Kniaz* were marionettes, bobbing up and down at the pull of invisible strings. First he of the eyeglass snapped out words, then the green ensign sang them out like a parrot, and the seamen ran about or barked orders. Vash peered over the bow and saw that they were approaching the dark blur of the wood where lay the Gypsy raft.

"Look here, Excellencies," he explained, "the devil himself is squatting down behind that bend. Only listen—"

Hastily he told of the meeting with Kolmar and his armed band, of the watch fire and the tidings of the Gypsies.

"May the hangman light my path if they aren't red hands – pirates. If you don't want your hides ripped, keep to the other side of the islands until you are past the fire."

The dry little man glared behind his glass and snapped out questions as a sap log shoots sparks. He ordered Makara and her brother up from the skiff and questioned them without result, because the Gypsies were afraid of the officers.

"What is the name of the leader of this band?" He demanded finally.

"Kolmar, lord lieutenant of Astrakhan." Vash made answer.

The green ensign scowled.

"That is a lie. Here stands his High Well-Born Excellency, Franz, Count of Fugenwald, who has been appointed Lord Lieutenant of Astrakhan by his Imperial Majesty, the Czar of all the Russians."

And he pointed to the erect little German, listening respectfully as Fugenwald rattled forth more long words.

"Moreover, his Excellency says to you that he entertains suspicion aroused by your coming. His Excellency has been warned against the outlaws of the Volga, and he has taken steps to resist them. These four carronades—" the ensign pointed to two pairs of twelve-pounders in position in the waist of the ship—"are charged with chain shot and iron. My twelve men of the Moscow *strelsui* are armed with pikes and pistols, and the twenty members of the crew have swords and axes."

"But for God's sake, go outside the islands. Look!"

Vash pointed at the tree-covered islets dead ahead of the *Kniaz*. But when the ship's captain turned inquiringly to Fugenwald, the German ordered him to keep to the inner channel, to pass close to the fire on the mound. Two seamen swung the long tiller over, and the *Kniaz* turned sluggishly toward the land. Fugenwald and the captain went aft to join a young Russian woman who appeared, wrapped in her cape, at the break of the poop.

"A lady!" muttered Vash. "Give us our swords and let us go."

The ensign shook his head.

"Nay. You two mangy dogs won't sneak off until we find out what your game is. If anything happens here, you'll be hung up on the hooks as a warning to all lawless men." He went to the rail to stare at the fire. "Eh, there are people signaling."

"What will they do?" Charny whispered.

It was the first time he had ventured on the deck of the ship and he did not like it.

"God knows." Vash spat out his sunflower seeds morosely. "These guards are militia – captain's a Russian – commander's a German, and the lady's his wife."

He looked around into the unfriendly faces of the pikemen, several of whom still stood by the Cossacks with drawn pistols. No love was ever lost between the Cossacks and the Muscovite militia. Unseen by the men, Makara slipped away along the rail and vanished into the darkness of the cabin passage.

By now the *Kniaz* was almost abreast of the fire and drawing in toward shore. Fugenwald was holding a spyglass to his eye. Charny climbed up on the spars amidships to see better.

In the firelight on the bank the two women, the priest and the boyars waved and shouted at the ship. One of the men ran down the mound, as if to throw himself into the water. And the cries of the women became distinct.

"Aid! Aid for the lost! Take us in, good people!"

The Countess Fugenwald was urging her husband to send ashore for these castaways who looked like nobles.

"In God's name!" The voice of the priest came over the water. "We were seized and robbed by lawless men. We have nothing left."

Shading his eyes from the lantern light, Charny studied the shore. The chests had vanished, and there was no sign of Kolmar or his men. Nor could he see any trace of the long boats. He glanced around for Makara, but she had disappeared.

Then came a rumble and splash from the bow of the *Kniaz*. The anchor was down, and the bark turned slowly in the channel, until the sail flapped lazily and it brought up, opposite the fire.

"What now?" Charny demanded.

"They've tied the vessel. They're going to send a small boat to the shore to talk to her friends. Hi – wait!"

But the tall Cossack was down from the spars and up the after-deck ladder with long strides. Grasping the burly ship's master by the arm, he swung him around.

"Eh, haven't you a nose to smell a trap? Loose the boat. Take a whip to her."

Removing his clay pipe from his bearded lips, the Moscow captain pointed with it toward the rail. Seamen stood by the two port carronades with lighted matches in their hands. The pikemen, fully armed, manned the rail, where torches smoked and flared.

"Where's the trap?" The captain growled. "You've been licking the pig this night, my man."

"He wished to turn us aside from rescuing these poor souls," echoed the Russian lady. Pearls glimmered softly on the collar that bound her throat.

Charny went to the rail and stared down. With two sailors, the young ensign was entering Makara's skiff to go to the shore to bring off the priest and the nobles. The ensign stood up, as the skiff pushed into the forest of rushes as high as a man's head along the shore.

And then with a splash a length of the rushes fell down. Orange flashes lighted the faces of the ensign and the two sailors as fire-arms roared and smoke swirled. A man screamed, and two portions of the rushes began to move toward the side of the *Kniaz*, a stone's throw away. Down in the gloom between the fire on the shore and the torches on the ship the two dark shapes drew nearer with oars swinging at their sides, and men tearing apart the screen of rushes that had hidden the two longboats. But the bodies of the ensign and the two seamen were visible, sprawled in the skiff.

"*Sarin na kitchka!*" voices roared from below. "Death to the white hands!"

Then the pirates were alongside the bark, throwing grapnels over the rail, clutching at the shrouds. Pistols blazed up from the side, and powder wreaths dimmed the torches.

"O Mary, Mother!" cried the Russian woman.

The captain let fall his pipe, shouting hoarsely. No one had fired the cannon, which could not have damaged the boats beneath them. Fugenwald, with an oath, clutched at his sword. But his commands, in German, went unheeded.

Something cold and hard was thrust against Charny's hand, and he gripped the hilt of his saber. Makara had brought it to him, her dark eyes of aflame with excitement.

"Strike, Cossack!"

It passed through Charny's brain that even the Gypsies could not fly from the ship. They were all in it together.

"Down with the torches! Shoulder to shoulder. Strike, lads!"

His voice cut through the tumult, as a sailor with a torch staggered and dropped, his face smashed in with an ax. The remaining torches were hurled down into the *saiks*, leaving only the great lantern in the moonlight.

"Back from the rail, you dog-brothers," Vash roared. "Behind the spars with you, bull-tails!"

The Muscovite pikemen, after discharging their pistols into the gloom – their eyes had been dazzled by torchlight – were struggling clumsily at the rail, their long shafted weapons of little use against the short pikes and knives of the Volga outlaws. Some of the sure-footed sailors were making good play with axes, but the pirates were coming over the rail with a rush.

Kolmar appeared in the shrouds, pistol in one hand, sword in the other.

"Slash the white hands, lads," he laughed. "Ho, women and gold for a frolic!" And, throwing back his head, he howled like a wolf.

Charny had been snorting and stamping with growing eagerness. This fighting at hands' strokes was to his liking.

"Make way for a Cossack!" He called, vaulting the poop rail. "*U-ha!*"

With both knees and the hilt of his sword he struck a Volga man, knocking him to the boards and slashing his body open below the ribs as he rose, dodging the thrust of a pike. The shaggy *burlak* raised the short pike to throw it, but the Cossack's saber whizzed, and the curved blade took off the man's hand.

"*U-ha!*" Charny's war shout. "Come down wolf, and you will howl—"

Kolmar had seen his two men fall, men of the *Kniaz* rallied to Charny's leadership. He hurled the pistol that he had just fired and jumped down into the clear space between the end of the spars and the after-deck. Snarling, he made at Charny, swinging a heavy cutlass.

Twice he cut at the Cossack's head, and twice he was parried. They were under the lantern, their backs guarded by their men on either side.

When Kolmar felt the weight of the Cossack's blade, he crouched warily.

"Fool," he called softly. "There's gold and gear under your hand. Come over to us. To the fish with the white hands!"

But Charny's saber flashed above his head, dripping blood.

"Your head will go first to the fish," he retorted, laughing.

The voice of Kolmar was the voice of the nobleman, and Charny was not minded to trust a voice any longer. He leaned back as the cutlass swept inside his blade, the point tearing across his chest. Instantly the leader of the outlaws cut down at his knees, and Charny jumped.

"Ho, the Cossack dances!" Kolmar shouted, pressing him.

A pistol roared near Charny, and he had the stench of powder in his throat. He parried a cut, and twisted his blade along about Kolmar's cutlass, locking the hilts and thrusting up. For a moment the two men strained, shoulder to shoulder, steam rising from Kolmar's yellow head. His utmost strength could not force down the Cossack's arm. But his free hand felt at his belt and rose with a knife.

Charny saw the thrust of the knife, felt the steel rip over his shoulder – and wrenched himself free. Kolmar's cutlass slashed down at him, but struck harmlessly against his side, all the force taken from the blow. For the Cossack's blade got home first on the man's bare head, splitting it above the jaw.

Kolmar dropped to his knees, when Charny struck again, severing the spine behind the ears, cutting the head from the body.

"Here's for you, red hands," he called, and caught the smoking head from the boards to hurl it among the Volga men.

A Kalmuk ran at him, but a stocky figure brushed him aside. Vash fought off the Kalmuk, shouting:

"*U-ha!* The Cossacks are dancing. Join in, brothers."

The rush of the outlaws had been stopped at the spars, while the rest of the crew had had time to come up. Some of the armored Muscovites were down, and the rest were fighting with desperation, seeing death at hand. Sight of their leader's head flying through the air brought the Volga men to a stop, and when Charny and Vash pressed around the end of the spars they gave way.

"Come on, dog-brothers," Vash urged.

The curved swords of the Cossacks rose and fell. The outlaws, leaderless, began to drop into the boats. Some leaped the rail, into the water, and climbed into the *saiks*, and in a minute they were clear of the deck, except for the groaning wounded who were soon silenced by the axes of the crew. Mercy was unknown on the Volga.

From the boats the outlaws retreated to the mound, beyond pistol shot. Charny was sitting, panting, on an overturned keg, when he saw Fugenwald striding past and heard a command. With a blinding flash and roar the two carronades were fired, the chain shot and scrap iron sweeping the knoll, scattering the surviving outlaws into the darkness. Only the bodies of three or four men were visible by the fire.

"Eh—" Vash grinned—"his High Mighty Excellency is starting to fight when everything's over. But it was you, dog-brother, who sent the red hands off howling."

"The head," Count Fugenwald explained precisely, "of the man Kolmar has been identified as that of a renegade and a river slayer who has shed blood like water in the northern district. From the scene of his crimes he fled into the steppe. He had the wits of a noble and the cruelty of a Kalmuk. It is apparent now that he laid a trap for this ship, dressing up five of his followers – for two women came with him into the steppe – in the garments of others he had put to death. So, by the discipline of my militia and the destructive fire my two carronades, we are victorious over the notorious Kolmar and his band."

Approvingly he tapped his eyeglass on the paper in front of him. He was seated on the afterdeck, and the morning mist was clearing away from the *Kniaz*, still at anchor in the river, gray under the first light.

Behind him in the place of the dead lieutenant stood the Russian ship's master who translated his Excellency's words to the two Cossacks who stood before him, silent but with restless eyes.

For an hour the whole ship had been ransacked for the jeweled collar and other valuables of the countess, which had disappeared during the tumult. Nothing had been found.

"However," went on that count, "you two lads bore yourselves well. I commend you and reward you – so!"

He picked up the paper that bore his seal and folded it, handing it to Vash.

"I have written," he explained, "to his Excellency the Governor of Astrakhan to free you, Vash, from patrol duty and bestow upon you the ranking of sergeant in his Excellency's town guard. As for you, Charny, you assured me that you have no duty except that of caring for his Excellency's horses. So I have suggested that you be raised from groom to master of the Zarit stables."

Vash turned the paper in his hands uneasily and passed it to Charny, who looked at it thoughtfully and tucked it into his belt. Both Cossacks were looking over the side, where a log raft was drifting slowly past the *Kniaz*. Behind the raft floated a skiff, and on the raft stood two horses, stamping restlessly. One was a black charger, the other a piebald pony, and their saddles had been removed. Charny nudged Vash, who found his tongue at last.

"We thank your High Well-Born Excellency," he said eagerly, "and we accept the letter joyfully. But we wish to be sent off in a skiff to that raft. Look, our horses are waiting for us there."

Fugenwald glanced through his glass and nodded amiably. After all, he would come to Astrakhan with a reputation.

The Cossacks climbed down into the skiff with alacrity. A few moments later they leaped from it to the raft, shouting farewell to the Russian seamen who headed back into the current.

"Now, you old son of a dog," Vash exclaimed to the anxious Yamalian, "you wanted to get away with our horses."

"As God lives, I heard you were dead."

"In a sow's ear, we were. Makara saw us on our legs."

"But the shore, my Falcon, it was aswarm with outlaws. Truly, I saved the horses for you."

Vash grunted and turned to confront the Gypsy girl, who would come out of the thatch cabin to look at Charny.

"Eh, little hawk, where have you hidden the pearls you snatched from that Russian dove?"

Indifferently Makara glanced at him: but her dark eyes glowed as she stepped before Charny, the wind whipping her dark hair about her throat.

"Will you take – pearls?" she whispered.

Charny smiled down at her.

"Nay, keep the pearls, little Makara. Pearls for a sword. Now I have had enough of the water. My road is on the land. Swing over, Yamalian, swing east."

When they had saddled the horses, and Charny had landed at a point on the east bank of the Volga, Vash followed him, leading the piebald pony.

"How will you get back again?" Charny asked.

The stocky Cossack pulled at his mustache reflectively.

"Then you're not going to Zarit—" he grinned—"to be master of the stables?"

Charny shook his head and drew Fugenwald's letter from his belt, handing it to his companion.

"Not I. You take it."

"I'm not going back. Too many lords and officers. I'll draw my rein with yours, you brother of a dog." Vash stepped to the river's edge and tore the seal from the paper. Then he tore the paper into pieces and scattered them over the water. "Now they can't make me sergeant of the militia."

Charny laughed joyously.